THE DARK SIDE OF DEATH

A JACK DUBLIN NOVEL

2014
Indie Book Award
Finalist

By

S T. PHILLIPS

This book is a work of fiction.
Names, characters, businesses, organizations, places, events, and incidents either are the product of the author's imagination or used fictitiously. Any resemblance to actual persons, living or dead, events or locales is entirely coincidental.
 Published in the United States by Sync ISD, LLC for Amazon's Kindle. www.syncisd.com
Cover design by Carl D. Pace III and John Wattenbarger
Cover photograph by David M. McCuin at www.panfoto.com

ISBN-13: 9780615597669
ISBN-10: 0615597661

ACKNOWLEDGMENTS

I want to take this opportunity to thank the many friends who took time out of their busy lives to help me finalize a dream. Without their help, this book would have never happened. Mike Maier, Ron Morris, Joe Schofield, Rachel Sacher, Jan Everingham, Linda Kahn, Dave Collins, Deane Cressman, Carla Lafferty, Rick Maier, Carol Matthews, Karen Pluta, Stu Snyder and Tim Browne read this book from its infancy, which I know must have been painful at times! They provided me with much-needed advice and encouragement.

A special thank you to Bill Gambrill, who gave me the final push and strongest advice about grammar and punctuation. His guidance was extraordinary, his support boundless. The final ending is largely due to his input.

Also, to my FTO (Field Training Officer) J.Wayne Merritt and Elwood "Woody" Gilger who gave me technical information about Black Hawk helicopters, which was crucial to the assault on Montserrat. Any factual errors are due to me, and not Woody.

Special thanks to my editor Robin Rosser for her diligence and perseverance.

A special thanks to all of my teachers and classmates, including the entire Mt.P alumni and extended Mt.P family, particularly the class of '71. Go Knights!

To my parents,
Betty and Bill Phillips
who taught me how to live, laugh and love;
and to my wife Maria
for her never ending encouragement
and unceasing love for me.

Author's Note

This novel has been meticulously proofread and edited; any errors in grammar, usage, or mechanics are neither my editor's fault nor mine.

1

It's easy to kill someone.

You just point your gun and pull the trigger. But each fatal bullet destroys two people: One dies, and the other lives to suffer.

Jack Dublin stood in front of his sliding glass patio doors. He peered out at the imposing monuments built centuries ago to reward political arrogance. In the distance, the Capitol and Washington Monument were waiting for the first fingers of light to shoot through the early morning darkness. Staring pensively into the shadows, he wondered when and how Senator Rothschild would get his revenge.

Jack knew one thing for sure. It was coming.

With one hand in the pocket of his Georgetown gym shorts and the other holding his coffee cup, he continued to sip his French-roast coffee. Having just returned from his daily five-mile jog, the gray "Fight Me I'm Irish" T-shirt Jack wore was soaked in perspiration.

Jack was 43 years old and in good health, both physically and financially. He was thinking about his retirement which had coincided with his recent inheritance of a small fortune. His paternal grandfather, whom he had not seen in years, left him real estate and stock potentially valued in the millions. Jack's future was looking bright, until he killed the son of U.S. Senator William Rothschild.

That night in February was uncharacteristically warm and M Street was overwhelmed with young, thirsty people looking for hookups. Jack was walking home from a personal business meeting where he had been discussing his recent largesse. He maneuvered his way through the dense crowd to slip down a side street. As Jack took a shortcut down an alleyway, he heard screams.

Quickly but quietly, Jack made his way further down the alleyway to investigate. The foul stench of restaurant garbage hung in the air. As he approached a narrow alcove, he stopped to listen and immediately heard a terrified young woman begging and pleading. Jack instinctively reached to the small of his back and grabbed the off-duty weapon he always carried, which was a Glock 9 mm. Model 26.

He heard men talking and laughing.

Without pause, Jack quickly came around to face them. A young woman, appearing to be of college age, was lying on her back on the grimy floor. The full moon sent light through a small opening in the roof, slightly illuminating the center of an otherwise dark storage area. Jack could see a man standing over her.

Her pants were pulled down to her ankles. She was whimpering.

The man was Rodney Rothschild, and along with him were two other accomplices standing in the dark.

"Police! Hold it right there, asshole!" Jack screamed as he pointed his gun at Rodney while displaying his badge.

The girl lifted her head to see Jack standing there.

"Help me, please!" she begged.

Rodney's back was facing Jack, but it looked as if he had started to unbuckle his belt before he was interrupted.

"Step away and keep your hands where I can see 'em. Don't make any sudden moves."

Rodney turned around.

"Get the fuck out of here," he scowled.

"Step away from the girl and you won't get hurt," Jack ordered forcefully.

Rodney Rothschild was about six foot five and at least three hundred pounds. His two cohorts appeared to be about Jack's size. Rodney stood still, as if he was pondering the alternatives. Finally, he stepped away from her and out of the light. He was now standing alone, cloaked in darkness.

His two friends stood on the opposite side.

It was difficult to see any of their hands or faces in the dark. Jack now had a dilemma: three large defiant men to subdue without a radio, handcuffs, or Taser. They read Jack's expression at the exact moment he realized this.

"So whadd'ya gonna do now, big shot?" Rodney asked. "You gonna take all three of us down by yourself?"

"Hurry up and get dressed," Jack told the girl.

Rodney and his friends began creeping slowly towards Jack. Keeping a firm grip on his Glock with his right hand, he reached into his pocket with his other, grabbed his phone, and quickly pressed 911.

"Hold it right there. Don't come any closer!" Jack ordered as the call connected.

All of a sudden, Rodney struck him in his left shoulder with a lead pipe he was concealing. Temporarily immobilized, Jack dropped his phone and fell to the ground in excruciating pain that radiated down his arm to his fingertips. Fear, a trait Jack never allowed, began to creep into his psyche.

Looking up to see the pipe coming towards him again, Jack rolled to his left. The pipe slammed to the floor, narrowly missing him. Rolling back into a seated position, Jack raised his gun and fired at Rodney with a triple-tap, three quick shots in progression just like he was trained. All of the shots struck Rodney in the K5 area, where the bullets ripped his heart and lungs apart, securing an immediate date with the devil.

The internal investigation cleared Jack of any wrongdoing, but Senator Rothschild took his case to the media. Bathed in lights accentuating his handsome patrician looks, the senator stood in front of a multitude of microphones from the major and local networks, deriding Jack and the Metropolitan Police Department. The senator argued his only son was a gentle and kind human being who would never be able to defend himself against the bogus allegations brought by Jack. The angry senator said a rogue cop took his son's life and should be put on trial to pay for his overzealous actions. According to him, the findings of the internal investigation and Justice Department were expectedly deplorable. He would not rest until justice was done.

Ordinarily, Jack would have received a commendation for saving a woman being raped. Not this time. He didn't even know her name (Sara Jane Hardy) until they fished her naked body out of the Potomac River a couple of weeks later. They said it was suicide. Jack never believed it.

Standing at the patio of his new condo, Jack continued to sip his coffee from a faded coffee mug. The blue script once read "World's Greatest Dad". It was chipped, gouged and cracked, but he still loved it, even though it was a bitter reminder of a good marriage gone bad and a fatherhood lost. The cup was a gift sixteen years ago from his son, Connor, who now lived in L.A. with Jack's ex-wife and her new Hollywood-producer husband.

Jack walked past Guinness, his sleeping Chocolate Lab, as he headed into the kitchen for one more cup. The new blue tile in his kitchen was cold to his bare feet.

The Capitol could still be seen from his kitchen counter. The sun was just starting to bring light to the city. His thoughts returned to the senator. Just how far would a powerful senator go to exact revenge? Now that Jack was retired, he hoped the senator would leave him alone.

Just before Jack started to take another sip of coffee, he felt someone else's presence. There was a sudden chill on his neck and shoulders, like the bluster of a harsh, winter wind. Slowly turning around to see who was behind him, he heard,

"Goodbye, Jack."

2

"Jesus Christ, Julie," Jack snapped angrily. "You scared the shit out of me."

"Well, I'm sorry Jack, but that's your problem," Julie retorted, unapologetically. "And now, unfortunately, it's my problem too," she added. "You're wound so God-damned tight, I'm afraid to say anything; it's like walking on eggshells. I refuse to live like this. I can't do it anymore!"

Julie's frustration was now fully-apparent to Jack. She had never talked to him quite this way, so cold and frank, and in such an abrasive manner. He bent over and began gathering the shattered remains of his beloved coffee cup while trying to process her anger. She watched him delicately place large pieces on the counter, as if he hoped to glue them back together.

She was dressed in the black running shorts Jack had bought for her and a white shirt with a logo for Lou's Bar, a jazz bar where they occasionally went to have a drink and listen to music. Her hair was pulled back into a ponytail. Her eyes were intensely black, like coal and she wasn't wearing any makeup. She never needed to. She was beautiful without it.

"You need to put some shoes on so you don't cut yourself. Let me get your sandals."

"Forget it," he said testily as their eyes met. "I don't need 'em."

Julie thought she would help and bent over to pick up some of the broken pieces.

"Please, don't touch anything!" Jack admonished. "I'll do it myself." Realizing how harsh he sounded, he added, "You just… you might cut yourself."

He held up some of the fragments, "Man, I'll never be able to put this back together," he said painfully.

"It's only a coffee cup."

He sneered at her. "Maybe to you it's just a meaningless, little coffee cup, but to me, it's a helluva lot more than that."

He sighed and added, "Connor gave me this cup when he was only four years old. It's the last vestige I have of him."

"I'm sorry," she replied, feeling guilty.

She grabbed some paper towels and dampened the coffee spread across the kitchen floor. She stood up.

"Look, I just wanted to say I'm leaving."

"What time will you be back?" he asked still bent over picking up the pieces.

"No Jack, I mean, I'm leaving," she said firmly. Julie reached around to the other side of the kitchen doorway and picked up her suitcase. She stood shaking it as if it had a bell on it.

Jack stood up, taking the shattered pieces left in his hand and putting them in the garbage. Sliding the other pieces on the counter with one hand into the other, he threw them all in.

"What do you mean, you're leaving? You mean leaving for good?" he asked in disbelief as he started to rinse his hands.

"Yes."

It was horrible timing. Julie was the only stability he had in his life right now. It seemed his whole world was disintegrating into dust which the wind was blowing in all directions. He stared into her eyes searching for a sign of weakness, something he could often manipulate to his favor. He didn't want her to leave, not now.

They had met in a bookstore in Silver Spring about two years ago when he saw her looking at a shelf of best-selling novels in the front of the store. Her beauty captivated him from the very first moment. She was about five feet, eight inches tall with a lithe body, and wearing shorts that exposed a pair of the most beautiful legs he had ever seen. Her buttocks were round and firm. She was wearing a short sleeve shirt with Asian lettering on it that accentuated her full and prominent breasts, but it was those long legs that got his attention. Her brunette hair was pulled through a Phillies baseball hat, another plus. He just couldn't take his eyes off her.

He started a conversation with her and before long, they started dating. Julie worked for the government and was a part-time aerobics instructor at a local fitness club. She moved into his apartment near Rock Creek Park three weeks later in a hurricane of sexual emotion.

"Why would you do that?"

"Jack, I need a relationship. One that is two-way. You're emotionally absent. You're like a ship without an anchor. Look, I know you've got a lot going on," she added. "But we weren't doing all that well before. You're an amoeba, Jack. You don't need anyone; you have yourself."

Jack felt he could always show his love through actions and not words. It's one of the reasons he always seemed to gravitate towards strong, independent women. He never thought affirmations were necessary.

"No, I don't have myself, Julie. I don't even know who I am anymore. I need you. I need you to help me," he pleaded. "Please. Don't go."

"Why? So you can ignore me again?"

"I don't ignore you, do I?" He could feel her skepticism. "I get it, but I don't ignore you."

"Jack, lately you don't even know when I'm around."

"That's not true. I miss you when you're not around." Jack softly argued, gently walking towards her.

"Shit!" Jack winced through his clenched teeth as he started to hop on one foot after stepping directly on a shard of the broken cup.

"Are you bleeding?" she asked.

He lifted his foot and held it with his hand as they both looked at his bloody heel.

Julie shook her head. "Sit on the stool, please." She put her suitcase down. Jack hopped over to the stool and sat. She grabbed the antiseptic and bandages from the top cabinet and carefully tended to his foot.

Their eyes met, and then she continued. "There you go," she said calmly.

Julie put the antiseptic and Band-Aids on the counter and picked up her suitcase. Jack stood up carefully and took the suitcase out of her hand. He set it down.

"Julie, I'm sorry if I broke your heart," Jack pleaded. "But this isn't how we fix it."

"Jack, I don't mean to burst your bubble, but you didn't break my heart. That's not why I'm leaving. I'm leaving because I don't want my heart broken," she said unemotionally. "Why should I give all my loving to someone who doesn't love me back? We aren't who we used to be. We've drifted apart; it's just not the same."

"Julie, I do love you back," Jack said, grinning as he raised his eyebrows up and down, trying to break her serious tone.

"Jack, it's not just about sex. It's about romance."

"We do a lot together. We go out to dinner, we travel, we go to jazz clubs," Jack smiled. "And, you have to admit, the sex is great," he said, pulling her close to him.

She pulled back reflexively, jerking her hands from his. "See? That's just what I mean. It always goes back to sex, and let me tell you, Jack, the sex might have been good in the beginning, but now, it's like you're not there either. You're just going through the motions and I need more than that!"

"That's not true." Jack reached out and took both her hands in his.

"Just stay," he said. "We can work it out. I want you in my life."

"Are you telling me you want to get married?" she asked with one eyebrow arched. "Is that a proposal?"

Jack paused and looked her straight in the eyes. He was cornered.

"No. Not now, at least. I need some time."

"Time? How *MUCH* time, Jack?"

"I honestly don't know."

"Well, while you're figuring it out, I will be at my house living my life without you," she said as she picked up her suitcase.

Jack called her name twice but she didn't answer. The front door opened and slammed.

He decided with everything going on, maybe it was time to really let her go.

Her timing couldn't be worse. It was Father's Day of all days. He hadn't spoken to his son Connor in years. He wondered how he turned out, what he looked like. Did he like sports? How were his grades? Was he going to college? Jack's thoughts always turned to Connor more frequently on Father's Day.

There were so many questions Jack would like answered.

Likewise, he hadn't spoken with his father for years either. It's funny how generations repeat themselves, though unlike his desire to see Connor, he didn't care to see Benjamin Dublin again. For all he knew, his father was dead. Either way, that part of Father's Day didn't much matter to him.

The last he saw of him was at his mother's funeral twenty-some years ago. Jack was a junior in college when his mother was killed in a car accident. His father called him at school to share the news without having the decency to drive two hours to tell him in person. He hated him for that.

For all intents and purposes, his father had died a long time ago.

His mother's death was devastating to him. It was Jack's mother, Isabella, who was always there for him. Unfortunately, she would never meet her grandson, Connor, who was born a few years after her death.

His father had been mysteriously absent for long stretches during Jack's life and his mother always seemed to make excuses for Benjamin, saying he had an important job as an international banker. She pointed out how thankful they should be to have a nice home and all the comforts to go along with it.

After a while, Jack had become accustomed to life without his father's presence. His mother was his champion. She motivated him to excel and never cut him any slack. She was a fiery disciplinarian when it was called for, yet loving and devoted. She was of Cuban descent and spoke several languages. He never understood how someone so intelligent, admirable and beautiful could allow her husband so much freedom.

Jack heard his cell phone ring in the bedroom. He hobbled across the kitchen to catch it. It must be Julie, since she was the only one who had his number. Following the shooting, he changed a few routines.

One included a new condo in Rosslyn, the other a new cell phone number.

He picked his phone up and looked at the number of the incoming call. It indicated “Blocked” making Jack hesitant to answer. How could anyone else have his number?

Jack decided to answer it.

3

"Hello?"

"Hello, Jack?"

Jack felt a sudden chill take command of his mind and body. He recognized the voice but couldn't place it. An uneasy feeling of darkness began to infiltrate and disturb his temporary peace. Was it the ruthless hand of the senator at work or just his paranoia?

"Who is this?"

"It's Bob. Bob Lewis. Is that you, Jack?"

Bob Lewis. It's a common name and it did sound familiar, yet Jack didn't remember a Bob Lewis.

"No, I'm sorry, you have the wrong number."

"No, Jack, wait! It's Bob. Come on, Bob Lewis. We worked a homicide together in '99. A woman was stabbed to death during a burglary and the perp tried to cash her Social Security checks. He was killed later in a shoot-out."

Jack remembered. Bob Lewis was an FBI agent he had worked with on the Shirley Rogers case when he had been assigned to detectives.

Shirley Rogers, an elderly black woman, lived alone in the Columbia Heights area. One day she answered the door and Jerome Stubbs, a nineteen year-old black male from the neighborhood who was strung-out on heroin, decided to stab her forty-nine times. When they got there, she looked like a human pincushion. Blood had coagulated into an inch-thick jelly, covering the living room floor.

Stubbs had decided to take her Social Security checks to finance his habit. During the break-in, he'd found Shirley's .25 caliber Bauer and had taken it with him. Sweet Shirley knew enough to have a handgun for her protection, even though it probably wouldn't have made any difference. Shirley would've only pointed it at someone. Being an intensely religious woman, she could have never pulled the trigger. Even if she had lost her sense of religious conviction for the moment, she probably would have been too nervous to use it correctly.

As it turned out, justice had been quickly served. The drug-crazed Stubbs decided to point Shirley's gun at two police officers who caught up with him in an abandoned house a couple of days later. Stubbs got off a couple of rounds, but it was no match for the firepower of the officers. He died from multiple gunshot wounds.

Stealing government checks was a federal crime and that's how the FBI came on-board. Cops always hate it when the "*Feebies*" get involved; that's the moniker cops knew them by. Although Bob Lewis was actually pretty easy to work with, the more Jack remembered.

He finally relaxed his shoulders.

"Okay. Yeah, this is Jack," he reluctantly responded.

"Man, how the hell are you? I knew it was you." said Bob Lewis with renewed energy.

"I'm good. Sorry, I didn't recognize you at first. It's been a long time; I'm not particularly inclined to answer the phone these days."

"Yeah, I can imagine. I read about your ordeal with Senator Rothschild, but you did your job, Jack. You saved that girl. You should've received a medal."

Jack thought about it.

"At least you're not the one taking a permanent dirt nap," Bob said with a chuckle.

"Yeah," Jack answered weakly.

Bob continued, "Listen, Jack, let me get to the point. I called you because you came highly recommended. I work for a security firm that needs good people. I know you've only been retired for a short time, but I've got something right up your alley. This will interest you."

"Interest me how, specifically?" Jack answered. "And who recommended me?"

"I ran into Lieutenant Sproat, told him I was looking for good people, and he recommended you."

"You mean Captain Sproat?"

"Yeah, geez Captain Sproat, right. Yes, he highly recommended you," Bob answered.

"Good people for what, exactly?" Jack asked, not realizing he sounded irritated.

"Well, I've since retired from the FBI and I work for WISE Security now. We're headquartered here in D.C. and work primarily with Fortune 500 companies doing everything from surveillance to executive security."

"I'm familiar with them," Jack responded.

"I'm making a lot more money now than when I was with the government. Hey, with your experience, there's no reason you can't be making some good money, too. We have investigators making $150,000 a year with expenses."

Jack thought some more.

"To be perfectly honest, I'm not sure what I want to do right now, Bob. I'm just trying to relax a little before I even think about it. Police work is the last thing on my mind."

"I can understand that. Look, I know what happened probably has you thinking twice about everything, but why don't you just start slowly. Maybe do a little surveillance to get your feet wet, and then see if you want to do more. There's great potential for travel, and not only that, upward mobility for someone with your talent is a guarantee.

"Jack, you have to do something. You can't just sit around. Psychologically, it's not good for you. It's not good physically, either. You don't wanna become a couch potato, do you?"

Bob paused to see how Jack would respond. Then he continued.

"Look, I have a simple surveillance tonight down in Georgetown. It's real close to you. You can spend about four hours there and it pays $100 an hour. Not bad for sitting in your car and listening to the radio. What do you think?"

"I don't know. What's involved?"

"There's this kid. I say "kid" but actually he's 28 years old. He's suspected of selling government information and weapons to the wrong people. All you have to do is watch and take notes. You don't get directly involved. You don't make any contact or anything. It's easy. Think you can handle it?"

"Yeah, sounds interesting, but I don't know if I want to get involved with anything to do with the government. Who's hiring you for this?"

"Jack, I'm not at liberty to say who's paying the bill, but you're not doing anything but surveillance. That's all you're doing. I'm not giving you anything heavy; it's an easy gig, really. I know you've been under a lot of pressure. This will let you get back into the swing of things at a leisurely pace. Do you have a digital camera?"

"Yeah, I have one," Jack answered thinking about the Canon digital SLR and attachments he had just bought.

"Great. Then all you have to do is watch the street and make a few notes. If you see anything, feel free to take some pictures. Also, you will be working with another agent."

"I thought this was for WISE, what does another FBI agent have to do with this?"

"No, Jack, she's a former....."

"She?" Jack instantly interrupted.

"Yeah, she. She's a former police officer we recruited. You don't have a problem working with a woman, do you? I didn't think Jack Dublin, the man about town, would have a problem with that. She's pretty hot. Too bad she's married."

"No. I don't have a problem working with a woman."

"Jack, we call our field officers, agents, too. The woman you're going to be working with is Peggy Garber. She was with Prince George's County for about eight years, lost interest, and started a picture framing business with her husband in Silver Spring."

"Picture framing?" Jack asked surprised. "That's a switch from police work."

"Yeah, I guess she's one of those artsy-fartsy types. Her husband has money. She wanted to do something she liked, so he helped open the business. She was tired of the cop bullshit. You know how that goes. Apparently she still wanted to keep her hands in police-type work and decided to take a position with us part-time. She is so good we've used her on some international assignments, so she does a lot of traveling.

To tell you the truth, I think her husband, who is from the Middle East, is getting a little tired of her being away. Since this case is local, she asked to be put on to stay close to home.

"Middle East?" Jack asked.

"Yeah, I'm serious, but now he's a naturalized citizen. He has more money than God, you know what I mean? She clearly doesn't need to work. You'll rendezvous this evening. You'll be in separate vehicles, but you'll have each other's phone numbers so you can communicate."

Silence filled the air for a few moments.

"Alright." Jack said, as he sat on the edge of his bed with his leg crossed, looking at his bandaged heel. "You know, maybe I *am* ready for a job like this. Surveillances are boring as hell, but it'll give me time to think about things. Let me get a pen to write down the information."

"That won't be necessary, Jack. Do you have a fax?"

"Yeah, I do."

"Give me the number and I'll fax all the information to you. If you have any more questions after I send it to you, just call me. My phone number will be on the fax."

Jack gave Bob his new fax number.

"I'm glad you've decided to do this."

"Do you need me to come in and fill out an application or something?" Jack said.

Bob laughed. "Jack, you're too much! Don't worry about it. I'm the Director of Operations over here; you don't need an application right now. We'll take care of all that tomorrow. Your experience is good enough for me. Deal?"

"Alright. You're the boss."

"Take care, and look, be careful," Bob said as he disconnected.

4

Jack thought about making more coffee, but decided to get a shower instead. After his shower, he checked his fax machine and saw one waiting. Jack grabbed it, went into the kitchen, and poured himself a tall glass of water. Moving into the living room, he sat down on his sofa and propped his feet on the coffee table. Guinness was next to him. Right now, she was the only companion he had.

The fax was on WISE letterhead with R.J. Lewis listed as Director of Operations. The information indicated the target as Robert Webster. His pedigree indicated he was a W-M, 28 years old, five feet and nine inches tall, weighing about 180 pounds with glasses and dark hair. Webster was a former Army private who was unsuited for the service, and was discharged early. He was suspected of selling weapons and information to a group of young local college students who were from the Middle East, specifically Pakistan. Webster's father is Colonel Warren Webster, a member of the Pentagon's inner circle. The Colonel was not thought to be involved.

The directive informed Jack to take a position at the south corner of Prospect and Potomac at 2100 hours and to not take action unless specifically required. A fellow agent, Peggy Garber, would be on the north corner near N street.

Classified Intelligence revealed the dissidents were thought to be purchasing SAMS (Surface to Air Missiles) and planning an attack somewhere in the world, quite possibly in the United States.

Jack read on.

They are very intelligent, wealthy young men with strong ideological beliefs being led by a student named Khalil Abrah, who aspires to be the next Osama Bin Laden. To accomplish this, Abrah knows he has to commit a massacre on a world stage. It is believed he may attempt an airline disaster, quite likely striking an airplane in the United States. Currently, Abrah is a student at Georgetown studying molecular biology. He has been seen in the company of other students with Middle Eastern heritage, including at least one female, whose identity is unknown. She typically wears a burqa, while the males wear traditional American clothes. Two members of the group are known as Amir and Abdullah NFI (No Further Information).

Jack put the paper down and took a drink of his water as he looked out towards the Monument, now fully illuminated by daylight. He didn't think the information was very thorough, nor credible. He wondered why WISE security was getting involved in what seemed like high-stakes surveillance. More questions ran through his mind. Why isn't the government investigating these college kids or the subject, Robert Webster? Or, were they? Who exactly was Robert Webster? How could Colonel Webster not know his son was selling weapons and probably secrets? Let's face it- it can't be easy to steal SAMS or missiles without a string of resources and people being involved.

Jack began to think further about Bob Lewis. Why did he call and how did he get his new phone number? He decided to call Bob back to reconsider the job. It didn't feel right to him. He grabbed his netbook, which was next to him on the couch, and *Googled* "WISE Security, Robert Lewis". Jack was happy the cable guy hooked up his cable the preceding day. He felt lost without it. Thank God, Julie was able to let him in since Jack was getting his car serviced.

Sure enough, Robert Lewis was listed as the Director of Security. Jack called the phone number on the fax.

"WISE Security, check-in desk," answered a man on the other end. "Yes, Bob Lewis please."

"Let me connect you."

He heard two beeps and, then there was silence. Jack waited.

"Robert Lewis' office," answered a woman.

"Yes, may I speak with Bob, please?"

"I'm sorry, he's not in today. May I take a message?"

Jack contemplated his message. There was too much information to formulate into something clear and now he felt embarrassed.

"No, that's okay, thanks," he said as he disconnected.

He thought about calling Captain Sproat at his old precinct and asking him if he really did recommend him to Bob Lewis for this security job, but it was Sunday. It was doubtful he'd be working. Captain Sproat was Jack's superior when he worked at the Metropolitan Police Department, or better known as MPD. The Captain was a commendable man and Jack thought highly of him.

He returned his thoughts to his new assignment. He picked up the papers and continued to read.

Bob stated he wanted Jack to only observe and take notes, but it would be advantageous to take pictures of the rendezvous between Webster and members of a Middle Eastern group. It was scheduled to take place at 2200 hours (10 P.M.) in front of Robert Webster's residence. Jack was advised: Take note of the time and items exchanged. Don't interfere. This information is classified, memorize your assignment and shred this document. It was also advised to carry a weapon while on duty.

On the cover sheet, Bob added an example of an incompetent investigator who allowed information to get into the wrong hands. As a result, the investigator was not only fired but also sued. Then in bold letters it read, "SHRED THIS DOCUMENT"

Jack's Glock 26 was still in evidence from the Rothschild shooting. Jack had a couple other semi-automatics but he remembered they were still at Julie's. He would take his Chief's Special. He'd received it as a gift from his grandfather when he graduated the academy over twenty years ago. It was nickel plated with a pearl handle that had a chip in it from when Jack dropped it once. Smith and Wesson had sought to develop a lightweight, concealable weapon with significant firepower. It was introduced in 1950 at an International Chief of Police convention, which is how it got its name. Jack liked it because it was a revolver and not an automatic. Revolvers never jam. He always kept it in under the mattress on his side of the bed.

He picked up the Sunday newspaper to check out how the Phillies did the previous night. They were his favorite team ever since he was a kid. He remembered Schmidt, Bowa and Carlton and the championship team of 1980. He still had his ticket from Game 6 when the Phillies won the World Series. He went with a friend and his father. It was a stroke of luck that a neighbor got sick and Jack got to go in his place at the last minute. He remembered the mounted police coming out along the sidelines to prevent all hell from breaking loose when Tug McGraw made the final out.

He got up and turned on the radio. Soon it would be time for *Breakfast with the Beatles.* He sat down, and picked up the *Post* again. He separated the sections, and grabbed the sports section.

He looked over to Guinness who was sound asleep.

Curiosity got the better of him so he got up to go get his gun. He looked between his mattress and box spring.

It wasn't there.

5

"Is he in?"

"Hold on," she said. "Is this Bob?"

"Yeah, Donna. How are ya?" Bob answered.

"Let me see if he's still on his other call," she responded.

After a reasonable pause, she came back on the phone.

"He said to call him on the other phone in five minutes. I think he's on the phone with the President," she whispered. "It shouldn't take long."

"Alright, I'll give him fifteen," Bob said. "Thanks."

Bob hung up. He smiled with self-satisfaction as he leaned back in his leather chair, lit a Cuban Montecristo Habana cigar and put his feet on the desk. He was proud that he could pick up the phone and talk with one of the most powerful senators in office without much difficulty. Bob felt almost as important as the President of the United States.

The FBI treated him with total disrespect by forcing him out, and now the stars were aligning for retribution.

He couldn't wait to be sitting on his yacht in the Caribbean, sipping on drinks and having his pick of women. His days as an FBI agent would soon be a footnote to his life.

Revenge is best served well-done.

Bob was sitting in his makeshift office at his home outside of D.C. in Beltsville, Maryland. Most federal employees didn't want to live in the District, so they bought homes in Prince George's County or Montgomery County. Now, years later, the homes were outrageously priced.

It was hard to fathom how new employees could expect to live in the suburbs without starving.

Thankfully, he bought his home years ago.

He made his garage into an office by doing some remodeling. He had the contractor put in extra sound barriers just to make sure Barbara, his wife, could never hear to whom he was talking or know what he was doing.

Bob and Barbara were married for almost nineteen years before their separation.

When they met, they were students at the University of Maryland.

He was interested in a career in law enforcement, and she was studying political science with a minor in accounting.

She had thought about pursuing a law degree, too.

Barbara was very attractive and was quite a catch for Bob, who was just average looking. She was very straight laced, and Bob had a wild side that appealed to her. They dated for two years after graduation and married. By then, Bob had become an FBI agent and Barbara had secured a job with the Justice Department. After five years, she decided that the IRS was better suited for her and she transferred to a position there.

When Barbara was 42 years old, she decided her biological clock was running out of time before she could have another child. She approached Bob with the idea of becoming parents again. They had one son, Robert, who was in a long care facility. When he was an infant he contracted an unknown virus, and now was totally disabled. She felt another child might change the cold climate of their marriage. But Bob enjoyed the finer things in life. He knew another kid would bring it all to an end, at least for another twenty years.

"Barb, I like our life the way it is," he said steadfastly. "If we were going to have more children, we should've done it years ago. What would you do? Quit your job?"

"I would like to quit, but if you think I need to work, I'll just take a leave of absence for a few months so we won't feel any financial hardship. I'll do whatever you want, Bob."

"And then what? Who's going to watch the baby when you go back to work? Your parents live in Delaware and mine are dead. We would have to hire someone and that cost money, you know? I think you've forgotten what's involved. Having kids is expensive. Think about what we'd be paying for Robert if it wasn't for your parents."

Barbara snickered at the timing of his acknowledgment in her parents' favor.

"I think I read somewhere the cost of raising a child from birth to college is over a million dollars," Bob continued. "That doesn't count the time and energy it takes. I talk with guys at work and all they talk about is going here, going there. Baseball practice, soccer practice, school work, doctor visits and hell, that's just while they're young. Then, they become teenagers. George Nickerson talks about his son like he's gonna be on the 10 Most Wanted List. Susan Eastburn talks about her son's cerebral palsy. That's something we can relate to. Christ, Barbara, the possibilities are endless and most of them aren't good!"

Barbara just looked at him. She should have known from college; Bob thought of only one thing: Bob.

Barbara's parents were never happy with their son-in-law anyway. He drank too much, smoked cigars, and was a loud, obnoxious jerk whenever they went on vacation together. They suspected he hit Barbara, too. Her mother wanted her to leave him, and come home. Finally, Barbara secretly decided a trial separation would be best for them, so she moved back with her parents.

In the last year, Bob called Barbara once a month. He had not seen her for several months. She had not filed for divorce yet, but if she didn't, he was going to. Once this job was over, he would never have to worry about money again. Like the FBI, Barbara and her parents would live to regret their contempt for him.

Bob picked up the phone and called the senator at the special number he had been given.

"Yes," answered Senator Rothschild.

"Good afternoon, Senator," Bob replied as he leaned forward in his chair.

"I don't have much time. Give me an update."

"Yes, alright; I think things are all set for tonight. Robert Webster, the Colonel's son, will meet on the block..."

"I don't have time to hear about the specifics!" the Senator interrupted. "Let's keep this brief; just tell me if it's going to happen."

Bob cleared his throat. "Yes, everything is in place. I don't expect any problems."

"Maybe you should expect problems, Bob, so you can counteract any if they occur," he said tersely.

"I've analyzed every scenario. There are back-up plans for every possible glitch."

"Good. Now, the money. Is it the same as we discussed?" the Senator queried.

"Yes, it is."

"They agreed to cash, correct?"

"Yes, they did."

"Now, when you receive it, you need to call me again so we can discuss the disbursement," said the senator.

"Is there any possibility we can obtain any more weapons? I have a feeling they are going to want more. I think we could capitalize on this…"

"I've thought about it. It's possible, but why are you so confident on taking more risk?"

"Easy," Bob replied, "more money."

"No, you don't understand. I can't risk any more exposure. And quite frankly I don't even like talking to you. Do you understand me?" asked the senator.

"Yeah, sure, but you could have designated someone else to talk to me."

"Yes, I've thought about that, but I'm interested in ensuring my cut Bob, and that this is done clean."

"Oh come on, give me a break," Bob answered, trying not to get angry.

"Don't talk to me like I'm some kind of idiot," the senator responded angrily. "You know damn well you could be getting more money and not telling me."

"Senator, you've been around long enough to know what those weapons are worth. Who's bullshittin' who?"

"I do know what they're worth, but I don't know if you've worked anything else into the deal."

"Like what?"

"Who knows? But if I find out you're fuckin' me, you'll live to regret it. Accidents happen, and I've got a lot of resources."

"You don't scare me, Senator. You brought me into this. If I really want to fuck with you, I could send you away for the rest of your life. I'm sure a little ol' former FBI agent could get immunity if he could deliver a United States Senator to the Justice Department. Who knows, maybe your wife would like to know about your mistress. Sandy, Isn't it?"

The senator wanted to jump through the phone and strangle Bob, but he had been around long enough to know if he lost his temper, he lost control.

"Alright, Bob. I don't think we need to play 'whose dick is bigger'. Just call me when you've made the transaction."

"Senator, I assure you, you will be the first to know. I will call you when the deal is done. Do you want me to call you the same way?"

"I'll have another phone. I'll get the number to you through the same channels. Oh! One more thing. You still have our friend involved?" the senator asked, still unable to say his name.

"Oh, yeah. He's never gonna know what hit him."

"That makes my day! I can't wait for him to go down."

"Me, neither."

"Thanks, Bob."

Bob focused his energy on the end result. He could care less about the senator and his threats. After this was all over, he would be able to live comfortably in the Caribbean for the rest of his life.

There was a knock on the door, breaking his train of thought. He looked out the peephole and saw Duke Callison.

Duke became a friend of Bob's years ago, when he worked for a security company. He was average height, slender build and had rugged looks. A man of many skills, Duke was an electronics and surveillance expert. When he was in the army, he worked in Ordinance. He was very familiar with all types of weapons, and was a qualified NRA instructor. Now, he worked for the government in a civilian capacity.

"Hey Duke, come on in," Bob said.

They went up the steps of Bob's modest split level home, into the living room, and sat down in a pair of Queen Anne chairs facing each other. There was a sofa and upright piano against one wall.

"Can I get you a beer?" Bob asked.

"Yeah, sure."

Bob went into the kitchen. "I have Heineken, Coors Light and Sam Adams," he shouted out.

"I'll take a Coors Light!"

Bob returned, carrying a can of Coors Light for each of them.

"Are you ready for tonight?" asked Bob with restrained excitement as he handed Duke his beer while sitting down.

"I am more than ready. I can't wait. Hell, you know me. I've got this all arranged."

"You realize we're taking some big risks tonight."

Bob clipped the end of another Cuban Montecristo and brought it to his mouth. He lit the foot, filling their small space with billows of aromatic smoke.

"I know we've been over it a hundred times, so I won't go over it again, but I need to ask you: Do you have the gun?"

Duke laughed.

"Not just any gun, Bob, but 'the' gun," Duke said with a satisfied smile on his face.

"Great. I don't need to know anything else," Bob smiled with contentment.

They continued drinking their beer.

"No need to be worried; my guys are ready," Duke said as he took a swig of beer.

Smoke continued to billow around the room.

6

Jack was upset about his missing gun. Hoping Julie had it, he would check with her tomorrow. He put Guinness in her crate. When Jack first got her, he crate trained her to protect his furniture. Guinness was 9 years old now and didn't chew anymore, but Jack didn't want to take any chances with his new furniture. Besides, he had read somewhere dogs feel more comfortable staying in a crate when the master isn't home.

"Don't you worry, Guinness. I won't be long," Jack said as he looked at her sad face.

Jack locked his front door, and started down the hallway to head out for his assignment, when he ran into a neighbor going into her condo.

"Hello there. Are you the new owner of the Shorts' condo?" asked the elderly woman.

"Yes, I am," Jack said, smiling as he offered his hand.

"I'm Miss McGarrity," she offered with a big smile while shaking Jack's hand. She had enough dentured white teeth to make any dentist proud. "I've been here for eighteen years. I've seen them come, and I've seen them go. Are you planning on staying here a while?"

"Oh yes, ma'am."

"I heard you're a retired police officer. Is that true?" she asked admiringly.

"Yes, it is," Jack responded proudly.

"That's great. We need some tough, young blood around here," she said wistfully.

Jack figured she was in her late seventies or early eighties. She probably was quite a beautiful woman in her day. She still looked great for her age. She was dressed regally with a fashionable blue blouse and matching pants. She was bejeweled with a pearl necklace and matching earrings. Her thinning gray hair was perfectly coiffed.

"Well, I'm glad to be here. If you need anything, please let me know," Jack offered.

"You're so gracious. You just moved here. I think I'm supposed to say something like that, aren't I?" she chuckled. "Would you like to come in and chat?" she asked hopefully.

"I would love to except I have an appointment at nine."

"I imagine someone like you has a lot of appointments," she said smiling. "Was that your girlfriend I saw helping you move in?"

Jack didn't want to talk about Julie's status, but for now, his response served its purpose. "Yes, that was her."

"Well, she's very beautiful."

"Thank you. Listen, I would like to talk with you right now, but I really have to go. Perhaps we can have coffee sometime," Jack said, as he started to walk away.

"That would be nice. Uh, you didn't tell me your name."

"I'm sorry. It's Jack Dublin," Jack said as he stopped his forward progress, but he didn't dare start walking back towards Miss McGarrity.

"That's a great name!"

"Thank you, Miss McGarrity. Take care now."

Jack continued walking towards the elevators. As he turned the corner he looked back, and saw Miss McGarrity still standing there by her front door, smiling and waving. "I think I found Gladys Kravitz," he thought to himself referring to the meddlesome neighbor in the sixties T.V. show *Bewitched.*

Jack got off the elevator and saw Henry, the concierge, behind the desk. Jack greeted him warmly. Henry looked like he was in his late sixties. Jack thought he was probably retired from the government, making a little extra money, since most people in this region seemed to be government employees. Henry was small in stature, with a slender build and well-combed white hair. He was dressed in a white short-sleeve shirt, red tie and dark pants. He wore dark rimmed glasses.

"Hello, Mr. Dublin. How's your day going?" Henry asked evenly.

"Great, Henry. How 'bout yourself?"

"Doing well, Mr. Dublin. Have a happy Father's Day! What's left of it, anyway."

"Same to you, Henry," Jack said as he descended the steps and walked towards the front door. Jack loved his new condo. Everybody in the building seemed friendly, and the view of Washington was terrific.

It was now 8:30 P.M. It would take Jack only ten minutes, fifteen max, to get to his assignment. He always made an effort to be on time. In his mind, if you weren't at least five minutes early, you were late. He was glad he had left early; otherwise, Miss McGarrity would have made him late.

He arrived at 8:46 P.M. and parked his car. The summer solstice was a couple of days away. Still, it was getting dark. Looking for Peggy Garber, Jack started to scan the area, trying to spot her car, before it got too dark. Jack didn't have a description of her car, but any good investigator could smoke it out. There were plenty of cars, and lots of activity, making it more difficult to figure out which one she was in.

Jack had written her number and Bob's number on a 3X5 card, even though he was supposed to destroy any written reference. Nobody would think anything of two phone numbers written on a 3X5 card if they found it.

At 9:00 P.M, he decided to call Peggy's number. It rang three times, before being answered with a pre-recorded message, indicating the number was no longer in service. He tried it again with the same result.

Jack thought about it, and figured he must have transposed a couple of numbers. He didn't want to seem incompetent right out of the gate, so he didn't try Bob's number. It should be an uneventful, boring night, anyway. He would call Bob in the morning.

As instructed, Jack brought a notepad, pencil, pen, book light and his new camera. He had also thought about bringing some bottled water, but realized he would probably have to use the bathroom and he couldn't leave the surveillance.

Jack watched the people moving around. Sons and daughters were coming and going to pay tribute to their dads. It was an old established neighborhood. The visiting "kids" were mostly in their twenties and thirties. It really didn't interest Jack. In a few hours, he would be back home in his new condo, sleeping.

The homes were Colonial architecture with front porches. Some were enclosed, and some were not. They sat up on gentle hills. It took twenty to thirty steps to get from the street to the front door. Parking, like most city parking, was tough unless you had a driveway. The homes in this area, most likely because of the way they were built on the hills, didn't have any driveways.

By 10:30 P.M, the neighborhood traffic had slowed down. Jack had casual time to think more about his life. Putting his police career behind him, he started to think about the future. Tonight already proved private investigation was too boring. Jack could hardly keep his eyes open even though he had been listening to the Phillies play the Nationals on the radio. As far as the future was concerned, this private investigation crap served little or no purpose, other than giving a security firm reason to justify its revenue.

Jack was always smart with his money, but going to law school when he was a police officer would have made things too tight financially. At forty-three years old, he was still young enough to consider a second career as an attorney. With twenty years of police experience, Jack would have a distinct advantage over most new attorneys.

Just then, a BMW pulled up in front of the target home, and backed into a parking spot directly across the street. Jack's instincts told him this vehicle was one to observe. There was a different feeling about it. His attention was now focused on the lone occupant getting out of the vehicle.

The driver, fitting the description of the target, seemed to be nervous by the way he looked around. Jack wondered if he knew he was under surveillance because of his suspicious actions. Jack's experience warned he was dirty; guilty of something illegal.

Finally, the target locked his car doors. Checking the driver's door to make sure it was locked, he walked around to the back of the vehicle and popped the trunk.

Reaching in, he removed two suitcases which appeared to be quite heavy since he was having difficulty handling them. Once they were on the ground, he closed the trunk. Struggling with the weight, the subject picked up the suitcases.

At that moment, another car came screeching around the corner. The target was just beginning to cross between his car and the one parked behind his, when the moving car came to a quick stop, blocking his path. Two men quickly got out of their car, and approached the subject. The driver remained in the car.

Jack watched intently, while blindly trying to reach his camera, which had fallen to the floor of the passenger side. He didn't want to miss what was going on, but he also wanted to get some shots. It was a matter of personal pride.

The men, who appeared to be Caucasian, backed the target up against his car. He was still holding on to the suitcases with a firm grip, while they talked.

They began screaming in his face, and the subject appeared to be alarmed. Jack couldn't hear specifically what they were saying, but he knew from the volume and tone, they weren't happy.

Clearly, they wanted what he had in his possession. The taller man reached out for one of the suitcases, but the target refused to let go. A struggle ensued. Just then, the driver got out, brandishing some type of weapon. Jack thought it was probably a knife. While continuing to fumble for his camera, Jack kept pushing it further away from his grasp every time he reached for it. Not wanting to turn on the interior light, Jack's attention was diverted fully to the floor. As soon as he leaned over, and felt around in the darkness for his camera, he heard a gunshot.

Jack immediately sat upright in time to hear and see the muzzle flash of two more shots. The target, presumed to be Webster, slumped against his car and slid to the ground. The driver reached into his car, and popped his trunk. While the other two men picked up the heavy suitcases, and lifted them into the trunk, the driver rifled through the prey's pockets. The assailants slammed the trunk lid and sped off.

Jack knew what he had to do. He immediately got out of his car and ran to the man lying in the street, getting there within thirty seconds. It was apparent the man was dying. Having been shot in the chest and abdomen, his breathing was labored and his color was pallid. Blood was pumping out into the street. Jack was soon wearing it. Wailing sirens could be heard in the distance.

The victim stared vacantly into space. Jack just held his hand. By the description he had been given, Jack knew it was Robert Webster. He had seen this empty look before, many times. It would take a miracle for Webster to survive. It was a miracle that wasn't going to happen tonight.

Jack looked around. Old habits never die. His police instincts took over. Evidence was the key to solving any crime. It was as if perpetrators always leave their autograph. Don't smudge their signature. Maintain the crime scene. It was the primary duty of the first responding officer.

Jack looked back at the victim but before he did, something caught his eye. He looked back at it, and saw it was a gun. Not just any gun. This gun had a pearl handle. His eyes examined the gun with renewed interest. The sirens were getting louder.

Jack couldn't believe it. It also had a chip in the handle just like his missing gun. The only way to tell if it was his would be to see if his initials were engraved on the metal part of the handle.

Jack's heart was pounding. The gun was several feet away. He knew from his training not to violate a crime scene, but he had to see the gun up close. He reached out, and pulled the gun towards him, as gently as he could. "JED" was clearly engraved on the handle. His initials.

"Put your hands up," screamed both officers, who were in a crouch stance, with their guns pointed squarely at Jack.

"NOW!"

7

Jack put his hands up slowly. He was fixated on the gun. He wanted to look at it closer, and hold it in his hands to prove to himself it wasn't his. Yet, he knew there weren't any Smith & Wesson Chief Specials floating around with a chip in its pearl handle, especially engraved with his initials.

"Lie on the ground and put your hands behind your head where I can see them, slowly!" one of the officers commanded.

Jack, who was on his knees, moved to the ground and placed his hands behind his head, just as he was told.

"I'm a police officer!" Jack shouted with his face in the pavement. Although no longer active, he still felt like he was. It'd only been a couple of months since his retirement.

"Don't move!" One officer holstered his weapon, while the other maintained cover. Finally, Jack felt one of his hands guided back and fitted for a handcuff. Then, the other was slipped into the other handcuff behind his back. The officer grabbed Jack's upper arm, and yanked him to his feet.

Jack turned to face the other officer. He didn't recognize him. He was so young and seemed like he was just out of high school.

"Listen, I am a retired officer with the MPD, I now work for…"

"Shut up!" barked the senior officer, a man by the name of Kowalski. He was about 5 feet 9 inches tall and stocky. He had blonde hair and looked to be in his late thirties to early forties. His jaw was square and his nose was large. Jack didn't recognize his ruddy face but had heard of him. Most people didn't like him because they thought he was a prick.

Kowalski then read Jack the Miranda rights from a laminated card. It was the card all officers kept, so if they testified in court, they could pull the card out and say they read it verbatim. It avoided any pitfalls on the witness stand. While Jack was cuffed, they started to pat him down.

"Do you have any other weapons or drugs on you?" Kowalski asked firmly.

"No."

"Do you have anything in your pockets that will cut me?"

"No."

The junior officer, who was wearing gloves for safety, began reaching into Jack's pockets looking for his identification. Jack wasn't carrying his retired police I.D. or driver's license. They were together in his badge holder wallet, back at the condo. An obvious oversight. He was only carrying fifty-three dollars. He continued to pat him down.

Once Jack was secured, Kowalski waved the paramedics in. The paramedics moved in and started to work feverishly on the victim. Kowalski called for a supervisor on his radio. Any time there was a shooting, the boss always wanted to be informed. Cars had already arrived in a fury. There were now enough officers for crowd control. Jack was pushed against the cop car and told detectives were on their way and to remain quiet.

"Looks like we're in for a long night," Kowalski shouted, to whoever cared to listen as he took his hand off the radio mike. "Take him over there and put him in the back seat."

The street was now being cordoned off with the traditional yellow tape for a crime scene. Flashing lights and a cacophony of police and ambulance chatter over a loud speaker filled the air. Jack watched Kowalski walk over to the paramedics near the victim. He was mumbling something, but Jack knew what he was asking when he saw one of the paramedics look up and shake his head no. People were coming out of their houses to try to get a glimpse of a dead man in the street. Oddly, there didn't seem to be any relatives of the victim coming forward.

"C'mon, keep walking to that car over there," the junior officer said, pointing at a black and white. They walked over to the car and the officer opened the back door. He helped Jack slide into the back seat by holding his right arm with one hand, and placing the other over Jack's head. As Jack sat down, he looked up at the officer. He saw "Walker" on his nameplate. Walker closed the door and went to the back of the car but Jack didn't turn to follow him. He just sat there. Alone.

He was sitting where he used to put rapists, murderers, prostitutes, drug dealers and thugs. The hard plastic seats were uncomfortable, just like they were supposed to be. Most departments had begun using these seats instead of soft leather or fabric. It made it more difficult for a detainee to hide any contraband missed during a pat down. It was also easier to clean up the blood, urine and vomit. You just hosed it down.

If there were any questions about his presence at the scene, he hoped Bob would clear it up. While sitting there, a few people walked by looking at him as if he were a murderer. Jack understood why. If you were sitting in the back seat of a police car at a crime scene with handcuffs, and there was a dead man in the street, you were guilty. Although it was callous, everyone, including him, thought that way.

He knew he was innocent and no charges could be brought against him, but he thought about the murder weapon. Was the gun really his? It couldn't have been. What are the chances? Or, was he just imagining things? He had to contact Bob Lewis as soon as possible.

Jack knew the detectives were probably on the way and he would remain isolated in the car until they got there. Thinking about what shift would be working, he knew it may be favorable for him if the lead investigators were guys he liked and respected, and vice versa.

A black unmarked Crown Vic pulled up. He saw Detectives Bill Keane and Nick Bucci get out. They started walking towards Walker, the junior officer. Bucci looked in and saw Jack. His mouth opened and his eyes widened in astonishment. He looked over to Detective Keane and waved him over. When Keane looked in, his reaction was identical to Bucci's. They walked back towards the rear of the vehicle. Jack heard them talking with Walker, but it was muffled and he was unable to hear exactly what they were saying.

Both Keane and Bucci walked back over and opened the door to Jack's side. Jack scooted across the seat and got out with Bucci's help.

"Jack, you've been read your rights?" asked Bucci.

"Yeah."

"You wanna tell me what's going on?" asked a concerned Keane.

"Bill, I was here as a private investigator, on an assignment for WISE Security firm. We had surveillance on the subject who was shot. I was watching from my car over there." Jack looks toward his car and nods. "As I was observing him, a car pulled up with two guys, who got out, and approached the victim. There was some type of highly animated discussion before an altercation broke out. Then the driver got out, pulled a weapon, and shot the victim."

"Did you get a tag number?" Keane asked.

"No, it was too far to see."

"Didn't you bring glasses with you?" Bucci asked referring to binoculars.

"No, I didn't think I would need them. I was told this was going to be a very simple surveillance," Jack said, slightly embarrassed.

"Jack, do you have a description of the assailants?"

"Well, it was dark and I couldn't really see them, but I think they were Caucasian," Jack answered.

"Could you I.D. them if you had to?" Keane asked, starting to get exasperated.

"Probably not," Jack said dejectedly.

"Can you at least give us a description of the vehicle?" Bucci asked, as if he was giving Jack an easy question.

"It was dark, but it looked like a Taurus or something like it."

Keane and Bucci looked at each other as if they were thinking the same thought.

"What are you thinking?" asked Jack, looking back and forth at them. "Possibly a government vehicle?"

They looked back at Jack. "Who knows? But that's an interesting thought," Keane answered ambivalently. "Jack, we're going to let the officer take you back to HQ. We have some more work to do here. When we get back, we will have to take a statement from you. Until then, I want you to collect your thoughts. Try to remember everything that occurred from the moment you arrived here until we did. Think about the men you saw, and the car they drove."

Jack was nodding his head. They made him feel like he was one of the investigators, instead of a detainee.

"Can you do that, Jack?" Keane asked with a furrowed brow.

"Absolutely," Jack answered in a positive tone.

They walked him back to the police car, and started to help him get in the back seat. As they opened the back door, Jack stopped and looked at them.

"You know, I had nothing to do with this," Jack stated, while looking hopeful for reassurance.

"We believe you, Jack," said Keane, trying to hide his skepticism. Bucci was nodding his head in agreement.

"Can you do me a favor then, and take these cuffs off?" he said, turning sideways with the cuffs behind him exposed.

"Jack, you know we can't do that," Bucci said regretfully.

Jack reluctantly started to get in the car. Keane saw the look on his friend's face.

"Tell you what we can do. If Officer Walker doesn't have a problem with it, we can handcuff you in front," Keane said leaning into the vehicle. "Is that okay?"

Patrolman Walker nodded his head affirmatively. He felt safe. The back doors were locked, and there was a cage between them. Jack turned around while they took his handcuffs off and cuffed him in the front.

"Thanks," Jack said with a sad smile. He got back into the car to begin his journey back to the place where he had worked for twenty years. It wasn't the way he wanted to walk in and see former co-workers. People he liked. People he depended on. People he once trusted.

8

It was a short ride back. On the way, Jack reflected on being in the rear seat. It was a view he never expected to have. The chatter on the police frequency handling emergency calls was minimal and that's the channel Patrolman Walker was tuned into. The officers at his scene had switched to another channel and Jack couldn't hear what was going on. Was it intentional?

"How long were you a police officer?" asked Patrolman Walker.

Jack moved his gaze to the rear-view mirror and met eyes with Walker.

"Twenty years."

"You must have seen all kinda things," Walker said with a grin.

"More than I care to remember," Jack said as he casually looked out the window, watching a young couple walk hand-in-hand along the closed storefronts.

"What units were you in?"

"Just about all of them. Patrol, C.I's, Sex Crimes…"

"You were in C.I's?" interrupted Patrolman Walker. Every cop who ever went on the force always had their eye on Criminal Investigation. It's even more popular now since CSI and other TV shows have glorified it.

"Yep."

Jack could have named more, but would have felt like he was bragging, which wasn't his style. Patrolman Walker began to act as if he were driving a celebrity around. Jack changed the subject.

"So, you married?"

"Not yet, but I am engaged."

"That's good. How old are you?"

"Twenty-three."

"You look like you're eighteen, no offense."

"I get that all the time," Walker said smiling.

"Why'd you want to become a police officer?"

"I have an uncle who's a Captain and he told me a lot of war stories that made me think it would be fun. Plus, you get to help people."

"Who's your uncle?" Jack asked curiously.

"Oh, you wouldn't know him. He's in Colorado."

"When did you come on?"

"I was in the last class."

"And how do you like it so far?"

"I'm still trying to get used to the shift work, but I like it."

"I hope it stays that way," Jack said with reticence.

As with most jobs, it's always exciting when it's fresh and new, but in time, even with the excitement of police work, you become jaded.

Walker pulled into the rear of the Metro Police Headquarters on Indiana Avenue. He parked near the back entrance and they got out. As they were walking in, Jack asked if he could have the cuffs removed once they were in doors. Walker hesitated and stammered, saying he would get suspended if anyone found out. He thought the virginal rookie would have been an easier touch. Not tonight.

The elevator was out of order so they walked upstairs to the Criminal Investigation Division. Jack was dreading the sight of his old office with all his former co-workers. They walked down the hallway until they came to the office. It could have taken forever and Jack wouldn't have minded. Walker opened the door and allowed Jack to walk in ahead. Fortunately, there were only three detectives in there.

"Jack, what the hell are you doing with bracelets?" said Billy Dawkins, as he saw Jack enter the room.

He was probably one of the only cops Jack truly trusted in the police department. Billy was a Vietnam Veteran and a damn good cop. He and Jack were partners at one time. Billy was one cool black dude. Whenever you needed some information anywhere in the rough areas of town, Billy was the guy you took with you. Everyone knew him as "Billy D" and he was definitely feared by most.

When they approached a door to inquire about someone they were looking for, Billy nonchalantly pulled his sport coat back and rested his hand on his gun, exposing his badge which was on his belt. When he politely finished asking questions, he always concluded with, "Tell him he's got twenty-four hours." Without fail, the word would spread through the neighborhood that Billy D. was looking for someone and sure enough, within twenty-four hours, someone would show up at HQ asking for Billy D. If it wasn't the one he was looking for, it was someone who knew the whereabouts of the missing party.

"I was at the homicide scene tonight."

"Well that's great Jack, but you're the one with bracelets. What's up with that?" he chuckled.

"It's a long story, but I was helping the victim when we..." He corrected himself, "Excuse me, I mean the officers arrived."

"Officer..." Billy leaned forward with a squint to look at the name tag. "... Walker. You can take those cuffs off my brother and you are dismissed. Damn, I need glasses," he said disgustedly.

"You've needed glasses for five years," Jack wisecracked. He felt a surge of relaxation in Billy D.'s presence.

"Hey, careful now, I'll tell 'im to keep 'em on," he said jokingly.

As soon as Jack had his cuffs removed, Billy reached out his hand and pulled Jack close to do the "Man Hug", a commemorative gesture given their partnership.

"God, it's been a couple years," said Billy D.

"At least," replied Jack.

"Well, have a seat".

Jack sat in the chair next to Billy's desk.

"Have they charged you with anything?" Billy asked pensively.

"Not yet," Jack answered, coming back to reality.

"Do you think they got anything on you?"

"No." Jack knew there would be no merit in discussing the murder weapon.

"Who's at the scene?" Billy inquired.

"Everybody and their brother."

"You know what I mean," Billy said. "Who are the C.I.'s?"

"I thought you knew," Jack answered with mild surprise. "It's Keane and Bucci."

Billy rolled his eyes and took his right hand and wiped his forehead as if he had a washcloth. "At least that's one thing in your favor. But I hate to tell you, Lieutenant Merrill's here."

Just then Keane and Bucci entered the office along with a few others.

Billy looked over.

"Well, look, here comes Frick and Frack," he said as he wrote down his number on the back of one of his business cards and handed it to Jack. "Here's my new cell phone number. If you need anything, call me any time, day or night," he said softly.

"Thanks, Billy," Jack said as he looked at the card before putting in his pocket.

"Jack, I need you over here" said Keane, as he walked past him and pointed to a chair next to his desk. "Thanks for keeping an eye on him, Billy."

Jack got up and sat at Keane's desk.

"Sit tight, we'll be right back."

Jack watched as they went into Lieutenant Dick Merrill's office and closed the door. He saw Lt. Merrill looking at Keane and Bucci as if he were listening intently. Then, he saw Merrill looking out through his window with a smug smirk on his face.

Lt. Merrill was one of the few people Jack despised. Years ago, Jack had told him something in confidence, and it got back to the source, ruining Jack's reputation with some of the staff and other police officers. Jack's secretive nature about his life outside of police work made it difficult for him to be trusted. Yet, he was loved by some, liked by most and hated by a few. Those few were a result of Dick Merrill's breach of confidentiality.

Lt. Merrill was an opportunist who thought nothing of ruining the reputation and career of another officer if it advanced his. He was useless as a street cop. Nobody wanted him for a backup. He was considered a coward. Yet, he was liked by some of the staff because he was a sycophant.

The Lieutenant's door opened and out came Dick Merrill, with a puffed out chest and a big grin on his face. He was tall and thin, and had bottle-black hair styled in a way that resembled a cul-de-sac. His nose was small and his ears were large. He wore glasses on the tip of his nose. He was followed by Keane and Bucci.

They walked over to Jack. Everybody in the room, including a few more detectives just arriving for duty, were now crowded around him. When the Lieutenant has something to say, everybody listens.

"Well, well, well," he said. "Look who it is. Jack Dublin. The man who can't stay away from his old office. In fact, he loves it here so much, that he shoots people just to get back in. What's the matter, Jack, can't stand prosperity?"

"Well, Lieutenant, it's you I really miss," Jack said with sarcasm.

"I bet it is. I always suspected deep down inside you had a thing for me," Merrill responded in kind.

Jack didn't respond.

"You really fucked up this time. We're going to nail your ass, at the scene of yet another murder, standing over the victim with a gun."

Jack remained quiet even though he wanted to get out of his chair and educate Merrill with a street beating.

"You're gonna love prison life, Jack. Don't forget to take your K-Y jelly with you."

Merrill started to laugh. The other guys just smiled.

"Take him and get a statement," he said as he started to walk away.

"Excuse me, Lieutenant," Jack called out. Merrill stopped and turned around.

"I think I know why your mother named you Dick."

The detectives in the room started to stifle laughs. Silence overcame the room.

"Why is that?" he asked.

"Because you were born one and grew around it."

A few of the detectives snorted with hands over their mouths trying not to laugh. Merrill started to simmer. His face turned beet red. He looked around the room at his squad. He couldn't think of any comeback before Jack spoke again.

"Y'know it always amazes me how the department, in its infinite wisdom, can promote someone who can't find sand at the beach," Jack said, enjoying the moment.

"Get him out of here!" Merrill said as he stormed back to his office.

Merrill got up and left the office. Once he was in his office, everybody told Jack how great it was to see him.

"Let's go to the interview room," Keane said seriously.

"I don't plan on being back here unless it's under different conditions. Take care, guys."

"Don't forget to call me," Billy D called after him.

Jack followed Keane and Bucci to the interview room. He had been there before. He knew the set-up. The room was fitted with a table and four chairs. There was a one way mirror on one wall. Jack figured Merrill might look in while he was giving a statement, but most likely nobody would be watching. They went in and Jack took his seat on the left side of the table, facing *away* from the mirrors.

"Jack, could you sit over here, please?" asked Keane, pointing to the other side of the table.

"Right," Jack said smiling.

Let the games begin.

9

"Jack, we need you to talk with us about what happened tonight," Keane said, taking the lead.

Jack had a predetermined statement in his head. He was going to give as little information as possible. If he were going to do it right, he would decline the statement and get an attorney. Yet, he knew his innocence and the facts would bear it out. He felt confident, even though there were innocent, incarcerated people who probably felt the same way before giving a statement.

This was different.

WISE, a respected and legitimate international security firm headquartered in Washington, hired him to do surveillance. Bob Lewis, a retired FBI agent who was a director for WISE, hired Jack directly. It would be a matter of record. Knowing Bob Lewis had something to do with his presence at the scene of a homicide, he needed to give the appearance of innocence.

Bob Lewis needed to be tracked down. If Jack refused to talk, Keane and Bucci would likely detain him for withholding evidence, preventing him from finding Lewis. Jack didn't have time for this. The sooner he could give them a statement and get out of there, the better off he would be. If they asked more about the gun, he would be evasive. After all, he doesn't truly know whose gun it is.

The statement began with the obligatory date, time and location of the statement; who was present; Miranda warning; and Jack's verbal confirmation of his identity, current address on file, pedigree and so on.

"Jack, tell us what happened tonight," stated Keane.

"Am I under arrest?" Jack asked plainly for the record.

"No."

"Am I a suspect?"

"No, you're just a witness to a shooting," Keane answered for clarification.

Jack wanted to confirm his status on the record. They called him Jack and not Mr. Dublin. This was a tactical decision and it did not go unnoticed. Maybe they thought they could lull him into making an incriminating statement. Jack was innocent and had nothing to worry about. Or did he? The mind can play games during times like these when you're under pressure.

"As both of you know, I recently retired from this police department. Early this morning, I was offered a job with WISE International, the international security firm here in DC, to conduct surveillance tonight at the location of the shooting. I arrived there at 2046 hours and began the surveillance. There was minimal activity until roughly 2235 hours. I saw the target arrive; he got out and popped the trunk to his vehicle, then took out a couple of suitcases and started to walk across the street. Then another vehicle quickly pulled up, and blocked him. The target stopped, two men got out and began speaking to him.

"Eventually a third man, the driver, got out of the car. The next thing I know, shots were fired and the target fell down. The shooter's accomplices took the two suitcases, while the shooter went through the victim's pockets. Then, they fled the scene. I got out of my vehicle and quickly ran to the target, which is now the victim, to see if I could render some type of first aid or get a statement. He was shot in the midsection and was bleeding everywhere. His eyes were rolling and he appeared to be going into shock. I was getting ready to call in, when I was told to put my hands behind my head by Officer Kowalski."

Keane was thinking about where to take his line of questioning. If he asked Jack if he had ever been involved in a shooting or whether or not this had something to do with his retirement, he knew he would cause Jack to stop talking. Right now, he was just a witness.

"Who is your supervisor at WISE?"

"Bob Lewis, retired FBI from the local office, here in DC. I had worked with him a long time ago."

Keane and Bucci looked at each other. Jack wondered what the inference was.

"What was your exact purpose for being there?"

"He sent me a fax stating the target was possibly involved in selling government information or weapons. I was told to record activities. That's it."

"How were you supposed to record the activities?"

"I was told to take notes."

"You weren't provided with a camera, or told to take one?" Keane asked.

"No." Jack thought he could evade the question because there were no pictures taken with his camera but then he remembered he had his camera in the car. "I was not provided with one but I took my personal camera there. It's in my car."

"Did you take any pictures?"

"No. I couldn't; everything happened too quickly."

Keane and Bucci glanced at each other.

Jack was starting to feel their suspicion. It was Bucci's turn to ask a few questions.

"Y'know Jack, knowing you like we do, I can't believe you didn't take any pictures."

"Like I said, it was my first assignment and it was supposed to be a simple assignment," Jack said maintaining his composure. He didn't want them to detect he was starting to get pissed off. When that happens, it's like sharks circling for the kill. "You can check out the camera when you take me back to my car."

"Was there anyone else with you?"

"No."

Jack remembered the other agent but he knew he'd have to get in touch with her himself before the police did. Everything must be handled with care. He had no idea what she knew or if she really existed. Later, if they discovered her presence, Jack could just say he didn't establish her presence and he didn't know for sure if she was really there.

"When did you start working for WISE?"

"Like I said, tonight."

"And this Bob guy, he sent you a fax? Is this how you were provided information about the person you refer to as a target?"

"Yes."

"Okay, we're going to need this fax."

"That's not possible."

"Why not?"

"I destroyed it."

"What?"

"I was told to do so by Bob Lewis. The document was classified, I was told to shred the fax after reading it. I followed through."

"I don't understand, why would you shred this fax?"

"Because I did as I was asked. I was told to shred it."

"Alright. Okay, no fax. What time did you arrive at the scene of the shooting?"

"2046 hours, like I said."

"That sounds pretty exact," Bucci said assertively.

"I deliberately looked at my clock in the car and it said 8:46. I then recorded it in my notes," Jack said flatly.

"Where are your notes now?"

"In my car."

"What else is in your notes?"

"Just the time of the target's arrival."

"What time was that?"

"If I remember correctly, it was at 2235 hours."

"What time did the assailants arrive, the ones in the Taurus?"

"I don't remember. But they got there within a few minutes of the target's arrival."

"But you did record the target's arrival?

"Yes, I did."

Bucci leaned back in his chair and crossed his arms while staring at Jack.

"But you didn't write down when the shooter's car arrived? Do I have that right?" Bucci asked smugly.

"Like I said, I don't remember. My notes will reflect whether I did or didn't."

Jack was starting to get angry. He didn't like being on the receiving end of these questions or getting the run around.

"Getting back to the alleged fax..."

"There is no "alleged" fax. I received a fax. That's what I'm telling you." Jack responded testily.

"Well Jack, I guess we'll have to call it an alleged fax since you can't confirm it with a copy. When you think of it, you destroyed evidence."

Keane stopped, and looked at Jack. Clearly, he was trying to play a psychological trip on Jack to see if he would say anything to provide more insight into the shooting.

This was not an interview. It was an interrogation. Usually, it was good cop, bad cop, but they were both punching him at the same time. No jabs, just right hook, left hook.

Jack tried telling himself they were just doing their jobs, but his Irish heritage was getting fired up. Yet, he knew it would be best to play rope-a-dope, like Muhammad Ali. Let them think they were winning.

Keane knew he was getting to Jack.

"What can you tell me about the target?" asked Bucci, who knew that Jack was getting angry with Keane.

"The target was Robert Webster. The fax I received said he was twenty-eight years old and believed to be selling weapons and secrets to a group of students who are of Middle Eastern descent."

"Did it indicate who these students are, or where they go to school?"

"Yes, but just basic information."

"And you no longer have the fax that contained this information?" Keane asked sarcastically.

"That's right. Glad you could follow along," Jack answered, returning the sarcasm.

"Okay, getting back to the camera. Let me understand this correctly. You were assigned to observe the target, or Robert Webster, and just take notes?" asked Keane.

"Yes."

"But they didn't give you a camera, so you took one and didn't use it. Is that what I am supposed to believe?" asked Keane while holding out his arms with disbelief.

"Look, you can try to make me look like a fool here guys, but this is all I have."

"That seems kind of odd to me, Jack. Isn't a camera a staple of surveillance?"

"You have to understand; I took this assignment half-heartedly and didn't even know if I was going to do any more work for WISE. It was kind of a lark for me. You know what I'm saying?"

"So you're telling me you did this half-assed and figured you wouldn't need a camera. Is that right?"

"Yeah, that's it exactly," Jack said through gritted teeth.

"Rumor has it that you have recently come into some wealth, is that correct?" Bucci asked.

"What about it?"

"How did you acquire this …prosperity?"

"It's an inheritance. If you want to verify it, go dig."

"It's a matter of record, so I'm sure we won't have to dig too much," Keane stated.

The statement continued. They talked some more about the vehicles and suspects. The interview ended an hour and twenty minutes after it began.

"We don't have anything further, Jack," Keane said. "We'll take you home now but I have to tell you, don't leave town. We'll have more questions."

"Just take me back to my car," he said disgustedly.

"Your car's been impounded."

"What the hell for?" Jack asked with his voice raised. Impounding a witness' car is hardly ever necessary and Jack knew this.

"Jack, this is a homicide. Okay? You were present. We had to impound it for now."

"Whose orders?"

"Mine," said Keane.

"We don't mind giving you a ride home," said Bucci. "You'll probably be able to get your car tomorrow after we check it out, don't cha think?" he asked looking at Keane.

"Fuck you guys! I'll get a taxi." Jack said angrily.

"Suit yourself," Keane responded ambivalently.

They left the interview room and walked down to the front door of HQ. No one spoke further. Jack walked out, looked both ways and started to jog. He never looked back.

"What do you think?" asked Bucci.

"He's innocent."

"Why are you so sure?"

"Because I think Jack's a good man. He was misunderstood by a lot of people, but he's honest. Besides, I wouldn't have been able to piss him off like that if he was really guilty."

They turned around to walk back to the office. Lt. Merrill was hurriedly coming in the opposite direction and stopped them both.

"Where's Dublin?" he asked excitedly.

"He just left."

"Are you serious?"

"Yeah. We took a statement and told him not to leave town."

"Just a witness? The gun at the scene is registered to him," Lt. Merrill said as he looked at Keane and Bucci for a response. They both looked at each other astounded.

"That's right. Jack Dublin is a murderer!"

10

The skies opened up and the deluge began. It had been a long day, yet Jack was not tiring. Even though he had been awake since early yesterday, he was still jogging thirty minutes after he had left Keane and Bucci at HQ. He wanted to get to Julie before she left for work. He was not looking forward to it, but he needed her help.

The streets were starting to show signs of day-to-day life. Delivery trucks were traveling the streets, and people were starting to leave for work. A patrol car cruised past him without any sign of recognition. It made Jack more paranoid. He knew it was a matter of time before they realized the murder weapon was registered to him.

He had little time to find Bob Lewis or Peggy Garber, if she truly existed. He needed to use a car, and didn't want to return to his condo. Hopefully, he still had some clothes at Julie's.

She lived in a fairly modest area between Georgetown and Silver Spring, with her townhome still in D.C. limits. It was a beautiful place to stay, as Jack often did. In the fall, the leaves were robust with color, and Julie's balcony overlooked a wooded area. It was a favorite time for Jack to stay at Julie's. He felt so comfortable with her. He preferred her townhome to his own place. Now that he owned a new condo overlooking the tidal basin, the pain of no longer staying at Julie's was diminished, but the pain of losing her was not.

Jack ran up to Julie's door just as it was opening.

"Jack, what are you doing here?" asked Julie surprised. She had just opened up her umbrella.

"Julie, I...I need your help."

"What's wrong?" she asked with genuine concern.

"Can we go inside where it's dry, and talk about it?"

"I'm leaving for work. I have to be there in twenty minutes. You'll have to make it fast," she said exasperated.

She opened the door wider and Jack hurriedly went inside, walking past her. Her home was stylishly furnished; the walls were covered with watercolors and eclectic works of art. The furniture was oversized and comfy.

"There's some coffee in the kitchen; I just turned it off," she added.

Once inside the door, he walked directly to the living room. Julie shut the door and put her umbrella down. She hoped he would go to the kitchen and not the living room. This meant he wanted to talk, and she was going to be late. Jack started to frantically pace back and forth. Julie had never seen him like this. She looked at her watch.

"Would you like coffee?"

"That would be great, Julie," Jack said still pacing.

Julie rolled her eyes and then went into the kitchen, poured him a cup, and fixed it how he liked it, black with one small scoop of artificial sweetener. When she gave it to him she said, "Jack, please, I don't mean to hurry you, but I have to leave."

"I'll try to be quick. I'm in trouble. I didn't do anything wrong, but I think I've been set up."

"How? What are you talking about?"

"Last night, I went on a surveillance..."

"What do you mean? I thought you were done with police work," she interrupted.

"Well, it wasn't sanctioned by the police. I was called by an old friend (at least I thought he was an old friend) who is retired from the FBI, and he asked me to help him by working a surveillance assignment for his security company. I went to the location where he told me to report. He said it was going to be simple; all I had to do was watch a man come home, walk into his house and write down the times. I've been bored and this was a distraction for me, and like I said, I thought it was going to be simple."

"What happened?"

"The man I was supposed to watch was murdered, right in front of my eyes."

Julie's eyes and mouth opened wide. "Oh my God!"

"To make matters worse, I think the gun that killed the guy was mine."

"Your guns are here. In fact, I want you to take them with you. I want them out of here. You know I don't like guns."

"Where are they?" Jack asked trying to remember what guns he had.

"In my bedroom under the bed, I think. You also left your police I.D. here too."

They both looked at each other and quickly went into the bedroom. They looked under her bed but didn't see anything except shoes. Jack started feverishly pulling out her boxes of shoes, and thankfully found his Smith and Wesson Model 1911, .45 caliber, in his canvas gym bag. He had bought this gun from another officer who needed the money. It was a $1500 gun which he bought for $600. He also found his Sig Sauer SP 2022 9mm. along with several boxes of ammunition for both guns.

He dropped the clips out of them and racked them. No bullets came out. He had left them without one in the chamber, out of respect for Julie. He inserted the clips, and racked one in the chambers. He placed the guns back in the gym bag.

"Did I leave any clothes here?"

"No. I took them over yesterday."

Jack just looked at her. He now realized, leaving him was prearranged. Julie handed Jack his I.D. which was in her nightstand. He was glad it was there and not back at his condo.

"What are you gonna do?" she asked, as she started back towards the living room.

"I have to try to find Bob Lewis or Peggy Garber."

"Who's Peggy Garber?"

"I don't even know if she exists, but Bob told me there was a woman by the name of Peggy Garber helping with the surveillance."

"How could she be helping if you don't even know if she exists?" Julie said with a strained look.

"I don't know."

"C'mon Jack, I have to get to work," she said running out of patience.

"I have to find them before the police find me. Jesus! Listen to me. I'm running from the cops. Not long ago, I was a cop. How pathetic!"

"C'mon. Walk me to the door. We have to leave."

"Julie, can't you call in sick today?"

"No! I can't! My boss is back today from an overseas trip, and we are supposed to have an important meeting. Besides Jack, yesterday you told me where I stand in your life. Nowhere!"

"Julie, listen to me. I killed a 22-year-old kid, who had his whole life ahead of him. Yes, it was justified, but nonetheless, I killed him. Have you ever killed anyone? Have you ever seen life leave a body, and know you were responsible?"

Julie shook her head.

"Right. Neither had I. I have to tell you, I've seen people with their brains splattered against the wall, decapitations, stabbings and I've gone to autopsies. I thought I was immune from feelings, but when you take someone's life, even though he deserved it and it was justified, it plays with your mind. The fact he was the son of Senator Rothschild made it much worse, because even if I want to forget about it, I can't."

Julie listened compassionately. Her feelings for Jack were still strong. She had never heard him express himself like this. He never gave her the impression he had any soft spots, except for his son. Yet, she instinctively knew Jack was not as callous as he liked to think he was.

"Julie, tonight was a set-up. Someone took one of my guns from my condo, killed the guy right in front of me, and then left it at the scene to frame me. I don't know who's behind it, but I intend to find out. First thing I have to do is talk to Bob Lewis, if I can find him.
Julie, can I borrow your car?" Jack asked switching gears.

"I want to help you but I have to go to work."

"What does that have to do with borrowing your car?"

"Nothing. You can borrow it but I need it back."

"I promise, I'll get it back to you."

"When?"

"When do you need it back?"

"How about tonight by eight?"

"I can do that," Jack said shaking his head.

Julie just continued to look at Jack to make sure he understood she was serious about getting the car back by eight. She then went into her pocketbook for her keys.

"You can drive me to work."

"I would love to," Jack said. He wanted to hug her but he didn't want to piss her off.

Jack drove Julie to the entrance of the building where she worked. Traffic had been heavy as usual, and the rain added to the drive time. He still managed to get her to work only five minutes late. When Jack pulled up to let Julie out, there was an awkward silence between them. They acted as if they were high school kids ending their first date.

"Thanks for taking me to work," Julie said.

"No Julie, thank you. Thank you for being so understanding. I don't know what I would do without you right now."

Julie just looked at him without responding.

"Listen, I will have your car back to you tonight."

"Do you think you'll have it back by eight?"

"I don't know where today is going to take me, but I promise to have it back by eight. Do you need me to pick you up after work?"

"No, I can get a ride home. Why don't you call me later to let me know about what time you'll be over?"

"Okay, I can do that."

They looked at each other not knowing what to do next.

"I've gotta go. I'll see you tonight."

Jack just nodded his head. Julie turned, got out of her car and went into her office building while Jack watched. His thoughts were confused. He really cared about Julie but then he returned to his predicament. He wanted to get over to Bob Lewis' office, but first he had to decide what he was going to do with the guns. He didn't want to be driving around with them in case he was stopped. He decided to go to his gym, which was close by, and put them in a locker.

After securing his guns, he went to midtown and parked his car in a garage. Jack then went to get something to eat at a Mom and Pop restaurant close to the Rollins Building where WISE International had their offices. This would allow Bob Lewis more time to get to his office.

While eating his breakfast, Jack read the newspaper. He was curious to see if there was any mention of the shooting. There wasn't. Jack figured the paper was printed before the story broke. He was happy because it bought him time. Nevertheless, he was still curious to find out how the shooting would be depicted, and how he would be mentioned in tomorrow's paper.

The streets were filled with people as always, people who appeared to be walking aimlessly yet having some intricate, complicated purpose. It always amazed Jack how many actually worked in the city. The majority were no doubt connected to the government in some way. Washington was still fascinating after twenty plus years.

Jack arrived at the Rollins Building at 10:15 hours. It was another large edifice in the city of monolithic buildings. The foyer was white marble and very pristine. A uniformed security guard stood sentry behind the front counter in the lobby. There were waist-high, metal gates that required keycard entry. Jack looked at the menu board by the gates, and began walking towards the gates. If he had the chance, he was going to hop over them.

"Sir," the guard called out to Jack.

Jack ignored him. Just act like you own the place and nobody will bother you.

"Sir," the guard called out again, this time louder.

Jack couldn't ignore him.

"Could you tell me what floor Bob Lewis is on?"

"Do you have an appointment?"

"Not exactly, but he should be expecting me."

"Let me check," the guard answered. He began mumbling to himself. "Let's see, I think he works in investigations, 12th Floor; here it is." He began dialing the extension.

"Mary, this is Mike downstairs at the security desk. There is a gentleman down here. What is your name, sir?"

"Jack Dublin."

The guard looked at him hesitantly before speaking on the phone. "His name is Jack Dublin and he is here to see Mr. Lewis," the guard said before pausing. "No? Okay Mary, Tha.........,"

Jack interrupted him, sensing he was about to be told he didn't have an appointment.

"Excuse me, before you hang up, could you ask her to tell him I'm in the lobby? I'm sure he wants to see me."

"Mar, Mr. Dublin would like......Okay," the guard responded. The woman on the other end had heard Jack.

People were filing past the guard, each showing their I.D. with an occasional "Good Morning, Mike."

"What? Okay, I'll tell him." Mike hung up the phone. "I'm sorry Mr. Dublin, but Mr. Lewis' secretary said that Mr. Lewis does not have an appointment with anyone named Jack Dublin."

It confirmed Jack's suspicions. Bob Lewis was going to ignore him. Why? And, who was really behind it, the Senator? Bob Lewis was not getting away that easy.

"Mike, Mr. Lewis has a good sense of humor. I think he's bustin' on me about something that happened last night. Could you call his secretary again and see if he'll see me now? I'm an old police friend of his," Jack said showing his retired police I.D.

Mike smiled. He looked like a man who wanted to be a cop, but for some reason never made it. Jack thought he probably understood the camaraderie of cops, the largest brotherhood in the world. Mike looked to be in his mid-thirties. Maybe he thought he still had a chance. He did have a military presence.

He tried again. After a minute on hold, Jack could hear the secretary saying something to Mike, but didn't know what it was until Mike looked perplexed. He hung up the phone.

"I'm sorry Mr. Dublin, but Mr. Lewis said he's never heard of you."

"That's insane. He hired me to do surveillance last night."

"Well, then, just show me your ID and I'll let you in."

Jack paused. "I don't have an ID. He said he was going to get me one this morning. Last night was my first assignment."

Mike looked at Jack dubiously and then smiled. "Mr. Dublin, with all due respect, it is highly unlikely that this company would hire anyone without giving them an ID. They're pretty strict here. WISE International is a company that works with Fortune 500 companies. It is the most respected security company in the world."

After last night, Jack didn't need to hear Bob Lewis didn't know him, much less have a security guard tell him about procedures. Jack needed time to think. He needed to see Bob Lewis and get his questions answered. Jack was not going to allow himself to be a scapegoat.

"Okay, thanks for trying. I'm just going to go over here and see if I can resolve this on my cell phone. Thanks again."

Jack moved over to a place close to the gates leading to the elevators but far enough away so he wouldn't get the guard's attention. He pulled out his cell phone and acted like he was talking with someone. More employees started to come through the door. As soon as Mike was distracted, Jack walked into a group of employees and got on the elevator. As the doors were closing, Mike caught a glimpse of Jack on the elevator.

"Hey! Come back here."

It was too late. Jack made sure he pushed the close doors button and pushed 12. He was going to see Bob Lewis, and he was not going to be stopped. The elevator opened on the 12th floor and Jack hurriedly went to the only open door on the floor. As he opened the door, he saw a receptionist behind a desk.

"I'm here to see Bob Lewis," Jack said rather hastily.

"Do you have an appointment?"

"No, I don't," Jack smiled as he flashed his retirement badge and turned on the charm. "I just got into town and I want to surprise the ol' boy. Where's his office?"

"Oh, his office is down that hall," she said pointing to her left. "But I don't know if I should let you go down there without getting permission."

Jack heard the bell for the elevator and looked over. He knew security would be hot on his trail. The doors opened and two uniformed security guards got off in a hurry.

"Believe me, it will be alright," Jack said as he started to run down the hallway in the direction of Bob Lewis' office.

"There he is! Hey you! Stop right there!" they yelled simultaneously as they started to run in Jack's direction.

Jack continued down the hall looking for an office with a name on it. He knew he had one chance. Jack ran just a short time and found a door with R.L. Lewis on it. He opened it. There was a secretary sitting at a desk in front of another office. She was on the phone and paused immediately.

"Can I help you?" she asked.

Jack started walking past her.

"Hey, wait a minute. You can't go in there," she said excitedly.

Jack opened the door.

"Alright you son of a ...," Jack saw a handsome black man sitting at a computer and he stopped in mid-sentence. He was light skinned with a pin-striped shirt, blue tie and suspenders. He looked to be in his late forties and in great shape. The Bob Lewis he knew was white and untidy.

"Can I help you?" the gentleman asked calmly.

"I was looking for Bob Lewis," Jack said with an astonished look on his face.

"I *am* Bob Lewis," he said. "What do you want with me?"

"I'm sorry; I'm looking for a different Bob Lewis."

"I am the only Bob Lewis that works for this company as far as I know."

The uniformed security guards walked into Mr. Lewis' office and each grabbed one of Jack's arms, standing on either side of him. It was apparent he was totally confused. The look on his face confirmed it to everyone in the room.

"Did you ever work for the FBI?" Jack asked as an afterthought.

"No. I worked for the Secret Service," he said smiling.

Jack stared at the desk and then the floor. He didn't know what to say.

"I'm sorry, I bothered you," Jack said staring aimlessly.

"Mr. Lewis, do you want to press charges against this man for trespassing?" asked the guards.

"No, I think this man apparently made an honest mistake. Just escort him from the building."

Jack said nothing. He just stared in space, giving no resistance, as the guards, hustled him out of the office and to the elevator. The entire ride down in the elevator, Jack never said a word. He acted catatonic. He knew he had been set up but he thought Bob Lewis, the one he knew, truly worked for WISE. They walked him past Mike through the front door.

"Sir, you are not allowed back in this building. If you come back, we will hold you until the police come to arrest you for trespassing. Do we understand each other?" said the older of the two guards.

Jack slowly shook his head affirmatively. They let go of his arms and walked back into the building. Jack just stood in the same spot they left him. He was still trying to gather his thoughts. What the hell is going on? Where the hell is Bob Lewis and how am I going to find him?

He started to walk in the direction of Julie's car, trying to clear his head when the thought came to him, Peggy Garber. At least that's what Bob Lewis said. Maybe it was just bullshit like the other information he had been told, but he still had to try and find her if, in fact, she did exist.

Jack sat on a bench to collect his thoughts. Bob had said she and her husband owned a framing shop in Silver Spring. He would look for the address and if one existed, he would go there. Maybe she could fill in the blanks. If that failed, he would call Billy Dawkins and see if he could look up information on her, and Bob Lewis.

Jack got up and started for his car. He needed to head back to his condo. He needed clothes and his credit cards to get more money.

11

"Lieutenant, we need to put a plan together first," Keane said. "Jack's not stupid. We can't just grab him. He knows the gun is his, and knows we're going to figure it out. Most likely, he's not going back to his condo. We need to build some more evidence to nail him good."

"Okay Sherlock, what do you have in mind?" Merrill asked mockingly.

"Let's go into your office and talk about it."

Keane and Bucci followed an angry Merrill to his office, closing his door for privacy.

"Let me tell you something. I know you guys don't want to believe it, but Jack Dublin is a murderer," Merrill started. "He shot and killed the Senator's son, then shot and killed someone else. At some point in time, he lost his marbles. To tell you the truth, I never thought he was stable to begin with. He's always been a whack job in my book. This confirms it. There is no doubt in my mind, he needs to be taken off the street, and put in a cell where he gets it stuck up his ass on an hourly basis. You two need to get a search warrant for his residence. I don't know where he lives, but wherever it is, find him. I want that search warrant to cover anything bigger than an insect. Do you two clowns understand what I'm saying?"

"Yes sir, we do," they said harmoniously. Everyone in the unit had been a victim of his condescending remarks to the point of turning a deaf ear.

"I want to nail that son of a bitch," he growled.

Keane and Bucci sat there not saying a word. There were times when you had to just nod your head, especially with an abusive supervisor like Merrill.

"Do you guys think you have enough probable cause or do I have to help you write the warrant?"

"No sir, I think we have it under control, but I need to ask a question," Keane said.

"What?"

"Do you think we have enough to charge him with murder now, or do you want to see what the search warrant yields first?"

"Good question! I think we have enough to charge him at the very least with conspiracy and go for the search warrant. We could probably put murder around his neck but I want to make absolutely sure we do this right. Hopefully, you'll find some incriminating evidence to solidify a homicide charge. Even if you don't, I think we have enough to get a conviction."

Merrill looked at them for a reaction. "Anything else?"

"No, sir."

"Then get your asses out of here and get the warrants. Bring back Dublin! I want you to call me when you apprehend him. I can't wait to look that pompous son of a bitch in the eye. I would love nothing better than to come to work tomorrow and see his ass in our cell."

"Yes, sir."

Keane and Bucci sat there waiting to see if he was done with his tirade.

"What are you waiting for? Get the hell out of here!" he yelled.

Keane and Bucci left his office and went back to their cubicles.

"Holy shit! Did you see how pissed the L-T is?" Bucci asked. "I don't think I've ever seen him this pissed."

"Yeah I know, and to tell you the truth, I'm pissed too!" answered Keane.

"I don't understand what the big deal is. We're gonna get Dublin. There's no doubt in my mind."

"You don't know what the big deal is?" asked Keane in amazement.

"Well, yeah, I know what the big deal is, but we've got it under control."

"We do? I think if we did, we wouldn't have to try to find him. He'd be sitting downstairs right now. It pisses me off that he sat here and lied to us the whole time. Then, by cutting him a break, we look like a couple of buffoons."

Bucci shook his head in agreement. "Why don't you write the search warrant while I write the arrest warrant?" asked Bucci.

"You're kinda gettin' the better end of that deal, aren't you?" Keane cracked derisively.

"You want me to do the search warrant?" Bucci answered seriously.

"No problem. I'll get it started and you can help me once you're done with the arrest warrant. We need to get his address. Maybe we can check the system for that."

"You won't find it there. He lives in Virginia, remember?" Bucci pointed out astutely.

"Shit! You're right. Let's check the statement and get his address. Then, maybe we can send a patrol unit over there to confirm. I think either he said, or someone else said, Jack lives in a condo. If that's the case, it shouldn't be hard to confirm. After we confirm his address, we're gonna have to get a police agency to assist us. I'd rather work with a local agency instead of VSP or the *feebies*," Keane said, indicating the Virginia State Police or the FBI. "They *could* get involved since it would be interstate. You know what that means once they're involved. We lose all control and they take the glory. Not to mention, Merrill would have our asses."

"I guess we have to get with the L-T again."

Keane sighed. "He's gonna flip out again. Let's find out where Dublin lives first."

After listening to the taped statement, they called the Winthrop House condos in Rosslyn. The manager declined to verify Jack's address based on confidentiality. They decided to call the Arlington police to drive over and verify. A uniformed police officer always seems to get more cooperation. Within fifteen minutes, they got a call back confirming Jack's address.

"I guess it's time to talk to the Lieutenant," said Keane.

They got up from their cubicles and walked to the Lieutenant's office. He was still sitting there going over paperwork. Normally, he would have been gone a couple of hours ago.

"Do you have the probable cause done on the search warrant?" he asked.

"No sir, we don't."

"Why not?" he asked pensively, as he put his pen down. He was too tired to yell.

"Well, sir, a small problem has come up," answered Keane.

"Like what?"

"Dublin doesn't live in our jurisdiction anymore."

"Where does he live?"

"He lives in Rosslyn."

"Shit!" the Lieutenant said as he sat and pondered the situation while tapping his pen against the desk. "Well, it looks like we'll have to use another agency to help us. Who has jurisdiction?"

"It's the Arlington PD. We called them to check Jack's address, which we took from his taped statement. We got a call back confirming it within fifteen minutes."

"Great, call their detective division and get someone to help you. Stay away from the state police if you can. I don't want their noses in this, and whatever you do, keep the fuckin' FBI out of this. If they smell this, they will take over the entire investigation. If you have any problems, let me know right away."

"Thanks, we will."

Keane and Bucci returned to their desks.

"You want a coffee?" asked Keane.

"Sounds good; you makin' a pot?"

"Nah, I'm just gonna get it from the machine in the break room."

"Hang on, I'll go with you," Bucci said walking over to his desk. He opened the drawer and took some change.

Walking downstairs, they discussed calling their wives to tell them they wouldn't be home any time soon. Keane was recently remarried to a school teacher. His first wife, a nurse, ran off with a doctor. This time he married a younger woman. She was attractive, madly in love with him, and pregnant with their first child. She appreciated his responsibilities as a cop, and was understanding to a fault.

Bucci, on the other hand, had been married for twenty-five years to a nice Italian girl. They had known each other since elementary school and were married right out of high school. They had three kids almost right away. All of them were great kids. Two were in college and the last one was a senior in high school. The youngest boy, Tony, was an athlete headed for a scholarship. Nick was ecstatic about it. Always complaining how expensive college was, he was a proud man who boasted that his wife Rita, never had to work. She was a stay-at-home Mom and as a result, his kids were never in any trouble, got great grades and had a terrific future. Now, Rita wanted to find a job, but Nick put his foot down. It was a recent source of strife.

When they arrived at the break room, each of them got coffee out of the vending machine and Bucci also bought a bag of peanut M & M's.

"I don't know how I can drink this stuff," Keane said, taking a sip and wrinkling his nose. "It's rank!"

"I know, diluted brown water. Hey, at least it's hot and wet caffeine."

"Listen, when we get back upstairs we've got to get crackin'. After we draw up the probable cause then we have to get in touch with the Arlington PD. They will have to stand with us to get a search warrant. Some of their officers will need to go with us to execute it. By the time we get all this done, it's gonna be afternoon before we can go home. I don't want to waste any time. I'm startin' to get tired just thinkin' about it."

"Still think Jack's innocent?" Bucci asked.

"I'm trying to keep an open mind, but the way I feel now, I want to bust his ass for causin' all this work."

"I think it's quite apparent we can't go on anything he said. We have a victim, a weapon, and the man who owns it standing over him. To me, it's a slam dunk. The more we talk about it, the more I'm convinced Jack did it."

"What's the motive?" Keane asked while sipping his coffee.

"We'll find out as we get deeper into the investigation, but for now, we don't need a motive."

When they got upstairs, the Lieutenant met them.

"I took the liberty of callin' over to Arlington PD. I'm friends with a major over there. He said they would be glad to assist us. A detective by the name of Postles has been assigned to help you. You may want to give him a call before too long so he can understand what's goin' on. Here's his name and number," Merrill said, as he handed the paper to Keane.

"Thanks," Keane said. "Is he on call?"

"Doesn't matter," the lieutenant said curtly. "Call him. I'm going home."

12

The meeting had been set for 7 P.M.

They started to arrive at 6:30 P.M, mostly by bicycle or on foot. Not all who came lived in the house. Some lived on campus. There were no cars of importance parked on the street, in order to minimize their presence. A Lexus SUV was parked in the garage. A taxi was parked out front. It was within walking distance of Georgetown University, where the majority of them attended college.

The gathering was comprised of ten members, all of Middle Eastern descent. The dubious colleagues were here on student visas; most were from Islamabad and the others from Muzaffarabad. Virtual neighbors in the mother country of Pakistan, they considered themselves the new rebels. The new association was a force to be respected by all, especially by the elders in the home land, and definitely by the filthy Americans. They were gifted, highly intelligent and committed; committed to a cause of vengeance.

The house looked just like any other townhouse on the tree- lined street. It was a nondescript, three-story colonial red brick, with a three-step porch and wrought iron hand railing. Inside, the living room was furnished with dated, Early American furniture. The walls were adorned with pictures of the Revolutionary War. A portrait of George Washington hung proudly in the entrance foyer. Anyone who entered would think they were entering one of the most patriotic homes in Washington D.C. It was up the street from the 1789 Restaurant which was frequented by the Washington in-crowd.

Khalil Abrah came down the steps into the brick-walled basement where the other members of his group had already assembled. Young, yet established in his manner, he was six feet tall and reasonably built, with an sparse dark beard. His face was handsome and proud. He was dressed in jeans and a white cotton shirt, and wore sandals.

Khalil detected their anger, frustration and confusion. They had just been swindled out of a half-million dollars. The boggled transaction also resulted in the death of an innocent young man. Even though the victim was an American, it was disturbing nonetheless because it potentially brought unwanted attention to them. The dead man was a young man who had been used for profit. The consequences were understood. Everyone has a price to pay. Yet ultimately, they would discover Bob Lewis was the man responsible for their predicament, and he would pay for their loss. Nobody would steal from them without punishment.

Khalil was angry too. However, he knew he had to maintain his composure. Each of them had different parents and came from different villages, yet they were unanimous in their destiny. He had to allow them to speak, to blow off steam. But they would have to listen to him as well. There was no choice; they needed Bob Lewis to complete the transaction. Once it was over and done with, they could dispose of him however they wished. In fact, he would proudly take the honor himself. Until then, Lewis still had the necessary components to complete their mission.

"Khalil, we need to talk," Abdullah said angrily, as he stood up from the table. Khalil had not yet taken his place. It was a verbal and potentially physical confrontation. Khalil was not intimidated.

"Sit down, please," Khalil said convincingly.

Abdullah was a man of stubborn conviction. He was about five feet seven and weighed well over two hundred pounds. Short and compact, he had an olive complexion, an unkempt beard and wore a white and red kufi. His nose was somewhat splayed and there was a mole under his right eye. The clothes he wore were unlike the rest of the people's clothes in the group. The attendees wore typical Pakistani clothes. Since he drove a taxi, Khalil depended on him to procure valuable information. Abdullah was like an undercover cop who penetrates the impregnable.

"That's what we're here for," Khalil responded calmly. He was weary of Abdullah. Any time there were questions from anyone else in the group, Abdullah was behind it. He seemed to be trying to erode Khalil's power. Yet Khalil was intelligent enough to know Abdullah's temper would be his downfall.

"Have you spoken with Florida?" Abdullah asked.

"Yes, I have," answered Khalil.

By not revealing too much information, Khalil knew it would incite Abdullah to show his true, angry, impatient feelings. The less Khalil said, the more Abdullah would become enraged, playing right into Khalil's hand.

"Well, are you going to tell us anything or do we have to guess?" Abdullah said indignantly, while looking at the others to gauge their emotions.

Khalil paused as he looked at his people. He sensed that Abdullah had not yet won their allegiance. They still looked at him as their leader, the veracious one whose guidance was sought and followed.

"I have spoken with Mohammed and he said when the crates arrived, they looked authentic. When he inspected the missiles, he said they had the government markings we expected. Without launching any of them, there was no way anyone would know they were impotent, including you, Abdullah," Khalil said with a calm evenness.

"Certainly you will protect your brother," Abdullah responded testily referring to Khalil's younger brother, Mohammed.

Khalil gave him a glacial stare of contempt. Abdullah picked up on it, and temporarily skated off the thin ice of antagonism.

"I am protecting all of us, not just my brother, and may I remind you Abdullah, you were the one who found Webster and brokered the deal. You wanted to make this deal as much as I did."

"For $500,000 we should have gotten more than limp dicks!" Abdullah shouted while pounding the table with one of his fists. His resentment was like a boiling cauldron.

While staring unaffectedly, Khalil remained calm and allowed a few moments for silence to return.

"I agree with you but we are not done yet," Khalil said composed.

"We should have killed Webster and saved the money. Death to the fuckin' Americans!" Abdullah yelled raising his fist trying to incite the gathering, but the reaction was tepid. There was just a mild murmur as they remained seated. Unlike Abdullah, these people were controlled with their anger, not by it.

"You have to pick battles small enough to win and big enough to matter," Khalil said.

"I think you're going soft, Khalil. You have been in America too long. Now you're starting to talk like them."

"It is important we don't deliver ourselves to the devils. Your way would have been a catastrophe. We would have been hunted down before we could get out of the city limits."

"I don't know who killed him, but at least we could have taken credit for his death. We didn't even do that," Abdullah said incredulously.

"What purpose would that serve?" asked Fadwa. She was the only woman permitted in the group. Khalil felt that her dark beauty would be a major benefit to the group and its purpose with her power of persuasion, a valuable asset. They met as students at Georgetown. Fadwa's major was molecular biology just like Khalil. He slowly came to know her and trust her.

"Now you have your girlfriend coming to your defense," said Abdullah, disgusted. He never liked her. He was suspicious. Never believing she was from Islamabad, he felt she was dangerous to their cause.

"I can speak my own mind, and I belong to no one," Fadwa responded self-righteously.

"Right now the police believe they have the person who killed him. It was in the news this afternoon. It said they had taken someone into custody who was a person of interest," Khalil said with conviction. "They didn't say anything about an arms deal. Now, it just looks like another street killing."

"It didn't say he was arrested," Abdullah answered, correcting Khalil.

"It's still early. The news may have more information today, but that's not what's important right now. We have some weapons that need to be armed, and I have some news. A man by the name of Bob Lewis has made contact with me by phone, and said he knows we were duped by Webster. He said he has the armaments we need to complete our mission."

"Don't tell me, I bet there's a price attached," Abdullah said sarcastically.

"Yes, there is."

"How much?"

"He wants an additional five million dollars."

"He's not going to get it from us. I refuse to agree to that," Abdullah said angrily.

"I agree, at least in theory."

"What do you mean?"

"The way I look at it, we are already in it for a half million, which is seed money. We tell him we will agree to his terms, but we will only pay after we are trained and test the goods."

"Are you crazy?" Abdullah said wildly.

"Let me finish. We will pay him when we get to Montserrat."

"What are you talking about?" asked Azir, who spoke for the first time. Usually, he sat and listened. Khalil knew he was a loyal warrior for the cause. He always listened intently to what everyone said before offering his opinion.

"That's part of what I wanted to talk about tonight. We have talked about how and where we were going to make our statement to the world. None of us could decide. Last night I had a dream. I dreamt of Americans on a ship and when I woke up I knew. Americans spend money lavishly on themselves and don't give a shit about people who are truly in need. They are bloated pigs. It occurred to me, the way to strike fear into them is by getting them when they are on vacation, when they are relaxed."

"How did you come up with Montserrat?" asked Tariq.

"I know that cruise ships travel through the straits every week, and Montserrat is virtually uninhabited since the volcano several years ago wiped out most of the island's population. It's a perfect spot that will allow us to fire missiles from there undetected. We can get in and get out by boat easily. We can strike quickly, and by the time the Americans get to us, we'll be gone. What does everyone think?" Khalil asked encouragingly.

The group started to talk about it with enthusiasm. Khalil didn't know if it was because it was a great idea, they were just anxious to make a statement, or they didn't like the idea at all.

"You still haven't said how we are going to get our money back," said Abdullah, still angry.

"We will tell Lewis we will pay him in Montserrat, but we won't. We'll kill him instead," Khalil said smiling.

"How do you know he won't have his own people there to kill us?"

"We are in control. We make the conditions. We tell him how many others are allowed. That's it."

"Do you think he'll go for it?" asked Fadwa.

"I think money dictates what Americans do. He is a pig like all Americans. He'll go for it. If not," he turned to face Abdullah, "then Abdullah, we'll let the valuable contacts you've made find us another arms dealer. I may be here to study molecular biology for future destruction but I must say, your value as a taxi driver and information gatherer is without equal," Khalil said, trying to placate Abdullah. "The connections you have made are priceless. You are our eyes and ears. You provide mobility within the power circles of Washington. You know how to get what we need. It is you, Abdullah, and the information you bring to us, that makes this group tick. You are unique."

"If we can't make this deal with this Mr. Lewis, we are out half a million dollars for nothing," Abdullah said less forcefully.

"That's true. That's why I want to finish the deal. But, if we can't, we will track Lewis down and kill him. And you, Abdullah, can do it slowly, with much pain."

Abdullah looked at Khalil and began to smile. The thought of killing Americans was almost erotic. Not since his days as a patriot in the hills of Muzaffarabad had he received such enjoyment. Killing was a spice he had hungered for. The anticipation began to overwhelm him.

In the end, Khalil told them he would contact Bob Lewis and make a deal. When the deal was complete, they would begin making final plans for Montserrat.

They were all in agreement.

13

Keane and Bucci went to Jack's condo to execute the search warrant after it had been secured through the Alexandria court. Assisted by Det. Postles and two uniformed officers from the Arlington P.D., they showed the warrant to Henry at the front desk and requested a key. He objected at first, but when they told him he would be arrested for obstructing justice, and that entry would be made with or without his help, Henry provided the key to Jack's condo.

Once they arrived at Jack's condo, they drew their weapons.

"POLICE!" Det. Postles yelled after opening the door. "POLICE!" he said again. Once they got inside, Keane and Bucci did a double take, looking at each other. Their eyes were wide with astonishment.

"Holy shit," Bucci exclaimed.

Keane just stood there speechless. He looked out over the living room from the landing. The condo had a very unusual layout. In the distance, through the floor to ceiling patio door windows, he saw the Washington Monument with the U. S. Capitol in the background.

"Ol' Jack must be doing alright for himself," Bucci whispered.

"No kiddin'!"

"Who is this guy working for anyway?" asked Det. Postles.

"That's what we'd like to know," Bucci answered while turning around to look at Postles.

They walked down the steps with their backs against the wall which led to the living room. This would not be an easy search if Jack was there and wanted to exchange gunfire. No matter how hard they tried, they were all exposed. One of their group would surely get shot before Jack would.

The entire time, their guns were pointed out into the room expecting Jack to come out shooting. A dog started barking, startling them. Guinness was in her crate and continued to bark.

"Jesus Christ, I think I'm gonna have a heart attack," Bucci said. "I'd like to shoot that fuckin' dog."

At the bottom of the steps, they walked through the living room and into the dining room. Connected to the dining room was the kitchen. From this point, they didn't talk. They used hand signals. They checked every room using the tactical methods they had been taught until it was cleared. Then, they holstered their weapons.

"Could one of you keep an eye on the front door?" Det. Postles asked the two uniformed officers.

"No problem."

"If anyone comes to the door, let me know."

"Yes, sir."

"Are you guys ready to get started?" Det. Postles asked.

"Yeah, we're ready. Can your guy record while we search? We'll do it one room at a time," Keane asked.

"Sure, we can do that," Postles said as he turned to the uniformed officer who remained behind. "Can you record the items seized for this search warrant in their computer?"

"Yes, sir," the young officer said as he took a seat at the dining room table. Keane had retrieved the computer from the hallway, where he had left it while they cleared the condo.

"Jesus, Bill. Look at this stereo system," Bucci said in amazement to Keane as he walked over to it.

"I wouldn't touch it if I were you."

Bucci just stood in front of it admiring it. "There's no reason why we can't listen to some music while we search," he said as he turned smiling at Keane and Postles.

"You'll probably break something," Keane admonished.

"I'm familiar with this system. It's easy. I'm not going to break anything," he said as he turned it on. After adjusting the volume he found the music station he was looking for. "I love this station."

Bruce Springsteen was playing *"Born to Run."*

"How appropriate," Keane said mockingly.

"What do you......Oh! I get it. Jack Dublin and Born to Run," Bucci responded with a chuckle.

"There's nobody like the Boss," Bucci said.

"Yeah, he's good," Postles said.

"Not good, great," answered Bucci.

"Springsteen is not the greatest," Keane interjected.

"Really?" Bucci asked dryly. "Who's the greatest?"

"Depends on what type of music you're talking about."

"Let's talk rock and roll."

"First, nobody can beat the Beatles," Keane said assuredly.

"Whoa, wait a minute. They haven't toured in forty plus years and two of 'em are dead. That's not a rock and roll band to me."

"Did they play rock and roll music or not, and does McCartney still tour or not?"

"You said Beatles, not McCartney, and if you think McCartney is the greatest, I disagree."

"How can anyone in their right mind say McCartney is not a great rock n' roller?"

"He may have been a great rock n' roller at one time, but not anymore."

"He still tours, sells out, and his tickets aren't cheap. To me, that's testimony he's the greatest."

"Bullshit! His tickets are so expensive that only geezers like us can afford them. You don't see too many young people at his concerts."

"OH! Now we're talking age requirements to qualify for greatest rock n'roller? These kids today wouldn't know rock n' roll if it bit 'em on the ass. All they listen to is that rap crap."

"I still say Bruce is the man," Bucci said resolutely.

For the first time, Postles spoke up. "What about the Stones?"

"Shit! I forgot about them. You're right. They're contenders," Bucci said vacillating.

"I can't believe you guys. What music is the world gonna listen to after we're dead and gone. Not the Stones. Not Bruce Springsteen. The Beatles! That's who they're gonna listen to," Keane said stubbornly.

"If we're talkin' about timeless music, what about Sinatra, Elvis and even Mozart?" Postles added.

"Who cares? We're talkin' about music now, today. All I know is if Bruce Springsteen, Paul McCartney and the Stones were all in town at different venues, I would buy Springsteen tickets," Bucci declared.

"Who cares? They would all sell out and make more money in one night than we will in our lifetime. Now that we've got that settled, let's get to work so we can get out of here."

They started in the back bedroom and began to go through each room, systematically recording each of the various items, not seeing anything much of interest related to the shooting. They took the fax machine, Jack's netbook and his computer. No weapons or anything else relative to the shooting were found.

During their search, the uniformed officer informed them a neighbor was at the door asking for Jack Dublin.

Bucci went upstairs to talk with her and decided she added no value to the investigation. She was just some elderly neighbor who probably was lonely.

. . .

Jack went to the garage where he parked before going to WISE and retrieved Julie's car. He pulled out of the garage and started toward his condo, deciding to take a chance to get Guinness and some of his things. He knew once he picked up some clothes, he would need to convince Julie to let him use her car a little longer. There would be a price to pay for her kindness.

Jack was willing to pay it.

He started towards Rosslyn. Passing the Rollins Building, he saw a couple of marked police cars out front and one unmarked car, in front of the building. The uniformed officers were walking briskly toward the entrance, along with a plainclothes officer. No doubt, they were called there by WISE security. Figuring it was about him, Jack felt confident time was on his side. He knew how things moved during investigations. Having a residence in Virginia would slow their process, and he planned to stay one step ahead of them.

Jack pulled into his condo parking garage about five minutes later and parked Julie's car. He walked carefully through the garage looking to see if there were any surveillance cameras. He detected none.

After walking through the hall to the elevator and using his pass key, Jack decided to stop by the front desk before going upstairs. He wanted to see if anyone had left a message. While at the desk, he would be able to gauge if there was a police presence in the building.

Getting off the elevator, he went over to the front desk. Several residents were there requiring Henry's attention. The staff was always very friendly and attentive. He made a mental note to remember them well at Christmas.

"Hi, Henry," Jack said to the concierge.

"Hello, Mr. Dublin," Henry said without smiling.

"You look busy, Henry. Anything wrong?" asked Jack curiously. He wanted to feel him out. Looking out through the front lobby windows, Jack didn't spot any police cars.

"No, Mr. Dublin," Henry said without making further eye contact.

"Has anyone left me a message?"

"No, Mr. Dublin," Henry responded while keeping himself busy behind the counter.

"You sure?"

"Yes, Mr. Dublin."

"Thanks. I hope you have a great day."

"Thanks, Mr. Dublin."

Jack went back to the elevator somewhat concerned by Henry's demeanor. Yet, Jack realized he had lived there for a short time, and didn't know Henry all that well. The doors shut and Jack pushed the button for his floor. The elevator began to ascend quickly, another plus of the building. Still thinking there could be a police presence in the building, Jack decided to try and get to his condo anyway. The curvature of the hallway gave him a vantage point that was fairly undetectable, allowing him to travel down the hallway, hiding in each condo foyer while listening and observing.

The elevator door opened. As Jack started to slowly maneuver down the hallway past Ms. McGarrity's condo, her door opened.

"Mr. Dublin, come in here," she said frantically while grabbing his shirt and pulling him.

Jack hesitated but entered her condo. It was exquisitely furnished with a surprisingly modern style. Ms. McGarrity closed the door and held her forefinger up to her lips. After the door shut, he heard what sounded like two men running down the hallway. Jack listened and then brought his curious eyes to Ms. McGarrity's. He now realized police were present. Henry must have called to alert them about Jack.

"There are police at your condo. You're not a murderer, are you," the feisty Ms. McGarrity asked in a whisper, while looking up at Jack inquisitively.

"I guess since I'm here, it's a good thing for you I'm not," Jack responded keeping his voice down.

"I didn't think you were, but people didn't think Ted Bundy was either."

"Why then, did you let me in?" Jack asked whispering back.

"Just a hunch. I've been on this earth for eighty years. I think I'm a pretty good judge of character," she said winking.

"How long have they been there?" Jack asked.

"About an hour," Ms. McGarrity said plainly.

"How did you know?"

"I went down to see if you were home. I wanted to know if you wanted to come over for that coffee you promised. That's when they answered the door."

"What did they say?" Jack asked, trying to determine his next course of action.

"Not much. They asked me a lot of questions though."

"Like what?"

"Did I know you? Did I know when you came and went? Did I ever see anyone else there? Things like that," Ms. McGarrity said smiling.

"What did you say?"

"I told them that I met you in passing, but that I didn't really know anything about you, which, quite frankly, is the truth."

Jack sighed. "Thank you. I don't know why you're sticking your neck out for me, but I am deeply indebted."

"You mind telling me what this is all about?" Ms. McGarrity asked questioningly with her eyes open wide.

They went into the living room and sat down. Jack told her about his situation beginning with shooting the Senator's son, and then brought her up to date on the recent shooting. All the time he was talking, Jack could tell Ms. McGarrity was listening intently because she nodded with affirmative understanding at various times.

"My God, Jack, you have been through a lot! Do you have any family that can help you?"

"No. My mother is deceased and I haven't spoken with my father in over twenty years. He may not be alive for all I know. I don't have any brothers or sisters either."

"What are you going to do?"

"I have to find the woman who was on the surveillance with me. I know her name. In fact, do you have a phone book I can look at?" Jack figured she didn't have a computer.

"Certainly," she said as she got out of her chair. "Can I get you something to drink?"

"A glass of water would be great."

"Would you like a little scotch to go with it?" she asked, while smiling mischievously.

Jack smiled. "No, that's okay."

She left and went to the kitchen. Jack got up and went to the front door, putting his ear against it trying to listen for any movement. Hearing none, he looked through the peep hole but couldn't see anything. Turning around, Ms. McGarrity was standing right behind him with a phone book in her hand, startling him.

"Here's your phone book," she said handing it over.

"Thanks. You scared me!" Jack said while taking the phone book. He was glad she had one, since they seemed to be scarce these days.

"I'm sorry, Jack," she said apologetically. "Your glass of water is on the table. I also put some cookies there for you. I made a few dozen for the social at the pool. Those are the leftovers."

"Thanks," Jack said as he walked over to the sofa and sat down. Flipping through the phone book looking for a Margaret Garber, he didn't see any listings for her. Then, he went to the yellow pages and looked at listings for picture framing shops. After turning some pages, he found "You've Been Framed" listed in Silver Spring, Maryland on Wisconsin Avenue. It wouldn't take long to get there. Writing the phone number on a scrap of paper, he put it in his pocket.

"That's a shame you missed the get together at the pool. There are some cuties that live here. Oh! That's right! You have a girlfriend already."

"Thanks, anyway," Jack said still focused on the phone book.

"Did you find what you were looking for?" Ms. McGarrity asked.

"Yes, I think so," Jack said as he took a bite from a chocolate chip cookie. "Man, these are good."

"Thank you, Jack. It's an old recipe my mother gave to me. I always get compliments on it."

Jack took a sip of water. "I wonder how long they're going to be here," Jack said thinking out loud.

"Why? Don't you want to stay and keep an old lady company?"

"Ms. McGarrity, you are great company, and I'm enjoying your cookies but I gotta find out who is behind all this, and I can't do it sitting here."

"Is there anything I can do to help?"

Jack thought about it for a few seconds. "Actually, there is. Can you go down to my condo and see if the detectives are still there? Then come back and let me know?"

"Sure. Is there anything I can say?"

"Just walk down and if they're there, just tell them you were curious to see if I came home yet. If they ask why, just tell them since I'm new here, you wanted to see if I knew about a condo association meeting coming up."

"I would be happy to."

Ms. McGarrity left and then returned within five minutes.

"I could see a couple of men in suits in your living room and I believe there were two in uniform."

"Could you tell what they were doing?"

"No. This time, I just saw the uniformed officer at the front door."

Jack paced back and forth. He wanted to get out of there but he certainly didn't want to risk being taken into custody.

"Tell you what. I need to get out of here so I can go talk to the woman who was at the shooting, and see if she has any information. Is there another way to get to the garage?"

"There's only the elevator and the stairs at each end of the hallway."

"I don't want to chance the elevator. Tell you what; could you take some cookies down to the detectives? While you are doing that, I will go down the other hallway and take the stairs to the garage."

"I can do that," Ms. McGarrity said, excited to be part of Jack's escape plan.

"Ms. McGarrity, I don't know how to thank you. When I get this straightened out, I owe you a dinner," Jack said smiling.

"I'm going to take you up on that, Jack," she said with a wink.

"Can I have your phone number?"

"Why certainly," she hastily volunteered.

"One other thing, can I give you a key to my condo?" Jack asked. Before she could answer he said, "Guinness is going to need to be fed and walked. I don't expect you to do it, but I know a young girl who may do it for me. If it's alright with you, I will give her your phone number and ask her to get the key from you. That way she can take Guinness with her."

"That would be fine, Jack," she said graciously. "Anything I can do to help."

Jack took her number, gave her a copy of his condo key and then gave her a hug. Ms. McGarrity looked up at him and smiled. Jack wondered if she had any children, but now was not the time to start that conversation.

She placed some cookies on a tray and walked them down to Jack's condo. Jack quickly went the other way, down the hallway to the stairs leading to the garage.

. . .

"She's a nice old lady," Bucci said. "She reminds me of my grandmother." He put the tray down with the cookies and they all took one. "Man, these are good," Bucci said. He helped himself to some more, putting a couple in his pockets.

They decided to finalize their search and exit the condo. Keane did a final walk through with Bucci. This was common practice since nobody wanted to be accused of stealing. They trusted each other, but they were working with officers from another police department.

There had been some officers who were terminated due to sticky fingers. They thought it would be easy to steal from crooks without being noticed. When confronted, they tried to justify it as due compensation. Many of these officers were suffering from financial burdens due to divorce, alimony and child support. Some were just psychologically twisted.

As they were leaving the kitchen, Keane noticed a piece of paper near the coffee pot. Written on it was the name Peggy Garber. Keane looked at it and wondered why it was there. He instinctively put the paper in his pocket. Perhaps it would have some value later on.

. . .

Jack carefully looked around the garage and didn't see anyone. Quickly, he maneuvered his way over to Julie's Jeep and got in. Just as he was getting to the exit, another car rapidly pulled out in front of him, blocking his exit. It was a dark colored Crown Victoria.

A government car.

14

A man dressed in a black suit quickly got out of the driver's side, and approached Jack in a threatening manner. Watching him, Jack thought it was odd he didn't pull a gun. Continuing to watch the man's hands, it became apparent he was alone, and wasn't a police officer.

"What the heck are you doing?" asked the man angrily. "You almost ran into me," he said waving his arms.

"You're the asshole who pulled out in front of me," Jack answered back with attitude. Clearly, Jack did not want to pick a fight with a man who was obviously a civilian, and who may delay his exit. Yet Jack, who was never able to take shit from anyone, couldn't restrain himself now.

In an instant, the man's demeanor changed. He looked at Jack as if he was measuring his face. "You must be the new owner here," the man replied quizzically. He was about fifty years old, with a solid build. His hair was dark, parted to the side, and Jack realized he was wearing a toupee.

"Are you the retired police officer that moved into the Shorts' condo?" he asked.

"I am, and I've been driving long enough to know you need to be more careful about backing out of a parking space, especially in a garage."

"My name is David Larchmont," he said smiling, as he stuck his hand out.

"I'm Jack Dublin," Jack said as he shook his hand hesitantly.

"Listen, I'm sorry we got off on the wrong foot. I'm president of the condo association.....and well..." he chuckled, "sometimes I go overboard trying to protect our residents. I didn't see your condo decal at first, and I thought you may be someone visiting." Luckily, Jack had given Julie a condo decal for her car. "We have one owner whose kids think this is the Indianapolis Speedway."

Jack wanted to hurry out of there. Since Henry didn't tell him about the detectives in his condo, he wasn't sure if Henry was watching him on an undetected surveillance camera.

"Listen, perhaps *I* was going a little too fast," Jack said.

"No problem. Hey! Do you know about the condo association meeting coming up? It would be a great opportunity for you to meet the other owners."

"Yes, I know about it but I have a prior commitment. Thanks for the information."

Just then a horn honked behind Jack that made him jump. Larchmont looked behind Jack, then smiled and waved at the driver.

"Tom Medori. He's always in a hurry. Give me a call and maybe I can bring you up to date on the Condo Association."

"Thanks, I'll do that," Jack said, thankful for the car behind him.

Larchmont went back to his car and pulled out of the garage. Jack made his exit and went in the opposite direction. Soon he was headed back to Georgetown on his way to Silver Spring. He could have just called the shop and asked for Peggy Garber, but he wanted to scope the place first.

Within a half hour he was parked outside "You've Been Framed." He looked inside, and saw an older woman in her sixties working the counter. There was one customer finalizing a purchase. When she left, Jack decided to go in. He began browsing around the shop. It had the typical paintings and photographs with some local photographers providing home-grown flavor.

"Can I help you?" the woman asked with a pleasant smile.

"Just looking, but perhaps you can answer a question for me. Is this shop owned by Peggy Garber?"

The woman smiled. "Yes, it is," she answered.

"Is she in today?"

"She's working at our new location in Georgetown today."

"New location?"

"Yes, we just opened a store on M Street."

"Really?" Jack said surprised.

"Yes, Peggy decided to open a store there. She's down there trying to get it ready to open next week."

"Hmmmm," Jack pondered. "I guess I'll have to stop down there to see her."

"If you would like, I can call her and tell her that you're coming," she said earnestly.

"No, that's alright. I don't know if I'll get there today. Does she work there tomorrow?" asked Jack, even though he knew he was going there as soon as he left.

"She'll be there all week and maybe next week too."

"At least she has left *this* store in competent hands," Jack said complimenting her.

"Thank you. I'm sorry I didn't catch your name."

"I didn't say it. It's Bob Lewis."

"Thank you, Bob. Stop down and see her. I'm sure she'll be glad to see you."

Jack didn't discern any awareness that the woman knew the real Bob Lewis.

"Take care," Jack said. He left the store and went to his car. He was chiding himself for using Bob Lewis's name. He couldn't understand why he would have done something so stupid. Maybe the woman knew the real Bob Lewis and knew Jack was lying. If she did, she would call Peggy right away, and it would make it difficult for him to meet with her.

Jack headed back to Georgetown. He figured there was probably a warrant for his arrest by now. He didn't want to be conspicuous by walking around Georgetown, but he had to talk to her. He was fairly comfortable that the MPD still didn't know Julie's car. Just then Jack's cell phone rang. He looked at the caller I.D. and didn't recognize the number. It didn't look like an MPD number so Jack decided to answer it.

"Hello," Jack said faintly, trying to disguise his voice.

"Jack, is that you?"

Jack recognized the voice right away.

"Hey, Julie."

"It didn't sound like you," she said.

"I just swallowed some coffee when I answered the phone."

"It sounds like you're driving."

"I am."

"Jack, you shouldn't drive, drink coffee and talk on the phone at the same time."

"Yeah, I know. I guess I'm just talented with my hands," he said, trying to make a joke to assess Julie's mood.

"Listen, you won't have to pick me up after work. Bonnie wants to go for drinks after work, and she can take me home." Bonnie was her friend from work. Jack had met her once and didn't care for her.

"Okay, are you sure?"

"Yes, Jack, I'm sure. How are you doin'?"

"Fine. I'm going to meet with the woman who was there last night," Jack said. He didn't want to tell her about the search warrant being executed on his condo.

"That's great, Jack. I hope she's able to help you. Do you know when you'll be returning my car?"

"Well, we agreed on tonight didn't we?"

"Yes Jack, we did. I meant what time? Will you have it back by eight, or are you planning on keeping it longer?"

"I don't think so, but if I have to, is it available?"

"If you really need it, I guess so, but I do need my car. Have you thought about renting one?"

Jack had thought about renting one but he was afraid to use his credit card. He didn't want to be traced.

"I guess I could."

"Well, let me know, okay? I will definitely need it this weekend."

"What's going on this weekend?"

She paused before answering. "Jack, I have plans to go away for the weekend."

Jack was hurt. For the first time, he truly felt her slipping away. Right now, she was the only person he had to talk to, and the only trace of stability he had in his life. He didn't want to lose her. Not now.

"Oh," Jack said, with disappointment apparent in his voice.

She sensed he was curious. "I need to take some time by myself. I need to think about me for a change. You've really hurt me, Jack."

"Listen Julie, I'm sorry. I need to think about things too. I know it's not fair to you, but it wouldn't be fair to get you mixed up with my situation right now, either."

"Jack, I think you're already getting me involved."

"Not really. I'm just borrowing your car."

"Anyway, please get my car back to me as soon as you can, okay?"

"Alright."

"Goodbye, Jack."

She hung up ending the call. Once he was cleared, he could concentrate on Julie.

After he parked on a side street, Jack made his way down M Street until he saw the storefront for "You've Been Framed." He nervously walked past it. If he went into the store and tried to talk with her, she might call the police. Then again, there weren't many alternatives. After deciding to feel her out first, he called the store while standing across the street. Jack hoped to catch a glimpse of her when she answered the phone.

"You've Been Framed, may I help you?" answered a woman, who from across the street looked to be in her mid-to-late thirties or early forties.

"Is this Peggy Garber?"

"Yes, it is. Can I help you?"

"Do you know a Jack Dublin?"

"No, I don't," she answered hesitantly.

"Do you know a Bob Lewis?"

When she didn't respond as quickly, he sensed her attitude changed. "Yes, I do. Who is this?"

"Were you on a surveillance last night?"

"Who is this?"

Jack could hear Beethoven's Moonlight Sonata in the background. It was one of his favorite classical pieces since the days when his mother made him practice the piano relentlessly.

"Just answer my last question, and I will tell you who this is."

"Yes, I was on a surveillance last night."

"Did a shooting take place?"

She hung up. Jack watched as she walked into a back room. He called again. She came out of the back room and answered the phone.

"You've Been Framed, may I help you?"

"Don't hang up. My life depends on it and maybe yours too."

"Who is this?"

"My name is Jack Dublin. I was at the surveillance last night. Bob Lewis sent me there. There was a shooting, and someone was killed."

"I know. I took pictures."

"What did you do with the pictures?" Jack asked quickly.

"I downloaded them, and sent them to Bob."

Jack winced at her disclosure. "Listen, I need to talk to you. Can we meet in a public place and talk? I think Bob is involved in something sinister."

"Like what?"

"Buying and selling weapons to the wrong people, and he may be providing classified information. For all I know, drugs could be involved too."

"How do I know you're not involved? Maybe you're the one with the weapons."

"If I wanted to kill you I could have by now. I found you, didn't I? I am a retired D.C. cop whom Bob called to do a simple surveillance. He left me holding the bag on the shooting. How do I know you're not connected in some way with what Bob is doing? Maybe you are setting me up to be killed."

"You called me. I didn't call you."

"Yeah? Tell me why Bob would have given me your name, and tell me you owned a picture framing business. He certainly didn't have to give me that information. I would have never known anyone was there last night."

There was a pause in the conversation.

"I don't know. Maybe he just wanted to keep you busy while he escaped to the shadows. Where and when do you want to meet?"

"How about The Sea Catch Restaurant at 6:00?"

"Tonight?"

"Yes."

"I guess, but how will I know who you are?"

Jack knew how to identify her, but he didn't want to alarm her. "I'll be wearing tan Dockers and a blue shirt."

"That will include just about everyone else in Georgetown. Can you wear something to make you stand out? Give me something to go on."

"I'll also wear a red Phillies cap. It has a white "P" on it. I'll meet you in front of the restaurant."

"Okay, Jack Dublin. I will meet you there, but let me tell you something. If you try anything, I'll kill you. Before I owned this business, I was a police officer, too. I know how to shoot, and I know how to kill."

"You won't have anything to worry about."

15

It was another hot day. The sun burned anything daring to walk beneath it. Yet, people still poured into the city undeterred by the heat. Full of money-sucking attractions, tourists were the transfusion on which Washington businesses relied.

Bob Lewis sat on the bench in front of the Washington Monument. He had been there about fifteen minutes, and was starting to become irritated sitting in the heat. He'd seen a photograph of Abrah, but knew with Muslims, they weren't always accurate. To him, they all looked alike after a while.

There was no reason to rehearse a discussion with Abrah. After all, he was a seasoned ex-FBI agent, and Abrah was just some rich kid from the Middle East.

Shortly after 1 p.m. (or 1300 hours as Lewis still liked to think of time)a young man in his mid-twenties, and appearing to be of Middle Eastern descent, approached the bench. He looked at Bob directly and did not change his focus. Bob looked at him the same way. Once he had come within ten feet, the young, dark-skinned man spoke.

"Are you Mr. Lewis?" Abrah asked while looking at Bob.

"Yes," Bob responded. Bob had thought of using an alias, but believed if Abrah was working for the government trying to set him up, it didn't matter. They would be close-by listening, ready to swoop in and arrest him, regardless of what name he used. They would determine his identity soon enough anyway. He would just have to follow his gut and take his chances. Still, the senator was his ace in the hole.

Abrah sat down. He didn't look at Bob. He just stared towards the Capitol. Bob examined him. He saw someone who appeared intelligent by the way he carried himself and the way he had spoken with authority.

"I have what you need," Bob said.

"I figured you did," Abrah responded while still looking straight ahead. "Otherwise, we would be wasting our time."

"I can get it to you whenever you need it."

"What is the price other than a life?" Abrah asked smugly.

He quickly turned his stare to the man sitting next to him.

"What do you mean by that?" Bob asked, irritated.

"One man has already been killed."

"Who did you kill?" Bob asked naively.

Abrah turned and looked Bob straight in the eye, smiling. "I didn't kill anybody....but you did."

"I didn't kill anyone," Bob said innocently.

"You killed Webster," Abrah said with sarcastic conviction.

"I didn't kill anybody named Webster," Bob said, still not taking any chances and definitely not confirming anything for some punk terrorist.

"Then you know who did."

"I don't know who killed Webster. Who is Webster?"

Abrah just looked at Bob and smiled. He slowly stood up. "Apparently I have the wrong man." He started to walk away.

"Wait," Bob said. "Sit down."

Abrah looked at Bob in a pretentious way, and then slowly sat down.

"You're talking about the young man killed a couple of days ago in Georgetown?"

"Don't play games Mr. Lewis. You know exactly who I'm talking about; otherwise you wouldn't have contacted me to talk about weapons."

Bob just looked at him, trying to decide what to divulge and what not to reveal. For all he knew, Abrah could be wired.

"Okay, okay. I thought *you* killed Webster to get your money back."

"Money is not an object with me, Mr. Lewis. Being betrayed is."

"Okay. So, you were betrayed, and then you killed him. Am I getting this right?"

"No, I didn't kill him. I just didn't know he gave me worthless missiles until after he was killed. So, what did you do with the money, Mr. Lewis?"

Bob smiled at Abrah, but didn't answer right away.

"All I can say is, I didn't kill Webster."

"That still doesn't answer my question."

"Listen, we're not here to talk about the past. I thought we were here to talk about the future."

"I'm listening."

"You have, to my understanding, weapons that are useless without some components that I happen to have access to. The fact of the matter is, I will replace the entire shipment for the right price."

"Go on."

"I need to know how many missiles you need."

"Let's talk units, Mr. Lewis. Let's just say I need the components for one unit."

"I'm not interested in selling components for one missile," Bob said through clenched teeth.

"I didn't think you were, but, right now, we're talking about one unit for purposes of discussion."

"Let me make this clear," Bob answered with unbridled anger. "I am not going to risk my ass to sell some ragtag group of kids components for one fucking missile. Do I make myself clear? I just told you I will replace the entire shipment you received. These "units" as you want to call them, are fully equipped armor-piercing missiles. They can destroy airplanes at ten thousand feet."

Abrah was unaffected by Bob's condescending attitude. Americans always think they can intimidate.

"Apparently, you have misunderstood my question. I would like to know how much it will cost to resolve my dilemma. I won't be able to answer your question until you give me the answer I need. Now, let me ask again. How much does it cost for the components to one unit?"

Bob feared the ability to sell all the missiles and make the money he wanted was going south fast. He was not interested in selling one missile, but if this was the way it was going to shake out, he needed to make a killing now.

"Three million dollars."

Abrah looked at Bob for a moment and then started to laugh.

Bob just looked at him and started to get angry. "Fuck you!" he said as he stood up and started to walk away. Before he got two steps away, Abrah called out to him.

"Wait, wait," he said still chuckling. "Come back, Mr. Lewis."

Bob came back and stood there, looking at Abrah with disgust.

"Sit down. Please, sit down."

Bob sat down. "I don't know who you think you're talking to, but I am not going to waste my time if you think you can buy components for one missile, and only one missile."

"Mr. Lewis, I am fully aware that you sent Webster to me without the necessary parts, thus making them useless. Therefore, you know the missiles I have right now aren't worth a, how do you say it, piss-pot. I also know that you took the half million dollars I gave to Webster. Whether you killed him or had him killed, matters not to me. What matters to me is that I need these components to accomplish my goal, or I need a completely new shipment. As I said, money is not an object to me, but I am not going to give it away. Also, I am not looking to buy weapons only once. If I like what you have to offer, I will come back to you for more. How much do you want?"

"For everything?" Bob asked now encouraged.

"Yes."

"Ten million."

"That's way too much. Way too much."

"Okay, counter it."

"Another million."

"Not even close."

"Look, I know you think you are the only game in town. You're not," Abrah said confidently.

"You know, you're right," Bob said sarcastically. "But I'm the only game in town that will train you how to use the weapons properly and make sure your identity is safe."

"Really? How can I be sure?"

"These weapons came from a military installation. You know that. Your people in Florida must have told you about the markings on the crates. I'm not going to risk being arrested. I made sure these can't be traced to me. If they can't be traced to me, they can't be traced to you. Eight million. Final offer."

"I think we are beginning to understand each other, Mr. Lewis. Who will train me and my people?"

"An instructor who is retired from the military and I. We will take you and one other person out to sea and demonstrate it for you. I know an area out of the shipping lanes where we will be safe to practice."

"Where is this area, roughly?"

"It's off the coast of Delaware. We will leave from a little town called Lewes. You can have another one of your compatriots stay on shore with the money. Once we see the money, we will leave for the ocean. If you don't like what you see, when we return, it's no harm, no foul. If you do, we want half of the money up front, and then we'll deliver the goods to you for the other half."

"Where will you deliver them?"

"Wherever you want, within reason."

"How about St. Lucia?"

"You're kidding, right?"

"You said anywhere."

"I said within reason. Can I assume that you are not targeting the U.S.?"

"You can assume what you want. Does it matter to you?"

"Not really. I put my blood, sweat and tears into working for the government, and they just stuck it up my ass sideways. So I really don't care."

"You just want to make money, right?"

"Yeah, so what?"

"You Americans really make me sick. You stick your noses into other people's business and portray yourselves as world saviors, but in the end it all comes down to money, doesn't it?" Abrah said sanctimoniously.

"You know, don't try and sell me your fucked-up morals. You recruit women and children to strap bombs on themselves so they can blow up innocent people, including themselves. For what? A cause? Some fuckin' cause! Give me a stack of money over a stick of dynamite any day."

Abrah just smiled at Bob. Americans will never get it. He raised his arm up as if to stretch, looking at his watch. The signal was given.

"Listen, I may have something else that may be of interest to you," Bob said surreptitiously.

"What might that be?"

"I have the classified technology to the drone system we're using to blast the shit out of your country," Bob said with subdued excitement.

"Interesting," answered Abrah.

"I have all the details."

"I'm sure that has a price."

"It does," Bob said, not letting Abrah know it was the same information being sold by our government to Egypt, Morocco and Saudi Arabia. He wanted him to think he had exclusivity.

"How much?" asked Abrah trying to disguise his interest.

"It's not cheap. After all, it's the latest and greatest weapon technology in the world. Do you know how many countries would pay to have this information?"

"Why aren't you trying to sell it to them?"

"I just got my hands on it and you're here. Are you interested or not?"

"Depends on the price."

"You just told me earlier that money is no problem."

"It isn't if it's spent on value. How much are we talking?"

"Twenty million."

Abrah pondered the price. He had the money. He was calculating how he'd use the new information, and how he'd sell it.

"Fifteen million," Abrah said.

After they negotiated back and forth, Abrah agreed to eighteen million.

They both stood up.

"When can I expect your call to go out in the ocean? I am anxious to learn. I need delivery soon."

"This week. I'll let you know," Bob said as they started to walk toward the street.

"What about the drone information?"

"I'll have that when we make final delivery on the missiles. Payment for that will be different."

"Really?" Abrah said in mock surprise.

"I will give you an account. When I have confirmed the money has been transferred, you will get your information."

Abrah just shook his head in agreement.

As they approached the street, there was a homeless man sitting there with a homemade sign that said, "I am a Homeless Vet. Please Help." It looked like he was Caucasian but it was difficult to tell since he probably hadn't showered in more than a month. His hair and beard were stringy and matted. He smelled disgusting.

"Can you spare a dollar, sir?" the bum asked, looking at Bob.

Bob just returned the look at him with disgust and didn't answer. Abrah reached in his pocket and gave the man a dollar.

"Thank you, sir," the man said.

"Fuckin' peasant. They're like pigeons. They walk around asking for scraps, and then they shit all over you. They ought to be shot so we can clean up this city," Bob said with disgust.

A taxi was approaching and Bob waved him down.

"Do you want a lift?" Bob asked Abrah.

"No, thanks. I'll walk back."

"I'll be in touch," Bob said as he got into the taxi. The interior had the malodorous smell of curry, but after being out in the sun and near that homeless man, it was like sitting in a flower garden. Middle Eastern music was playing on the radio. Bob got his cell phone out and made a call. He glanced momentarily at the driver just as the phone was answered.

"I just met with him and it looks like a go," Bob said.

After he listened for a few seconds he said, "I'll tell you when I get there." He listened some more and then terminated the call. As the sitar music moaned on, he thought to himself, "Jesus Christ! The fuckin' ha-beebs are taking over."

"Where to Mister?" asked the driver.

"Just drive towards Georgetown. I'll let you know when we get closer," Bob ordered as he stared out the window contemplating his future.

Abdullah placed the Washington Post over the binoculars he had used to spot the hand signal from Abrah. As he pulled away from the curb, Abdullah just smiled. Things were starting to go as planned.

16

The day was starting to cool down. Jack had plenty of time before he met Peggy at the restaurant. Since he was familiar with the layout, he knew where to go for an escape if it became necessary.

The Sea Catch was a favorite of Jack's. Situated along the C & O canal, the building was one hundred and fifty years old. It was made of both brick and stone. It started out in the mid-1800's as a shipping warehouse, and then, during the ensuing years, it housed a manufacturer of punch card machines. The owner later merged with two other companies and became known as the "International Business Machine Corporation" or IBM.

Now it was an exceptional restaurant. Jack always enjoyed their seafood. If you were lucky enough to get a table outside along the canal, you could sip your wine with a terrific view, particularly in the spring and fall. It was a very romantic place to take a date, but Jack was not thinking about romance now. He needed information.

This restaurant allowed for many avenues of escape. It was generally crowded and had several exits allowing for Peggy's comfort and Jack's safety.

Jack kept his hat in his pocket as he sat across the street in a coffee shop, watching to see if anyone suspicious showed up. If Peggy had tipped anyone off, he would just leave and try to figure something else out.

He sat there for a good hour and a half, drinking coffee, reading papers and magazines, while trying not to get too involved in them. A little after six o'clock, he saw Peggy cautiously walking down the street. She looked furtively behind herself once and kept walking, never looking across the street. Jack watched her walk down to the breezeway that leads to the restaurant. She paused, and once again looked behind herself then turned toward the restaurant. Jack waited a moment and didn't see anyone suspicious-looking following Peggy. He exited the coffee shop and trotted across the street, putting his Phillies hat on.

As expected, the courtyard was teeming with hungry patrons. He saw Peggy standing near the front door anxiously looking around at the assembled people. As Jack approached from the street, she caught his eyes. She continued to stand there and watch him, without averting her eyes. Her expression was one of caution. As he got closer, he realized how attractive she was. No wonder Bob hired her. She was about 5 feet 10 inches tall and very well built. Her brunette hair was shoulder length. Her features were dark. She wore a black skirt and white button-down shirt that accentuated her breasts. She also wore a black blazer which no doubt covered her gun. Still, Jack wondered why she was wearing black in the hot summer.

"Peggy?" asked Jack.

"Yes," she answered, and offered her hand with a hint of a smile.

As Jack looked around, a couple of people whose name was just called got up from a bench in front of a brick-encased planter. The bench faced a row of stores. There was a gift shop on the lower deck, and an art gallery on the upper deck. Georgetown is known for its shops along M Street.

"Let's go sit down," Jack said as he motioned towards the bench. She walked over and he followed.

She spoke first. "I'm glad you called me."

"Really?" Jack said surprised.

"Yes. Bob has been acting really strange lately."

"Let's back up. How do you know him?"

"My husband told me about him. He came into our shop about a year ago. He and my husband began talking about art, and then one thing led to another. He said he was looking for a part-time investigator. Bob told me it wasn't hard work, primarily insurance claims. You know, when someone fakes an injury we go out, do surveillance, and take video. It paid one hundred dollars an hour, cash, and my husband knew I missed police work. I thought it would be fun. It seemed innocent enough, but lately he had me doing other stuff."

"Like what?"

"Well, like errand type stuff. It had nothing to do with security. It was picking up and dropping off packages, things like that. He was starting to freak me out the way he looked at me."

"Do you know anything about Bob?"

"Just what he told me, that he was retired FBI, and that he had his own security firm."

"He didn't tell you the name of his firm, did he?"

"No, but I didn't care. It was just something I did for fun. He always paid cash. I don't need the money. My late husband has left me well off. I just enjoyed keeping my hand in police work."

"Late husband?"

"Yes, he died about three months ago."

"I was under the impression he was still alive. How did he die, if you don't mind my asking?"

"In a car accident."

"Was there anything suspicious about his accident?"

"No, not really. The police said he must have fallen asleep and driven off the side of the road. They couldn't tell me much more." She paused and looked away to collect herself. "The car was consumed by fire, and it was difficult to retrieve my husband's body."

Jack was momentarily struck by the twist of fate with his mother's death. Their minds were momentarily not in the game. Jack needed both of them to think about last night.

"What is your police background?" Jack asked changing the subject.

"I worked for the Prince George's County Police for two years before meeting my husband. He didn't want me to work anymore. He owned some businesses and wanted me to help him."

"What kind of businesses did he own?"

"A Persian rug store, an import store, and of course, the framing store. He used to own a restaurant too, but got out of that business. He said it required too many late hours and he didn't want to be away from me so much. I guess that's why he tried to curtail my moonlighting activities."

"Did he travel a lot?"

"Some."

"Did he ever take you with him?"

"Sometimes, when he went to Europe. Even though he was from India, his family was in London."

"Did he ever go to the Middle East?"

"Sometimes."

Jack had so many questions to ask. "Do you think Bob was involved in illegal activity?"

"It's quite possible. The places he had me going to were owned by a lot of Middle Eastern types, but I didn't think anything of it because like I said, my husband was from India."

"Where was Bob's office?"

"You know," she said, "I don't know," realizing it for the first time. "He would always come to the shop to pay me, pick up any packages, and give me my next assignment. He and my husband got along very well."

"What did he tell you to do last night?"

"It was a little strange. He just said he wanted me to take a video of any activity pertaining to a Robert Webster. He said he was suspected of selling weapons to terrorists. This was different from the insurance things he had me doing before, but I gotta tell you, I was kind of excited to do it."

"What did you see?"

"I saw a man drive up, get out of his car and start walking across the street, carrying two pieces of luggage. Another car pulled up and two men got out. There was a confrontation, and somebody shot the first man. They took the luggage, and got into the car and drove off."

"Did you see a man run to the victim?"

"Yes, but I didn't pay too much attention to it. I was pretty rattled."

"Did you take a video?"

"Yes, I gave it to Bob when he stopped by the shop today."

"Do you have any way of contacting Bob?" Jack asked, glad to hear he was still in the area.

"Yes, I have his cell phone number. But he said he wouldn't be contacting me for a while."

Jack looked around at the other people waiting to go into the restaurant, while she rooted through her pocketbook. He wanted to see if anyone was watching them. While Peggy was looking, Jack heard what sounded like a "thump". Jack looked back at Peggy, as she slumped over and fell off the bench. She was bleeding in the front of her blouse. Another shot whizzed by Jack's head and hit the dirt behind him in the planter. Jack looked up, saw a man turn and start running along the walkway above. People started to scream and run in all different directions. Instinctively, Jack reached for his weapon and then realized he didn't have one. He looked back at Peggy. She was most likely dead. He grabbed her pocketbook and started to run. The man above was gone, and Jack was not going to stick around.

Jack started to run towards 31st Street. He figured he would circle around and get in his car to head out of town. He was still running with Peggy's purse. It had Bob's phone number and he wanted it, desperately. Already he could hear sirens. Two officers were starting to run towards the restaurant. Jack also knew the shooter was still close by. He didn't get a real good look at him, but he looked like he was a white male in his late thirties, tall with a slender build wearing black pants and a gray polo shirt. He had brown curly hair. Jack had always been sharp when it came to identifications.

Jack turned down 31st Street and headed toward the river. He realized he looked suspicious carrying a woman's purse, so he stuffed it down the back of his pants. There was no time to look in it now. He had stopped running but was walking briskly, trying not to draw attention to himself, occasionally looking back to make sure he wasn't going to be shot in the back.

Now half a block away, he looked back one more time. As he turned around, he was hit in the face. Momentarily stunned, Jack fell to the ground. As someone rolled him over, he felt the purse being taken. Just as the assailant was starting to move away, Jack put his foot up and tripped the man. It was not the same one who shot at him. There were people outside eating al fresco, witnessing the struggle.

Just as the man got up, a couple of college-age kids tackled him and took the pocketbook from him. They punched him a couple of times before he ran off. Jack was just starting to get to his feet. One kid came over to Jack and handed him the pocketbook, giving him an awkward look. The kid was built like a football player.

"Here's your .....purse," he said.

"Thanks," Jack said. As an afterthought he said, "It's my wife's."

"I figured it wasn't yours," he said, smiling.

"Thanks for getting it back for me."

"We saw him sucker punch you. It wasn't right."

"Well, thanks again."

"Aren't you going to report it to the cops?"

"No. After all, you let him go."

Realizing Jack was right, the kid smiled again, "I know, but at least we gave him something to remember us by."

"Yeah, you did! Listen, I have to go. Thanks, again."

Jack started to walk down the hill. He was certain M Street was pretty chaotic by now. He would have to find a place to stay until going back to Julie's Jeep. He decided to walk along the canal until he could get to a spot underneath the Francis Scott Key Bridge which connects Georgetown and Rosslyn. There, he would go through Peggy's purse without any interference, until he found Bob's number.

17

Keane came into the office after executing the search warrant on Jack Dublin's condo, exhausted from working almost eighteen hours straight. He wanted to go home, get a shower and go to sleep. Bucci was down in evidence turning in the seized items. He was dead on his feet, too.

"Hey Keane, did you see the package on your desk?" asked.

Lt. Harris, the dayshift lieutenant.

"Yeah," he replied as he picked it up. "Do you know anything about it?"

"Someone dropped it off at the desk downstairs. It looks like a DVD."

He thought about pushing it aside but decided it may have something to do with Jack Dublin. He looked at the outside of the package and didn't recognize the handwriting. It was in a bubble wrap envelope. Cautiously looking inside the package, he saw the DVD and then pulled it out carefully while looking at it. There were no markings on it. Temporarily setting it aside, he had no idea what was on it.

Keane sat down and rested his tired head in his hands. He tried to collect his thoughts, focusing on finding out where Jack Dublin was. It was hard to believe, but now he was thinking Jack was "dirty."

Keane looked back at the DVD and pulled it out of the package again. This time he felt in the package and pulled out a small slip of paper he didn't see the first time. It simply said "Jack Dublin" in a typewritten note. Keane's eyes widened.

Keane gingerly gathered up the DVD and envelope and got up from his desk in a hurry. He told another detective to tell Bucci to meet him down in the video room as soon as he returned.

He walked hurriedly down the hall to an empty interview room, exchanging hellos with a couple of people, before walking into the dark room and turning on the light. He placed the DVD in the laptop. Shortly after it came on, the picture showed a dark street with dimly lit street lamps. The view was from a point slightly higher than the center of focus. There were occasionally people walking by, some with dogs. All of a sudden the focus changed to the inside of a vehicle. Apparently the person taking the video forgot to turn off the camera and placed it in the foot well of their vehicle. There was classical music playing on the radio. Keane fast- forwarded the video but kept track of the elapsed time on the display counter. It was approximately twenty-three minutes. He saw a change in the picture on the screen and cursored back.

He stopped it and hit play. What he heard was what sounded like a gunshot and then a woman cursing. Keane presumed it was the woman in the car recording the video. Then, he observed the focus change on the picture, and eventually saw a man standing over the victim. The camera zoomed in on that male. He was looking around the scene furtively. The man was, without a doubt, Jack Dublin.

Jack then knelt down alongside the victim and was saying something which was inaudible on the video. Next, he saw police arrive. In a series of commands, he saw Jack taken into custody.

Keane leaned back in his chair and put his hands on his head, staring into space. He couldn't believe he had raw video of the very same shooting with Jack Dublin center stage.

Keane stopped the video. He would look at it again, but for now he just wanted to think. It didn't show Jack shooting the victim. It could still support Jack's statement but now there was definitely another witness. It was a woman. What did she see? More importantly, who is she? Could this be the Peggy Garber whose name was on the slip of paper in his pocket? He would call her when they were finished looking at the video a few more times.

Just then Bucci entered the room.

"Hey, Simpson told me you were looking for me. From the look on your face, it must be pretty good. What've you got?"

"Sit down," Keane said re-energized, as Bucci took a chair. "Someone left a DVD for me. I just looked at it and it's from the crime scene."

"Our crime scene?" Bucci asked with renewed interest.

"Yeah, our crime scene."

"Anything good?"

"Take a look," Keane said as he played it again.

They both looked at the video again from the point of engagement with Jack Dublin. They looked at each other in disbelief trying to discern what the final impact would be on the case.

"We gotta show this to the Lieutenant when he comes in," Bucci said. "This is incredible! It may just be the break we need to nail it down."

"I'm not so sure of that. I mean, Jack's story still matches this video when you think about it."

"Still, it has to mean something and we'll go over it with a fine tooth comb. Maybe we'll hear or see something else," Bucci said.

Suddenly, the adrenaline flowing in their bodies had them supercharged. They rushed back to the office.

"Hey, Simpson, do you know how this package got to the office?" asked Keane.

"I'm not sure but I think someone brought it up to Scanlon who then put it on your desk. Shouldn't you guys get some sleep?"

"We will, but for now we need to follow up on this."

They left the office and found Scanlon pouring a cup of coffee. Keane asked him if he put the package on his desk.

"Yeah, I put it there."

"How'd you get it?"

"Tully gave it to me when I came in. He said some babe brought it in and asked to give it to you. Tully was busy and asked if I could give it to you. I said no problem and brought it up and put it on your desk."

"How many people handled it after you got it?"

"As far as I know, nobody."

Keane didn't say anything else. He turned and left to go downstairs and speak with Tully. It was almost shift change but he was still on the desk.

"Hey Tully, did you get a package for me today?"

"Yeah man, I sure did. Some babe with great sticks came in and asked if I could relay the package to you. I said I would do anything she wanted. She smiled and then turned around and walked out. I gotta tell you, watchin' her walk out was enough to give me a hard-on. On a scale of 1 to 10, she was a 15."

"Other than the fact you have a perpetual hard-on, can you tell me anything about her? Color, height, weight, age, color of hair, long, short. Anything?"

"She was a white female; I'd say she was about 35 to 40, five feet forever, you know tall. Maybe 5 feet 10. I don't know her weight but for her height it was proportionate. Well proportionate! She was wearing a black mini with high heels and white top. She had great tits, too!"

"What about her hair?"

"It was short and blonde."

"And, you gave the package to Scanlon?"

"Yep."

"Anything else you can think of?"

"Not at the moment."

"If you think of anything else, let me know will ya?"

"Sure."

Keane started to turn and walk away.

"Hey, Keane, do you know the woman?"

"Not as far as I know. She didn't give her name, did she?"

"I asked her, "Who should I tell him it's from and she said just tell him a friend."

Keane's face looked pensive. He had no idea who she was.

"What time did she come in?"

Tully looked at the log book and then looked at his watch. "It was about two hours ago."

"Thanks," he said as he turned to go upstairs.

"Hey Keane, let me know if you need any help finding her!"

Keane just kept going upstairs, raising his hand and waving.

When he got upstairs, Bucci was standing next to his desk.

"Hey, what is this about?" Bucci said as he started to point at the envelope.

"DON'T TOUCH THAT!"

Bucci quickly removed his hand like he had touched a hot stove. "Jesus Christ, is there a bomb in there?"

"No. Sorry. That's the package. I just don't know who sent it and I need to have it dusted for prints. It's the envelope the video came in."

"Get another envelope, and I'll drop it in."

Keane got a large evidence envelope and Bucci very carefully picked it up by the corner and dropped it in. It had already been properly labeled. They would send it to the lab for analysis.

"You wanna go watch the video, again?" Bucci asked. "After that, I don't care. I'm pumped but I'm going home. I can hardly keep my eyes open."

"Yeah, let me get a cup of coffee."

They went to the video room and watched it several more times until they were convinced nothing else was new. The main thing they observed was a car at the bottom right leaving the scene just as the camera focused on the street. It was parked up the street from the shooting. There didn't appear to be anyone getting in the car during the entire video. Someone must have been sitting in the car the whole time. They now believed there may have been accomplices.

They went to Lt. Merrill, who just arrived to begin the next shift, and asked to talk with him in his office. They told him about the video. He told them to process the envelope, and review the reports from the previous night to determine if there were any witnesses. He asked if they got the warrants for Jack Dublin. They told him they did, but now believed Jack wasn't the shooter because the video showed another vehicle with possible accomplices, and it looked like Jack ran to the scene.

He reminded them the gun at the scene next to the victim was Jack's. Kneeling next to the gun at the scene was none other than Jack Dublin. They screwed up by not holding on to him and getting some evidence that would have cleared him or proved he was the shooter. He didn't mince words.

While they were standing there, the shift Captain walked in. He wanted to get an update but interrupted them instead.

"Listen, I hate to interrupt your conference but there's been a shooting on M Street. Initial reports indicate a woman is the victim. A witness gave a description of the shooter and it sounds like someone who is very close to the description of Jack Dublin."

They all exchanged glances. Lt. Merrill was the only one smiling. "Well gentlemen, you're not going home yet."

18

Jack walked hurriedly down along the canal. There were some restaurants and bars but also retail stores and condos. He considered ducking into a bar, but thought it would be one of the first places the police would look.

He continued walking under the highway steel girders and archways that ran parallel to the Potomac until he arrived at the Francis Scott Key Bridge. There was a chain link fence where they were doing work underneath. He jumped the fence and found refuge there and would remain until night returned. Darkness would be his best friend.

It made him think about working the street. His favorite shift was the midnight shift. All the hardworking, honest citizens were home sleeping or working. It was mostly just cops and dirt bags. One to one, mano a mano. Jack loved it.

The street was where you made your reputation. It's where you made a difference. Camaraderie and respect were built on the street. If you were perceived as weak or cowardly among your brethren, you were labeled as such and weeded out of the circle. It was predator and prey, within and without.

Right now, Jack was both. He needed to find Bob Lewis before anyone else did so he could beat the shit out of him! Now his only connection to Bob was dead and Jack was also tied to that murder. It didn't matter if the bullet was meant for him or not. It was certain everyone wanted a piece of him now.

Jack expected to see vagrants under the bridge, but instead there were just occasional joggers, bicyclists and lovers walking hand-in-hand along the Potomac. Once Jack felt secure, he sat down and looked through Peggy's purse.

There were the usual items you would expect to find in a woman's purse such as makeup, toiletries and keys. There was also an address book with slips of papers inserted in various alphabetical slots, but no slips with Bob Lewis's name in the "L" slot. Continuing to search, he never found anything remotely close except a few unidentified phone numbers without names. Jack found a couple of secret compartments but none of them revealed any important information. Finding Bob Lewis was going to be next to impossible.

Once night arrived, Jack decided he would walk towards his alma mater, Georgetown. This would allow him to circle around to his car. It was several blocks away. As he crossed M Street, he looked in the direction of the shooting, but he couldn't see that far due to a bend in the road. Even though it wasn't the weekend, the streets were populated with a healthy number of people.

He crossed over M Street and walked up the famous "Exorcist" steps. It was where the final scene was filmed in the movie when the priest jumped out the window to his death. If someone didn't point it out to you, you would never know. Once he got to the top of the steps, he was close to "1789", a restaurant on 36th St. He crossed the street and started to walk past it.

The famous restaurant was close to the campus of Georgetown. It was a political nesting ground. As he started to pass the entrance, an FBI friend of his was coming out with his wife. It was Rick Dryden. They knew each other well. There was no way Jack could avoid him.

"Hey Jack, how ya doin'?" Rick asked.

"Pretty good, Rick. How are you, Nancy?"

Jack leaned over and gave Rick's wife a peck on the cheek. Jack and Rick had become friends by accident. Jack was at a Nationals game. When he went to pay for some food, he used his wallet which had his I.D. and badge. Rick saw it and asked him what department he worked for and they began to talk police work. Rick was single at the time but dating Nancy. They ran into each other at the games and developed a good relationship that extended beyond baseball, going to dinner several times. Jack was dating someone named Jane at the time. Eventually, like most people, they lost contact.

Jack couldn't detect any indication that Rick knew about his most recent problems. They hadn't spoken in a few months. Rick had called and left a supportive message for Jack after he shot the senator's son.

"Jack, you seem a little uptight, are you sure you're doin' okay?"

"Yeah, yeah," Jack said nodding his head affirmatively.

Rick's tone turned serious. "You know, Jack, you got a raw deal with the senator. I can't believe you got blistered in the press like that. His kid had it coming to him. High on drugs, attacking you; as far as I'm concerned, it was beautiful police work."

"Well, I didn't set out to kill him, but there was nothing else I could do."

"You were just defending yourself. That's what we're trained to do, right?"

"Yeah, that's right."

"I heard you retired. I called and left a message for you. I hope you got it."

"Yep, sure did. Thanks." Jack changed the subject. He wanted information while he had the chance. "Hey listen, I heard Bob Lewis retired."

Rick smiled shaking his head. "Jack, he didn't retire. He quit before he was fired."

"Fired?"

People were leaving the restaurant. "Yeah," Rick said looking around. "Let's get out of the doorway."

They moved up the street a little until they were clear of the entrance.

"Jack, Bob was going to be fired because he was suspected of being an operative for a terrorist group. Now from what I understand, they couldn't prove it, but they must've had something on him to get him to retire. From what I heard, he's trading information and weapons with some nasty individuals. Right now, I heard he's conducting business from St. Lucia and living the good life."

"St. Lucia?"

"Yeah, he's living on a boat. I should say yacht," Rick started to smile. "Guess what he named it?"

Jack shook his head and shrugged his shoulders.

"*Busted.* The guy sure does have a twisted sense of humor."

"Yeah, I'll say," Jack answered thinking of the "You've Been Framed" store and the set up with WISE International. "How did you know about the boat and where he's living?"

"Our SAC (Special Agent in Charge) talked about it when Bob left the office. He wouldn't say too much more about it but he did show us a picture of the boat and said it was Bob's."

"Has anybody seen him recently?"

"Around here?"

"Yeah."

"Not that I am aware of. I think he'd be crazy to stick around here."

"Didn't he have a family?"

"Yeah, his wife Barbara is a nice lady. She deserved a lot better than this. She left town shortly before Bob resigned. I heard she moved to Delaware. They have a son who is disabled and I'm pretty sure he's in a long-term care facility in Delaware. I think she was from there and she moved back with her parents while Bob's living in the Caribbean enjoying the good life. How a man can walk away from his wife and handicapped son is beyond me. Guys like that don't have a soul. Eventually, they get theirs or, at least, you hope so."

There was a pause in the conversation before Rick spoke. "Hey, what are you doing now since you're retired?"

"Nothing, just enjoying some time off."

"I can't wait until I get there. I've still got 12 years to go until I'm 55 and can retire."

"It'll be here before you know it. Well, listen it was good talking with you."

"Jack, it was great seeing you, too. Take care of yourself and let's get together again. Are you still dating the same woman?"

"No."

"That sounded pretty definitive!"

"Let's just say I haven't been able to find a woman as beautiful as Nancy. You take care of this beautiful woman of yours. You're a lucky man."

"You don't have to tell me twice," he said as he looked lovingly into his wife's eyes.

Jack hugged Nancy and shook Rick's hand.

"Take care."

Jack walked away. He couldn't believe what he just heard. Bob Lewis in St. Lucia! If this is true, Jack needed to get down there somehow and find him. It had sounded like he was in D.C. according to Peggy Garber. Jack figured if had been here, it was to tie up loose ends before heading to the Caribbean. At least the FBI hadn't targeted Jack yet, or so it seemed. Rick has a supervisory position and if there was a BOLO (Be On the Lookout) on Jack, Rick would surely know.

Jack walked around the campus and the residential part of Georgetown for hours, wanting to make sure it was safe to go back to Julie's car. He didn't want to make her angry. It was already around 1 a.m. and Jack was surprised she hadn't called him. Looking at his phone, he saw he had missed a call around ten o'clock. He wondered what kind of reception she would give him when he got to her house. Hopefully, she would let him stay there for the night.

Finally, he came to M Street from an alleyway and peered out to see if there were any police officers in the vicinity of his vehicle. Since it wasn't his car, it was quite possible they didn't know he was using it. Nobody was around it. As soon as he could get in it, he would go to Julie's and ask to stay there until he could get a plane ticket to St. Lucia. He didn't know how he was going to get it without being traced, but he would figure that out.

Jack looked both ways again and felt safe. He trotted over to the car and put the key in the lock.

"Hold it, right there!!" officers screamed at him. The street lit up like a Hollywood production. "Put your hands up!!"

Jack did as he was told.

"Get down on the ground with your hands out to the side."

Jack knelt down and then lay on the pavement with his arms out to his side. Soon he was wearing handcuffs, again. Twice within 24 hours. Now he was under arrest.

19

It was a short ride back to HQ. Jack was again sitting in the back seat of a police car, wearing humiliation like a permanent tattoo. Just last night, Jack was interviewed by Keane and Bucci. Now he was back again. This time there were no professional courtesies. Jack was placed in a holding cell. There was a drunk sleeping it off on the other metal bunk.

Even though it was early, there was a buzz in the building. Jack could instinctively feel it. The cops were electric with the thought of one of their own arrested and in a cell. Jack saw many uniformed officers walking by his cell, looking in the small window of the heavy metal door. The cells were not within the normal walking area of working cops. They had to make a special effort to walk by.

Jack knew he would be all over the newspapers and TV. His face would be plastered everywhere, his name spoken with disdain by everyone he knew. Friends, few that he had, would be shaking their heads in disbelief. None would come to his aid.

Keep your expectations low, and you're never disappointed.

Jack decided to try to sleep, hoping to be rested for what was going to be another long day. He knew he was going to be charged with murder and sent to prison, at least for a short time. Until a lawyer was retained and the defense process began, there would be no release. Yet, he was confident once the facts revealed themselves, bail would be considered. He would find Bob Lewis and clear himself once he was released.

Jack was awakened by the unmistakable sound of cell keys opening the cell door. Although he did not know what time it was, he knew he would be taken for arraignment, and a bail hearing. Looking up he saw Keane and Bucci looking at him in a cynical way.

"C'mon Jack," ordered Keane.

"What's goin' on?" asked Jack while wiping his eyes with his palms.

"We're taking you upstairs."

"For what?"

"We're headed for the courthouse."

They'd already tried to get a statement from Jack, and he'd refused. There was nothing he could say to convince anyone, so why bother. It was quite apparent the investigation had taken a turn away from Jack's favor, and anything he said at this point could have negative implications. Hell, if he were on the other side of the situation, he would have doubts, too.

Jack got up and walked to the doorway of the cell. They told him to hold out his hands. He did, and was handcuffed. He saw that Bucci also had ankle restraints in his hands.

"Do we really have to do ankle cuffs?" asked Jack despairingly.

"'fraid so Jack. This is a capital case. Besides, when we walk out of here, don't you think the media would have our heads? They would say we gave you special treatment. Ain't happenin'."

Jack turned around and placed his hands on the wall, lifting his feet one at a time. There was no need for directions. He had done it so many times to prisoners, he knew the drill.

The ride to the courthouse took about five minutes. Fortunately, they were able to avoid the press while leaving HQ. There was a private entrance at the courthouse allowing them to bypass the media outside. Jack was taken to a holding cell in the courthouse. He sat there in stony silence. How could an innocent, honorable man be treated like a convict? It was a question he had asked himself many times over the last couple of days.

He sat there for about an hour before he heard voices and footsteps coming towards him. Jack assumed they were talking about him, but wasn't sure. Shortly, he heard keys in the lock of the cell door. The bailiff and a man Jack recognized as an attorney stood outside looking in at him. Jack had seen the well-known attorney before, but didn't know why he would be there for him.

"You Mr. Dublin?" asked the bailiff.

"Yes."

The bailiff opened the door all the way revealing the attorney and a woman.

"This is your attorney, Mr. Prescott. He wants to talk to you."

Archibald M. Prescott, one of the leading attorneys in Washington D.C. and perhaps the nation, stood there looking imperiously at Jack. He was accompanied by a voluptuous Caucasian woman, who was wearing a red dress that came mid-thigh, and accentuated her curvaceous body. She was, in a word, striking. Her hair was jet black and her doe-shaped eyes were blue. Her legs were incredibly long. Her face looked remarkable with delicate ears, and a small perfectly formed nose. Her lips were brooding, sensuously accentuated with ruby red lipstick. She was carrying a leather folder. For a minute, Jack forgot about his problems.

Archibald Prescott was a diminutive man, yet seemed tall in stature. He stood about five feet seven. Everyone knew him, from the poorest man on the street to the most powerful in Washington. A proud African American, he was one of the most famous criminal attorneys alive. He hadn't been seen lately, and it was rumored that he was terminally ill or worse, had gone to work for one of the larger law firms in Washington, specializing in political work for Congressmen. It seemed like a contradiction for a man of honor with historical distinction. Yet nobody could blame Mr. Prescott if he finally sold out.

He was dressed in a black suit that no doubt cost a few thousand dollars with a white shirt and conservative red tie. He also wore his ever-present carnation in his lapel. Today it was red, to match his tie. He had caramel-colored skin, a bald head with a neatly trimmed salt and pepper beard, and a mustache. His eyebrows always seemed to be raised, and his eyes were half open as if he was unimpressed with you. When he spoke, he had an aristocratic way that confirmed his Harvard education.

The bailiff led them down the hall to a private room. Jack shuffled along with his leg restraints, his hands still cuffed. The bailiff unlocked the door and opened it for them.

"Mr. Prescott, I will be standing right here outside the door. It will be locked. If you need me, just call me or tap on the door."

"Thank you" were the first words spoken by Mr. Prescott. "Could you please remove my client's handcuffs?"

"Mr. Prescott, you know the policy."

"I also know you are going to lock the door behind us, preventing any possibility of escape for my client. Not to mention his leg restraints will undoubtedly make it difficult for him to run, should he acquire the inclination."

"It's also done for your safety."

"I can assure you, I do not feel threatened or endangered by my client. Now please remove the handcuffs," he ordered.

The bailiff reluctantly did as was requested. After all, it was Archibald M. Prescott.

Jack went over to the table and sat down as the bailiff left the room.

"Mr. Dublin, I have been hired to represent you in this legal matter. This is my assistant, Marnie Bloom. She will assist in the investigation from our office. Her credentials are impeccable, I assure you."

"Who hired you? I know I didn't, and I also know you're not cheap," Jack asked turning his look from Marnie to Mr. Prescott. Mr. Prescott was nonplussed.

"Mr. Dublin," he paused, "our law firm has an interested benefactor, who occasionally takes an interest in cases such as these. This person is willing to post your bail, should we be so fortunate as to get bail, and to pay our expenses."

"I don't need anyone to pay my way. I have the money to pay for myself."

"Mr. Dublin, while you may have recently inherited some substantial funds, your ability to access them will be difficult. They are frozen assets, or will be shortly."

Jack looked stunned. He hadn't thought of that.

"Why? Why would someone take an interest in me?"

"That question could only be answered by the benefactor. Unfortunately for you, the benefactor has chosen to remain anonymous."

Jack sat there shaking his head. He had no idea who it could be.

"Mr. Dublin, you are in a tenuous situation. Perhaps you don't appreciate the true gravity of your circumstances. With the evidence against you, there exists very real potential of an extended incarceration. With that being said, I believe in your innocence."

"Why is that?"

Ms. Bloom spoke for the first time.

"Mr. Dublin, we have spoken with the investigators and we firmly believe in your innocence. In my opinion, they do not have enough evidence to affirm your guilt."

"What exactly do they have?"

Marnie spoke again. "They have a gun believed to be owned by you, at the scene. They have a video that shows you at the scene standing over the victim. Although the fatal shot most likely came from your gun, there is no evidence that you fired it."

"I'm no rocket scientist, but that sounds pretty incriminating to me. Not to mention, a woman sitting next to me at a restaurant gets shot. By the way, has anyone found out her condition?"

"She expired," Mr. Prescott answered.

"Oh, and I failed to mention, the victim in your first shooting is the son of a Pentagon official, General Webster," Marnie said.

"Now that we're giving numbers to shootings I've been involved in, how does the second one affect me?"

"I believe you shot and killed Senator Rothschild's son, in self-defense of course. The victim in the shooting with which you are charged is the son of General Webster. Although there doesn't appear to be any direct correlation between the two shootings, it does appear vaguely connected in the sense that you may have some type of vendetta against the government."

"That's insane! What could I possibly have against the government?"

"I don't know, Mr. Dublin. Perhaps you could enlighten us," Mr. Prescott said with a raised eyebrow.

Jack looked at him. He wasn't happy with the way Prescott was speaking to him.

"Why are you here?" Jack asked, annoyed.

"Mr. Dublin, you probably don't remember, but almost twenty years ago, we had a DUI trial together. During cross examination, you gave an answer that would have clearly won the case for the prosecution. After seeing the reaction on the faces of both the prosecutor and me, you realized it was misunderstood. But you clarified your point, even though you knew your statement could have reversed the opinion of the judge in favor of the defense. You have integrity. I also know my client tried to bribe you that night, but it never came out at the DUI trial. In the end, Mr. Dublin, the truth prevails, doesn't it?"

"How did you know about the bribe offer?"

"My client was also my brother."

"How's he doing now?"

"He's dead, Mr. Dublin. He was an addict. He thought he could get away with anything. Drug abuse is an insidious disease. It usually gets you in the end."

There was a palpable pause before Mr. Prescott spoke again.

"I believe you are an innocent person who is being utilized for devious purposes. In other words, Mr. Dublin, you are a fine upstanding citizen who was perfect for the ruse. Call it timing and opportunity."

"Where do we go from here?"

"Let's get the arraignment over with, and address the bail situation. If you are fortunate enough to be released on bail, the interested party has agreed to underwrite your bail with conditions."

"Strings. I knew there had to be strings."

"You will be chaperoned by Ms. Bloom, who works for a security firm and for my office. My client wants some reassurance that you are not going to jump bail. I want you in my office as soon as possible for interviews. It is important that we investigate this matter as quickly as possible, comprenez?"

Jack looked at Mr. Prescott. Why was he using French? To impress? Clearly, Jack was not impressed and responded accordingly.

"Si, yo entiendo pero quiero preguntar algunas preguntas, tu entiendes?" Jack said in Spanish. (Yes, I understand but I want to ask some questions, understand?)

"Si, preguntame." (Yes, ask me.)

Jack then asked him in German, who was going to investigate his story.

Mr. Prescott answered in German that their firm has several investigators to examine the claims of their clients.

Jack could have spoken in a couple more languages but chose not to. Apparently, Mr. Prescott was not impressed with him either.

"Mr. Prescott, what makes you think I'm going to get out on bail?"

"Mr. Dublin, your charge is only conspiracy at this time. Not murder. The judge, who heard from the detectives, would not allow a homicide charge based on the evidence. He did allow conspiracy. You certainly appear to be an erudite man. Have you ever heard of leverage? They are certain you know something you're not telling. They think you know who the murderer is, and what the motive is. With this charge, you face some prison time. They think you will be willing to plea bargain."

"But my gun was at the scene."

"Pretty damaging evidence, I know. My sources indicate a search warrant was completed at your residence earlier today. If they had found evidence implicating you as the murderer, they would have charged you accordingly. Since they didn't, it is apparent they do not have any other substantial evidence against you. In fact, it may be just the opposite."

The bailiff opened the door.

"Mr. Prescott, you and your client are wanted in the courtroom."

The bailiff placed the handcuffs on Jack and secured him.

"You will take these handcuffs off my client before we enter the courtroom, correct?"

"Yes, sir, I will."

Mr. Prescott turned to Jack and smiled. "You know, your language skills are superior. I had heard you were quite the linguist. Thank you for confirming it. I hope everything else I've heard about you is also accurate."

20

"Hello," Senator Rothschild said, answering the phone as if distracted.

"I made contact, and we are on our way," Bob Lewis informed him.

"What are the details?"

"I made contact with the leader, and spoke to him down at the Monument. We negotiated a payment upon delivery, which I expect to take place soon. I don't know what their plans are, but they're not a group to be feared, at least by us."

"What is the amount they are willing to pay?" the Senator asked anxiously.

"We're only talking five million," Bob answered reluctantly.

"That's all? I thought we were going to get at least ten million," he answered stridently.

"I'm not real happy about it either, but he knows we know he can get weapons elsewhere. As he said to me, "You're not the only game in town."

"This is bullshit, Bob! I was expecting considerably more. That's coffee money, Bob! Five million dollars is all you could get out of them? I mean, they're just a bunch of itinerant kids, who no doubt have deep pockets. I just can't believe it!"

Bob was starting to feel paranoid, like the senator was making sly innuendos about his honesty. He had to be careful about how he responded.

"Look, Senator, I tried everything I had in my toolbox to get him to compensate with more money, but he actually got up to leave during the negotiation. I saw our opportunity going down the toilet. I told him to sit down, and after further discussion, I told him to reconsider the value he was getting for his dollar. He didn't budge."

"It sounds like a one-sided negotiation to me."

"Senator, I have been involved in hostage negotiations, not to mention many other negotiations. I am no neophyte."

"Sounds to me like he's taking us hostage," he said mockingly.

There was silence on both ends that seemed much longer than the ten seconds it was. Bob was angry but trying to contain himself, and allow the senator to vent with his sardonic comments.

The senator broke the silence.

"Y'know Bob, I'm starting to wonder if the view is worth the climb on this one."

Again, there was silence. Bob didn't want to answer angrily. Then a thought came to his mind.

"Senator, my contact has heard of a new upgrade in SAMS. Do you know anything about it?"

"I have heard some discussion about a nuclear...I wouldn't call it a warhead, but an attachment. I was reluctant to bring it up."

"Why would you be reluctant to bring it up? It could be a pipeline for some more cash," Bob said excitedly.

"I know, but I don't know how we can get our hands on them without being noticed."

"Perhaps if you could get an upgrade in my contact's clearance, he could get his hands on some."

"Bob, these aren't your average outdated, armor-piercing weapons. These are sophisticated, state of the art nuclear components. They are closely monitored. There are ten tons of red tape you have to go through just to get close enough to sniff them. There are literally about twenty-five very stringent checks and balances."

"I think if you can get a higher clearance for my man, he will, at the very least, be able to assess the situation. If we can't get our hands on the latest and greatest, then we will just have to go with what we have."

"I'm not going there for less than twenty million. Feel them out before I go to any trouble," the senator said firmly.

"I will make the presentation and see what they say. If they're not interested, I'm sure I can find other takers."

The senator laughed for the first time.

"Just how many terrorists do you do business with?"

"You'd be surprised."

"How soon can we get paid?" Rothschild asked with regained composure.

"As soon as I can teach them how to use the weapons."

"Teach them?"

"Yeah, they need training."

"You mean to tell me they don't know how to use them?" the senator asked in disbelief.

"I guess not, but maybe it's a ploy. They may know how to use them, but want to make sure after the last episode, they are fully armed and ready to go. Or, they may think they can get a little revenge, by taking me and my guys out, so they can have the weapons and keep their money. If that's the case, we will be ready for them."

"I thought it was a requirement for kids in the Middle East, y'know, like driving cars here in America. Every kid has to know how to shoot a rocket launcher before they're sixteen," the senator said jokingly.

"Apparently not."

"We need to make sure we get delivery on the money," Rothschild said, returning to seriousness.

"Don't worry; they won't see the weapons until we see some cash."

"How are you going to train them? I mean, it's not every day a person sets off rockets in the neighborhood."

"You won't have to worry there, either. We are going to take two boats out to sea..."

"Wait, you're going to do this out at sea?" asked the senator with concern.

"Yeah."

"How close and where?"

"Don't worry. It will be far enough out at sea that no one will be around. I know the shipping channels as well, and we will be clear."

"Where?"

"Out of Lewes, Delaware."

"Don't they take charters out of there?"

"Probably, but it doesn't matter. We will be far enough out that the tuna charters, and whoever else wants to go out there, will be closer to shore than us."

"What are your plans?"

"We're going to take another boat out that's ready to become a reef, and then practice on it."

"Practice? What do you mean? Shoot at it?"

"Yep, that's the plan."

"Are you crazy? The Coast Guard will see a ship on fire."

"Maybe, but by the time they get to it, it will be gone. I'll be there and I will make sure it's sunk by the time any Coast Guard gets there."

"You gotta be careful about airplanes too."

"Listen, I know what I'm doing," he said sarcastically. "I've thought of that, too. I've checked every airport with flight paths traveling in our area including New York, Philadelphia and Washington. My IT guy has a formula using triangulation and algorithms. There aren't any I'm concerned about in our time frame. Of course, if I see any private aircraft in the area, we'll wait until they pass."

"Don't get so defensive. My ass and career are at stake. I have a lot to lose."

"You're not the only one. I don't want to spend time in prison. That includes federal prison."

"I'm glad to hear you have a formula. When do you plan on doing this?"

"This week, if possible. Maybe on Tuesday or Wednesday. I don't want to do it on a weekend. Too many people out trying to find weekend salvation."

"When will you receive payment?" the senator asked anxiously.

"Half when we return to shore and the other half when we deliver the payload."

"How soon after you train them are you going to make delivery of the weapons? I want to get this deal completed."

"Anytime they want them after that. I expect within a couple of weeks."

"Any problems that you can foresee?"

"One, other than the ones we mentioned earlier. They want to take delivery in the Caribbean. Maybe St. Lucia."

"You're kidding, right?"

"No. I'm dead serious. They don't want to take them here."

"Why not? I thought they'd be anxious."

"It makes sense when you think about it. Why take a risk here? This way, we take the risk. While I'm thinking about it, we should get paid more since we are taking the risk. Anyway, they can receive the weapons, and we can get our money out of the scrutiny of the U.S."

"This actually could turn out to be perfect. I am going on a cruise down there in a couple of weeks, and I'm taking a staffer down with me. I've been invited to tour the newest cruise ship, which will be making its maiden voyage from San Juan to Barbados and back. Hold on, I have the itinerary here somewhere."

Bob could hear the senator rustling through some papers. "Here it is. We're going to hit five islands: St. Thomas, St. Maarten, Antigua, St. Lucia and Barbados."

"You're taking a staffer?"

"Yes."

"Are you taking the wife?"

"It's business. No, I am not taking my wife."

"Well, that's interesting."

"What about Dublin?" the senator said changing the subject.

"What about him?"

"Have you been able to make plans for him?"

"Right now, he's in custody."

"Where?"

"Metro P.D. has him for murder."

"That's good, but how are we going to get to him if he's in custody?"

"It will be more difficult, that's for sure."

"We need him out, on the street."

"That may be difficult."

"Is there anything you can do to get him out?"

"Maybe. It depends on whether or not he gets a bail."

"Do what you can to get him out. If you can't, do what you can to get him, period."

"I'll see what I can do. I have someone in mind."

"Really?"

"Yeah, I might be able to get to him while he's in custody."

"Just make sure he's no longer around to see the light of day."

"I know, I know."

"Listen," he said changing the subject again. "Maybe we can make a money transfer while I'm down there. We can meet at one of the islands and deposit the money into an offshore account."

"We might be able to arrange that."

"Obviously, if I deposit money in an island bank, it's more discreet."

"I hear you." Bob said understandingly.

"Just out of curiosity, did they give you any idea about what they are going to do with the missiles? You know, what they're going to hit?"

"Not a clue."

"Let's stay in touch this week," the senator said signing off.

"Will do," Bob said hanging up the phone. He sat there pondering the phone call and started to laugh. "Triangulation and algorithms... I can't believe he fuckin' bought it!" as he continued to laugh heartily.

21

Jack shuffled from the elevator, feeling like he was walking to an execution, his execution. At least he was still wearing his clothes and not the universal orange jump suit that prisoners always wore to court.

The hall from the elevator to the door that led directly to the courtroom was occupied with curious onlookers. They were mostly bailiffs and police officers. He recognized most of them. He didn't say anything to any of them and they didn't speak to him either. Most of the cops looked at him with disgust. In the cop world, you are trained to feel everyone in cuffs is guilty, but a former cop wearing them was almost as bad as being considered a pedophile. He felt like Lee Harvey Oswald being transferred to court and expected the ghost of Jack Ruby was close-by.

This time they had the wrong man.

There are times during an officer's career when you feel pressure to make arrests in questionable cases for many reasons. Supervisors want the stats to show their success as a unit and police department.

Jack never operated that way. As an investigator, everybody was guilty until proven innocent, but before they got charged, Jack had to be certain in his mind the defendant was truly guilty. Not only that, he played by the rules. If he perceived the slightest chance a case could be reversed by his actions, he would take the safer route and not place a charge, even if it didn't win him favor with his brethren.

Once he was a lead investigator on a homicide where the victim had been stabbed to death. The perpetrator used a small knife, and it went far enough into the victim's body to just nick the heart. The victim bled to death in an apartment hallway. All the evidence pointed toward the suspect, who had just turned eighteen.

When they got him back to HQ, the suspect was placed in a private cell. Before Jack and his partner could get back from the scene to interview him, the boy's father and an attorney were there at HQ, demanding to speak with the suspect before a statement was taken.

Jack went to the lieutenant and cited a constitutional case, Escobedo vs. Illinois, where an attorney demanded to see his client before an interview could take place. The police in that case kept moving the defendant around to avoid the attorney. The case was overturned and the defendant in that case was retried.

The lieutenant ordered him to just read the Miranda rights, and if the suspect asked to speak with an attorney, don't take the statement. In other words, just go for it. Jack knew that months down the road, he would be the one trying to explain how he blew the case. The stigma of a man guilty of murder being released was not one Jack wanted to have on his conscience. He didn't want to look at the victim's family and explain the failure. Most importantly to Jack, he didn't want an innocent kid who had just begun to live life, lying in his grave while his killer walked free.

Jack again pleaded with the lieutenant to call a prosecutor for confirmation. The lieutenant said it was 3 o'clock in the morning. After further arguments, the lieutenant reluctantly contacted the prosecutor on call and gave him the information. He agreed with the lieutenant.

Jack and his partner went down and took a statement. The suspect didn't request an attorney after receiving the Miranda rights, and admitted stabbing the victim, but said it was self-defense. It was a complete lie. Everyone knew the suspect was a little tyrant with a Napoleonic attitude who enjoyed terrorizing his teenage community. He enjoyed striking fear in people, especially those bigger than him. The victim had size and height on the suspect, but was about as threatening as a puppy.

The suspect was charged with homicide and sent to prison to wait for trial. When the case eventually made it to trial, he was found guilty and given a life sentence. Two years later the sentence was overturned because the appellate court said he should have been advised and allowed to speak with the attorney at HQ.

Another trial took place. The problem became finding people who had testified at the original trial. Some had died. Some had moved. Some had disappeared. Those that were found couldn't remember exactly what happened.

The defendant with proper coaching now looked like a choirboy. He sat with a deer-in-the-headlights look and the jury bought the self-defense theory sold by his new attorney. He was acquitted. Jack never believed in his innocence, and the kid was later killed when he took on someone who got tired of his shit.

Now Jack was in the center of something larger then he could possibly understand. He was now ingenuously accused in the murder of a Pentagon Colonel's son. Furthermore, shooting the senator's son in self-defense was now being reconsidered as a questionable act.

Jack was led into Courtroom 5 with which he was quite familiar. It was the largest courtroom on the 4th floor. It was an older courtroom with updates of walnut wood panels placed over lighting, giving the impression the panels had squished the light out from the sides, splaying it over the textured walls. Jack always hated the décor in this room. He thought the interior designers got it wrong. It should have been wood walls with textured panels. When you sat in a courtroom for hours over years, you had the tendency to analyze even the most inane topics.

When Jack entered the room, he was surprised that there were so many people there. He hurriedly searched the gallery to see if there were any familiar faces before looking down solemnly. He saw just the usual clerks, court reporters, bailiffs, reporters and, of course, Keane and Bucci.

He walked over and sat down next to Mr. Prescott after his handcuffs were removed. They spoke briefly.

"All rise, court is now in session. The Honorable Jacob Steinberg presiding."

Jack heard the sound of a hundred people standing up at once and thought immediately about the sound of people at his church rising on cue in their pews. Only this time, the choir was not going to sing.

There was an energy in the room that was almost explosive. Those who were lucky enough to get in, not only saw a dishonored former police officer being arraigned for a capital type offense, but they also got to see a clash of titans.

On one side of the aisle, a tall upcoming golden boy (and Caucasian) prosecutor was about to go against an established diminutive African-American attorney who had a storied past.

Archibald Prescott was like a rattlesnake lying coiled in harmless repose but once disturbed, he would strike quickly with deadly results. It was the black self-assured David versus the slower pompous white Goliath.

"You may be seated."

"Good morning," said the judge. He was authoritative looking from his perch. He had been a federal prosecutor for eighteen years before becoming a judge, and he was a hardliner who didn't tolerate any nonsense. Some judges encouraged a little banter but not Judge Steinberg. He had gray wiry hair, a matching beard and always looked unkempt, but his case acuity was razor sharp.

After the obligatory response the judge asked the prosecutor, George Sarley, if he was ready to proceed. When he answered in the affirmative, the judge glanced over at Mr. Prescott and smiled.

"Are you ready Mr. Prescott?"

"Yes, your honor" was his response as he stood and then sat down again.

"You can proceed, Mr. Sarley."

"Your honor, the people of the District of Columbia have charged the defendant John Dublin with conspiracy to commit murder. In view of the serious nature of these charges, we are asking for the defendant to be held without bail."

There was a collective "Ooh" in the courtroom.

"We have reason to believe he is a flight risk."

Judge Steinberg then looked at Mr. Prescott.

"Mr. Prescott, your response?"

Mr. Prescott stood up as Mr. Sarley sat down and addressed the judge.

"Your honor, the charges brought against Mr. Dublin are borne without merit. Mr. Dublin is a highly respected, retired police officer who served the people of this district with honor and integrity for twenty years. While he no longer lives in the boundaries of the district, he lives close-by in a recently purchased condo in Rosslyn. He has no intention other than to restore his impeccable name by remaining here to answer to this, at best, questionable charge."

Mr. Sarley immediately stood up.

"Your honor, Mr. Dublin's "impeccable" name is one tarnished with the shooting death of United States Senator Rothschild's son. And, not only are we here for this shooting, he was present at another shooting yesterday," he said theatrically, "that resulted in the death of a woman who may have had some knowledge about this case. It seems that just standing close to Mr. Dublin can result in gun lead poisoning."

There were some chuckles from the courtroom. The judge banged his gavel bringing order to the courtroom. He then glared at Mr. Sarley without saying anything. He didn't have to. Sarley took his seat.

Mr. Sarley got back on point. "Mr. Dublin has also recently acquired substantial sums of money in his personal financial accounts. We believe with his penchant for shootings and his questionable attained wealth, he is quite capable of fleeing this country."

"Your honor, Mr. Dublin obtained his wealth through an inheritance, and with regard to the unfortunate shooting of Senator Rothschild's son, my client was cleared of any wrongdoing. With all due respect, these charges are the result of poor investigation, and my client should not even be subjected to this unwarranted humiliation. As to the other allegations, there have been no charges. Until there are, Mr. Sarley's ridiculous comment is nothing more than frivolous conjecture."

"Poor investigation?" Sarley asked incredulously as he shot out of his chair. "How do you explain your client innocently standing over a murder victim with a gun that he owns?"

"He..."

Before Prescott could respond, Judge Steinberg interrupted by banging the gavel several times.

"Gentlemen, gentlemen. We are not here to argue the merits of the case. We are here to set bail only. It seems to me, Mr. Sarley, that whether or not Mr. Dublin lives one mile to the north or one mile to the south of here, does not make him any more of a flight risk than if he lived five miles away and still lived in the district. Additionally, there is no indication that Mr. Dublin acquired his money illegally. I do not hear you taking a position that Mr. Dublin obtained his wealth by linking it to this case. You have avenues available to you to hinder Mr. Dublin from getting access to his funds. Therefore, this court is setting the bail at one million dollars."

"Is that cash, your Honor?" asked Sarley.

"Your Honor, we respectfully request a lower bail since you, yourself, said he does not present a flight risk," asked Mr. Prescott before the judge could answer Mr. Sarley. He wanted to interject first before the judge could decide in favor of the prosecution, even at the risk of being admonished for interrupting.

After giving Mr. Prescott's response consideration, he responded.

"I am not reducing the bail but I will make it secured instead of cash." He had thrown the prosecution a small bone. Mr. Prescott got the filet.

"Thank you, your Honor," replied Mr. Prescott.

The secured bail allowed Jack to put up ten percent with a bail bondsman instead of thirty-three percent if it were cash.

"Mr. Prescott, will your client be able to make this bail?"

"Yes, your Honor," answered Mr. Prescott.

Another collective "Ooh" went through the gallery.

"Then it is a condition of this bail that Mr. Dublin will not be allowed to leave this area any further than a five-mile radius. Is that understood? I believe he can defend himself more than adequately by remaining within a five-mile radius. If he needs to leave the area, he must first obtain permission from this court. Is that understood?"

Everyone answered in agreement.

"I believe this concludes our hearing. Thank you."

"All rise."

With that, the courtroom came alive with chatter.

Jack looked around the room quickly as the bailiffs moved in and put the cuffs on. He saw a couple of people he thought he knew. It was the person he didn't see that would have an impact on the rest of his life.

22

He sat in his ergonomically-fitted Pininfarina chair. Like many of his possessions, it was one-of-a-kind and had cost enough to pay for a family of five to take a Caribbean cruise. It had been custom made for him and his temperamental back. The years spent operating in the field had left their stubborn mark, and his chronic pain would endure through his remaining years.

All said, Ben Dublin's physical appearance was remarkably youthful for his sixty-seven years. He worked out for forty-five minutes, five days a week and but for a few pounds around the middle, he kept himself in terrific shape. Although his hair had turned chrome-colored with the years, it remained thick and the man's eyes were still piercing blue and engaging. Women, thirty years his junior, still found Ben quite desirable. Bifocals rested precariously on a sharp nose, and undulations of skin were starting to hint furrows along his face. As is true for everyone, the unavoidable pull of gravity, and time that moved faster now, it seemed, were steadily dragging him to his inevitable abode below the soil. Some things cannot be denied.

Still, there was work to be done, and grasping the arms of his chair, Dublin pulled himself closer to the desk. Ben's suit, like most of his belongings, was custom made. He was wearing a medium gray Alexander Amosu creation, custom tailored from a blend of rare animal wools from the Himalayas and the Andes, along with a pale pink Charvet shirt, accented with a Stefano Ricci silk tie. His hand-made Berluti shoes and rose-colored carnation in his lapel highlighted the day's ensemble, reflecting his impeccable taste.

Staring apprehensively at the desktop, Ben's mind had shifted back again to his son's predicament. He struggled with a decision to get involved, to help, but there was one major difficulty. His son wholly hated him, and viewed him with utter contempt, convinced he had murdered his wife, Jack's mother. In spite of everything, Ben wanted to help his only son.

Suddenly, Dublin felt the vibration, and reached into the inside coat pocket of his suit. Not recognizing the caller ID number, he answered but did not offer any greeting. It was not his habit to answer calls arriving from unfamiliar numbers.

"Lucky?" asked the familiar voice.

Paralyzed for an instant, Ben thought about ending the call.

"Lucky?" the caller repeated louder.

After pausing a few more seconds, Ben answered in a faraway voice, "Yes."

"Jack is in trouble," was all Ben heard. "But I'm sure you already know," the caller finished.

It was a voice Lucky recognized from the past, but had not heard in many years. It was the Artful Dodger. They had been brothers once, united by a common ideological bond, love of country. But it was another kind of love that had made them adversaries, their love for the same woman. In love, as in war, there can be only one winner, and at times, a poor and vengeful loser.

"I'm aware Jack's in trouble. What can you tell me I don't already know?" Ben tersely questioned.

"Right now, he is charged with conspiracy to commit murder. That's the most immediate problem," the Artful Dodger answered, not as curtly.

It was obvious the two men didn't like each other much. But, they had a common concern for Jack. Mick Jennings was worried about Jack, and had called Jack's father trying to be helpful even though he received the anticipated cold reception.

The two men had worked together on a few covert ops. It was during those times the men had gotten their nicknames. Ben's had come from the simple fact he was *lucky* and Mick had been tagged with the

Artful Dodger moniker because he was very slick and elusive in the field. Each man had saved the other's life, more than once. Their work had been mostly Cold War stuff in Soviet Russia and the Communist Bloc. Back then, the men had been great friends, comrades-in-arms fighting a hated enemy. But, it had been their mutual love for beautiful Isabella, whose heart Lucky had won, that had caused the trouble between them.

"Why are you calling me? What do you expect me to do? I've been out of this game for a long while now."

"For starters, because his bail was set at a million dollars."

Ben stood from the chair, and walked slowly to the expansive windows overlooking the city, attempting to digest what he'd just been told. After years of silence, the Artful Dodger had emerged from the darkness. Ben resolutely pushed the angry thoughts that hearing his voice had dredged up, out of his mind. Jack was all that mattered.

"What else can you tell me?" Ben asked in a civil tone.

"First off, we can't just stroll in there with a bag of money and get him released. Shit, Ben, he's been arrested, released, and arrested again, all in twenty-four hours. He's in deep. Jack is into some big shit, and the Metro P.D. and the DA are out to nail his ass. It's complicated Ben, trust me on this. I'm pretty sure you're all he's got."

"I suppose," Ben sighed.

"Listen Ben, you know I've got eyes and ears everywhere. And my guy inside the MPD tells me this fucking jerk, a Lieutenant Merrill, has really been out to get him. He's got it in for Jack, and I hear he will do anything he can to bury Jack for good."

"From what I've heard, a false charge of conspiracy is the least of Jack's problems, now," Ben said clearly.

"Maybe it's time to tell me what *you* know," Mick quickly returned.

"What I know is Jack's involved in something much bigger that being slapped with a potential murder rap that in the end won't stick. And you know it, too!" Ben said with fervor, his tone charged again, louder and irritated.

"I'm gonna lay it out for you, at least as much as I can. I know I owe you that, and Jack, too."

"That would be nice," Ben said, interrupting sarcastically, while still standing at the windows.

Mick realized it wasn't the time to get into a pissing match, so he held his tongue and kept talking.

"I've been temporarily assigned to our ODAT people, Office of Domestic Anti-Terrorism, and we've been working with the Feds, IAI (Internal Affairs and Investigations), over at the FBI, and with their domestic anti-terrorism group, too. My counterpart over at Langley has truly been helpful. He's a good guy, and has been easy to work with. This whole thing has been complicated from the get-go, and it's just too important to allow all the standard interagency bullshit to get in the way, you know?"

"Just get to the point!" Lucky briefly interrupted, still quite irritated.

"We've had a very complex and comprehensive ongoing investigation, but Jack stepped into the shit, and now it's all over him. He had no idea what was going on. An ex-FBI agent named Bob Lewis purposely pulled him in. Lewis was using him as a fall guy, to drop the shit in his lap."

"I was told all about that too," Ben interjected again, in a tone indicating his continued frustration. "Tell me something I don't know."

"We've had our eyes on Lewis for some time now. The indications were, he was involved with stolen U.S. weapons, and was interested in peddling them. We became aware of a few possible local terrorist groups, but didn't have enough on any of them to bring them down. We couldn't just trust our intelligence, and then drop a smart bomb on a house in Georgetown, like we do in Afghanistan. Finally, one of them became of special interest, and we were able to infiltrate the group with one of our operatives. They aren't just a ragtag band of rich, snot-nosed college kids from affluent families. They have deep pockets, and plenty of sophistication and intelligence capability to counter our moves."

"So what's the situation there?" Lucky asked, his tone again eased just a bit.

"We're not sure. We think she, our mole, might have been compromised. At the time of her last contact with us, she was very uneasy, and was fearful she had been followed."

"Why doesn't that surprise me?" Ben interrupted with sarcasm.

"Believe me, she's an outstanding agent, very cautious and intelligent. She's not one to be easily intimidated. We have a designated signal to confirm she's okay. Unfortunately, we haven't seen it for a couple of days. And that's unusual. In fact, it's never happened before, so we're obviously concerned."

"You still haven't told me what Jack has to do with all this. You know and I know, he's got some bullshit charge on him for something he didn't do. Everybody knows its bullshit, except the cops. So send someone down there, tell them what's going on and get *my son* out of jail. You don't need a million dollars from me. It shouldn't be that fucking difficult!" Ben said raising his voice.

"Like I said, Ben, it's not that easy. Jack is in it with both feet. When Jack got involved, he really opened it up for us. It's a whole new can of worms now, and we need him."

Ben pondered the situation as he went back to his desk and sat down. "So tell me how this is going to go down," Ben responded calmly.

"We have to get Jack out of jail. And like I said, due to the circumstances, we just can't just go in and do it ourselves. Once he's out, I think Jack will lead us right to Lewis. Once that is done, we will monitor Lewis."

"You make it sound so easy, but we both know it won't be. It's going to be dangerous," Ben claimed in a worried voice. "Besides, why the hell does Jack have to find him? You've got the resources of the entire CIA!"

"You would think we wouldn't need him, but for all our awesome superiority and resources, they have intelligence too. And Lewis, being an ex-Fed, knows how to make himself scarce when he needs to. One other thing, we think Jack knows something we don't."

"How's that?"

"He ran into Rick Dryden and his wife right after the Garber shooting. The guys I'm working with over at Langley don't have Dryden on board with them. There's no need. Jack and Dryden had a long talk outside the 1789 restaurant, about six hours after the Garber shooting. We've got no idea what they talked about, but that's part of the reason we think Jack knows some stuff we don't. Dryden knows Lewis, and there's a possibility he told Jack something. And Internal Affairs doesn't want to question Dryden, not yet. You know how that goes, once IA talks to somebody, everybody starts talking."

"What kind of protection is Jack going to have?" Ben asked tersely.

"I'm doing what I can do, but you know yourself, we can only do so much. Hell, I saved his ass once already. Right after the Garber shooting, Jack thought it was just a couple of big football types who happened to be there to help him, when he was mugged. They were my guys, Ben. I almost didn't send them. And, if I had decided to stay more backed off from the situation, Jack might have been killed right then and there. You know yourself, Ben, people go down on ops like these. There are always casualties and collateral damage. Ben, I guess I'm just trying to say I can't promise anything. Like it or not, it's the best I can do. Believe me, if there were any way to do this without Jack, we'd do it."

"Mick, you may not be able to promise anything, but I can. If anything happens to Jack, you'll be the last one I kill!" Ben promised with conviction as he ended the call.

"What about Jack's bail?" Mick quickly asked, but was unable to finish the question before Ben had cut him off. He pondered the last words Lucky said and he had no doubt, it was not an idle threat.

23

Jack went back to the city jail and was placed in the same cell as before. This time, he was alone. Apparently the drunk was having better luck. The cell smelled like a cesspool. He looked in the toilet and saw it was backed up. Instead of calling for someone to come fix it, he walked over to the bench and sat down, dejected.

Jack had no idea how long he would be there but he knew another minute would be too long. Getting bail could be a long process. It always depends on a few things: Did the person posting with the bail company have proof of the money needed to post? If not, did that person have a deed? If not, it could take a while to get one, or proof of one, from the recorder of deeds and their employees were usually in no hurry to help.

Meantime, the clock was ticking, and at five o'clock the court personnel stopped and didn't care if someone spent the night in jail. If his bail wasn't raised by five he would just have to wait and get out the next day.

It was usually the fault of the bail company. They had a habit of waiting until the end of the day to get someone over to the courthouse to post, even if the money was in their hands. Of course, Jack didn't know what the relationship was between Mr. Prescott's office and the bail office. He suspected the bail company didn't want to get on Mr. Prescott's bad side.

Jack sat there and pondered the entire situation. He went over in his mind each minute detail again, beginning with the time he received the call from Bob Lewis. Having a five mile radius to work from would make it difficult to find Bob Lewis, and he couldn't rely on anyone else.

As he continued to think about his dilemma, he heard footsteps. It sounded like two people. They were talking in a casual manner but weren't close enough for Jack to hear what they were saying. As they got closer he heard a police officer talking with someone who was about to be placed in Jack's cell.

"Alright, have a seat and you'll see a judge sometime today," said the older police officer who Jack didn't recognize. He opened the door and a large man in his early thirties with a muscular build entered taking a seat opposite Jack. The officer closed the door and walked away.

Jack was beginning to feel like he was living in a land of giants. The man was about six foot six inches and must have weighed about 275. His chiseled body was no doubt the result of many hours in the gym. He was wearing a tight fitting, sleeveless black t-shirt which put his tattoos on display. They were multi-colored and went down to his wrist. The tattoos expressed anger. Impressions of razor wire encircled his upper arms. He wore jeans and light-colored work boots.

The last thing Jack wanted was someone else in the cell with him. The solitude had been fitting and now it was going to be disrupted. Jack sat silently trying to exude an "I don't want to be bothered" attitude. The other man shuffled around looking at his feet and adjusting his posture. He got up and walked over to the door looking both ways out of the window. After a few moments he went back, sat down and began to fidget. Jack could feel the other man looking at him, yet he didn't look up to meet the other man's gaze.

"So, what are you in here for?" the man asked Jack with a strong voice.

Jack didn't answer.

"Excuse me, but what are you in here for?" he asked again this time giving his voice more volume.

Jack slowly raised his head until his eyes met the other man's.

"I don't want to talk about it."

"I'm in here because I got picked up for a parole violation."

"Really?" Jack said disinterested.

"Yeah, I was driving down M Street and they say I ran a red light, which I didn't, but when they ran my name they saw I was wanted for a parole violation. What a bunch of shit! I miss two meetings with my parole officer and he bangs me with a violation. Can you believe that?"

"Hmmmm," Jack muttered.

"Man, you don't say much, do you?"

"I don't have anything to say."

There was a short period of silence. Jack hoped the man got the message. But he didn't.

"Y'know you look familiar," the man said with a quizzical look on his face.

"That so?"

"Yeah," he said with an inquisitive look. He was drumming his fingers on his thighs. "Wait! I know who you are," he said angrily. Jack just looked at him. "You're that fuckin' perv who sticks his dick in young kids."

"I don't know who you're talkin' about but it's not me," Jack replied disinterested.

"Yeah, you're the one. I've seen your picture on T.V."

Jack thought the man probably saw his picture on T.V. associated with the shootings and combined it with another news story about a child molester. Jack looked over and the man was taking his boots off. He noticed that the laces were still in them with the boot tag still on a small chain. This was unusual since they always take your belt and shoelaces before they stick you in a cell. Jack looked up at the small plastic protrusion in the ceiling that encased the security camera. He was hoping that someone was watching.

Jack kept his eyes on the man who seemed to be working himself up into a frenzy.

"Why are you taking your boots off?" Jack asked. "You know they can see everything you're doing from that camera," he said pointing to it.

The man looked at Jack with demonic eyes. He didn't even glance in the direction of the camera when Jack was pointing to it.

"I hate fucking perverts!" he shouted.

"Yeah, well I'm not a pervert," Jack said. "So calm down."

He certainly did not want to do battle with this guy who clearly had age, size and muscle to his advantage.

Jack continued to watch as the man pulled something out of his boot. He couldn't immediately discern what it was but he knew it was a weapon of some sort. The man held the object in his cupped right hand. The cell was about ten-by-eight and any confrontation wouldn't allow a lot of moving around. Jack had used his black belt Tang So Doo moves before, on the street, but it had been a long time. The best defense right now was diplomacy. These situations were beginning to seem oddly familiar to him.

"Look man, I am not a child molester. I was arrested for murder."

The other man stopped what he was doing and started to laugh.

"That's real funny," he said. "A child pervert is going to persuade me he's a murderer. Well, let's see what a child pervert can do."

The man stood up and Jack looked in his hand. He was holding a shank he had removed from his shoe. Jack stood up too, taking a defensive stance. The man hunched over and began to slowly approach Jack. He held the shank in his right hand.

He took a simulated lunge at Jack who responded by backing up. The walls were beginning to close in on him. The man began to smile.

"What's the matter, perv, afraid you're gonna have something shoved up you for a change?"

Jack didn't respond. He had always been taught not to engage in verbal conflict. Maintain your focus on the aggressor and his weapon. He would use hand strikes, kicks and blocks to defend himself but the area was tight.

Jack yelled, "Yo!" He was hoping that someone was watching the security camera and would come to intercede.

The man laughed again and kept the sinister smile pasted on his face.

The man was keeping his distance but Jack knew it wouldn't last. He knew the attempt to kill was coming and he wanted to be ready. He didn't want to use excessive force but his opponent was definitely in great shape and a couple of kicks would not neutralize him. It would take more than that. Jack could feel the metal bench touching behind his knee and he knew he was out of room. He was close to the wall.

The man lunged at Jack quickly but Jack was quicker. He took his left arm and blocked the shank while wrapping his arm around the man's bicep and placing his left hand on the man's pectoral muscle. With his right hand Jack viciously shoved it under the man's jaw and pushed up until his head twisted backwards at an unhealthy angle crumpling the man immediately to the floor. Amazingly, the man still held the shank in his hand but released it slowly after his head hit the floor. Blood started to come out of the man's mouth. Jack looked down at the helpless man not knowing what to do. It was over that quick.

"Help!" Jack yelled again.

Shortly afterwards the cell door opened and police officers rushed into the cell, pushing Jack up against the wall. Another officer came and checked the other man's pulse.

"Quick, somebody call an ambulance!"

"He tried to kill me," Jack tried to tell them through clenched teeth as his face was pushed up against the wall.

"Get him out of here!" screamed the officer attending to the man on the floor.

The two officers took Jack and forced him out of the cell. With one officer on each arm, they raised them behind Jack so he was facing the floor. They took him out into the hall and down to the next cell which was unoccupied. They pushed him in and shut the door.

Jack didn't care how badly the man was hurt. Live by the sword, die by the sword. Jack looked out the cell window until he saw paramedics arrive and take the man out on a stretcher. The officers followed them down the hall.

Jack hoped it didn't interfere with his bail. He needed to get out. Right now, with everything happening to him, he would be happy just to get the hell out of D.C. If he could jump bail, leave the country and start a new life on an island without fear of having to come back to the United States, he would give it serious consideration.

Jack went over to the bench and sat down with his back against the wall literally and figuratively.

He would not sit there long.

24

It was 6:30 in the evening.

The television was on in one of the first floor bedrooms with news leaking into the hallway about the continuing effort to assist the people of Syria where thousands of people died as a result of government genocide. The following news story talked about the President and the U.N. trying to work in concert to place sanctions on Iran, in an effort to curtail its nuclear capabilities.

Abdullah enjoyed hearing this. With the illegitimate purchase of U.S. government weapons, he knew they would soon be the lead story. It would be a story that would be as strong as an earthquake and as devastating as a nuclear explosion. If he died in the process, so much the better. Abdullah was prepared to die a martyr.

The group had a scheduled meeting at their rented Georgetown house for 7:30 that evening. It was scheduled that way so everyone could take a breather from class and get something to eat. Initially, it was a ritual to eat together every evening. This allowed them to strengthen their connection. After a short period of time it became obvious with everyone's schedules and commitments, it would be difficult to maintain the dedication. So they agreed to have their community meal on Sundays. Meetings were generally on Wednesdays but could be called at random by Khalil.

Tonight, Khalil would inform the rest of the group what had occurred at his meeting with Bob Lewis. Their objective was on schedule. Soon, they would wake up the world.

Before the rest of the group assembled, Abdullah took Khalil aside to talk to him. Khalil was wearing his usual white cotton short-sleeved shirt and dark blue denim jeans. He had sandals on. This was the attire he usually wore day in and day out, changing only the color of his shirt to help him fit in with American students, although he never made any effort to befriend anyone. In student surroundings, he was friendly but detached. Since he was a handsome man, women tried to approach him but his comportment usually kept them at bay. Once in the secure surroundings of his home, he would wear a turban and a galibiyya which was a tunic that extended to the ankles. He could still wear his jeans and sandals underneath. Generally, he also carried a special kuk misbaha that had been given to him by his father when he became a young man. This religious tasbih of thirty- three beads was made with the incredibly hard and round kuk nuts.

Abdullah was waiting for Khalil. He was compelled to tell him about his suspicions of Fadwa before too much information was divulged to the group. He knew it was a sensitive subject. It is difficult to come between a man and his lover but when lives are at stake, he had no choice. Abdullah hoped self-preservation would win when contested against Khalil's sexual desires.

"Khalil, how sure are you of Fadwa?" asked Abdullah.

"What do you mean?" answered Khalil indignantly. He didn't like Abdullah's tone. He was well aware of Abdullah's contempt for Fadwa. Perhaps he was just jealous, Khalil thought.

"I mean, are you sure she can be trusted?"

"Of course."

"I want to show you something," Abdullah said. He turned around to make sure nobody was listening or watching but still felt it was too risky. He asked Khalil to follow him down the hall to the laundry room. Once they were alone, he then took some photographs out of his pocket and gave them to Khalil.

Khalil started to look through them one by one. He examined each photograph with intensity. His reaction was one of disbelief. His eyes widened and seemed to burn with anger, not because Fadwa's loyalty to the cause was doubted, but also because Khalil loved her. Now he was seeing photos of her without her chador burqa. She was wearing jeans, polo shirt, and a baseball hat sitting in a booth talking with another man, obviously American. It was clearly her. She had the same birthmark at the corner of her upper lip and scar on her eyebrow.

"Where did you get these?" asked Khalil still in disbelief.

"I took them myself," Abdullah answered.

"Where did you take these?"

"They were sitting at a Starbucks in Silver Spring."

"Silver Spring?" Khalil asked surprised.

"Yes, I followed them."

"What for? I mean, how did you know about this?"

"I am not sleeping with her Khalil. I can look at her with a rational eye. There is something about her that I found to be dangerous. I followed her for a few days and when I saw her meet with this man at the Smithsonian, I became more convinced that she was working against us. So, I continued to follow her for a couple of days. She is a spy, Khalil."

Khalil just stood there with a concerned look, speechless while putting one hand in his pocket and holding on to the pictures. Starting to pace while looking down at the floor, he wanted to find a rational answer, but anger was starting to seep in and take hold, preventing him from finding one.

"We have to do something, Khalil. How much have you told her?"

"Just the same as everyone else, except you of course," he said staring at Abdullah. "Don't give me that look."

"I am not giving you any look, Khalil."

"Yes, you are. You're giving me that look of distrust. It's the same look you give Fadwa."

"I trust you and believe you. I just wanted to make sure. At least she doesn't know the particulars about the strike; that's a good thing."

"When did you take these pictures: before or after our last meeting?"

"Before, why?"

"I just want to make sure she didn't know about our plans before her meeting with this man."

"Why?" asked Abdullah.

"Because she may have told him about Montserrat."

"She definitely met with this man before our last meeting because I remember thinking about her and the man while we were having our meeting."

"Good," said a satisfied Khalil.

Khalil was pinching his neck. He did this whenever he was nervous. He was still trying to understand everything that had just happened. The woman he loved was betraying him. A broken heart was something that could be repaired, but his was crushed. Yet it paled next to his safety and his mission. Khalil was now convinced she was trying to get him killed, or worse in his eyes, arrested.

"What are you planning to do?" asked Abdullah.

"We have no choice. We have to neutralize her," Khalil said with conviction.

"What do you mean by that?"

"She has to be.....eliminated," Khalil said with difficulty.

"Now you are becoming the leader I always knew you would be," Abdullah said with one of the few smiles in months on his usual surly face.

Khalil just shook his head. He was still in a fog.

"Do you want me to do it?" asked Abdullah.

"Give me time to think about it," Khalil said. He was still walking back and forth.

"What about the meeting we are having? Don't you think you or we should take care of her first?"

"Maybe we just postpone the meeting for now and then think of a plan to take her out," Khalil said not even wanting to think about the meeting.

"Aren't you going to question her first to see who she is working for?" asked Abdullah who had returned to his sullen ways.

"Yes. I am going to give her a chance to explain herself first, and then if I am not satisfied, I will make her tell us who she has given our information to."

"You are not serious, are you?" Abdullah asked believing that Khalil was starting to weaken.

"Why not?"

"Ask her to explain herself?" asked Abdullah raising his voice.

"Quiet, keep it down."

"You are letting love interfere with your brain, Khalil," Abdullah said as he lowered his voice. "There is no explanation. She has deceived you and us. It all makes sense now, she's working for someone. Why do you think that man was killed? She gave them information. That's how they knew about the deal. She has to be working for that Lewis man."

Khalil pondered Abdullah's words.

"Let's see," Khalil said. "Go get her and take her to the 3rd floor. I will meet you there."

Abdullah and Khalil probed each other's eyes for a few moments searching for answers. They were looking for an easy solution to their problem. All they found was an unwanted answer. Abdullah turned and marched off promptly.

Khalil stood there momentarily and then started up the stairs. It was a long climb.

The third floor was gutted out and empty. They had used it for storage at one time. Now it was dry-walled but unfinished, spackled and taped, ready to be improved. Members of the group had done the work themselves so as not to draw any unwanted attention from outsiders. The floor was still covered with painter cloths. There were some historical and religious items of faith in a box by the door. Shortly after he reached the room, Abdullah and Fadwa arrived.

"What is this all about?" asked Fadwa clearly not happy with Abdullah.

Khalil just paced for a few moments letting the tension in the room build. He resembled a fighter before a fight: psyching himself to do battle where he clearly did not want to, but was forced to.

"Fadwa, do you mind telling us what these pictures are about?"

He walked over casually and handed her the pictures. She looked him in the eyes and knew he was enraged. His calm demeanor belied him. She took them in her hands not knowing what she would see, but knowing it was placing her in danger. She began looking at them without giving any indication of concern. She looked at them slowly, one by one, buying time.

"What do you want to know?" she asked defiantly.

"Who is this man you are with in the photographs?"

"He is a professor."

"At Georgetown?"

"Yes," she answered thoughtfully.

"What is his name?"

"Henry Sadler."

"Abdullah, look up his name of the website and see if he is truly a professor."

"You're not going to find him there," she said.

"Why not?"

"Because he's not a professor there at the present time. He's on sabbatical."

Khalil slapped her hard against her face. A slight trickle of blood formed around the corner of her mouth. She gave him a look of astonishment as she wiped the blood with her fingers.

"You are a liar," Khalil screamed.

"Why would you say that?" she asked looking offended.

"Why are you wearing those clothes?"

"He asked me to come that way."

"Since when is it so important to abandon your faith and wear what someone, an American, wants you to wear?"

"You, yourself, wear American clothes," she said quietly.

He slapped her again.

"You are not placing me on trial. It is you, Fadwa, or whatever your name is, who is on trial."

"It was a mistake."

"What does this man mean to you?"

"I met him a long time ago, before I changed my name and my religion. He was my boyfriend."

Khalil and Abdullah looked at each other. Then Khalil slapped her again.

"What do you mean, changed your name?"

She clearly had made a mistake. She now knew she was defending her life which was hanging in the balance. In a moment of weakness, she had blurted out a tiny portion of her true identity. Now, she had to dance on her feet before dancing no more.

"I was born in this country, not in Pakistan," she said.

Again, Khalil slapped her.

She turned her head slowly back to face Khalil while Abdullah stood behind her. Her cheeks were red from the strikes she took.

"My father was from Pakistan, Islamabad. My mother was American. They raised me Catholic at my mother's request. My father never converted to the Catholic religion even though my mother pressured him. Eventually, she accepted his refusal.

"I loved my mother, but I worshipped my father. My mother died when I was thirteen. It was a critical time for a girl growing up. It was tough on my father. Not only did he lose his wife, but now he had a daughter going through puberty. To help himself deal with the difficulty, my father leaned on the Muslim community. He converted me to Islam. I have found Islam to give me depth and meaning. It has answered my questions about life, beauty and truth. Islam has chosen me. I now understand the true meaning of life and death."

"Why do you continue to lie?" asked Khalil unmoved.

"I am telling you the truth," Fadwa said emphatically, emboldened by the release of information.

"Who do you work for?"

"I work for Allah," she said with determination.

Khalil looked intensely into her eyes as his welled with tears. Abdullah slowly drifted back to the door. He knew from looking at Khalil, her interview was over.

She glanced back at Abdullah and then turned around to Khalil. "You must believe me..."

She faced Khalil and then felt Abdullah's hand on her left shoulder. It was not to comfort her or to lead her back out the door. It was to steady her.

It was fast and methodical. Her eyes widened in disbelief as the three-foot sword of Allah entered her torso. She looked down at the sharp tip, which extended by a foot, past her body. After a few moments,

Abdullah slowly pulled the sword from her mortally wounded body and looked at Khalil.

Fadwa looked at Khalil in disbelief before she entered eternity. Foamy blood trickled from her mouth as she slumped to the floor. Once she hit the floor, blood started to run from her upper body, and spread on the floor like red paint from a paint can that had been tipped over.

There was not even a trace of remorse on Abdullah's face, just a look of professional satisfaction. He picked up a rag and tried to clean the three-foot blade. It had a black handle with a gold tip and no metal guard for the knuckles. It was three-and-a- half inches at its widest crescent.

"You fool, we never found out who she was working for."

"She would have never told us. She was no good, Khalil," Abdullah said plainly. "She needed to die. She was an enemy of Allah."

Khalil stood there trembling.

"What do you want me to do with her?"

"Get rid of her," Khalil said his eyes still wide with horror.

"How?"

"I don't care," Khalil said as he walked out the door.

25

Jack sat on the bench in the cell, wondering what else could happen to him. Now, with his bail possibly in jeopardy, Jack was looking around at the cinder block walls contemplating life in a prison cell. The way things were going, he was going to live in one for quite a long time.

Over the years, he had sent many men to prison, never thinking about them again once they were sentenced. His job was to eradicate civilized society of scumbags. Once they went to trial and received their sentences, his job was done.

Yet, there was a contingent out there who felt trials were nothing more than a rubber stamp. Police officers were held in awe by most people to the point of minor celebrity status. The demeanor of officers on the stand was enthralling to most members of the law-abiding jury, whose only encounters with the police were from T.V. and movies.

Now, he was on the other side of the law. He had shot and killed someone, had been seated next to someone who was assassinated by a shot most likely meant for him, had his home searched via a search warrant, and had been placed in a cell a couple of times, once having to defend himself from an assault. Was there anything else? Jack was beyond humiliation. He was disgraced.

Jack was taking on a new outlook about the criminal justice system, not just thinking about the criminals, but also the people who make a living working for it. He started to scrutinize the cops, the prison guards, the court personnel, the judges and last but not least, the attorneys. What a filthy, polluted quagmire of innocence and guilt!

He now openly believed what he had always believed but had suppressed into his subconscious. It all comes down to power and money. Judgment is usually not fair and equal. It's the result of whoever wanted to impose their will the most. There would always be all kinds of motives, incentives and rewards. It was the driving force of the system. It was the game.

He was now focused on the attorneys in the food chain. If an attorney wanted to derive a large income and all the accoutrements of success, he had to compel the court to purchase his goods, by making them believe his view of the story. If he or she was successful, the client base multiplied as did the income.

The opposing side did the same, which made the battle seem almost fair. The prosecution usually had a larger budget to deal with the case, unless the defendant had deep pockets to amass the same type of weapons. Most people didn't. What was lost in battle was the pursuit of innocence or guilt. Veracity was irrelevant.

Jack heard the sound of heavy keys in the hallway and soon the cell door was opening. He looked up and saw Captain Sproat standing there in a tan suit with a brown printed tie and highly polished brown shoes. Jack immediately stood up to show his respect.

"Sit down, Jack," he said. "No need to stand up for me."

"Sir, I disagree with that but I am going to sit down if you don't mind. It's been a long day."

Captain Sproat smiled. "I know it has."

He left the door slightly ajar and came over and sat next to Jack. He looked at Jack sympathetically. It visibly pained him to see Jack in his current predicament.

"Jack, you've been getting yourself into a lot of hot water lately."

Jack was crying on the inside. Not only because he was fearful of the outcome, or because he felt like he was letting himself down, but also because a man he respected was disappointed in him. A man he thought of as a father.

"It's been tough, Captain."

"I know, Jack," Captain Sproat said as he patted Jack's forearm. "But, I think you're going to come out of this nightmare alright."

"Do you know something I don't know?" Jack said kiddingly but really curious to see if there was a thread of encouragement there.

"Just a gut feeling, Jack," he said. "Although you can't keep beating the crap out of people."

"You mean that guy in the other cell?"

"Something like that."

"Captain, I don't know if you saw that guy or not, but he was the size of a redwood, and he had a shank. He came at me and, to tell you the truth, I thought I was gonna die. I hope his jaw is fractured. He thought I was a pervert. I would have loved to shove that shank up his ass!"

"With his injuries, he'll be lucky if that's all that's wrong with him. You don't think he came here by chance, do you?"

"Captain, with what's been happening to me lately, I don't know what to think anymore. I can't tell you what day it is. I don't even know who I am anymore."

"Jack, one of the things I always liked and respected about you was your integrity and your toughness. You're a tough son of a bitch! Don't ever underestimate that. It will get you through tough times, like now. But Jack, you're also an intelligent, well-educated man. I always thought you were too smart for this job and I always thought you needed to be promoted. It just didn't work out that way. Of course, you didn't have to stop taking the promotional exams. It's kind of hard to get promoted unless you're on the list."

Captain Sproat started to cough violently. Jack saw some bloody spittle spray out onto the floor. The captain stood up and walked over to the urinal, spat into it and then flushed it. It was clearly blood, deep red blood.

"Are you okay, Captain?" Jack asked with deep concern.

"I'm fine, Jack," he responded, taking a handkerchief out of his pocket and wiping his mouth.

"I don't call spitting up blood, 'fine'."

"It's nothing that some rest won't take care of, Jack."

"Have you seen a doctor?" Jack asked apprehensively.

Jack watched him walk back and take his seat. He was more gaunt then when he saw him just a couple of months ago. Jack had never seen him wear a suit at work either. He always proudly wore his uniform. The captain was changing his pattern of behavior. It's usually a sign of something and usually not something good.

"Yeah, I have."

"What did he say?"

Captain Sproat just turned to Jack and smiled.

"Not much. Don't worry Jack, I carry my own lumber," the captain said.

"Sometimes a man needs help because the size of the lumber is too large for one man to carry."

"When it is, I just cut it down into smaller pieces. It's easier to carry that way. Just be glad, Jack, that you're retired."

The captain was shifting gears.

"I know you didn't want to retire, especially the way it was kinda forced on you, but believe me, it's for the best."

"What do you mean by that?" asked Jack hoping to get some insight into his shooting investigation involving the senator.

"What I mean, Jack, is I spent almost forty years with this department. I was a loyal team player. Yeah, it got me promoted to captain but for what? My wife and I sleep in separate bedrooms, and have for years. She hates me but stays because at this point she has nowhere else to go. If she had been smart, she would have divorced me years ago. Marriage shouldn't be an endurance test. It should be about love and mutual respect among other things."

"Yeah, but you got some good kids out of it," said Jack trying to salvage the captain's self-esteem.

"That's what I hear," the captain said mordantly as he looked at Jack. "Don't get me wrong. They're good kids. Heck, adults now. But, they really don't have time for me and who can blame them. I never had time for them when they were growing up. I was hardly ever there for their sporting events. I didn't go to parent-teacher meetings and I never went to any school functions. I missed the whole purpose of being a father. I'm nothing more than a sperm donor."

"I'm sure you feel guilty. I know about that myself, but don't underestimate yourself. You are a good father."

"I would like to think so at least from the standpoint they had a nice home, went to good schools and didn't lack for food or clothes."

"See?"

"But now, Debbie is married and never comes over or calls. When we visit, she and her husband seem like they can't wait for me to leave. Robert is in the Navy and, of course, he's never home and Jeff works so much he's never around. I've never seen him with any girls. I hope he's not gay."

Jack started to laugh.

"Just so you know, I ran into Jeff about a month ago at the movies. He had a hot-looking chick on his arm and they looked very cozy together."

"Did you talk to him?" the captain asked.

"We just said hello. I think he's very private, Captain."

"I guess."

"For what it's worth, I always considered you like a father," Jack said sincerely.

Captain Sproat looked at Jack with appreciation. He decided to switch gears.

"Jack, let's talk about the situation at hand. What the hell happened in the next cell with the other guy?"

Jack recounted the entire event starting with the fact the guy was enticing him into an argument by calling him a pervert. Jack recounted that he still had his laces in his work boots, and he pulled a shank from one indicating someone was negligent in his/her duties. He concluded with his self-defense move which immobilized the man.

"Sit tight, Jack," the captain said as he left the cell, locking the door behind him.

Jack didn't know what to think.

About ten minutes later the captain returned, and opened the door. He motioned for Jack to come with him. Jack quickly stood up and went to the door. He was curious to learn where they were going. When he got to the door, the captain was standing in the entrance way of the previous cell. Captain Sproat disappeared into the cell, and naturally Jack followed. When he entered, he was looking for blood but it was cleaned up.

"Jack, I spoke with the officer in the control room by the name of Doug. When we went to review the tape of the incident, there was a malfunction. The camera didn't pick up anything," Captain Sproat said plainly.

"That's just great! How am I supposed to defend myself against charges he and his family will make, let alone the department?" Jack said, clearly angry.

"Let me get this straight, the guy in the cell with you walked over, and for some strange reason, cupped his hands together, filled them with water and started splashing water all over the floor, right?" the captain said as he filled his hands with water and started splashing it on the floor.

"Huh?" Jack asked completely puzzled.

"He started talking nonsense. Right?"

"I don't know what you're talking about."

"Then, he slipped and fell hitting his chin against the bench, falling to the floor and striking his head which rendered him unconscious. Is that correct?" Captain Sproat said with a sly wink.

Jack was now on the same page.

"That is exactly what happened. Poor son of a bitch slipped and fell," Jack said.

The Captain looked out into the hallway and yelled for the janitor. Shortly thereafter, he arrived.

"Dave, I need you to mop up this water. The man fell in here because it was slippery."

"Captain, I just mopped up the blood in here. There was no water then," Dave said.

"Perhaps I didn't make myself clear, Dave. The man who fell in here slipped and fell in some water that he put on the floor," the captain reiterated.

"But Captain…," Dave stopped in the middle of the sentence when he saw the look on the captain's face. "Y'know, Captain, I must have missed it when I was in here earlier. I'm sorry. Let me clean it up before you, or this gentleman, slip and fall. I wouldn't want anyone else to hurt themselves."

The captain smiled. He led Jack back to his cell next door.

"Jack, I have to go now. Let me check and see when you're getting out of here," the captain said as started to close the door.

"Captain," Jack said.

The captain hadn't locked the cell door yet. He pulled it open and looked at Jack.

"You're one tough, wily bastard," Jack said smiling, adding "Thanks."

"I don't have the corner on that market, Jack," the captain said as he closed and locked the door.

26

In the next hour, no other prisoners were placed in the cell with Jack. He was grateful for that. It's amazing what little pleasures make you happy when your freedom has been denied. He needed the time to meditate, to gather his thoughts. Suddenly, he heard the clanging of the keys, and thought his luck had run out until Captain Sproat appeared at the door again.

"C'mon Jack, there's someone here to see you," the captain said smiling and motioning with his arms for Jack to get up and follow him.

Jack hesitated, and then got up. He didn't know what to expect. Since it was Captain Sproat opening his cell this time, he expected to see Billy Dawkins waiting for him but was surprised to see Marnie instead.

"Do you know this, lady?" the captain asked.

"Yes, I do," Jack answered happily.

Captain Sproat pushed the door wide open.

"Mr. Dublin, your bail has been secured and I am taking you back to our office," she said officiously.

"Right now, I'm ready to go anywhere you want."

Jack was disappointed she acted so coldly official.

"We need to go to the front desk to get the rest of your belongings," the captain said as he escorted them down the hallway.

It was a hallway Jack had walked many times as a cop and now as a prisoner.

There wasn't much property for Jack to retrieve. They had his belt, shoelaces, watch, money, wallet and some other incidentals. The captain stood by while Jack signed the release form. After Jack put on his belt and watch, and re-laced his shoes, he placed the other incidentals in their proper pockets. The captain then walked Jack and Marnie to the exit of the building.

"Captain, I want you to know I appreciate everything you've done for me."

"It was my pleasure, Jack, but don't make this a habit."

"Don't worry. I don't plan on coming back into this building again."

"I'm glad to hear it because if you do, I won't be able to help you."

Jack looked at the captain pensively.

"Jack, today is my last day. I'm retiring."

Jack smiled now.

"It's about time. You deserve it," Jack said relaxed.

"I've got a lot of bridges to build while I still have the time."

Jack tried to comprehend the implication but didn't want to probe. He appreciated a person's right to privacy. If the captain wanted Jack to know any more information, he would have offered it.

"Captain, I hope we can get together and have a cup of coffee some time."

"I hope so, too, but let's make it a beer," the captain said with a grin. "It was a pleasure to meet you, Miss," he said to Marnie holding out his hand.

"The pleasure was mine," Marnie said shaking his hand.

"Jack's a good man."

"Captain," Jack acknowledged as he approached him and hugged him. He was shocked how thin and brittle he felt.

Jack and Marnie turned and left.

There were two reporters across the street when they walked out of the police station. As soon as they saw Jack, they rushed over with their cameraman. Jack hoped they were the only reporters at the station.

They began asking a lot of questions while thrusting microphones in front of Jack, asking him if he was guilty and wanting more details of the shooting. Jack just said he was innocent and looking forward to his day in court as Marnie pulled him towards a waiting car.

They got in the back seat and the car drove off. Jack thought it was a good sign there weren't more reporters, and the ones the TV station sent were the second-stringers. He mentioned it to Marnie. She acknowledged him by nodding her head but she was busy texting on her phone.

Jack just sat in silence for the rest of the trip.

They went back to Mr. Prescott's office where Jack found welcome sanctuary from the media and the police. Mr. Prescott's office was in a new building located in the heart of the District, close to the Capitol. His office was, ironically, not far from the Rollins Building. The name of the firm on the wall said "Morris, Maier, and Prescott Attorneys at Law". The office had the customary rich entrance and the usual, incredibly attractive receptionists. The waiting area was luxuriantly furnished and tastefully done in a modern motif.

A man and woman were sitting in the waiting room. The heavy-set man, wearing tan pants and a yellow shirt without a tie, was reading a magazine. He looked to be in his mid-fifties. The thin, attractive black woman was in a business suit, and Jack thought she must be an attorney as she seemed to be reading a legal document. She was wearing reading glasses. They didn't look like they were together. Phones were ringing and there were many people Jack assumed to be office staff walking up and down the hallways.

Marnie and Jack walked down the hall to a conference room and sat down. She had hardly said anything to him on the way over. He had asked her a couple of mundane questions and she gave brief answers, which was disappointing.

Marnie asked Jack if he wanted anything to drink. Her demeanor was now businesslike. When he said he would like some coffee, she called the receptionist and asked for a pot to be delivered.

She asked him to wait there while she excused herself. When she left, he sat there and swiveled in his chair to look around. The windows were floor-to-ceiling and provided an interesting view of the Monument. Other than that, it was your typical conference room. A large table had twelve chairs spaced equidistant around the table.

Jack didn't know what to expect from this point, wanting to extricate himself from their supervision even though he was grateful. But, he was also anxious to resolve his dilemma and wasn't sure how helpful they could be from an investigative standpoint. Not only that, he was a little paranoid.

Someone was out to get him, and he figured it was the senator. Archibald Prescott was a high priced attorney, the kind who gets paid by people in power. People like senators. Mr. Prescott's allegiance was still in question. Jack would make sure he was careful and deliberate with his answers to any of their questions.

He saw a beautiful young woman with blonde hair carrying a tray headed towards the glass door. She wore a tight dress that revealed ample cleavage. He got up in a hurry and went to the door to open it for her. She brought the tray inside and set it on the table.

As she walked by he smelled her fragrance, recognizing it from someone in his past.

The tray held a pot of coffee, cream, sugar, sweetener and three cups with spoons. He thanked her, and she smiled. She told him if he needed anything else to call her. Of course, she didn't say how to contact her, and he decided not to ask.

Jack poured himself a cup of coffee, added some diet sweetener and stirred it mindlessly with a spoon. He took one sip and realized it was top-of-the-line coffee. It tasted like French roast, probably from the coffee emporium down the street. Jack bought his coffee there. As he was taking another sip, the door opened. Marnie had returned with Mr. Prescott.

"Good afternoon, Mr. Dublin," Mr. Prescott said as he reached out and shook Jack's hand. Marnie followed close behind him, shutting the door. He was wearing the same shirt and tie without his suit coat, seeming more average, more tranquil than in the courtroom. He was also wearing colorful and expensive suspenders that added to his sartorial splendor. Jack remembered his paternal grandfather calling them braces and how upset he would get with Jack when he called them suspenders.

After he fixed himself a cup of coffee, he turned to Jack and said, "Well Mr. Dublin, what do you think should be the next course of action for us? After all, you are the experienced investigator at this table."

Jack pondered his answer. He noticed Marnie just sat down and didn't make herself a cup of coffee. He was somewhat surprised Mr. Prescott was asking him to take the lead, knowing what he wanted to do. Jack wanted to go to Delaware and talk to Bob Lewis's wife. He also knew he was not allowed to go any further than five miles. Jack didn't want to tip them off. He knew he was leaving for Delaware as soon as he could separate himself from them.

"You know, I was going to ask you the same question. After all you're going to defend me. You must have some plan in mind."

"If I may interject?" asked Marnie.

Mr. Prescott nodded.

"I think we need to take a statement from Mr. Dublin and determine what it is the police feel they may have, then investigate the holes and most importantly, find Bob Lewis," Marnie said.

"I agree," said Mr. Prescott. "Ms. Bloom, I trust you can take the statement and then pick Mr. Dublin's brain to shed some light on an investigative approach."

He then turned to Jack.

"Mr. Dublin, I'm sure you understand the predicament you're in. I can defend you by using the law to our advantage but I am not an investigator. Ms. Bloom has some experience, but you are the expert, and you are the one in the cauldron. Any information or ideas that you have will provide us with tremendous opportunities to resolve this case satisfactorily."

"I agree. I also have someone on the Department that I trust and maybe he can help me."

"Very good, but I must caution you, do not trust anyone at this point. I don't care how well you know this person."

"I understand, but this guy has always helped me. We used to be partners."

"It doesn't matter. You don't know what kind of pressure he may be under."

Jack reluctantly shook his head to placate Mr. Prescott but he would always believe Billy D. would never betray him.

"Very well. Ms. Bloom, I trust you will take the statement, and let me know tomorrow how you believe we should proceed."

"I will."

"Mr. Dublin, you have my resolute promise to gain your acquittal. We will prevail."

Mr. Prescott stood up and placed his coffee on the tray. He had only taken a couple of sips. He shook Jack's hand while looking Jack in the eye as if to confirm his promise.

After he left, Marnie took a statement from Jack that lasted over an hour. There were no outstanding revelations. Jack appreciated her manner and methods. She was very thorough and professional. Maybe he had underestimated her. He wanted to find out.

27

"Let's get out of here," Marnie said as she completed the interview. "Do you want something to eat?"

"I was thinking more along the lines of a beer," Jack replied.

"Sounds good to me," she said with a faint smile.

Marnie gathered up her notes and the tape recorder she used to take Jack's statement. She asked Jack to sit tight while she went back to her office and put them away. When she finally returned fifteen minutes later, it looked to Jack as if she had freshened up by reapplying some make-up and lipstick, but he didn't say anything. He was flattered to think she would do it for him.

"Sorry, I took a little longer. I ran into an associate who needed my advice on a matter."

Jack smiled and said, "No problem."

They left the office and walked to a little pub called Killarney's that was close by. It wasn't crowded. It was an Irish pub; the walls were covered with Irish memorabilia and photographs of serene Irish country scenes. Most importantly to Jack, they sold the Irish Holy Trinity on tap: Guinness, Harp and Smithwick's.

The bartender told them to sit anywhere they wanted, so they walked to a booth in the back. There was nobody else seated close to them.

"I thought you might like this bar," Marnie said.

"It's perfect! I love Irish pubs," Jack said happily.

The waitress came and gave them menus.

"Can I start you off with a drink?"

Jack looked at Marnie in deference.

"I'll just have a cup of Earl Grey tea."

"And you, sir?"

"I'll just have a Half and Half," Jack said.

"I just want to make sure, is that Guinness with Harp or Bass Ale?"

"Guinness with Harp. If I said Black and Tan, it would mean with Bass," Jack said trying to educate her.

"Just to let you know, our Shepherd's Pie is on special tonight for $11.95. I'll give you a few moments to look over the menu while I go get your drinks."

She turned to walk away, but Marnie spoke before she left. "I'm not having anything, but if you want something Jack, go ahead and order."

Jack quickly reviewed the menu and saw it was pretty standard fare for an Irish pub.

The waitress returned with their drink order.

"How is your Shepherd's Pie?" Jack asked.

"I love it. It's one of my favorites," the waitress answered. She looked to be in her early twenties. She was a little overweight, but Jack wasn't sure if it was because she was pregnant, or just enjoyed a lot of Shepherd's Pie.

"Sounds good. That's what I'll have," he said as he closed his menu and handed it back to her. She took their menus, placed them under her arm and walked away.

"So, Jack, tell me about yourself," Marnie probed, looking intently at Jack.

"Is this an interview?" Jack asked, smiling.

"Call it what you will, but I think it is important we get to know each other, since we'll be working together, more or less."

"That means you'll have to answer my questions, too."

"I suppose I will, as long as they're not about sex, religion or politics," she said smiling.

"Well, hell, what's the use?" Jack said smiling with his hands held out to the side.

She just smiled, and shook her head.

"What do you want to know?" Jack asked.

"The usual stuff, like all about your family, your education, your time with the police department. Y'know things like that."

"I thought you already knew all about me. That's what you insinuated back at the courthouse."

"Maybe I want to find out from you whether or not our information is good."

Jack took a long draught from his freshly poured Half and Half. He let the cold brew slowly caress his tongue. And then he began his story.

"Well, let's see," Jack said tapping his chin in jest. "Where do I begin? Once upon a time, there was a boy named Jack who had two parents. One was named Ben and the other was Isabella. He was Irish and she was Cuban. They lived together as husband and wife in a small state named Delaware. One day Jack's mother died a suspicious death. His father was not around when it happened, so they say."

Jack's demeanor changed. He stopped playing around.

"I believed it at the time, because my father was never around anyway. But now, I believe my father knows more then he told the police. I miss my mother terribly, and I haven't spoken to my father in years.

"I was married a short time and have a son, who I haven't seen in a long time. My ex-wife moved to California, took him with her, and married a wealthy movie producer. As far as the police department goes, I did a serviceable job for twenty years before I shot and killed a U.S. senator's son in self-defense. Long before the shooting, I probably could have been promoted, and should have, since I think I was just as smart as those in the administration. I just didn't want to drink the company Kool-Aid. Now I'm in the hot seat because I was set up by Bob Lewis, who is probably working for the senator, or someone else who wants to make my life miserable. The rest is history as they say. Now, what about you?"

"Wait! You didn't really tell me anything. What about your education? Did you go to a private school? Where did you get your classical training?"

"Aha! You do know some things about me."

"Well," she said smiling, "what are you waiting for?"

Jack was enjoying himself. It was the first time in a long time that anyone was interested in him for who he was. Yet, he also knew Marnie was delving into his life for background. Maybe she just wanted to get the job done. Jack was always suspicious, but he wanted to believe Marnie was truly interested in him. Besides, he wanted to know her better. A lot better.

"Like I said, I lived in Delaware. I went to public schools. I graduated from Mt. Pleasant High School. I was taught self-discipline from my parents, primarily my mother because she was the one who was around. She made me take piano lessons at a local, but respected music school, and I practiced relentlessly. I was leaning towards a music career, but she wanted me to go to school at Georgetown and pursue a law degree."

"It seems your mother had the greatest influence on you."

"She did. She was a wonderful person, always happy, yet with a fiery personality, ready to erupt when provoked. It was never dull with her. After all, she was Cuban," Jack said.

"What about your father?"

"Not much I can say about him. He wasn't around much. He was an international banker. When he was around, he was pushing me to play sports. I'm thankful for that direction. But, my mother and he battled over it. She was always afraid I would do harm to my hands, like break a finger or something. He understood the importance of my piano training, but he also realized the positive impact sports can have on a young man. My father did give me my love for competition. I played football, basketball, and baseball but really excelled in baseball. I played second base, and pitched on the high school team. We were the champions my senior year."

The waitress returned with the Shepherd's Pie. She set it front of Jack and walked away.

"What was the relationship between your mom and dad like?" quizzed Marnie.

"When I was young it was very good," Jack said as he began to eat. "As I got older, I sensed a lack of love between them. Maybe it was always that way. Maybe I was just too young to know the difference. I suspect he had girlfriends. He was very handsome and outgoing."

"Did they have many friends?"

"Now that I think of it, no, they didn't. They didn't really connect with anyone in the neighborhood, but remember, my father was hardly around. My mother did talk with other parents from my school, you know, parents of my school friends."

"So, I guess they didn't socialize much?"

"Not too much. Like I said, my father was not home too often."

"What about relatives like aunts and uncles?"

"My father was an only child. My mother had one brother but I never met him. My mother told me he was much younger than her. So, for all intents and purposes, there were no siblings. My grandfather was an influence on me, though."

"Which side?"

"My father's side. He owned a couple of bars, and he liked to tell stories. He had quite a few, too. Great sense of humor. With the money he was making, he invested in real estate and became quite wealthy. He bought a piece of land in Lake Havasu City in Arizona. I remember he told me it was ten dollars down and ten dollars a month back then, so he bought a whole bunch of lots. The desert was his oasis. He didn't like Florida. He said there were too many old people there. He called it God's waiting room. Of course, he told me this when he was 75."

"How did your mother die?"

"She died in an automobile accident. I think my father had something to do with it. Of course, I'll never know."

"Why do you think that?"

"When I was home for a weekend visit shortly before her death, I heard them arguing. It was not uncommon to hear them arguing at this point, but this time it seemed really intense. I don't know what they were arguing about, but I know my mother was not happy with something my father did. A couple of weeks after I got back to school, my father called me. He told me my mother was killed in an accident while he had been out of town. He didn't cry or sound upset. It was weird. He seemed like he was trying to read my mind, like he was more concerned about what I was thinking, than the fact that his wife, and my mother, was dead. I just had bad feelings about it. I never trusted him after that."

"How could he have caused her death in a car accident if he wasn't around?" she asked with doubt.

"I have never been able to figure it out. I'm not so sure he really was out of town. I always wanted to talk with the police, but I figured they would never give me the information. Besides, I believed they would have investigated it thoroughly."

"If you thought they would have investigated it thoroughly and your father was never charged, why would you think he had something to do with it?

"I don't know. Just call it an intuition and let's leave it at that."

They sat for a few moments in silence. Jack started to pick half-heartedly at the remainder of his dinner.

"You know, that is one of my biggest fears," admitted Marnie in a rather unexpected manner.

"What's that?"

"That I will be a victim of the dark side of death."

"What do you mean, 'dark side of death'?" Jack inquired placing his fork on his plate. He couldn't eat while Marnie was divulging something which seemed hidden deep inside her.

"The dark side of death is when you die from unnatural causes," Marnie replied. "They're always horrific deaths.

Y'know like plane crashes, train wrecks, explosions, shootings, stabbings, car accidents, things like that."

Jack's brow furrowed, as he nodded his head affirmatively. He was trying to let it sink in. He had never heard the term before.

While Marnie pondered her next question, Jack asked her,

"What about you?"

Just then, Marnie's cell phone rang. She looked at the incoming number.

"Excuse me," she said as she got up from the table and walked out the front door.

Jack finished his shepherd's pie and drank the last of his pint. As he was paying the bill, Marnie walked back in.

"You didn't have to pay that. I could have put it on the firm's account," Marnie said, as she came in and tucked away her phone.

"That's okay. All you had was Earl Grey tea," Jack said.

"I know but..."

"Tell you what, you can pick up the next one," Jack said.

"I'm sorry. I had to take that call."

"Mr. Prescott checking up on us?"

She paused. "Yes, that's it. He wanted to know where we were and how it's going."

"How *is* it going?" Jack asked with a smile on his face.

"Fine, Jack, fine. Do you have any suggestions of where to go at this point?"

"We need to find Bob Lewis."

"How do we go about that?"

"I'm going to use my contact in the police department and see if he can get me some leads."

"Just be careful," she said sincerely.

"Listen, I have a pretty good handle on people. He is someone who has always had my back."

"I just hope he's not the kind that is holding a knife or gun behind your back."

"Not Billy D."

"Why don't you walk me back to the office? I'll get my car out of the garage and give you a ride home."

"Okay. Then what?"

"Then I drop you off, and I go home," she said protectively.

Jack smiled, "No, I mean, what are the plans for tomorrow?"

"Oh," Marnie said. "We have some follow-up to do."

"Who? You, or you and me?"

"You and me."

"Like what?" Jack asked.

"Like interview some neighbors who may have heard or seen something the night of the shooting. It would be great if we could get our hands on a police report. It may identify witnesses amongst other information we could find pertinent."

"Let me talk to Billy, and see what I can find out. Maybe he can get us some reports."

28

It was 1:00 in the morning.

Bob Lewis deliberately waited this long before informing Khalil where and when to meet, in order to minimize Khalil's preparation. He told him to meet at the dock at 5:00 A.M., providing detailed directions to its location in Lewes, Delaware. He told him not to bring any more than four people, and no weapons. They would be trained by an Army Ranger who had been assigned to special OPS.

Bob wanted to make it perfectly clear they were getting their money's worth; they were being trained by an expert. He also wanted to make it clear to Khalil and his band of misfits, if they had any intention of circumventing the agreement, there would be harsh consequences. They were taking two boats out to sea. Only one boat was coming back.

Bob and Duke were headed to Lewes in Sussex County, Delaware. It's a small town that is home to about two thousand people. However, in the summertime it quadruples becoming overpopulated. It's a mixed blessing for the townspeople. They love the quaintness of being a small town with their small shops, but they love the revenue from the magnanimous visitors. Usually the visitors only frequented the area during the summer, so it provided a little respite for the townies during the colder months. It was the balance they needed.

It was an area that was small and charming. Notwithstanding an occasional bar room fight, it was still a sleepy, little hamlet.

They prepared food and drinks for their excursion; they didn't want to present any possibility they could be recognized by stopping at a convenience store, particularly now with the widespread video surveillance in most places. They didn't stop at any coffee shops on the way. Their gas tanks were filled earlier in the day. The boats' tanks were filled and also ready.

They had a couple of thermos bottles filled with coffee and were enjoying it, when they pulled off Rt. 1 and turned into the town of Lewes. Within a short time, they were at the intersection of Savannah Rd. and Pilottown Rd.

"Hey, I hear that's a pretty good place to eat," said Callison as he and Lewis rode past the Rusty Anchor Restaurant.

"It is," Lewis said. "I've eaten there a couple of times. We used to have some meetings there with people from the office. On the weekends, you can't even get into the place for a couple of hours. It's packed, and I'm talkin' year 'round. But let me tell you, it's worth the wait. I usually get something that has just about every kind of seafood you can think of - shrimp, lobster, flounder, crab, clams, everything."

"Maybe we can stop there on the way back."

"We'll see; I don't think I'll feel like it after this encounter. Pass me some more coffee."

The pick-up truck lumbered down the highway, towing the 34 ft. Sea Ray target boat. It was seaworthy enough to make it out to their ocean destination, but that was about it. On board was one SAM rocket launcher with six warheads. Once they were far enough out to sea they would transfer the SAM to the 57 ft. 2000 Bayliner which was en route to a rendezvous from its private dock in Ocean City, Maryland. There was one more person who was going to join Lewis and Callison. His name was Bill Franklin and he was taking the Bayliner from Ocean City out to sea. He was retired Navy, and he would meet up with them after making contact by radio.

They wanted to keep their eyes on Khalil and his partner from the band of junior terrorists. The fewer people involved minimized the leaks and potential for mistakes. It was the reason they didn't bring more people. Besides, if this ragtag bunch of terrorist kids tried anything, it would be their final cause. Bob Lewis had investigated groups like these and Duke Callison was as hardened a partner as anyone could want. He had been to Nam and also Desert Storm. He was close to sixty years old but he was still lean and mean. He had killed many people and was as ruthless as they come, even to the point that Bob sometimes worried about his own safety.

"You know we're taking some big risks here," Bob told Duke.

"I know, but what specific risk are you talking about?" Duke questioned.

"This rocket launcher is pretty lethal and I'm sure it gets pretty hot."

"And your point is?"

"We're on a fiberglass boat in the middle of the ocean. The heat from these SAMS needs to be carefully pointed away from the boat."

"Don't worry. I've got it all figured out.

"What's the range on these?"

"Anywhere from one to eight kilometers," Duke readily answered. "These suckers can go to ten thousand feet."

"Yeah, but we're not firing at aircraft."

"Don't have to."

"Yeah, but they're gonna be hot after they're fired aren't they?"

"When we've finished firing, we'll toss them in the ocean," Duke said smiling.

Bob looked at him in astonishment. "You're kidding, right?"

"You worry too much."

"Exactly! We're talking tens of thousands of dollars going into the ocean."

Duke just continued to smile. "Relax. I've got more where these came from. Besides, they're paying for it anyway."

Bob just continued to stare at Duke and then turned his attention back to the road. They rode down the road in silence for a few minutes, sipping their coffee.

"Did you find out what happened at the courthouse?" Bob asked breaking the silence.

"He didn't get the job done, obviously," Duke said miserably. "I thought he would have no problem with Dublin. Hell, he was twice his size and he has no problems with people his own size. I once saw him take on two guys his size simultaneously and make short work of it. Within thirty seconds, they were both dead."

"What do you have planned now?"

"As soon as he's released, I got a guy tailing him, waiting for the right moment to take him out."

"Good. Let's hope he doesn't fail."

As they traveled through town, a police car made a U-turn and turned on its emergency lights.

"Fuck, we're getting pulled over," Duke said as he looked back through the rear window.

"Relax, probably just some good ole boy who's bored. I'll flash him my badge and turn on the charm."

Bob pulled over to the side of the road and realized it was a Delaware State Trooper and not a local yokel. This would require a different approach. The trooper pulled over behind him with his strobe lights flashing and his radio squawking. He sat in his car for a few moments before he got out and approached.

While the trooper was in his car, Bob told Duke to be wary. If the trooper asked to see the interior of the boat, they would have to take a dead trooper for a ride with them out to sea. They didn't want it to go down like that, because he most likely had called in their license plate. Still, they were not going to take any chances. They could always change their plates.

Duke pulled his .45 Beretta Storm Tactical gun with black matte finish from his bag, and placed it under his feet. He would keep it there until the trooper walked away from the driver's door. Then he would pick it up and place it squarely in his right hand, waiting for the opportunity to take the trooper out.

"Can I see your license and registration?" the young trooper asked Bob.

"Sure can. Is there a problem?" Bob asked as the trooper shined his light in the cab.

"You were going about 15 miles over the speed limit back there."

Bob pulled his license out of his police I.D. making sure the trooper noticed his badge.

"Are you a cop?" asked the trooper.

"I'm retired FBI just going down to do a little fishing with my friend here."

The trooper still took his license and leaned in and asked Duke for his I.D. as well, while shining his light in Duke's face. When he gave it to him, the trooper looked at both of them with his flashlight never breaking a smile.

"What do you have on board your boat?" he asked as he returned their I.D.'s.

"Just some beer and some tackle."

The trooper started to walk back to the boat, shining his light into the bay area. He started to circle around and Bob started to get out of the truck.

"Is there anything you need to see?"

The trooper didn't answer immediately, as he walked around to the back of the boat. He shined his flashlight all around the back of the boat, stopping to focus on a certain spot near the galley. The door had popped open at some point during the ride. It was where the SAM's were situated. Duke was ready to exit the truck. He switched the gun into his left hand and placed his right hand on the door handle. He could hear the conversation through the back window which they had slid open earlier for ventilation. If he heard the trooper say he wanted to inspect the boat, Duke would exit and nonchalantly walk back towards the trooper and shoot him in the head. No qualms about it. He knew a chest shot was useless; the trooper was wearing a vest.

"No, but you may want to secure that galley door before you drive any further. Make sure you slow down. Have a nice day," he said as he handed the licenses to Bob.

The trooper turned to get back into his car never cracking a smile.

Bob stood at the back of his truck, and then hopped up into the boat to secure the galley door. As he was getting back in his truck, the trooper drove past. He waved as the trooper sped past them.

"What an asshole!" said Callison angrily.

"I guess he doesn't like *feebies*," Lewis said, smiling as he put his truck into gear. "At least we didn't get a ticket."

They were surprised when they got to the dock ten minutes later, to find their group was there waiting for them.

Khalil and Abdullah were standing there with two other men, one named Amir. They were driving a gold Lexus SUV. Bob and Duke pulled up and then backed their boat down the ramp. Duke got out, disconnecting the boat from the trailer. Once the boat was in the water and tied, they got out and approached Khalil.

"Do you have the money?" asked Bob.

Khalil didn't say anything, he just waved his hand and one of the other men brought a briefcase forward and opened it. It was filled with one hundred dollar bills. They closed the case, and then took it back to the car.

"Very well. We are going to meet with my boat out at sea. It's headed out there now with a friend of mine piloting it. We will travel out to sea and then transfer back to my boat, leaving this boat at sea. Then, we will motor back an appropriate distance to take practice shots at hitting it with the weapons. I only brought enough ammunition to practice six times. We don't want to draw any attention to us. You should be familiar with the equipment by then. Once we are finished, we will return to the dock, and you will give us the down payment. Once we are both satisfied, you can tell me where you want the rest of the equipment and ammunition delivered, and it will be done. Then, you will pay us the balance. Understood?"

Bob didn't bother to tell them there would be additional cost for delivery. He wanted their appetites for the missiles to be whetted before dropping that detail of the deal on them.

"You only brought enough ammunition for six practice rounds?" asked Khalil rather perturbed.

"Listen, we are going out into the ocean. There's a risk involved. I have a fairly good idea where to go, where we will not have any interference from other ships, but I can't plan for aircraft. The target boat will be on fire before it sinks. I don't think any of us wants to get questioned by the Coast Guard. Six rounds will be more than enough to familiarize you with the weapon. Any more questions?"

"No."

Soon they left the dock and were on their way out to sea. Six hours later when they arrived at the spot, Bob radioed Bill Franklin via walkie-talkie and they pulled alongside each other. The seas were gentle and the day was clear. The weather prediction was correct for a change. It was one of the reasons they picked this day to go out. Duke set the anchor and they transferred to the larger boat, taking the crate of ammunition with them.

It was difficult for Bob to fathom that two young men of Middle Eastern descent with ties to terrorists were not familiar with these types of weapons. He thought they were well-versed in all types of firearms and bombs. At least he'd found two with deep pockets who were as clueless as they were rich.

Once they were about a quarter of mile away, Bob told Bill to cut the engine. No other ships were visible. Bob wanted to work fast while they had the clearance. Duke went below and brought the SAM up. He went over the basics of the weapon and how it worked, giving them more detail than they needed and taking more time then Bob wanted. After he was finished giving instructions, he took Abdullah to the rear platform and placed the SAM on Abdullah's shoulders, making sure the heat from the device was pointed away from the boat they were on.

Once he had the okay, Abdullah fired a shot that went to the left of the target and sent a plume of water into the air in the distance. Now he placed the weapon on Khalil's shoulder. He took a turn and also sent a geyser of water into the air. Khalil and Abdullah looked at each other with satisfaction.

"I deliberately had you fire off target, to give you an idea what this weapon feels like. Besides, we don't want to hit the boat the first time. Now I'm going to show you how to fix your sight coordinates."

Once Duke showed them how to fix the sights, he let them try for themselves. First Abdullah fired, hitting the captain's chair at the top. He smiled. Now the competition was on. Khalil took his turn and missed the boat totally. Abdullah was enjoying his dominance with the weapon, and took his last turn with confidence. His next shot hit the very tip of the bow and some pieces flew in the air.

Finally, it was Khalil's last shot and he took his time and aimed his shot. Once he fired, they watched the top of the cabin roof fly into pieces but the ship was still floating. Bob looked at Duke with concern. What do they do now? They can't leave the boat floating like that.

Duke smiled and went below. When he came up he was carrying one more rocket. There was a look of relief on Bob's face.

"I guess I'm gonna have to show you boys how it's done."

Duke loaded, did the proper calculations, and fired his shot. It went true and blew the ship into a ball of fire. He turned around and looked at Khalil and Abdullah. They nodded their heads in approval.

"Let's get back to shore," Bob said as he gave the order to start the engine and turn back to go home. The trip home would be shorter since they didn't have to wait for the slower boat. Bill Franklin turned a western heading and throttled it to full speed. They would be back before sundown.

29

Marnie dropped Jack back at the entrance to his condo building. She told him to get plenty of sleep because they had a lot of work to do the next day. Jack was tired. He knew he would have no problem falling asleep; he was more worried he wouldn't wake up in time for Marnie. She wanted to pick him up at eight o'clock but Jack requested nine. Realizing what he had been through the last couple of days, she relented.

As he passed the concierge desk, he saw a young woman. She looked like she was in her early thirties. She was heavy-set and wore her hair up. She had a cute face behind stylish glasses. She greeted Jack with a huge smile full of beautiful teeth that shined bright. She was definitely pleasant, not sober like Henry.

He acknowledged the concierge whose name was Lourdes and didn't detect any sign she recognized him as a problem from the news earlier in the day.

Any damage was already done by now. Jack felt content and safe sleeping at home tonight. There would be no reason for Keane and Bucci to come back and place him under arrest. The worst that could happen now was being placed under surveillance. He wasn't concerned. They could follow him all they wanted.

He didn't think about it until he got off the elevator, but as soon as the doors opened and he turned the corner to enter the hallway, he remembered Ms. McGarrity. Jack carefully walked softly past Ms. McGarrity's front door. He made sure he didn't take the keys for his condo out of his pocket; fearful jangling keys may alert her. He knew people her age were up at all hours of the night and he certainly wasn't in a mood to talk. If she tried to engage him in conversation, he was concerned he wouldn't be civil. Thankfully, he made it past her door without any encounter.

As he walked down the hall to his condo, he noticed one of the bulbs in the sconce lights was burned out. The hall was fairly dark at night time without the light. He would mention it on his way out in the morning to the concierge, who probably would be Henry. Jack knew if he was going to live here, he would have to break the ice with Henry sooner or later.

Jack opened the door and immediately felt there had been a presence of unfamiliar people in his condo. He hit the light switches turning on the downstairs lights while descending the steps slowly, attentive to any sound or movement. Things still appeared pretty much in order; however, he realized some items had been moved in the living room, which he had expected. Jack started walking back to his bedroom. He had barely slept there enough to be totally comfortable since the condo was relatively new to him and he had spent most of his time at Julie's. Turning on the hallway light, he walked down the hallway past the second bedroom and powder room. Switching on the bedroom light, he saw his bed. The covers were bunched up in the middle. Some of his drawers were left open. He wasn't surprised. At this point Jack could care less; he just wanted to get a shower and some sleep.

Jack pulled out the cell phone Marnie had given him. He knew he should call Julie to try to set things straight. He felt badly about the situation between them, but now was not the time to call her. He didn't feel like arguing.

Jack took off his clothes, went into the bathroom and turned on the shower. While he waited for the water to get hot, he looked at himself in the mirror. It seemed like he'd aged ten years in the past couple of days as he rubbed his face.

In the shower, he couldn't remember if he locked the front door behind him, but decided he did and just continued his shower. The hot water felt good. Jack realized he needed a shave and got out of the shower dripping wet to find his razor. He always shaved in the shower.

Once he was finished, he walked slowly over to the closet door and then quickly opened it. Everything looked like it had been inspected but it was still fairly neat and orderly.

He went back to the bed and made it, then pulled the covers back. Lying in bed, he realized he needed to call Billy D. Jack needed information and Billy said he would help. Jack hoped the offer was still good, as he found Billy's business card with his private number on it and dialed it.

"Hello," answered Billy.

"Billy, it's Jack."

"Jack who? Jack shit? Jack off? Who?"

"Jack Dublin."

"Oh, that Jack. The one who's in a lot of shit and may as well Jack off," Billy said sarcastically.

"Look, Billy, I need your help," Jack said sincerely.

"Man, from what I've been hearing you're gonna need more help than what I got to offer."

"What are you hearing?" Jack asked curiously.

"That it's not healthy for anyone to be around you for one thing. Seems like anyone who comes in contact with you ends up dead."

"Billy, I didn't kill anybody. You gotta believe me," Jack pleaded.

"Whether you pulled the trigger or not, you're responsible. Whatever shit you're tied up in is killing people."

"I've been set up."

"Of course you're gonna say that. How do I know any better?"

"C'mon Billy, you know me well enough to know that I didn't have anything to do with any deaths other than the senator's son, and he deserved it."

"Jack, rumor also has it that you are in cahoots with terrorists. That you're buying and selling weapons to them."

"Who's puttin' that out, Merrill? It's all bullshit."

"Really? Then how come you're living high on the hog. I hear you've got a place over Rosslyn worth about $800 thou. How'd you get a nice place like that on a cop's pension?"

"I inherited it from my grandfather."

"You wouldn't be selling any oceanfront property in Arizona would you?" Billy said mockingly.

"I know it sounds like bullshit, but it's the truth."

"How much? If you don't mind my asking."

"You mean how much did I inherit?"

"Yeah."

"Let's just say enough that I can bank my pension."

"Must be nice."

"Listen, I need a favor," Jack begged.

"Like what?"

"I need to find Bob Lewis, the former FBI agent who set me up, but I don't think that's going to happen any time soon. But, if you could find out where his wife is, that would be a great help. I can give you her name. I think she's in Delaware."

"You want me to get fired?"

"Hell no! But you did offer to help the last time I saw you."

Billy was starting to feel bad. He had been tough on his friend. He knew that if the tables were turned, Jack wouldn't think twice about helping him.

"Jack, I'll do what I can but I'm a little paranoid. Merrill wants your ass bad and if he ever found out that I was helping you, he'd have my ass, too. And my job!"

"Billy, are you at work now?"

"As a matter of fact, I am. I came in to clean up some cases I've got backed up."

"Is it crowded in there now?"

"No, just me and Cross for the moment."

"Just do a quick NCIC on Barbara Lewis and see if you turn up anything. Also if you could call the Delaware State Police and find out if they know anything. The *feebies* may have sent them a BOLO (Be on the lookout)."

"Alright, I'll do what I can." There was a pause before he spoke again. "Jack, I know I'm bustin' your balls, but I want you to know I think you're innocent."

"Thanks, Billy. It means a lot. When do you think you can get back to me?"

"I'll try to call you back tonight."

"Great! Billy, I owe you one."

After he hung up, Jack called Carla, the dog-sitter, to check on Guinness. He explained he would need her to keep her a little longer and she said she could.

Jack finished the call and decided to call Julie. He knew he'd have to face the music sooner or later. He dialed the number and waited for her to pick up but instead it went to her voicemail. He quickly thought about it and decided to leave a message. While he was leaving the message, Julie picked up.

"This has got to be good," she said angrily.

"Julie, I have been arrested for conspiracy to commit murder, I think. I'm really not sure," he said as he was thinking.

"You're not sure?" she asked cynically.

"It's all so confusing. They talked about a lot of charges but I don't know which one they went with, but it doesn't matter. I didn't do anything. It's just a matter of being in the wrong place at the wrong time. Did you get your car back?"

"Yes, $276 later."

"I'll reimburse you."

"Send me a check. You have my address."

"I'll bring it to you tomorrow."

"Jack, I don't want to see you anymore. You're too screwed up, with too many problems."

"Julie, I know it may seem that way, but this situation is going to change, for the better."

"I hope so for your sake, but for me it's time to move on. Right now, you are too self-absorbed."

"Well, yeah. I am facing some serious charges, bogus, but serious nonetheless. I have to protect myself."

"And I have to protect myself."

"Julie, when this is all over I want to make it up to you. I want to prove to you that you have me all wrong."

Just then his phone beeped. He looked at it and saw it was Billy calling.

"Jack, I loved you and…"

Jack interrupted her.

"Julie, I'm sorry to interrupt you but I have an important call coming in about my case. I have to take it, but I promise I'll call you back."

The phone went dead from Julie's end. Jack clicked through to Billy.

"Billy, what's up?"

"Jack, if I have the right Barbara Lewis, she is staying in a place called Greenville. I have an exact address but I'm not sure it's hers."

"Great, give it to me."

Jack wrote it down. It was strangely familiar to him.

"What about the State Police, any info there?"

"Not yet, but I'm still checking."

"Thanks, Billy."

30

Jack had trouble getting out of bed. It felt good to finally sleep without stressing about getting arrested. At times, it seemed like his problems would never go away, but he was always the optimist and was convinced they could be fixed. Today was going to be the beginning of the end of his problems. He would find Bob Lewis and clear his name, if he didn't kill him first.

Jack went down to the lobby and waited for Marnie to show up. He got there at 8:50 A.M. He saw Henry and told him about the light out in the hallway. They didn't say anything else to each other. Jack wasn't ready to let Henry off the hook yet and apparently Henry felt Jack was a menace.

9:00 passed and so did 9:15. He started to pace. Jack called Marnie's cell phone and it went straight to voice mail. He decided to give her until 9:30 and if she hadn't arrived by then, he would take a taxi to Prescott's office. At 9:29, Marnie pulled up in her BMW.

"Nice to see you're a punctual person," Jack said as he got into the car.

"Sorry, I had to stop by the office and the traffic slowed me down," she replied as she looked to her left for other cars.

"Thank God I don't sit on the bench. Those excuses never fly with judges."

"Well, I guess you didn't sleep very well," she said clearly annoyed as she pulled out of the driveway.

"Why do you say that?" he answered defensively.

"It seems like you have a bit of an attitude."

"My life's in the shitter. Yeah, I'd say I have a bit of an attitude. You would, too. But you know what, today is going to be a great day. I feel it."

"I can understand why you'd feel depressed," Marnie said more sympathetically. "And, I'm glad to hear you're ready to turn things around. That's what I'm here for. We are going to get your life back."

"I intend to," Jack said smiling at Marnie.

"I haven't spoken with Mr. Prescott this morning but he has placed his trust in us to follow our instincts. What do you think we should do first today?"

Jack deliberated. "I have an address in Wilmington for Barbara Lewis. I should say "possible" address in a place called Greenville."

"That's great. That's a good start, wouldn't you say?"

"Yeah, but I'm not supposed to leave the area, remember?"

Marnie frowned. Jack was right. If he was caught leaving the area, his bail could be revoked and he would be incarcerated until trial. It was highly unlikely a bail modification would be successful.

"What do you think?" Marnie asked Jack.

"It's not on me. It's on you. You're supposed to be watching me to make sure I don't leave the area, but if it's up to me, I'm going to Delaware."

Marnie was silent as she let her thoughts marinate.

"Let's go to the office first; I can talk to Mr. Prescott, and get his input."

Jack shook his head looking out the window as if to say, "Yeah, right."

"Hey! Where's that positive attitude?"

Jack just turned and looked at her dubiously.

When they arrived, Marnie took Jack to the kitchen area to get a cup of coffee and Danish, and then left him there while she hunted down Mr. Prescott. Jack drank his coffee and ate his cheese Danish. He looked around and found a *Washington Post.* He began reading about the politics of the day and then read the sports page. The Phillies had won and he was happy.

Marnie returned and informed Jack they would have to do some local leg work and check out some local haunts of Bob Lewis. Jack didn't bother to ask where she obtained the information. He believed it couldn't be that credible. Still, he felt he would humor her for the day, and then try to persuade her to do things his way. If she wasn't convinced, he would go his own way. For now, someone had paid his bail, and Jack felt obligated to placate her and Mr. Prescott.

They went to the business "You've Been Framed" first.

Jack thought they may be closed due to the death of Peggy Garber but, surprisingly, they were open. They went in and asked for the manager. They decided not to mention Jack's identity, only identifying themselves as investigators. If the manager wanted to draw the conclusion they were cops, so be it. Jack would ask the questions and Marnie would write.

When Jack and Marnie went through the front door, they approached the counter and asked the older woman for the manager. She didn't ask the nature of their business. She just smiled modestly and left the counter to fetch the manager. Returning in short order, she said the manager would be right out.

Shortly thereafter, an effeminate man in his sixties with gray coiffed hair sashayed towards them. He was short and thin wearing a pink collared shirt with wide blue stripes and tan slacks. His glasses were tethered around his neck and they rested on his chest. They also had a pink frame. He was wearing sandals.

"How can I help you?" he said clasping his hands in front of him.

"We're looking into the death of Peggy Garber, and we'd like to ask you a few questions."

"There were officers here yesterday. Don't you talk to each other?" he asked in a contemptuous way.

"It's important during an investigation to get multiple viewpoints. That way, if someone didn't ask the right question, someone else, in this case us," Jack said gesticulating by waving his hand back and forth at himself and Marnie, "might think of something else."

"What is it you would like to know? I mean, there really isn't anything else I can tell you."

"Do you know or did you ever hear the name Bob Lewis?" Jack asked.

"No, I can't say that I ever have."

"Did you know Peggy's husband?"

"No, I never had the pleasure."

"How did you get hired here?"

"I filled out an application. Peggy liked the fact that I had experience with art. I had met her a couple of months ago at a show," he started to smile as he relived the moment. "We hit it off from the very first moment. She knows my partner. They worked together in retail a long time ago and that's how we started talking."

"You didn't answer my question: How did you get hired?"

"Calm down, I was getting to that. She told me she was opening this store. I don't know if you know it or not, but she has another store in Silver Spring. It's a lovely store and it's doing remarkably well for that area. Anyway, she said she would need a manager, and after she reviewed my qualifications, she hired me."

His smile turned to a frown. "And then, she was murdered," he said as his eyes welled up with tears. He took out a handkerchief and started dabbing at the corner of his eyes.

"I just have a few more questions Mr…" Jack stopped. He couldn't believe he didn't get his name first. "I'm sorry, I don't think I got your name."

"It's Royce Ringlé." He spelled it out as Marnie wrote it down.

"Has there been anyone suspicious in the store lately?" Jack asked.

"No more than usual," Royce said looking at a puzzled Jack and Marnie. "I mean c'mon, it's Georgetown. We get a lot of unusual people in here, and they're not just locals either."

"Did anyone in particular stick out?"

"No," he responded irreverently.

"Did Ms. Garber act strangely in the last few days before her death?" Jack asked.

Royce gave him an irritated look.

"What I mean to say is, did she act any differently the few days before her death?"

"No. Ms. Garber was an outstanding woman, a woman who cared about other people. She was generous to a fault. She did not "act" at all. She was the genuine article. So to answer your preposterous question, no she did not "act" any differently at all. Are you almost done with me?" he asked, becoming persnickety.

"Just about. I don't mean to appear disingenuous, Mr. Ringlé, but if someone was out to get her, I would think she may have been troubled and under pressure. It may have surfaced in her behavior. That is why I asked the question. You do want us to find her killer, don't you?"

"Of course. Excuse me for being a little upset. In the short time I had the pleasure to know her, I adored Peggy. I would have done anything for her. All she had to do is ask. I guess I'm a little sensitive."

"Was there or is there now, any indication she was having financial difficulty?"

"None whatsoever. From what I know she was in excellent financial health."

"Did her habits change at all?"

"What do you mean?"

"Did her routine change at all? Did her appearance change? Anything like that."

He thought for a moment and then smiled. "She bought some delightful new shoes to go with her powder blue pant suit. All of us commented on them."

He started to describe them but Jack cut him short.

"What I mean is, did she appear unkempt in any way?"

"No, she was always dressed to the nines."

"I know it has to be tough on you and the other employees. Do you know how the store is going to operate now?"

"We don't know. It's all up in the air. She has a cousin who lives in Minnesota who is here now to attend to her funeral arrangements. I guess she'll let us know what's going on."

"Well, I don't think we have anything else at the moment but if we do, would it be alright to stop back and talk with you again?"

"Certainly. I don't think I got your names, either."

"This is Marnie Bloom and I'm …John Smith."

"It was nice talking to you Marnie and John," he said as he offered his hand. "I sure hope they keep that man, that Jack Dublin I think his name is, locked up and just throw away the key."

"I don't know that he is the one responsible, but I'm sure we'll get to the bottom of it."

"I sure hope so," Royce said as he became emotional again.

"Have a nice day," Jack said as he shook Royce's limp hand.

They walked out and when they were out of sight of the store, Marnie started laughing hard.

"What the hell is so funny?" Jack asked seriously.

"John Smith? Why didn't you just tell him I was Pocahontas and we were here looking for directions to Jamestown?" she was in tears laughing so hard.

"Calm down."

"I'm sorry, I can't help it," she said holding her stomach.

"He caught me off-guard. I couldn't tell him Jack Dublin, for Christ's sake. What can I say, it was the first thing that popped in my mind," Jack said starting to chuckle at himself.

31

By 4 o'clock and, after making other insignificant stops, nothing substantial had been discovered. Marnie had a defeated look on her face. During their time together, driving around D.C., Jack learned Marnie had been adopted. She said her mother died when she was an infant, and her father was killed when she was four. A friend of the family raised her, and for that she was eternally grateful. Her "father" (as she called him) was a remarkable man of integrity, who ensured she always was afforded a good life. Her "mother" was also an outstanding woman who remained at home to care for her. Unfortunately, she died of breast cancer a couple of years ago. Marnie applied for a job at the Prescott Law Firm when she graduated from college and has been there ever since. Her assignments varied and she liked it.

"Listen Jack, I know today wasn't very productive," she said, and before she could say anything else he interrupted.

"I think we, or I, need to get in touch with my friend on the department, Billy D., and ask him for some direction."

Jack believed he knew what path to take, but he didn't feel confident with Marnie as an investigator. He needed another sharp investigative mind to help him. Maybe he was missing something. If he was, Billy would know.

"Do you think he'll meet us?"

"Probably."

"Give him a call but be careful Jack. You don't know what he's obligated to do with any incriminating evidence."

Jack thought about it and then placed the call.

. . .

They met at a coffee shop in Maryland at Billy's request. He was spooked although when he shook Jack's hand and gave him a hug it seemed genuine. Then Jack introduced Billy to Marnie.

They ordered coffee and took a booth away from the other few customers.

"Tell me what you got," Billy asked.

Anything you say to someone can be twisted and used against you, especially if someone is out to get you, but Jack had full faith in Billy. It was an inherent sense of trust. When you're a cop, it becomes instinct. Jack began to tell him the whole story. When he was done, Billy took a sip of his coffee and pondered the story.

"Let me tell you Jack, you're in deep shit. You ain't got dick," Billy said before apologizing to Marnie.

"What do you mean?" Jack asked.

"I hate to tell you, brother, but with what you've got, you're gonna get fried."

"Wait a minute," Marnie said jumping in. "He didn't fire the gun that killed Webster. He didn't fire the gun that killed Peggy, whatever her name was. And, he's never spoken with any terrorists to sell weapons or information."

"Yeah? Well, how do you explain him kneeling over a murder victim with his gun close by, and "*it is*" Jack's gun. He doesn't really have any good explanation for being there. He owns a condo that costs a fortune. You don't live like that on a police pension. He's sitting next to a woman who looks like the girl next door, and she gets killed. Meantime, weapons are being sold to a group of terrorists who appear to be tied to these murders.

"Just wait until they put the picture of Jack kneeling over a murder victim with his own gun in sight, looking like a deer in headlights. And then, the picture of Miss Girl Next Door on the screen in the courtroom before a jury who no doubt will be selectively chosen to include little old ladies and men with hard-ons."

Marnie started to speak up to defend Jack, but Jack put his hand up.

"What would you do if you were in my shoes?"

Billy saw the look on Jack's face and couldn't say what he really wanted to say.

"First, you hire a good attorney. You've already done that. You've got one of the best, if not the best, attorney in town. Second, find that son-of-a-bitch Bob Lewis and bring him in."

"Can you help me?"

"Jack, there isn't much I can do but keep my ear to the ground. You know I have to be careful. I don't want to lose my job. I've got a family to feed. Hell, I'm so scared now, talking to you, I'll probably have to clean my underwear when I get home."

"I appreciate it, Billy. I really do. You know they told me I can't leave the area, and his wife is in Delaware..."

"Stop right there. You know, if it were me I'd travel around the world to find that son-of-a-bitch no matter what. What's the worst they can do to you? Put you in jail for life?"

They started to laugh a bit at the irony.

"Jack, you don't have a choice. Take the chance and go after him. For God's sake, don't kill him. You'll never clear your name," Billy said comically.

They laughed again, and then Billy got serious.

"Jack, I believe you. I've known you for twenty years. You wouldn't kill anyone unless you were threatened or you were saving someone else. You've demonstrated that. I don't know this Bob Lewis, but you can't let this guy get away leaving you holding the bag. I promise you I will keep my eyes and ears open. If I hear anything, I'll call you and let you know. Just give me your number."

Marnie looked at Jack as if to say maybe you shouldn't give him the number, but Jack did. Billy left before they did. They sat for a few minutes to discuss strategy.

"Y'know now he has your number. They can probably track you. He knows you're going to leave the area and break the rules of your bail. If he wants to turn you in, you'll be sitting in jail waiting for trial. Is that what you want?" Marnie asked.

"Everything you said is true. But you can't measure a person's heart. I know Billy. We were partners for years. I trust him. He would never do that to me. Besides, this is a throwaway phone. It can't be traced."

"Are you sure?"

"Absolutely."

They finished their coffee and headed for Delaware, but not until Jack stopped by his gym to pick up his gym bag containing his guns and ammunition. He was tired of being unarmed.

32

Marnie pointed her car in the direction of the Beltway. It would be nearly 9:30 before they got to Wilmington. It took them almost four hours due to traffic at rush hour through the Baltimore tunnel. Jack was feeling tired from the previous days' ordeals and tried to sleep, but it was difficult in a compact car.

Marnie was still driving a cobalt blue BMW Roadster. Jack couldn't help but wonder how someone like her, who worked for a law firm in her capacity, could afford a car like a BMW. When he made mention of the cost of the car, she told Jack it was leased to the office. She said it was a pool car and she was allowed to drive it only when necessary. His case qualified as necessary.

"With the price of gas, I imagine it's pretty costly," he stated.

"I don't really have to worry about it, since the firm pays for the gas," she said nonchalantly. "Have you ever owned a BMW?"

"On a cop's salary? You gotta be kiddin' me! I usually owned used cars. The only brand-new car I ever owned was a Toyota Celica. Do you remember them?"

"Not really."

"Yeah, I guess you wouldn't. They stopped selling them around the late nineties."

"How old do you think I am?" Marnie asked with a grin.

"You really want to get me in trouble, don't you?"

"I'm just curious to hear what you'll say, that's all. I won't take offense to any answer you give."

"Hmmmmm, let me think," Jack said as he thought about his answer. "I'd say thirty."

She started to giggle. "Well, I thank you for your answer."

She didn't say anything else. Jack waited, but an answer wasn't voluntarily forthcoming.

"Well, are you going to tell me, or do I have to beg for an answer?"

"I'm thirty-six."

Jack was pleasantly surprised. He liked the fact she was closer in age to him. "You look good," he said truthfully.

"Thank you," she answered smiling.

There were a few minutes of silence before Marnie spoke.

"You know, Jack, I know this is a bad topic. The election is a couple of years away but there is talk that Senator Rothschild is lining himself up to make a run for president."

"It will be a sorry day in this country if that son-of-a-bitch gets elected," Jack said bitterly.

"I agree, but politics being what it is, you can never tell. I never thought the current president would get elected, but he did, and now with the problems in the economy, the Republicans are making some headway in the polls."

"Y'know that pisses me off. No president can make unilateral decisions, I don't care what party affiliation you are. That means Congress is the one who holds the ball. It's in their court, and as far as I'm concerned, they're all crooks. It's big business that makes the decisions for our country. They have the deep pockets, so they will buy their way into Congress's pockets. We have to live by it, because they put so much crap into a bill, we will never know what's truly in there, or what the intent is, other than to screw the middle class. And by the way, how does a fat cat oil man from Oklahoma promote himself, when oil prices are going through the roof along with the price at the pumps? People gotta say to themselves, why elect someone who is getting rich by stickin' it to us?"

"Good question."

Jack just looked out the window at the passing scenery trying to calm down. He managed to fall asleep soon after Marnie switched on the radio to a classical music station.

As they approached Wilmington, Jack began to stir. He was pleasantly surprised to see Frawley Stadium, where a minor league team of the Kansas City Royals organization plays. One day he would have to make a trip up and see a game.

"Jack, we can't go looking for Barbara Lewis tonight. It's already 9:30. Watching you sleep makes me tired. We need to stay somewhere. I've heard the Hotel DuPont is nice," she said glancing over at him.

He looked at her with mild surprise.

"You're right about that, but it's pretty pricey."

"I don't care about that; I'll get reimbursed."

"Aren't you concerned about revealing we were in Delaware?"

She pondered his question. He was right. It would inform Mr. Prescott they had disobeyed not only his instructions, but more importantly, the court order. By the time he found out, it would not be of any major consequence.

"Obviously since we've come this far, I think the information we're going to get is worth the risk. I'll delay getting reimbursed and submit it later. Hopefully that way, we can keep it under wraps."

Jack told her to get off the Delaware Avenue exit. Marnie looked over at Jack, who was smiling.

"What are you smiling about?" she asked.

"How many rooms are you getting?"

"Two. So don't get any ideas."

"I believe in cost-saving measures. I think we should get one room and I'll sleep on the couch," he said still smiling.

"I bet you believe in saving water too, don't you."

"Absolutely!"

They pulled into the lane for valet parking, under the portico, and got out of the car. Jack took his bag out of the trunk and carried it. The bellman offered to take it but Jack refused. Once they were inside, Marnie charged two rooms. Jack stood by and listened. They were not on the same floor. He knew it wasn't Marnie who planned it that way. They were heavily booked due to a convention, and there were only single rooms on different floors.

Marnie was in 511 and Jack was in 711. As Jack turned away from the front desk, he accidentally bumped into a man behind him who was also just checking in. After Jack excused himself, he looked at the man and thought he recognized him, but dismissed it. Cops always see people they think they recognize. He was an ordinary man who looked like the business type.

Behind him was a tall black man, possibly in his mid-thirties, wearing casual clothes. His hair was worn in a box braid style and was neatly tied behind his head. He definitely didn't look like the Hotel DuPont type, but with a convention in town you get all kinds of people. He was conspicuous by his size and his dress. He got Jack's attention.

"Do you know him?" Marnie asked.

"Which guy, the black one or the white one?"

"The white guy."

"He looks familiar but probably not. I'm finding as I get older, everybody looks like somebody I know. You want to meet in the bar after we check out our rooms?"

Marnie looked him in the eye. He gave an intentional innocent puppy dog look sticking out his lower lip.

"Okay, but don't get any ideas," she said smiling. "Remember, I said I'm tired."

"On my honor," Jack said as he crossed his heart with his finger, and then held up three fingers like he was a Boy Scout.

Jack went with her to her room to make sure she got in, even though she told him it wasn't necessary. He then took the stairs mistakenly to the sixth floor and walked down the hall to 611. As he was trying to put the key in the wrong room door, the man who had been behind him at the front desk, was walking down the hall, pulling a suitcase with his left hand. The manner of his walk looked like a man intent on finding his room quickly. Jack kept fumbling with the key and the door would not open. The man started to reach with his right hand into his suit coat. He had a serious look on his face. Just as the man began to approach him, a maid opened the door.

"I'm sorry, I didn't know the room was being made up," Jack said.

"No problem, Mr. Schneider, your room is ready now," the emerging maid stated as the man passed by.

Jack gave her a surprised look and then watched the man leave through the hallway door. "That's not my name."

"This is Mr. Schneider's room," she said with a look of concern. "I've never met him but he's a regular who always insists on Room 611."

Jack looked on the door and realized he needed to go up one more floor. "I'm sorry. I'm in 711. I need to go up one more floor." He smiled at her and turned for the elevator.

Jack decided to take the elevator, laughing at himself. Paying attention this time, the numbers in the elevator were large and guaranteed he would get to the correct floor, as he shook his head smiling. "*What an idiot I am!*"

Once Jack got situated in his room, he called Marnie's room and told her he would meet her in the bar next to the Green Room. When Jack got to the bar, only a couple of people were in there. Now sitting at the bar, he ordered a Glen Morangie on the rocks. He never ordered beer at upscale bars when he knew he could get great scotch.

A few minutes later Marnie came in and ordered a Cosmopolitan. They took their drinks to a table in the back. There were only two people in the bar, an older couple probably in their seventies. Jack always liked to see who came in hoping to see a celebrity who was performing at the Playhouse. Marnie sat alongside him. She said she didn't like her back to the door either.

Marnie looked around at the deep rich wood that paneled the bar and liked what she saw.

"This is a very nice hotel," she said as if surprised.

"You sound as though you didn't expect Delaware to have any nice hotels," he said.

"This hotel has a long history. I can tell."

"The theater here has had a great number of Broadway shows. A lot of times producers would try their shows here before hitting Broadway. That way they could tweak it. Many of the legendary stars have been here: Katherine Hepburn, Lucille Ball, Orson Welles, Henry Fonda,

Bette Davis and many more. It's a great hotel. I remember when my parents used to bring me here sometimes for Sunday brunch," Jack said as his voice trailed off.

"You OK?"

"Yeah, fine. I guess I was thinking back to happier times when my parents seemed happily married, seems more like a hallucination now." He paused and then changed the subject, telling Marnie how one year he came to the Wilmington Sports Writers Banquet in the Gold Ballroom, with a friend and the friend's father. He saw a lot of the local sports heroes of the time like Mike Schmidt, Pete Rose and Ron Jaworski along with other notable figures. It was quite thrilling to see sports legends you worshipped, sitting right in front of you signing autographs. He said his high school prom was in the Gold Ballroom as well.

As they talked, the man who Jack bumped into at the front desk walked in, sat at the end of the bar and got a drink. He was sitting fairly close to them but not within earshot. Shortly afterward, the man with neat dreadlocks walked in and sat at the bar alone. He had to be an easy six feet six with a muscular build. He seemed to scan the room looking for someone. Jack was feeling paranoid.

"Are you ready to meet with Bob Lewis's wife tomorrow?"

"I can't wait, if you want to know the truth," Jack said as he refocused on Marnie.

"What do we do if we don't get the information we need?"

"Holy shit! Marnie, you don't have to be so negative."

"I'm not being negative. I'm just trying to think ahead. I want to do whatever we need to do to get you vindicated. If she is not cooperative, then we need to be prepared to go to the next step. Do you know what that is, because I don't."

"Yes, I do, but for now let's concentrate on Barbara Lewis," Jack replied.

They sat for a while and finished their drinks before deciding to call it a night. When they were on the elevator, they decided to meet in the lobby at 8 A.M. When Jack got back to his room, he couldn't stop thinking about Marnie. He had become so comfortable with her, and wanted to spend more time with her, be with her. He thought of an excuse to call her room.

"Hello," she answered.

"I was thinking that maybe we need to talk some more about our interview tomorrow with Barbara Lewis," Jack said. "You know, discuss strategy."

"I was thinking about it, too. Why don't you come down to my room, and we can talk about it," she said.

"I'll be right down,"

Jack arrived at her door in a minute.

"C'mon in," Marnie said as she answered the door. "I was just getting ready to call it a night." She had a white robe on. Jack couldn't tell if she was wearing anything underneath but he hoped to find out. He sat down in a small wooden chair next to a table.

"What did you have in mind?" she said coyly. "About tomorrow," she added.

"I think you should let me do the talking," Jack said. "Tomorrow."

"Really," she said with a faint smile.

"Yes, it's always good to have someone lead, and the other follow. You shouldn't have two people trying to lead a conversation at the same time. Do you know what I mean?"

"Okay, sounds good to me. Anything else?"

"Let me think," Jack said with an expectant pause.

Marnie went over to the bed, sat on the edge and crossed her legs. She started to take her earrings off. As she sat there, her robe parted up to mid-thigh of her left leg, and revealed she was naked except for perhaps panties.

Jack got up from his chair and walked over to Marnie. He sat on the bed next to her. Neither one spoke. Marnie looked at him with a confused look. Jack put his arm around her and pulled her towards him. She showed no resistance. He started to lean in slowly to kiss her. She watched him, looking into his eyes and then at his lips. He began to lean in to kiss her and Marnie jumped up.

"What are you doing?" she said irritated.

"What do you mean?" Jack answered surprised.

"Get out!"

Jack looked at her with his mouth partly open. He was dumbfounded. He got up slowly and began to walk towards the door. When he got to the door, he turned around to apologize and a pillow hit him in the face. The zipper of the lining caught his eyebrow. He put his hand up to his eye and then pulled it back. He was bleeding.

"My God Jack, you're bleeding," she said regretfully. She ran to him and put her hand on his shoulder. He had covered his eye. "Let me take a look."

Jack took his hand down and it revealed a small cut that was trickling blood.

"Come into the bathroom," she said taking his hand and leading him there. "Sit down."

Jack sat on the toilet seat. Marnie took a washcloth and began to run cold water over it. She squeezed it and placed it on his forehead. After a minute or two, the bleeding stopped.

"Jack, I am so sorry," she said.

"Don't worry about it."

She took him by the hand and led him out of the bathroom and they walked towards the door. When they got to the door, she looked up at him with a desire she couldn't disguise. She placed her hands on his arms and started to speak.

"I'll see you in the morning," Jack said evenly, as he turned to the door.

33

It was an arrangement that worked well for Bob Lewis.

He needed to sell the house because of his looming divorce with Barbara, and yet he needed a place to live. He didn't want to move everything that remained in the house. There was a lot of junk, and it was difficult even thinking about it. He thought about getting one of those junk buyers, but didn't want a lot of strange people traipsing through his house. If he missed something, a paper, a computer disk or something like it, he could be implicated in illegal activity. There was no doubt he would go to jail, and his dream would never become reality.

As it turned out the new owner, a young man who was vice president of a computer firm, was transferred to India shortly after signing the contract to purchase the Lewis home. He didn't want to relinquish his sizable security deposit for withdrawing from the contract, so he asked Bob to find a renter.

Ultimately, Bob worked a deal for himself to stay there for one year after the sale. This allowed Bob to maintain his "business" and not appear in the system as the home owner. Any law enforcement agency would be unaware he remained there. He could fly under the radar, get a P.O. Box, and have service such as electric and cable established in the new owner's name. There would be no trails. As far as most people were concerned, Bob Lewis didn't exist.

Now that the year was almost up, and the landlord indicated he was going to take residence there, it was a perfect time for Bob to pack up his belongings and move to St. Lucia just as he had planned. This time, someone could buy the contents he didn't want or need. At this point, it didn't matter if they found anything incriminating. He would be long gone. His checks would still be sent to his bank, and he would do a wire transfer to his bank in the islands. The arms deal would be consummated; he would be financially set and living his dream. Bob was ready for life outside the United States.

He was feeling confident. His "clients" were now trained to use the SAMS. They understood how effective they were. They had made their down payment and it was a certainty the rest of the money would be paid with the delivery of the remaining SAMS. He knew he could always get more weapons since Duke Callison was going to remain in the States.

The weapons were already en route to St. Lucia through secured channels, and would be aboard his yacht in the next couple of days. Bill Franklin would already be there on Bob's yacht to receive the goods.

Bob decided to call the senator.

"Good afternoon, Senator," Bob said smugly.

"I can tell by the tone of your voice that you have good news," he replied.

"Why do you say that?"

"Because I detect an hint of arrogance."

"It's something you're quite familiar with, so I am not surprised." There was no response. "I do indeed have good news. We have received payment and the goods are on their way. We will receive the remainder upon final delivery."

"When do you anticipate this exchange to take place?"

"Within the week."

"Can you be any more specific? As I told you before, I am going to be down that way next week."

"I couldn't remember when. Is this the cruise you were talking about?"

"Yes, I have been invited to be a guest on the newest ship in the Star Cruise Fleet, when it makes its first voyage through the West Indies. We're stopping at five islands"

"Congratulations; I understand it's the largest ship ever built."

"It is," he said excitedly. "They say it has cities replicated onboard and you can do just about anything you want, including surfing," he paused. "That was something my son loved to do whenever he visited family on the West Coast. Don't ask me why, but he did. Can you imagine a big ol' country boy on a surfboard? An Okie, too?"

"Must have been a sight to see," Bob said trying to sound interested.

"Anyway, they say the only thing that could sink this ship is nothing short of a nuclear warhead," the senator said.

"You better be careful about what they say. They said the Titanic was unsinkable, too."

"Yeah, I know," the senator said laughing. "But I'm not worried about that. Last I heard, there aren't any icebergs in the Caribbean. I'm only going to be on that ship for a week. I'm going to relax and enjoy myself. Where can you meet me?"

"I don't know. When are you going to be near St. Lucia?"

"Hold on, let me get my itinerary," he said as he put the phone down returning in short order. "It says here that St. Lucia is our third stop on that Wednesday which would be the 11th."

"I didn't realize you're out of session."

"Yeah, there is nothing pressing, and I have been authorized to go, so I'm going."

"I guess the wife will be thrilled."

"I already told you, she's not going," the senator responded.

"Really," Bob said with fake amazement.

"This is a business trip of sorts. She is staying home, spending my money on bullshit, I'm sure."

"Are you going alone?"

"What I do is none of your business," the senator answered angrily. "Besides, I already told you."

"Relax. I don't care who you're fucking. I'm only interested because, if I am giving you large sums of money, I want to know who's going to be present. Unless of course, you don't care who knows you're getting millions of dollars from illegally sold United States armaments to a terrorist group."

"Okay, okay. I get the message. And, let me make this clear, after this transaction is complete, I don't want to see you or hear from you again. Do you understand?"

"Perfectly."

"It's better that way for both of us," he said trying to reduce any animosity.

"Understood."

"Now, how are we going to make a transfer?"

"Do you want me to wire the money to an account?"

"Y'know, something tells me I shouldn't make a wire transfer because it could be traceable."

"I doubt it, but you tell me what you want, and I'll make it happen."

"Why don't you get me a suitcase, put the money in it and secure it?"

Bob laughed. "You're kiddin' right?"

"I'm serious. I can take it to a bank somewhere down there, open an account and nobody will be the wiser for it."

"You think it's that easy?"

"Why wouldn't it be?"

"Well, I guess if you walk into a bank with a few million in cash, some banker will take it and keep it quiet."

"Absolutely."

"I guess you'll be alone when you do it, so there won't be any witnesses."

"I don't know why you're fixated on who I'm with, but yes, I will be alone. She likes to stay on the ship and be waited on."

"Senator, I'm just trying to be a friend. You don't need any problems when you get back to the States. Your political career is contingent on being squeaky clean."

"I couldn't agree more, but it will be nice to know I have some money in a safe place for when I need it for my campaign."

"What you're getting is not a great deal of money these days."

"Yeah, but when you're in a campaign, it's a war. You can never have enough money. Besides, it's not the *only* money I'll have, y'know."

"Unlike you, I don't need a lot of money to keep me happy. Just my boat, a woman, and some booze and I'm set. I'm not gonna just kick back though. I might for a little while, but then I am going to start a business like fishing charters, and make more money. Who knows? I might even sell more weapons."

"That's great Bob. I'm impressed," the senator said unimpressed. "Listen, I have to go. I have a meeting with the media. We'll need to talk some more to nail down the location, date, and time for this transaction. Don't call me, I'll call you."

The senator hung up before Bob could say anything else.

. . .

Senator Rothschild marched up to the microphones with his usual flair of self-importance. He was dressed in a grey suit, white shirt and a red, white and blue tie. The purpose of this news conference, other than to promote himself, was to discuss the war on terrorism.

He knew he would be gearing up his candidacy for president upon his return from the Caribbean. He wanted to give time to his exploratory committee and his advisers to effectively choreograph his strategy. They knew there were other candidates who were also going to announce their intentions. Even though it was early, they wanted to make sure Rothschild had center stage first. Yet improper timing could disturb his potential donors and grass root supporters. The tête-à-tête with the people who powered his machine had to take place first, and not everyone was available before his return from vacation. Certainly he would talk with many donors on the phone, but there were two potential sizable donors he wanted to fortify first with private consultations. Not only was their money important, but their public support could garner enormous dollars and votes. When it comes down to it, money is always the driving factor. Nobody becomes president without the support of healthy donations, but you also have to be a viable candidate. Benefactors don't hedge their bets; they only put their money on sure winners. Senator Rothschild was a winner.

He adjusted the microphones and looked at the cadre of reporters. What he was about to say would have an impact on his future.

"Ladies and gentlemen, the war on terror is far from over. It has almost become a cottage industry for those Middle Eastern countries that continue to offer a weak resistance to the Taliban and Al Qaeda. There is no doubt in my mind, there are other militant groups springing up to overtake and replace these groups. They are lying dormant waiting for the next opportunity to kill innocent Americans.

"The current administration continues to respond by misappropriating our troops. We need to send an message to these terrorist groups with tough actions and sanctions against those countries that allow our security to be threatened by their inaction against terrorism on their own turf.

"Additionally, we must turn our attention to homegrown terrorism. There exists, here in America, a realistic threat to our security from domestic Muslims, who reside amongst us and are loyal to jihad. I mean no disrespect to the law-abiding Muslims. The disaffected Muslims continue to be recruited by the misdirected allure of promised martyrdom for murdering our citizens. They live amongst us. They could be your neighbors.

"As Americans, we are entitled to live and breathe freely without the threat of terrorists. We are also entitled to have the means to provide for our families through jobs. Everyone deserves respect and dignity.

"I will not rest until these basic tenets of human life are realized here in America, the greatest country in the world."

The questions started to come fast and furious from the piranha-like reporters.

"Senator Rothschild, is there any truth to the rumor you will shortly announce your candidacy for president?"

"As you know, I have created an exploratory committee and it is analyzing my options. I will be making an announcement sometime in the near future regarding my candidacy. I have to go now. Thank you for your interest." He gave his brilliant ten thousand-watt smile as he waved, turned and left the podium.

Bob Lewis was smiling like a Chessie cat as he turned off his television after watching the grand performance. If America only knew, he thought.

34

"Jack," Marnie said, as Jack answered the phone in his room.

"Hi Marnie," he answered. "What time is it?"

"It's almost eight o'clock."

"Oh shit! I guess I need to get moving," Jack said excitedly, as he jumped out of bed.

"Can you meet me downstairs in a half hour?"

"Yeah, I can do that."

"See you then."

Jack got up and began to get ready. As he showered, he ruminated about the previous night, but didn't give it too much weight.

He found Marnie in the coffee shop reading the paper.

"Anything good in the paper?" Jack asked nonchalantly.

"No, not really. The Braves are kicking ass. Other than that not much going on."

"They can kick ass all they want, the Phillies will still win the division this year."

"I don't think so," she said with sarcasm. "They're already five games behind."

"Doesn't matter, it's only June. The Braves don't have the pitching that the Phillies do. And, the Philly offense is better."

"You're dreamin'."

"Take my word for it, the Braves will run out of gas."

"We'll see."

Nothing was said by either of them about the previous night.

Jack wandered over to the counter and got a coffee and a bagel.

"Are you from Atlanta?" Jack asked as he sat down. He knew sports fans all over the country had their favorites, but he detested the ones whose favorite team was from an area different from where they grew up. Where's the loyalty? That's why he would be a Phillies' fan for life.

"No. Actually I was born outside Atlanta, but my family moved to Washington D.C. when I was a toddler. My godparents became my guardians, as I told you yesterday. They lived in Washington but I went to Oglethorpe, a small college in Atlanta."

"How long were you in Atlanta?"

"Until I was twenty-three. About one year too long."

"Why's that?"

"No reason really," she said with a hint of gloom.

"No, really. Why did you say it like that? There must have been something that went wrong down there."

Marnie paused and then said, "My fiancé was killed. He was a fireman in the city. He was killed in a training exercise."

"That had to be tough. How long ago was that?"

"About thirteen years ago."

"I take it you've never married."

"No."

"Because of your fiancé or because you just haven't found anyone?"

"I'm pretty much over Jack, although he will always be in my thoughts. I just haven't found anyone and no one has found me."

"Wait a minute. Your fiancé's name was Jack?" Jack asked.

"Yep, sure was."

Jack smiled, "Interesting."

Marnie changed the subject. She wanted to lead Jack away from distractions and focus on his predicament. "So, what do you think we should do? Just go up there, and knock on the door?"

"Why not? It's a start. What did you have in mind anyway?"

"Well, I thought we could start by going to the door, asking if her parents could confirm that she lives there, and then take it from there."

"Isn't that what I just said?" Jack said kiddingly.

"Are you done?" Marnie said mockingly.

"Let me finish my coffee and bagel and then we can go. Did you eat already?"

Marnie nodded her head, positively.

They checked out of the hotel about a half hour later and retrieved their car. Marnie drove. It was about a twenty minute drive to the house. On the way up the Kennett Pike, they passed many old, iconic, affluent landmarks. There was a little nervous tension in the air from the previous night. Neither one of them knew how to act in front of each other since they were now in close quarters. Nothing said was probably best.

It was a clear day, and the humidity was already getting thick. Jack pointed out the exclusive Wilmington Country Club, and gave Marnie his version of its history. He talked about how private it is. You have to know someone on the inside to become a member. Only the elite were members, and anyone else who played there as a guest felt like he had received special dispensation from the Pope.

"Do you play golf?" Jack asked.

"A little," Marnie answered.

"Maybe we can play some time."

"Maybe."

Jack couldn't read her. Her manner had changed since they left the hotel. He intuitively knew she wanted to be with him, but she was more disciplined than he was.

"Have you ever played there?" Marnie asked tilting her head towards the country club.

"No, I never did, but I remember my father was a member there."

Next they passed Winterthur Museum, once the home of Henry DuPont whose property extended to the Wilmington Country Club, which in fact, purchased land from him to build the golf course. Winterthur was now a museum, which was also home to the Point to Point race in May. Jack had never attended, but heard it was a very popular day of horse races that enabled the middle class to rub elbows with the upper crust of Delaware.

Further up the road was a local watering hole, Buckley's Tavern. Jack knew once they passed Buckley's, they were close to the home of Barbara Lewis's parents. The area was filled with mansions occupied by staid, old-money individuals and families. The Hollingsworth mansion was wooded and concealed from the main road. Most people would fly right by Selborne Drive, and never know there were about twenty homes back there with acreage to spare. It was the seclusion sought after by the aristocracy.

The road curved left and then right. They saw a sign that was marked "400" and they drove up the long driveway. They expected some barking dogs but none appeared.

It was a huge, stone mansion with turrets at one end and a gate house at the other. There were a few cars in the circle. There was a late model black Mercedes, a cream colored Lexus, and an old Ford pickup with a trailer attached carrying landscaping equipment. They got out of the car, and approached the large front doors which looked like they could have been from a monastery in Europe. The doors had brass hinges and iron markings.

Marnie took one of the large rings and used it to signal their presence. They could hear what sounded like a large dog barking inside and they looked at each other. Jack turned while they waited and saw the license plate on the Mercedes. He got Marnie's attention and shook his head towards the car. She saw it had Maryland tags and raised her eyebrows.

A refined looking man, who appeared to be in his seventies, soon answered the door. He was about six feet two, bald on top with silver grey hair on the sides. He was in good shape for a man his age. He was wearing a dark blue Ralph Lauren polo shirt with lime green pants. It was the Greenville look, Jack remembered from high school days. The "look" usually included Docksides with no socks. The gentleman looked squarely at Marnie, hardly noticing Jack.

"Can I help you?" he asked rather high-handed.

"Yes, I am Agent Bloom with WISE International in Washington D.C., and this is my partner, Jack Dublin," Marnie said plainly, but struck with how odd it sounded to say "my partner".

"We're looking for Barbara Hollingsworth Lewis," Jack said taking control of the conversation.

"That is my daughter. Why are you looking for her?"

"We need to talk to her about her husband," Jack stated.

He rolled his eyes. "That son-of-a-bitch…" his voice trailed off. "I assure you, she is not involved in any of his shenanigans."

"Sir, we know that. We're only interested in speaking to her about him."

"Soon to be ex-husband," he said, as he looked at Jack closer. "Did you say your name was Jack Dublin? Did I hear right?" he asked with a confused look.

"Yes, my name is Jack Dublin."

Mr. Hollingsworth looked at Jack, examining him. Jack tried not to smile. Mr. Hollingsworth had his forefinger across his lips, and touching his nose as he continued to inspect Jack. "I just read not too long ago in the Washington Post, I think, about a Jack Dublin who shot and killed a U.S. senator's son. Did you ever live in Wilmington?"

"Yes sir, I did. I lived in Wilmington over twenty years ago."

"Where did you go to school?"

"I went to Mt. Pleasant High School."

"Then you must be the one the Post referred to."

"If your question is, did I shoot and kill Senator Rothschild's son? The answer is yes," Jack said without restraint.

Mr. Hollingsworth continued to look at Jack contemplatively. His eyebrows were furrowed as he continued to stare. Jack had no idea where this was going, but it could only go one of two ways. Either he felt Jack mistakenly killed a senator's son, or it was justified. Nevertheless, Jack knew whatever his opinion was would soon dictate whether or not they would have access to Barbara Lewis.

"You know, I'm a Republican but I can't stand that self-righteous son-of-a-bitch. In my mind, he is responsible for our country's loss of family values, especially coming from the Bible belt. Whether or not his son was attempting to rape an innocent young girl, and I have no doubt from what I read he was, how do you defend someone like that? Let's say the senator is right about a "misunderstanding". How the hell do you justify your son getting high on drugs and alcohol? If I was a betting man, I'd bet his son was also using steroids. Thank God, I never had sons to raise. Two girls were enough of a headache. But still, I don't condone his actions. I'm sorry you had to take a beating on it. I can't imagine the hell you went through."

Jack looked at him and thought if you only knew. The hell is still in progress.

Mr. Hollingsworth just stood there for a moment. Jack wondered whether he was going to invite them in or tell them to get off his property.

"Why don't you both come in?" he said generously. Mr. Hollingsworth led them to the living room. The hallways were extremely high and extremely long. The ceilings must have been twenty feet high and the hallways seemed to be as long as a football field. The walls were adorned with expensive paintings. There were also several sculptures in the hallway. Some were on pedestals and others were recessed in grottos. Both the paintings and the sculptures were Asian influenced.

They made it to the living room where they were instructed to sit. The room was exquisitely furnished, also with an Asian elegance and accentuated by a large fireplace.

"Mr. Hollingsworth, we are trying to locate Bob Lewis. We understand your daughter is, or was, married to him, and we would like to question her in order to get more information about him. We also understand she has moved back here with you. Is that correct?" asked Marnie.

"She's not here right now," he said rather cryptically. Jack and Marnie didn't know if it meant she lived there, but was not at home, or she didn't live there at all.

"Her mother and I hardly see her."

Just then Barbara entered the room.

35

They all stood up.

"Barbara! I didn't know you were here," Mr. Hollingsworth said with mock surprise.

"Dad, you're always trying to protect me," she said smiling and shaking her head.

"They're here to ask you some questions about Bob. They're from an investigative firm in Washington," he said pensively.

"Hello, Mrs. Lewis. I'm investigator Bloom and this is Investigator Dublin. We're with the WISE Investigative firm in Washington D.C.," Marnie said with a smile.

Jack looked at Marnie and wondered why she used the WISE name. It was the second time she had done it.

Barbara reached out and shook their offered hands. There was a moment of silence before Marnie seized the opportunity to get down to business.

"Ms. Lewis, could we have a moment to speak with you about your husband, in private?" she asked.

"Are you saying I can't be present during this conversation?" asked Mr. Hollingsworth indignantly.

"Dad, please. Let me talk with them in private," Barbara said pleadingly.

Mr. Hollingsworth looked at both Marnie and Jack with contempt and then walked briskly out of the room. Jack and Marnie looked at each other with raised eyebrows.

"Don't mind him. He's very protective, and he hates my husband for what he has done to me and my son," Barbara said defensively.

Marnie and Jack looked at each other again with surprise.

"Did I say something wrong?" Barbara asked.

Jack's mouth was open but before he could utter a word, Marnie spoke up.

"Our information indicated that you didn't have any children."

Jack looked at Marnie with the kind of look meant to stifle her from asking any more questions. When they talked strategy earlier, it had been agreed he would do the talking, and she would only supplement him if necessary, yet she was jumping in and taking the lead. Apparently, she forgot the plan. Maybe she was just nervous or maybe she had something to prove. Nevertheless, Jack was going to take control of the interview. Marnie caught his jaundiced eye look, and acquiesced.

Barbara smiled.

"That is the story Bob wanted everyone to believe, and he has been successful with it, but the real story is we have a son named Robert. I will never call him Robert Junior because he's much better than my..." she stopped and pondered her sentence, "husband. I just can't get used to the thought of Bob being my ex-husband."

"I'm assuming by the way you said it, that Robert must be living with you," Jack said.

"Yes and no," Barbara responded. "Robert is mentally and physically challenged. When he was young he caught a virus that still, to this day, hasn't been identified, and as a result he needs care around the clock.

"For Bob, it was devastating. He couldn't handle the fact that his son would never play baseball, go on fishing trips, get married or have children. Don't get me wrong, he wasn't the only one affected. It took me a long time to accept it, but through prayer and a couple of loving parents, I was able to survive.

"Bob, on the other hand, was destroyed. He just ran in the other direction. He was, and is, in denial. Our marriage started to crumble. I loved Bob and wanted to do whatever he needed to keep him happy. I would have done anything to keep our marriage alive. I thought maybe if I could find a place for Robert where he would be well cared for, at least until I could work on Bob to accept him, it would save our marriage. My parents told me about a place here in Delaware, which cares for people with disabilities. It's a beautiful place, staffed with wonderful, loving people. I knew Robert would be well cared for, and it would be close enough for me to visit."

"That must have been a tremendous burden on you," Marnie said with the compassion of someone who could relate on a deep level. She gave Jack a sad look.

"Yes. I have felt a great deal of guilt ever since I gave in to Bob's demand. He couldn't bear the sight of Robert at home. The sooner Robert became institutionalized the better chance we had at saving our marriage. Of course, I now know Bob would have never accepted Robert.

"I came up frequently to visit Robert. My parents, God bless them, have covered the expenses of Robert's stay and made a point to visit him almost every day. It proved to be difficult for my father, since he is the president of one of the largest banks in the world, but my mother visited often. They, of course, despised Bob for being so self-centered. I'm sure they weren't happy with me either for trying to keep the marriage alive.

"I wanted another child. I thought it might improve our situation. I asked Bob if he wanted another child but he refused. He was adamant. No more children. He was too scared to take a chance. He figured we might have another child with health issues."

"That must have been a tough time," Jack said supportively.

"I don't know if you could imagine the struggles I went through. I was trying to please everyone, which was impossible. Every day, I had difficulty looking at myself in the mirror. I suppressed my feelings until finally, I knew I had to do what was best for Barbara."

"Barbara, may I call you Barbara?" Jack asked.

"By all means," she answered.

"Barbara, I know it's been tough for you, and I imagine it became quite difficult to live with Bob with all this happening. Did he have any friends?"

"No, not really. We never went out to dinner with anyone. When we did go out, it was just by ourselves and that wasn't often."

"Did he ever go out by himself?" Jack asked.

"All the time. It got to where he would go out and not return until after I was asleep."

"Do you think he was seeing anyone?"

"You mean, like a woman?"

"Yes."

"Anything's possible, but I don't think so. I think he was just so lost that he wandered around in a fog."

"He had a boat, didn't he?"

"Oh yes, he loved that boat. In fact, I think that is where he went a lot of the time, when he was gone on weekends. He kept it in Maryland before he took it to the Caribbean."

"How were your finances, if you don't mind my asking?" Jack inquired diplomatically.

"You would think we had money since my parents paid for Robert, and we had two good jobs and no other children. My father could have made life easier for us, since he's so well off, but the fact of the matter is, he didn't like Bob and he wouldn't invest in us when Bob could reap some rewards if we divorced. Bob, on the other hand, had no problem asking my father for money. He asked him for loans a couple of times but was turned down. We were always struggling. For one thing, that boat was a huge drain on our finances."

"Did he ever discuss with you what his plan was when he retired?" Jack asked.

"He wanted to live in the Caribbean on the yacht. We traveled down there quite a bit."

"Where did he want to live?" Jack inquired.

"He always loved Montserrat, but when the volcano took place in '95 he shifted gears, yet he always vowed to return to Montserrat. He knew that island, and he always thought it would return to normalcy."

"Do you think that's where he is now?" Jack probed.

"I haven't spoken with him in a couple of months, but he said he was going to St. Lucia to live on the boat. He said if I wanted to join him I could. I told him I would never do that. I'm family-oriented, and I would miss being around Robert and my parents for long stretches.

They're getting older, you know what I mean? I just want to be here for Robert and my parents if they need me."

"Why did Bob mention St. Lucia?"

"After the volcano at Montserrat he started going to St. Lucia. A friend had told him about the island. He loved the people, the climate, the ocean and most of all his boat. He was always restless though. He wanted a bigger boat and he wanted to live in a huge house overlooking the ocean. He knew we would never be able to afford it, but he said he would find a way. That is what I always loved about Bob," Barbara said smiling. "For an FBI agent he was always filled with wanderlust. He was ill-suited for police work, at least in my mind. Problem was, I was never hung up on material things. I just dismissed it as an unrealistic dream, and I thought he would eventually realize it, too."

There was a pause in the conversation so Marnie asked permission to use the bathroom.

"Sure, it's down the hall to the left. You know where you came in, just to the left. Do you want me to show you?"

"No, that's alright. I think I can find it."

Marnie left the living room and made her way into the entrance foyer. She then went down the hallway taking in all the sights. There were expensive paintings and sculptures occupying the entire house. In some respects, it was like a museum. She prized a mosaic that covered an entire wall. The house had character, and she loved it.

Meantime, Jack picked up where he left off.

"Where did he keep his boat in St. Lucia?" asked Jack. This was the crucial information he wanted.

"He loved Marigot Bay, even though I told him it was too ritzy for me. My father didn't become extraordinarily wealthy until after I left for college. Believe me, I never wanted for anything, but I believe in working for what you have. I don't believe in taking handouts. I believe in the simple life."

"When did you notice anything different about him?"

"Like what specifically?"

"His behavior, like, did he start becoming secretive? For example, did he start making or taking phone calls in private? Did he get up in the middle of the night and leave the house? Did he seem to get angry over small things? Things like that."

"He always got calls, and sometimes left for days, but I just figured it was FBI business. I guess now that you mention it, it was becoming more frequent."

"What did he tell you when he left the FBI?"

"He said he decided to retire."

"That was it? He didn't say anything more?"

"He said he had a job offer with a high-end security outfit in Washington."

"Did you believe him?" Jack asked.

"I did. I didn't have any reason not to, at least not then. But his absences became frustrating. I couldn't handle that. I thought since he was no longer with the FBI, his absences would decrease. Instead they increased. Then, we started to argue more often. We started to sleep in different bedrooms. Finally, I told him I wanted a divorce. I was hoping it would change him. I thought if he really cared he would pay more attention."

"What happened next?"

"He said I was being foolish. I don't think he believed me."

"Have you filed for divorce?"

"Not yet," she said timidly reading Jack's mind. "My parents think I have. I know, I know. What am I waiting for? I guess I'm a hopeless romantic. One who believes that when you marry, it's for life."

"Yeah, but it doesn't have to be a life sentence," Jack quickly added.

"My feeling is, once you make a commitment, it is forever."

"I guess this is a religious belief?" Jack inquired.

"Yes. I'm a dyed-in-the-wool Catholic and proud of it," she said without reservation.

"Okay," Jack said quickly getting the conversation back to Bob. "Did you have any suspicious visitors at the house?"

"Just once. It was a guy who looked very country, if you know what I mean."

"Describe him."

"Well, he was about six feet tall and slender. He had a mustache that was long. I think his name was Duke."

"What did he want?"

"He asked for Bob and I invited him in, which I know is stupid, but he seemed to know Bob by the way he asked. I don't know, I just felt he must be an undercover officer or something. Anyway, I called for Bob and when he came downstairs, he asked me for privacy. He said they were going to the study. We had an office right to the left of the entrance foyer."

"When Bob came downstairs, did he seem surprised to see the guy? How did he react?"

"He wasn't surprised this man was at the house. He said hello and the guy's name, which I'm pretty sure was Duke because I remember thinking "John Wayne". Then Bob basically asked me to leave them alone."

"What was Bob's demeanor?"

"He didn't seem happy or surprised or angry. He just seemed... even."

"Did you hear any conversation?"

"I was tempted to go to the door and listen, but if Bob caught me, he would have been extremely angry."

"You say that like you've seen him angry."

"Believe me; you don't want to be around when he's angry. He's never hit me, but he can be quite intimidating. He will get in your face with the look of a crazed lunatic and yell. It scares me half to death."

"So, you think he's at Marigot Bay?" asked Jack.

"I don't know for sure, but I would imagine that's where he is."

"Is there any specific place, y'know like restaurant, bar or tackle place that he frequented?" Jack asked.

"He liked a restaurant named Da Vinci's. We went there for dinner a couple of times. He also talked with a man who owns a tackle shop there. His name is Captain Barney."

Jack wrote down Da Vinci's and Captain Barney.

. . .

While Barbara and Jack continued to talk, Marnie made her way to the bathroom. She made a wrong turn, and realized her mistake but heard Mr. Hollingsworth talking on the phone. He was in his study with the door ajar.

"I'm telling you he is right here, right now," he said in a hushed voice.

Marnie got closer to the door and listened. She knew he was talking about Jack.

"What do you want me to do?" he asked followed with several "Mmm hmm's. I guess that's why they call you 'Lucky'," he said with subtle laughter.

Marnie listened a few moments longer, but he was finishing his call so she hurried to the bathroom. Shortly after she closed the door, she heard footsteps go by the door towards the living room.

When Marnie returned to the living room, Mr. Hollingsworth was standing in the doorway.

"Excuse me," Marnie said as she tried to make entry into the living room.

"Oh, I'm sorry," he said as he moved out of the way. "Would anyone like a drink?"

"No, thank you," Marnie answered. "We must get going. Jack and I have a lot to do if we are going to catch up to your husband," she said looking at Barbara and then Jack.

Jack looked at her mystified.

"I don't mean to be meddlesome," Mr. Hollingsworth said as he began to chuckle. "Actually, I guess I do. What are your plans at this point, since Bob is probably out of the country?"

"That's a good question. We don't have the authority to bring him back here, but we would like to talk with him before the FBI does. We have a different agenda. We need to know about his involvement in a murder, in order to protect our client," Marnie said as she looked at Jack.

"Murder?" Barbara said in disbelief. She looked as if she had just been told of Bob's death.

"Yes, there was a homicide and he may be involved directly or indirectly. We don't know yet. That is why we want to talk to him," Jack said authoritatively.

"I can't say I'm surprised," Mr. Hollingsworth said. "He's a useless bastard."

"We really must be going," Marnie reiterated.

Jack stood up. Barbara got up slowly, still looking shocked by the earlier statement about Bob's involvement with a murder.

Mr. Hollingsworth walked them to the front door.

"Is there a number where you can be reached if I have any further information for you?" asked Mr. Hollingsworth.

Jack thought about it and then gave him his cell phone number. At this point, any information would help.

36

Jack and Marnie got into the car. They didn't talk until they hit the end of the driveway.

"What the hell is going on?" Jack asked angrily. "Why on earth did we have to leave on short notice? What the hell happened in the bathroom?"

"Which question do you want me to answer first?" Marnie retorted as she turned on to the highway.

"What happened to you back there?" Jack asked.

"When I went to the bathroom, I got lost. I mistakenly wandered down a hallway which apparently is where Mr. Hollingsworth's office is. I heard him on the phone. I don't know who he was talking to but he said, "They're here now." Then after a couple of "uh huhs" he said "I guess that's why you're called Lucky." Then after that he said "What do you want me to do?" I was going to listen further, but I was afraid he'd find out. So I went back down the hall and realized I had passed the bathroom. Shortly after I went in, I heard him pass by."

"Holy shit!" Jack said. "I wonder who he was talking to."

"I don't know, but I would think the way he talked about his son-in-law, it wasn't him."

"You're right about that. I think it's safe to say it's not the terrorists either. You know who that leaves."

"Yep, sure do. The police."

Just as Marnie said it, a marked Delaware State Police car went speeding past them on Rt. 52 with its flashers on. By now they were too far from the entrance to Selborne Drive, to see whether or not the trooper pulled in there. They weren't going to take a chance and go back.

"Maybe there's an accident further up the road he's responding to," Jack said, although his face indicated he believed otherwise.

Marnie gave him a doubtful look. They rode in silence. Neither one of them had anything to say. Jack was thinking and Marnie was nervous.

She decided to turn the radio on. It was tuned to a local rock station. Led Zeppelin was just finishing up with "Whole Lotta Love" as the local news came on.

"And now, this just in," the newscaster said. "Wilmington Police are investigating a homicide that occurred at the Hotel DuPont sometime last night. No further details are available at this time, but we will let you know as soon as more information becomes available. In other news, the largest cruise ship..."

Marnie turned off the radio.

"Oh my god!" Marnie said. "Jack, what are we going to do?"

"We didn't commit any murders last night," Jack said trying to calm himself down as well. "I've got to call Billy. I want to know who was killed, as well as any other information he can get for us. Do you remember the sinister-looking white guy in the bar last night?"

"Yeah, I do."

"I had a feeling he was watching us, but didn't want to say anything because I didn't want to upset you."

"Do you think it's wise to call Billy?" Marnie asked.

"At this point, we don't have a choice. Give me your phone."

Marnie handed him her cell phone but not before asking, "Why aren't you using your phone?"

"Just in case they have a trace in place."

She gave him the phone, wondering why earlier he said his was untraceable. Jack dialed Billy's cell phone number. After a couple of rings Billy answered.

"This is Billy," he said.

"Billy, this is Jack," Jack said with a serious business tone. "I need a favor."

"What do you need?" Billy asked helpfully.

"There was a murder last night at the Hotel DuPont in Wilmington, Delaware."

"Jack, I know where the Hotel DuPont is. You don't have to tell me it's in Wilmington."

"Seriously, Billy. I need you to contact the Wilmington Police and find out what you can about the murder."

"What specifically do you want to know?"

"Find out the sex, ethnic origin, room number and method used on the victim. Was it a knife? A gun? If so, what caliber and where it struck the victim? Can you do that?"

"I'll see what I can do. I may have to make something up, but I'll see what I can find out. Are you okay?"

"I've been better and I've been worse. Can you expedite this, Billy? I need to know as soon as I can."

"Let me get on it right now and I'll call you back. Still the same number?"

"Yeah, use this one."

They hung up. Jack gave Marnie her phone back and then told her how to get to the Concord Pike. He wanted to get out of the Greenville area as soon as they could. They went on the back roads.

"Where are we going?" Marnie asked.

"I'm hungry. We're going to get something to eat and think this out."

Once they were on the Concord Pike they traveled to the Charcoal Pit Restaurant. It was a well-established and very popular local restaurant that was insanely busy on nights and weekends during the school year. It was just a little quieter now in the summer. Jack figured if the police were looking for them, it would be best to be in a heavy traffic area so they could blend in.

The hostess showed them to their booth. Jack couldn't help but smile. He remembered all the times he had been to the Pit, as it was known, after his high school games with a variety of friends. It was the place to be seen.

"From the smile on your face, I can see this brings back memories," Marnie said.

"Oh yeah, it does," Jack said.

"I'm glad to see it has taken your mind off our situation," she said seriously.

It brought Jack back to reality. They ordered sandwiches and drinks, and then talked strategy.

"What are you thinking?" Marnie asked.

"I'm thinking we need to get back to Washington as soon as possible."

"Why?"

"What else are we gonna do? Bob is out of the country. We have no way to get down there without getting caught. And we have no idea what happened at the hotel last night. The way my luck has been going, I want to be as far away as possible."

"It's not going to change the fact that we were there last night. They're going to find that out when they check the guest list. You know they're going to try and interview us."

"They have your name, not mine."

"Not exactly."

"What?"

"I had to put your name down for your room."

"Why did you do that?"

"They required it."

"You paid for it."

"I did, but they needed to know the occupant's name for the other room."

"And you gave them *my* name?"

"I had to. You're Larry Whitwell, aren't you?"

Jack laughed. At least she was smart enough not to put his real name down on the guest list.

"How'd you come up with that name?"

"I met him when I lived in Atlanta. He was a firefighter."

Just then their food arrived. Neither one of them wasted any time eating their food. They were both hungry. They didn't talk for a few minutes perhaps realizing they had to eat fast and get back on the road.

Jack's phone vibrated.

"Jack?"

"Yeah, it's me, Billy. What have you got?"

Marnie sat there wondering why Billy didn't call on her phone.

"The victim's name, this is kinda confusing. First, they told me the guy's name was Larry Whitwell, but the detective I was speaking to got interrupted and corrected himself, and then said the victim's name was Henry Schneider. He was shot in the head with a 9 mm. They think the perp may have been using a suppressor because so far nobody heard anything."

Jack was speechless. He had a worrisome look on his face. Marnie looked at him with concern. He looked as if he swallowed something that tasted terrible or like he was having a heart attack. She could hear Billy on the phone in the background calling Jack's name.

"Jack," Marnie said. "JACK!"

Jack came back to earth.

"Okay, Billy, thanks a lot."

"Jack, there's something else I need to tell you. Keane and Bucci are on their way to Delaware. They heard you're up in Wilmington asking questions. Don't ask me how, but they did. I swear it wasn't me. You know if it was, why would I tell you and why would I call the Wilmington Police for the information on the hotel homicide? Jack, you gotta get back here before Keane and Bucci find you."

"Okay, Billy, thanks a lot." Jack ended the call.

"What's going on Jack?" Marnie wanted to know.

"The victim at the hotel last night was named Schneider."

"So?"

"After I walked you to your room, I went to mine. Only I made a mistake and went to the wrong room. The maid opened the door just as I was getting ready to put the key in the slot. She thought my name was Schneider since it was his room."

"Okay, so you had the wrong room."

"Not just that, but as she called me Mr. Schneider," Jack changed his thought. "Do you remember the sinister white man I bumped into as we left the front desk?"

"Yeah I remember him. He was one of the men in the bar last night we already talked about."

"Yeah, that's him. Well as I was trying to get into Mr. Schneider's room by mistake, the guy I bumped into at check-in was approaching me and put his hand in his pocket. I thought he was getting a key out because he was on the same floor, but he walked past me when the maid appeared at the door and kept going. He wasn't on the same floor. I didn't think anything about it until now. He was going to kill me! Instead, he must have backtracked and killed Henry Schneider by mistake."

"That's a pretty stiff penalty for bumping into someone," Marnie said trying to get Jack to loosen up. It didn't change his demeanor at all.

"I wonder who sent him," Jack said as if speaking to himself.

"All I know, Jack, is we have to get back to Washington. This is getting crazier by the minute."

"Speaking of crazy, Billy told me Keane and Bucci are on their way to Wilmington."

"How come? Do they know you're here?"

"Apparently so."

"How would they get that information?"

"Don't ask me, but they did."

"I think Billy dimed you out," Marnie said disgustedly.

"I don't think so. If he did, why would he give me that information, and why did he call the Wilmington Police for us to give us information on the homicide?"

Marnie shrugged. There were so many unanswered questions.

"I think we need to go back to the hotel," Jack said seriously.

Marnie looked at him like he had three heads.

"Are you nuts?"

"I don't mean to check in," Jack said to clarify. "Let's just park in the garage across the street, and go sit in the bar. The police are not going to know we were registered guests last night."

"What is this going to prove?" she asked.

"I want to see what's going on. Maybe we can get some intel."

"Like what?"

"I don't know, but I do know I don't know anybody here, so I think we're pretty safe."

"The risk isn't worth the reward. In fact, you haven't said what we are going to get out of it. Don't forget Keane and Bucci are on their way." Marnie reminded him.

"Listen, all I know is somebody set me up, and somebody is trying to kill me. Whoever killed Henry Schneider is probably long gone. Until he hears the true victim's identity revealed, he's satisfied I'm dead, so I don't think we'll have to worry about him."

"I still don't know why we should go back there."

"I don't know exactly either, but something is pulling me there. I need to go there and observe. Somehow I think someone is going to appear that's going to help me solve the puzzle."

"So, we're going back there on a hunch?"

"Something like that."

"A dangerous hunch if you ask me. I think we're going into the lion's den, but hey, you're the cop with the experience."

Jack's phone rang. He figured it was Billy with more information.

"Hello," Jack answered.

"Jack, this is Peter Hollingsworth. Do you have a minute?"

"Yes, I do," Jack said as he mouthed "Peter Hollingsworth" to Marnie.

She looked confused at first not knowing what Jack was trying to say, but shortly the light went on and she mouthed "Oh" and nodded her head.

"Jack, I know you and Ms. Bloom want to get Bob in the worst way. I assure you, not any more than I do. The sooner he's in jail, the sooner my daughter will wake up and realize what a no-good son-of-a-bitch he is, and extricate herself from him. With that in mind, I want to offer my plane to fly you both down to St. Lucia."

"Mr. Hollingsworth, I'm overwhelmed."

"Don't be. I am a wealthy man. I earned it the right way. I worked for it and as a result, I am able to take certain liberties that are not available to many people. I want to do this. I want to help bring my prick son-in-law to justice."

Jack's mind was racing.

"Why are you helping us, and not the FBI?"

"Quite frankly, I thought about it but I'm afraid someone he may still be friendly with would tip him off."

"We don't have passports with us."

"That won't be necessary. The Prime Minister owes me a favor. I helped his country with some banking situations, and he has not forgotten it. I just hung up from him a few moments ago. He assured me safe passage for you and Ms. Bloom for the next forty-eight hours."

"I will need to take my weapons with me. I'm sure he won't like that."

"You're right. He didn't, but when I explained the situation he was finally persuaded. Let's just say my banking prestige will come in handy at the conclusion of this little event."

"I don't know what to say. I'll have to talk with Ms. Bloom."

"Why don't you ask her right now? I'm sure she's sitting right there. I'll hold on."

"We'll have to talk it over. It's going to take more than a few minutes."

"Alright. Call me back. Do you have my number?"

"Yes sir, I do."

"Very well, I will be waiting for your call."

Jack ended the call and looked at Marnie.

"You're not going to believe it."

"What?"

"That was Mr. Hollingsworth as I'm sure you figured out. He wants to fly you and me down to St. Lucia in his private jet."

"Wow! Talk about service," she said. "But wait, how can we trust him? He's the one who was informing someone about our presence, and the next thing you know a State Police car goes zooming past us in the direction of the Hollingsworth house."

"We don't know, of course, that the police were headed to his house either," Jack added.

"Well, that's true but c'mon. What are the chances?"

"I don't know what to do now."

They sat in silence for a few moments before Marnie made an excuse to go to the restroom.

Jack sat there, grateful for a few moments alone, so he could think things through. He truly didn't know where to turn. He was finding it difficult to place his trust in anyone except Marnie at this point.

"Did you get any more phone calls while I was gone?" she asked nonchalantly as she returned.

"No," Jack answered. "Thank God. I don't need any more calls to confuse me."

"Y'know, I think we should take Mr. Hollingsworth up on his offer." Marnie said.

"That's not what you said before," Jack said confused.

"I've given it more thought, and I think we should go with it."

"What changed your mind?"

"Just a hunch. You get hunches, don't you?" she added teasingly.

"Yeah, but I have a cop background. You don't."

"I'm still allowed to think that way. Just call mine women's intuition."

"Yeah, I guess. What if it's a set-up and there are cops there to arrest me?"

"I wouldn't worry about it."

"That's easy for you to say. You're not on trial."

"True, but maybe I know what I'm talkin' about since I'm not on trial. Trust me. I won't let anything happen to you."

Jack wanted to believe it.

37

"Gentlemen, I'd like you to meet Detectives Keane and Bucci. They're from the Washington D.C. Metro P.D." Lt. Collins said as he made the introduction to Detectives Steve Rosiak and Earl Cook. They all shook hands and sized each other up like dogs sniffing each other the first time they meet. Every police agency thinks they're the best.

They were at Delaware State Police Troop 2 on U.S. Rt. 40 which is the investigative headquarters in New Castle County for the State Police. It was one of the newest troop buildings in the state. In actuality, Jack and Marnie were suspected to be closer to Troop 1 Penny Hill, north of Wilmington, which was about twenty miles away, but Troop 2 had the investigators who would escort Keane and Bucci around. They weren't aware Selborne Drive was not in the State Police jurisdiction. It's where they were ordered to report when they got to Delaware.

Lt. Collins was a fifteen-year veteran who delegated responsibilities to his squad. If you were going to pick a poster boy for tall, good-looking with a well-toned physique, he was straight from central casting. He selected Rosiak and Cook to assist, not just because they were good investigators, but because they were the only detectives on his squad who had worked at Troop 1 as patrol officers, and were familiar with the area. Everyone else on his squad was from Troop 6 or downstate.

Rosiak and Cook were not pleased with the assignment. They had caseloads to manage and didn't have the time to cart around a couple of detectives from out of state. They reluctantly complied. Besides, they had no choice.

"You guys need some coffee?" Lt. Collins asked.

"I could use a cup," Bucci answered.

"I'm good, but if you could point me in the direction of the restroom, I would greatly appreciate it," Keane said. "The two-hour ride has done a job on my kidneys."

"Sure, go down the hallway and it's on the right," Rosiak instructed.

"Thanks," Keane replied and headed in that direction.

"The coffee is over there," Cook pointed out to Bucci.

"Thanks," Bucci said. He poured himself a styrofoam cup full of coffee and then added three sugars. After stirring it, he returned to the spot where Rosiak, Cook, and Collins were standing. He felt like they were staring at him, but he didn't care. Most likely he would never see these guys again. Shortly after he walked over, Keane returned.

"Guys, why don't you take them to the conference room, and let them tell you why they're here, and what they need from us? Give them all the help you can," Lt. Collins advised Rosiak and Cook. He turned to Keane and Bucci and shook their hands. "Gentlemen, I'm glad the Delaware State Police can help you out. If there is anything else you need, you just let me know."

With that he turned and disappeared behind a door which undoubtedly was his office. Bucci thought he sounded like a public service announcement. He was probably all spit and polish and no substance. He figured that's the way it works everywhere. The pretty boys always get promoted and leave the shit details to everyone else.

They walked to the conference room which was located through a set of double doors and down a hallway. They went in and sat down on opposite sides of the conference table. The room was sparsely decorated with only a few pictures of DSP ranking officers. Computer connections for laptops were situated in the middle of the table. Keane thought it was a bit antiquated even for his department.

Rosiak looked to be in his late thirties. His clothes appeared to come off the shelf of a department store. His shirt was too big, even though his girth pushed the limits around the waist. Home cooking, and a wife who watched the budget, seemed to be his current lot in life. His wedding ring confirmed his marital status.

Cook, on the other hand, was not wearing a wedding band. He looked to be in his early thirties and just from his cockiness, you could tell he probably was the type who would never settle down, at least not for long. His designer clothes showed he took great pride in how he impressed others.

Their guns were Smith & Wesson M & P 9 mm. Rosiak wore his on his belt, and Cook had his in a shoulder holster.

"Okay, how can we help you?" asked Rosiak in an indifferent tone.

Keane took the lead. "We're looking for a man by the name of Jack Dublin. He is in the company of a woman by the name of Marnie Bloom. They're traveling in a BMW with DC plates bearing CAM-618. We think they're here because they want to question a Barbara Lewis about a homicide in which Dublin is a suspect. He has been charged with conspiracy. He's at the very least an accomplice, and may even be the trigger man."

Keane paused before continuing.

"He's not allowed to leave Washington. He's got a million dollar bail on him," Keane said firmly.

"Isn't that what bail bondsmen do? They go after people who jump bail. Why are you here?" Rosiak asked as he leaned towards them trying not to show any disrespect.

"We need to get him back to Washington to avoid an embarrassing situation for our department. While it may not be illegal to mount a defense, he has violated a court order by breaching the terms of his bail," Keane stated, feeling like he was on the witness stand.

"Okay, but guys jump bail all the time. Why would your department send you to get him? I still don't quite understand the dilemma," Rosiak said.

"Normally that's what happens, but when you shoot a U.S. senator's son, you get a lot more attention," Keane answered strongly.

"Wait a minute, I remember reading about that," Cook said eagerly as he leaned forward in his chair. "I pay close attention to police shootings and that was a big one. It had all the ramifications of political intrigue. A rape in progress, followed by a shooting in self-defense of a senator's son who was high on drugs by an off-duty police officer.

Sounds like good police work to me. Who cares if the dirt ball was a senator's son?" Cook said. "Besides, I thought Dublin was cleared."

Keane was trying not to get frustrated.

"He was, on those charges. I'm not trying to be argumentative. Jack Dublin was someone who I worked with on the department. I respected Jack but this is not about the senator's son shooting. Jack is potentially involved in a weapons deal with terrorists. There was another shooting where a Pentagon official's son was murdered. That is what the one million dollar bail is about. That's why we're here. It just so happens, my bosses want to get Jack back to avoid another black eye in the press," Keane explained.

Bucci spoke up. "Imagine if someone on your department shot somebody in a high profile setting. Whether it was a good shooting or not, makes no difference. The media will paint whatever picture they want. Most of the time, it's the cops that are made to look bad. You know that. Now suppose your officer is vindicated, but the press still is not convinced, and then he goes out and gets involved in another questionable shooting within a few months. Don't you think your brass would want his ass?"

Rosiak and Cook were nodding simultaneously as they pondered the scenario.

"How do you know he's in Delaware?" Rosiak asked.

"We got a tip from someone. He is believed to be somewhere in an area called Greenville at the Hollingsworth home."

"Peter Hollingsworth?" Rosiak asked.

"Yes." Keane answered. "Why, do you know him?"

"I know of him. He's one of the biggest employers in the state. He's a president of a bank and is known for his donations to local charitable causes. He is very well liked, from the little guy on the street to every starched shirt in every boardroom in Delaware."

There was a pause in the conversation; Cook finally spoke up.

"What do you want us to do?"

"Have you put out a BOLO?"

"Yes, we did to all the troops. Once before the morning shift, and there will be another one put out before the afternoon shift. Also, we made contact with the city and county police, and gave them the information."

"Any luck yet?" Keane asked already knowing the answer.

"Not yet, but you never know." Cook answered. "It all depends on manpower. Quite frankly, it's like finding a rare fish in the ocean. Guys on patrol don't usually pay attention to BOLO's, because they figure it's old news and the targets are long gone."

"Do you think we could take a ride up to the Hollingsworth home?" Keane asked.

"Yeah, we can do that," Rosiak responded. "Is there anything else we need to know? Never mind. We'll talk on the way up. Let's go."

They all got up from the table simultaneously. Bucci drained his coffee. They went to the parking lot and got in a Crown Victoria. It had nice cloth seats so Keane and Bucci got to ride in style. Their cars were beat to hell.

During the drive to the Hollingsworth house, Keane and Bucci apprised Rosiak and Cook of all the details of the shootings. Then they talked about general cop topics. How big is your department? What are your service weapons? What was the pay scale? They talked about the difference in policing from a state point of view to a large city point of view. Cook was asking questions about Washington and the politicians, like he thought it was Hollywood. Keane and Bucci told him they had never had to deal with politicians before until Jack killed the senator's son. They met Senator Rothschild once during the investigation. He seemed pleasant enough under the circumstances, but they knew from the constant questions coming from their supervisors that he was applying the maximum pressure.

"What about the girl?" Rosiak asked.

"You mean, Marnie?" Keane asked in return.

"Is that her name? The one who's with Dublin?"

"Yeah, that's her. We don't know too much about her. Apparently she graduated from college, applied for the Secret Service and did not meet their qualifications for some reason. She was living in Atlanta with a fireman who was married but separated. He, at least they say, committed suicide. But from what we can determine, it wasn't an open and shut case. She became a person of interest since she was present at the time it occurred. She was questioned, but ultimately no charges were filed."

"How did she get involved in this case?" Cook asked.

"She apparently works for one of the most prestigious law firms in Washington, and she has been assigned to keep an eye on Jack."

Rosiak turned the car onto Selborne Drive. He turned his head to inform Keane and Bucci they were almost there, advising them to allow him to make the introductions, and then he would turn the interview over to them. Shortly thereafter, they pulled into the driveway.

They got out and walked up to the impressive doors and knocked loudly. Mr. Hollingsworth answered the door looking exasperated. Before Rosiak could say anything, Mr. Hollingsworth spoke.

"Don't tell me, let me guess," he said cynically. "You're with the Boy Scouts, and you want to sell me something, or maybe you're police officers looking for a man named Jack Dublin. Which is it?"

"I'm Detective Rosiak, and this is Detective Cook, and we're with the Delaware State Police. These gentlemen are with the Washington D.C. Metropolitan Police. This is Detective Keane and this is Detective Bucci."

Each of them had their I.D. folders out with pictures and badges to prove their identity. Clearly they were not happy with Mr. Hollingsworth, but they were mindful of where they were. Smart-ass comments like that in another part of the county would have resulted in a physical confrontation, but this was Greenville, land of the millionaires and billionaires. Plus Mr. and Mrs. Hollingsworth were friends of the governor.

"Is it possible we could come in and talk with you about Jack Dublin?"

"I'm sorry, but I have already been delayed twice, and quite frankly I have things to do," he responded. "Like I told the other policeman..."

"Wait, what other policeman?" Rosiak asked interrupting.

"The State Trooper who was here earlier."

"There was a Delaware State Trooper here earlier?"

"Yes, I told him that Jack Dublin was here a couple of hours ago. Listen, I really have to get going," he said as started to walk out the door towards the driveway.

"Mr. Hollingsworth, did you get the trooper's name?"

Mr. Hollingsworth gave them a sarcastic smile. "You have to be kidding me. I can't even remember your names."

Rosiak turned to Cook and asked him to check with RECOM, to find out who was there earlier.

Keane intervened. "Mr. Hollingsworth, with all due respect, my partner and I came up here all the way from Washington. Mr. Dublin is a potentially dangerous person. We'd like to ask you a few questions."

"I understand completely. Call my office and we will schedule an appointment early next week."

"That may not be soon enough."

"It's the best I can do. Now, if you'll excuse me," Mr. Hollingsworth said, just as a limo pulled up into the driveway. He started to walk towards the limo, where a driver had come around to open the door.

"Steve, a vehicle matching the description has just been spotted on the Concord Pike in the vicinity of the Concord Mall," Cook yelled as he relayed the information to the group.

Mr. Hollingsworth turned his head as he heard the news, and then said to them, "Good luck."

The detectives walked quickly back to their car and got in. Detective Rosiak got on the radio.

"Recom, have that unit standby until I get there."

"10-4," Recom responded.

"Also Recom, send any available units for back-up."

"Be advised, there are no other units available," Recom replied.

"10-4." Rosiak answered as he looked at Cook. "Let's haul ass."

Detective Cook floored it and they were on their way.

For the first time since they arrived, Keane and Bucci were keyed up.

The limo slowly pulled out of the driveway, ahead of the detectives, and meandered down the road. As soon as they approached the Kennett Pike, the limo turned south and so did the detectives. They thought about passing the limo, but they didn't want to irritate Mr. Hollingsworth any more than they already had. He was a powerful man who could pick up the phone and make life miserable for them.

Instead they waited, and as soon as they could they turned onto a back road, and sped towards the Concord Pike.

When they arrived to meet with the patrol unit, they discovered the suspected car was not the matching plate. It was an Ohio plate, which looks similar. Another patrol unit rolled up as they stood there. Rosiak immediately told the two patrol units to start checking parking lots along the Concord Pike advising them not to duplicate their efforts. He told them he was going to go to the other end and start his way north. They would start just south of the Fairfax Shopping Center.

The Charcoal Pit was located across the street from the Fairfax Shopping Center.

38

Jack looked at Marnie, trying to determine his next move. On the one hand, Jack wanted to trust Mr. Hollingsworth enough to get on the jet and fly to St. Lucia. On the other hand, he didn't know if Mr. Hollingsworth was working with the police, and was leading him into a trap that would snare him long before he left the country. It was exhausting to think about everything.

"I don't know if I'm ready to accept his offer, based on what you heard when he was on the phone, back at his house," Jack said.

"What's the alternative?"

"I don't know," Jack said as the waitress returned and asked if they wanted anything else.

Jack looked at Marnie and smiled.

"I think we're wasting time, especially if Keane and Bucci are on their way," Marnie said with conviction.

"I wish I had time for one of your hot fudge sundaes but I think I'll pass. We'll just take the check please," Jack said to the waitress before turning to Marnie. "Look, right now I am like the needle in the haystack. They don't know Delaware. I need time to think about the situation. Part of me says to go back to Washington, and let them try to prove their bullshit case with what they have."

"I don't think that is the best philosophy, right now. You didn't do anything wrong and look at you. You're the person in everyone's sights. If you're innocent...and, I believe you are or else I wouldn't be here, we need to find Bob Lewis. C'mon Jack, don't you have any balls?"

Jack glared at her.

"Sorry Jack, I didn't mean it that way. I'm just trying to get you moving in the right direction."

"Don't misinterpret deliberate thought before action as a lack of balls. I want to make the right choice. I already fucked up once. I should have thought more about taking the surveillance job that landed me here in the first place. I should have said to myself, 'Jack, why the hell is someone you haven't talked to in several years so concerned about you that he's offering you a job?' If I had taken the time to think it through, I would have smelled the skunk."

"Jack, you had just been involved in a devastating shooting. Your head wasn't screwed on right. You were still trying to get over the death of a young man."

"Y'know, shooting and killing the senator's son is not what's bothering me so much. It was a good shooting. It's these last shootings that I had nothing to do with. My brother officers stabbed me in the back. I'll never forget it."

"Jack, that's all the more reason to find Bob Lewis. He is another police officer who set you up. We need to find him. We need to bring him to justice and clear your name."

Jack's phone rang.

"Jack?" asked an excited Peter Hollingsworth.

"Yeah, this is him."

"Where are you?" he asked with obvious concern.

"I'm in the area of Concord Pike."

"Jack, you need to let me pick you up right now, and take you to the airport. You need to get on my plane – now! I hope you're not near the Concord Mall. There were a couple of detectives from D.C. at my house five minutes ago. They were with two Delaware State Police detectives. They think you are at the Concord Mall, and they are on their way there now. You need to get out as soon as possible."

As the waitress brought the check, Jack looked at Marnie. She could see the alarm on his face. She knew it was serious.

Jack finally realized it was getting too dangerous to stay in one place. He reached in his pocket for some cash as he motioned Marnie to get up because they were leaving.

"Do you know where the old Merchandise Mart is on Governor Printz?" Jack asked.

"Yes, I do," Mr. Hollingsworth answered.

"Meet us there in a half hour."

"I'm on my way."

Jack ended the call as he threw a few dollars on the table. He instructed Marnie to go get the car. He would bring her up to date when they were on their way. She left and he paid the bill. She pulled up out front, and he got in the car. Once he was seated, he reached back into his bag, and felt around to make sure his ammunition was there. Then he realized his weapons were in the trunk. He didn't carry his guns and ammunition together in case he got stopped. It was illegal to have a gun with ammunition in close proximity. He wasn't going to take any chances.

Until now.

He made Marnie pull over into the Fairfax Shopping Center parking lot, as he discreetly got out and grabbed his gym bag. He took out his Sig Sauer 9 mm. Once he was belted in, he instructed Marnie to drive on while he made sure his gun was loaded. It would only take fifteen minutes to get to their destination. He wanted time to evaluate the situation before Mr. Hollingsworth arrived. Jack anticipated the police may be there. As they approached the Merchandise Mart, he had her slow down. When they came down the hill he would be able to determine the layout, and if police were there, without giving away their identity.

As they came down Edgemoor Road, Jack looked over and saw two New Castle County Police vehicles parked next to each other, pointing in opposite directions. Jack couldn't be sure if they were waiting for him, or if they were doing what a lot of cops do, sitting there talking. He didn't want to take any chances, so he told Marnie to make a left into Edgemoor Terrace, a small residential community. As they did, he turned around, looking back to see if they noticed the car and if they were coming after him. They didn't move.

Jack told Marnie to pull over on a side street while he called Mr. Hollingsworth.

"Mr. Hollingsworth?" Jack asked as the phone was answered.

"Go ahead, Jack."

"We can't meet at the Merchandise Mart. There are two County cops sitting there probably writing reports, but I am not taking any chances. How about meeting us at Sears on Market St.?"

"It's not a Sears anymore. It's the State Department of Labor, but I can meet you there. It's right across from the Wilmington Drama League."

"Okay, where are you now?" Jack asked to gauge the time.

"We just crossed over the Concord Pike onto Murphy Rd."

"I'll see you soon," Jack said.

Jack gave directions to Marnie to get them to the old Sears parking lot. On the way there, he told Marnie his plan. He still didn't trust Mr. Hollingsworth because of the phone call Marnie overheard when they were back at his house.

He told her that she was going to get out at the entrance facing the Drama League. Jack was going to drive to a location that still gave him an observation point. He would be able to detect if he was being set up. Marnie would be in no danger. It was Jack they wanted.

He told Marnie to get in the limousine, to make sure there were no authorities to arrest him, or anyone else associated with Bob Lewis to harm him. He would then follow them from a distance, while talking with her on the phone ensuring their safety. Once they got to the airport, he could assess the situation further. If it was clear, he would drive up and get on the plane with her. Marnie agreed.

He dropped Marnie off, drove across the street and parked next to the service entrance of the Drama League, allowing him a total view of Marnie. He decided to call Marnie.

When Marnie answered, he told her to keep her phone alive with his call. Jack told her he wanted to hear any discussions in the limo. He instructed her to keep it down by her side, inconspicuous. If she wanted to at some point, she could tell Mr. Hollingsworth she wanted to call Jack.

Shortly afterwards, Jack saw her put her phone down by her side. Their call was still active. He could hear street noise.

Then he saw a black stretch limo pull up. He saw the driver get out and approach her. He heard him ask her to get in. She walked over to the door which was now open, and she got in. Mr. Hollingsworth was the only occupant.

"Where's Jack?" asked Mr. Hollingsworth somewhat surprised.

"He's going to meet us there."

"How does he know which hangar is mine?" he said irately. "He's going to screw things up!"

"Don't worry. You should never underestimate Jack Dublin," Marnie said. "If you don't mind, I'd like to call him now."

"Yes, get him on the phone."

Marnie acted like she was dialing Jack's number.

"Hi Jack," Marnie said.

"You're doing great," Jack said. "I'm right behind you. Is there anyone else in the car with you other than Mr. Hollingsworth?"

"No."

"Let me talk to him," Mr. Hollingsworth insisted reaching for the phone.

"Jack, where are you?"

"Don't worry Mr. Hollingsworth, I'm right behind you."

Mr. Hollingsworth turned to look out the back window. He could see the BMW several cars behind in traffic. They were headed north instead of south towards I-495. It meant they were headed back in front of the Merchandise Mart where the county cops were.

"Why didn't you come with Marnie?"

"Let's just say I'm a very careful man, Mr. Hollingsworth. Why are we headed north instead of south? Isn't the New Castle Airport in the opposite direction?"

"Yes, Jack, it is, but I don't like to travel through the east part of town so we are headed back to the Edgemoor exit, and then south on I-495."

Just as Mr. Hollingsworth said, they turned onto southbound I-495. Traffic was heavy but Jack stayed fairly close.

"Jack, I can't believe you don't trust me. Why would I give you access to my plane? Why would I make arrangements for you in St.

Lucia? If I wanted to get you back to the Washington police, I could have done that already."

"I'll trust you completely when I set foot in St. Lucia."

It wasn't long before they got off at the Rt. 13 Southbound exit. Traffic was very heavy. This time of year, cars were everywhere, heading to the beach. Rt. 13 was always clogged, yet this time there was an accident causing traffic to back up. They were crawling along as they approached the accident at Rt. 13 and Bacon Avenue, a hotspot for accidents. It was just as Jack suspected. There was only one lane open and traffic was crawling.

Once they were past the accident, Mr. Hollingsworth's driver sped up to get to the airport. Jack was still stuck in the traffic jam. As he approached the accident, he couldn't help but look to see if there was anyone hurt. As he slowly approached the intersection, he noticed several troopers at the scene. They seemed to be discussing the accident when one turned away from Jack, but then looked back as if to double-check his tag.

As soon as Jack got past, he looked in his rearview mirror and noticed all of them looking at his vehicle.

He knew it was a matter of time before one of them broke off and tried to stop him. Jack sped up. He hoped there wasn't another trooper up ahead. By now, Jack could barely see the limousine and didn't know what to do. He knew the main terminal entrance was not the one he should use as he lost sight of Mr. Hollingsworth's limo.

"Where are you now?" Jack asked into the phone, but quickly realized their connection was lost.

He looked in his rear view, and in the distance he could see flashing lights, but he wasn't sure if it was the state troopers at the accident, or if one was coming in his direction. He continued to look back and finally realized one of the troopers had left the scene of the accident to come after him. It was still at least a mile back.

Jack quickly dialed Marnie's phone and got her voice mail. He was starting to panic. He tried her again and this time got through.

"Marnie, where are you?"

"Jack, let me give the phone to Mr. Hollingsworth," she answered.

Jack looked in the rear view mirror and realized the trooper was gaining on him.

"Jack, once you pass the airport, there is a small access road that will bring you to my hangar. Turn before you get to the Burger King. The jet is on the tarmac ready to go."

Soon Jack saw the access road and turned right. He didn't use his signal. Jack was now heading towards the hangars on the other side of the airport. As he headed up the access road, he looked in his rear view mirror and saw the trooper pass the access road, but he knew it wouldn't be long before the trooper backtracked.

Jack was halfway down the road when he noticed a jet with a black limousine next to it. He slammed on his brakes and backed up to turn in the gate. As soon as he got through the gate, an employee closed it to prevent anyone from getting further access. He drove up the ramp, and as soon as he got to the top, he saw Marnie talking with Mr. Hollingsworth.

He turned the car off, reached in the backseat and grabbed his bag containing his guns and ammunition. He got out and ran toward them. Mr. Hollingsworth yelled at Jack to give the keys to a huge man who was running in his direction. Jack fought the urge to pull his gun. He took a defensive stance. Once Jack realized he was not an enemy, he gave him the keys.

Jack walked over to Marnie and Mr. Hollingsworth. The noise of the jet engine made it difficult to hear what was being said. As he approached them, Mr. Hollingsworth turned to him and said,

"Listen Jack, when you get to St. Lucia, a man will come on board to check your passports. Of course you don't have them, but don't worry. He is a friend of the Prime Minister who will acknowledge your invisible passports once you get off the plane."

"You're not coming with us?" Jack shouted.

"No. My job was to get you on this plane. My job is done. Just make sure you get that son-of-a-bitch. I don't care if he's dead or alive," Mr. Hollingsworth yelled back.

Jack looked at him and then they shook hands.

"Hurry up. We don't know how close the State Police are," Mr. Hollingsworth said.

Jack turned and followed Marnie onto the G650 Gulfstream Corporate jet. They taxied and within five minutes they were airborne headed toward St. Lucia.

39

Once they were airborne, they both let out a sigh of relief. Their biggest task was ahead of them but for now they needed to relax. For the next four and a half hours they were away from trouble.

Jack had never been on a private jet. He was amazed how roomy it was. Now he realized why executives craved the perks and fought to keep them. The Gulfstream 650 had a capacity of nineteen passengers. It had a range of over 7000 miles and a cruising speed of up to 560 miles per hour.

The attendant came up to him and Marnie, and asked what they wanted to drink. Marnie ordered water and Jack ordered a beer.

They sat across from each other. Jack couldn't help but smile as he looked out the window. They were now over the Atlantic Ocean. Marnie looked tired. Jack was wide awake, at least for now.

"Why don't you go to sleep Marnie," Jack suggested. He had to hand it to her. She had stuck by him during this whole ordeal. As he thought about the last few days, he realized she had been in harm's way also. She never complained. She was pretty tough.

"Jack, I am beat, and I probably will fall asleep soon, but we need to discuss strategy first."

"I've been thinking about it. I guess we have to rent a car to get around, and we have to find a place to stay," Jack said.

"Actually, that's all been taken care of."

"Really? How did you book a car and a place to stay already?"

"I didn't. Mr. Hollingsworth has a place in St. Lucia, and his driver is picking us up at the airport."

"How'd you know that?"

"He told me while we were on our way to the airport."

"That guy is unbelievable. Still, I am not feeling real safe with him."

"Yeah, I can't disagree there."

"Well, once we're situated, we need to find that Barney guy, and see if he can lead us in the direction of Bob Lewis," Jack said.

"True, but we probably won't get to St. Lucia in time to find him today, because when we get there it will be close to nine o'clock p.m.," Marnie said.

"I guess we'll get something to eat and then find him in the morning."

"Sounds like a plan," Marnie said with a yawn.

The attendant brought their drinks and then disappeared. Jack poured his Harp beer into a frosted pint glass, while Marnie poured her Perrier water into a crystal glass of ice. Every whim seemed to be honored on the private jet.

Jack looked around the cabin at the white leather seats, defined with blue trim and wood accents. He wondered how much an aircraft like this cost. There were several monitors for computers which appeared to retract into woodwork. The lighting was perfect, and could be softened with an easy touch of a dial. Everywhere Jack looked, he was amazed. He started to play with his seat and discovered it reclined into a bed. Once he realized it, he pointed it out to Marnie.

It wasn't long after he showed Marnie how to recline her seat, she was asleep. Jack opted for another beer before he drifted off to sleep.

They were awakened by the pilot coming over the P.A. system, announcing they would be landing in about fifteen minutes. They both shook out the sleep-induced cobwebs and looked out their windows. Marnie got up and went to the bathroom. Jack wiped his face with his hand, and waited for Marnie to get back.

Looking out the window, he could tell it was close to dusk. The hot orange sun was already dipping below the turquoise horizon. He also remembered they were supposed to be met by someone from the Prime Minister's office to take care of their lack of passports.

Marnie soon returned looking refreshed.

"How'd you sleep?" Marnie asked.

"Pretty good. Not long after you fell asleep, I did too."

"We must have had a real smooth flight because I never felt or heard anything," Marnie said somewhat amazed.

"Me neither. Now comes the tricky part. Let's hope Mr. Hollingsworth got his part right. I don't want to turn around and head home, *and* I don't need to get thrown in jail here because we don't have passports."

"I'm not concerned about it. I'm concerned about finding Bob Lewis."

"I guess we'll have to wait until morning now," Jack said somewhat dejectedly. "One thing's for sure. I know I'm hungry. When we get off, we need to find some food."

The landing was smooth. The wheels hardly screeched as the jet touched down. The best pilots always painstakingly made every effort to prevent any noise or motion when landing, and Mr. Hollingsworth certainly could afford the best. They taxied to the end of the runway as the pilot steered the plane into a 180 turn. Stopping halfway up the runway, Jack looked out the window, and could see there was no terminal or other planes. It was so odd, that for a moment he wondered if they were even on St. Lucia. He had no way of knowing where they were, except some place tropical, since palm trees were not in short supply. The attendant walked back to Jack and Marnie and told them to sit tight because the authorities were about to board.

The door opened and the steps were lowered. Two black men in colorful uniforms entered the aircraft looking very stern. The older one, who was dark-skinned and looked to be in his forties, walked in front. The younger, corpulent one, who looked to be in his late twenties or early thirties, walked closely behind. They walked down the aisle toward Jack and Marnie.

The older one spoke up. He had an authoritative voice and an arrogant attitude to match.

"Show me your passports," he ordered.

Jack and Marnie just looked at each other confused.

"Your passports, please," he reiterated with a raised voice.

"I'm sorry, I don't understand," Jack said. "We were told the Prime Minister had given his approval for us to enter your country without passports."

The older one looked at Jack without emotion, and then looked back at his underling. He then turned back to Jack and started to laugh. The younger officer joined in.

Jack didn't find it funny. Marnie could see the ire in Jack's face.

"Excuse me," Marnie said, but they continued their laughter.

"EXCUSE ME!"

They stopped laughing and returned to their plain, impassive look. They were not happy with Marnie's demeanor, but it achieved its purpose. It got their attention and prevented Jack from coming out of his seat.

"Listen, if you will check with your superiors you will find we have been given special dispensation from your Prime Minister, to remain here for forty-eight hours without presenting our passports. I don't think it would be wise for your career to question your Prime Minister," Marnie said confidently.

The older one just stared at Marnie for a few moments. Clearly he did not like his authority put to the test in front of his underling.

"I would think I would have been informed of this information prior to your arrival on my island. I am not going to call the Prime Minister and disturb him at this hour."

"Have it your way, asshole," Jack said under his breath.

"What did you say?" The older officer looked at Jack, not knowing what he said but realized it was sarcastic in nature.

"I was just admiring the pretty colors on your ribbons," Jack said mockingly about the uniform decorations.

Just as he approached Jack, another officer came on board. This man was so tall that he had to bend slightly to keep from hitting his head on the cabin ceiling. His appearance was genteel but foreboding with a full head of silver-gray hair and sideburns. His uniform had more brass and ribbons than the other officers.

"What is going on here?" asked the new but definitely superior officer.

"Colonel, these people do not have passports," the older officer said with bluster.

"Captain, I will handle this. You are dismissed."

"But, Colonel," he replied.

"Captain, these good people are personal friends of the Prime Minister. You are dismissed," the colonel said with command. They left summarily, but not before the captain looked back, giving Jack the distinctive feeling he did not want to encounter the captain during his stay on the island.

Once they left, the colonel came over and sat down in a seat adjacent to Jack and Marnie.

He smiled briefly before speaking.

"Let me be clear," he stated. "Mr. Hollingsworth is a great friend to the Prime Minister and to this country. We are greatly indebted to his generosity. It is because of him, and only him, that special providence has been granted to you. The Prime Minister wanted me to convey this message to you."

Jack and Marnie were listening intently as the colonel continued.

"He knows what your mission is. He knows the dangers involved. Not just to you, but to him, his reputation, and our country," he said as he turned his focus to Jack. "He knows you have brought weapons into our country. We are hopeful that you will stay and leave without the use of force. If you do use deadly force on this island, we cannot promise any protection or sanctuary. You **WILL** be off this island in forty-eight hours or else you will face grave consequences. Do I make myself clear?"

Jack and Marnie looked like two scolded schoolchildren. They both nodded their heads affirmatively. The colonel then stood and smiled again.

"Welcome to St. Lucia," he said as he turned to depart.

"Excuse me," Jack said. "May I ask a question?"

The colonel stopped, and slowly turned around to address Jack. He was wearing an impatient, forced smile.

"I don't believe there is anything I said that could be misinterpreted. There are no questions, Mr. Dublin. Your clock is running.

I strongly suggest you get your gear together and disembark. Mr. Hollingsworth's chauffeur is waiting for you."

With that, the colonel left. Jack and Marnie looked at each other. Clearly they both felt the intimidation and they understood the message. Like a dying man, they were on borrowed time.

They didn't have much gear. They stood up and began to walk off the plane. Marnie turned and looked at Jack and then asked, "Aren't you forgetting something?"

Jack gave her a confused look and then realized he had left the bag with his weapons and ammunition on the plane. He rushed back and grabbed it. Marnie was already down the steps and out to the car. It wasn't a limousine. It was a Toyota van.

A tall, slender black man in his sixties quickly came over to Jack. He had a very pleasant face, and was wearing a taupe-colored island shirt with a slightly raised design. It was a Guayabera shirt, the kind of shirt with two breast pockets and two waist pockets. His pants were light-colored like his shirt, and neatly pressed. He wore dark brown sandals, appropriate foot attire for the tropics.

"My name is Walter," he said in a heavy island accent. "I work for Mr. Hollingsworth, and he told me to assist you and the lovely lady in any way I can. May I take your bag?"

"I've got it, Walter. My name is Jack and her name is Marnie. The first thing you could do for us is find us some food," Jack said as they hopped into the van.

"No problem, but I think we should go to the house first so I can show you your living quarters."

"How far is it?" Jack asked.

"Only about twenty minutes. Do you think you can last that long?"

"It depends. After we get there, how long before dinner?" Jack asked.

"I can make you some dinner, or you can go to Da Vinci's, which is five minutes away from the house. I am a good cook, but I highly recommend Da Vinci's."

"Okay. I'm sure your cooking is great but I'm guessing your advice is better. So, I say we go to Da Vinci's. Is that alright with you, Marnie?"

"Sounds like a wonderful idea to me."

Jack wanted to check out Da Vinci's. He remembered it came up in a conversation associated with Bob Lewis. His wife said it was the restaurant he frequented. With any luck, who knows? Maybe it would be a quick trip back home.

40

Within ten minutes, the van was climbing a mountain. Reggae music was playing on the radio. The air conditioner was on full blast, and it was cool inside. Jack and Marnie looked back through the window at the city of Castries below. It was dark now, and it gave them a great view of the twinkling lights of the city. They could also see a cruise ship in the harbor, which Walter said was rare for this time of year. He said it must be the last one before next season.

"Looks like we have an escort," Walter said.

"What do you mean?" Marnie asked while Jack looked at the vehicle behind them.

"That car has been following us since we left the airport," Walter said. "Although that's not uncommon since this is the only real road between Castries and Marigot Bay, but there just seems to be something different about this one."

Jack pulled his Sig 9mm out of his bag and held it across his lap with his left hand. He was sitting on the right side of the van. If they tried to pass it would be on the right, since they were traveling on roads residing under the rules of British government. Jack wanted to be ready, just in case the car's occupants had some sinister intent in store for Marnie and him.

"What's different about this one?" Jack queried.

"I have been on this island and this road many times. I have never seen a Hummer, especially with a red paint job," Walter said as he continually glanced back and forth, between the rear view mirror and the road ahead.

"Let me know if they try to pass," Jack said to Walter.

"No problem."

"Can you see how many people are in it?"

"It looks like there are two or three."

"Are there any other cars on the road?" Jack asked, hoping there were. He figured another car in close proximity might prevent the occupants of the suspicious Hummer from taking any actions that may require gunfire, since there could be witnesses. He was still thinking about the conversation he had on the plane with the colonel as he loaded his weapon.

"That's what I mean. There are two or three cars."

"You said it was a red car," Jack said as he turned around again to look. He did see three cars now.

"Do you think I should pull over?" Walter asked concerned.

"No. Just keep on driving. How long before we get to the house?"

"We still have about ten more minutes."

"Can you pick up the pace a little? If they maintain the same distance, then we know it's probably us they're after."

"Okay," Walter responded as he stepped on the gas. He looked in the rear view mirror, and it appeared they were putting some distance between them, but they were still following.

About ten minutes later, they arrived at the Hollingsworth home. It was gated, and it took some time for the gates to swing back to allow them access. Walter pulled up close to the house. The gates were already closing as Jack got out and looked toward the road. He saw the red Hummer and the other two vehicles pass, sensing the last vehicle was a police vehicle. Jack wondered if the captain was keeping a close eye on Marnie and him.

He turned around and saw Marnie walking around the driveway in awe of the Hollingsworth house. Once Jack looked at the house, he was impressed, too. There was a two-car garage to the right where the driveway curved in a slight decline from the road. There was a breezeway extending from the garage to the house. In front of the house were all types and colors of tropical flowers and plants, which served as a brilliant and fragrant accent against the banana yellow exterior of the house. The dominant color of the flowers was red. The lighting was impressive, too. Lights shone upwards from various points in the shrubbery. There was also lighting at the corners of the house, illuminating the perimeter. A large dog could be heard barking.

Jack could see a woman walking inside the house. It was also lit up. It seemed every room on the lower level was illuminated, inviting them inside. Once they went into the house, Walter introduced them to Ila. She was a black woman who appeared to be Walter's age. She was short, had a round shape, and was wearing light-colored tropical clothing, similar to Walter's. Jack wondered what the relationship was between them, but since Walter didn't introduce her as his wife, he was satisfied she was just another employee of Mr. Hollingsworth's. She was very pleasant, had a warm smile, and also seemed to be willing to accommodate Jack and Marnie with their requests.

"I am very pleased to meet you. May I get you something to drink?" she asked.

"Ila, I think they are more hungry than thirsty," Walter said. "I am going to show them their rooms, then take them to Da Vinci's for dinner. We must hurry before they close. Could you call them, and alert them we will need a table for two?"

"Certainly," Ila answered smiling.

"Come with me, and I will show you where you are going to sleep," Walter told Jack and Marnie as he walked towards the stairway.

Jack and Marnie followed Walter up the steps. He turned the lights on as they ascended the stairs. Once they reached the top of the landing, they could see it opened into a large area with several exposed doorways leading to several different bedrooms and bathrooms. Walter pointed out one locked room. He said it was secured because it was Mr. Hollingsworth's study. He then showed them the master bedroom, even though it was also off limits. It was large and sparingly, but smartly furnished.

He first showed Marnie her room, which was about twenty feet by twenty feet, and it had a queen-sized bed with a floral print bedspread. Most of the furniture was rattan. It wasn't the inexpensive kind Jack was familiar with. It was probably made on the island. In the center of the ceiling was a paddle fan. The primary color feature of the room was a pastel peach.

"There should be some clothes to fit you in the closet, if you would like to change," Walter said.

Walter told her to meet downstairs in ten minutes.

Walter then took Jack down the hall and showed him his room. It was smaller, looking to be about sixteen by sixteen, with a double bed. It also had expensive rattan furniture with a paddle fan on the ceiling. The primary color feature of this room was pastel blue.

Walter told Jack he also could change into some different clothes in the closet, and to be downstairs as well, but before he left, Jack asked Walter a couple of questions.

"Do you and Ila stay at the house?" Jack asked.

"Only Ila. I live about five minutes away. Not to worry. I will be here in the morning before you wake up to take you wherever you want to go."

"When we arrived I heard a barking dog," Jack said with a concerned look.

"That is Attila. He is a Doberman Pinscher. He is in a kennel on the side of the house. Once we are in for the evening, he will be allowed out. He is our form of security. Do not go out of the house unless you tell Ila. He is not a friendly dog. Please remind me to tell Miss Marnie."

"I heard you," Marnie said from behind Walter.

Jack looked and saw Marnie had changed into a long, white, body hugging summer dress with a plunging neckline revealing some cleavage, evidence of her generous breasts.

"I forgot to mention, there is a bathroom at each end of the hallway. I will see you downstairs." Walter walked away and went downstairs.

"How do you like the accommodations?" Marnie asked.

"They'll do in a pinch," Jack said smiling, "although you got the better end of the deal."

Marnie walked into Jack's room and looked around.

"Oh yeah," she said in jest. "You have a lot to complain about."

Jack smiled, and then said they better get downstairs. Marnie said she would meet him downstairs in a couple of minutes. She wanted to brush her teeth. He told her he was going to find something to change into, and then meet her downstairs. Jack looked in the closet and found a *Tommy Bahama* island shirt and pants that fit. He also found some sandals. This Hollingsworth guy really thinks of everything!

Jack went downstairs, and saw Walter talking with Ila. They turned to see Jack standing there, and looked as if they were deer caught in the headlights. Jack was beginning to think there was more of a relationship between these two than he originally thought.

"Ila has reserved you a table for two."

"Great!"

As soon as Marnie came downstairs, they left for Da Vinci's. It was a short ride before they were taken into the restaurant by Walter. He introduced them to the maître'd. Walter said he would be back to pick them up in an hour, since the restaurant was closing in fifteen minutes.

"I apologize," Jack said as he turned to the maître'd.

"No apologies are necessary, sir," the maître'd said with his melodic island voice. "We are always pleased to accommodate friends of Mr. Hollingsworth. Allow me to show you to your table," he said. They waved to Walter who smiled, turned, and left.

They were taken to a table next to a picture window. Once they were seated, Jack ordered Glen Morangie on the rocks, and Marnie ordered a Pinot Grigio. There was only one other couple in the restaurant, and it looked like they were leaving.

Their view was breathtaking. Since the island was lit up, they could see down into a valley where two edges of mountains almost touched, but were separated by an opening that formed the bay where yachts were moored. It was the area to which they would venture tomorrow to find Captain Barney and his boat. Hopefully, he would have information about Bob Lewis.

Looking around, a smiling Marnie turned to Jack and said, "You should get in trouble more often. I think I could get used to this."

Jack smiled in return and said, "I would just like to get my life back."

Soon their drinks came and they ordered dinner. No menus were necessary at Da Vinci's; the wait staff recited the meal choices flawlessly to their guests. They both ordered fish dishes. Even though Jack felt like something more substantial, like a steak, he knew the fish was probably outstanding, and he wasn't disappointed.

Jack was surprised when Marnie ordered a bottle of 2008 white Montrachet from Burgundy, France that cost over $200. He was glad the law firm was picking up the tab, savoring every sip of the Montrachet, as it hit his palate.

During dinner Marnie brought up the topic of his father. Jack didn't want to talk about him, but Marnie persisted.

"Why are you so interested in my relationship with my father?"

"Jack, I like you and I believe everyone who has a parent who is still living should do everything they can to resolve their differences. It's not healthy otherwise."

"Listen, I think I understand where you're coming from, since both of your parents are deceased, but your situation is different. Your father didn't murder your mother."

"Jack," she said frustrated, "you don't know that for sure. You have made the assumption based on your love for your mother and your disdain for your father, but that doesn't mean he killed your mother."

"Let's change the subject," Jack said as he was getting exasperated by the conversation. He didn't want to spoil the evening.

Soon it was time for dessert. Jack passed on dessert. He ordered a tawny port as an after dinner drink. Marnie ordered coffee. The waiter walked away. He was the first person on their short stay on the island who looked unfriendly, but they figured it was because they were keeping him late.

"You're ordering coffee?" Jack asked surprised. "It's about two thousand degrees outside."

Marnie smiled. "Y'know, that's what I like about you. You're so different from me."

"I don't think we're that much different."

"We are."

Jack took it as a condescending remark. The waiter returned with their drinks and brought the check also. Marnie gave him a credit card, and he left.

"What are you saying? Our differences make me an idiot?" Jack answered irritably.

Marnie looked at him and smiled. "No. Not at all, but for example, you like red wine and I like white. I like coffee and you like port after dinner. I always look for sunshine, you look for rain. Things like that."

"What do you mean by the sunshine and rain comment?"

"I'm always trying to be positive and you're not."

"Wait a minute, whose life is hanging in the balance here, yours or mine?"

"Jack, don't take it personally. I am not criticizing you. I'm just saying we're different people. That's all. Another example, you like the Phillies and I like the Braves. I'm a Democrat and you're probably a Republican. I believe in pro-choice and you're probably pro-life."

Jack laughed. "You really like to cover all the bases don't you? Politics, religion, baseball, food, wine. But I might add, you have made some incorrect assumptions."

"Really? Like what?" Marnie answered disbelievingly.

"That is going to be the fun part. You're going to have to figure it out," Jack said as he sipped his port.

The waiter returned and Marnie signed the credit slip. The waiter gave them an obligatory "thank you" and left. They sat there in silence looking out the window at the view as they finished their drinks.

Marnie turned to Jack and asked, "Jack, what do you think makes the world go 'round?"

Jack paused to look at her. He didn't have a clue where she was going with this.

"Centrifugal force," he said jokingly.

She smiled gently at Jack and patiently asked, "No Jack, really, what do you think is the power that makes this world go around?"

Jack thought briefly and said, "Money."

"Really?"

"Absolutely. What do you think?" Jack asked curiously.

She hesitated and looked at him with intensity. With a hint of a smile, she continued to stare at him, never leaving his eyes.

Jack began to realize she was going to say something unexpected, something of impact. The mood had suddenly changed. It was like the quiet after a loud thunderstorm, when the sky is no longer dark and threatening. The sun begins to appear and the sound of birds chirping begins to emerge from the periphery. Life begins again.

While they gazed at each other, she slowly and gently reached across the table, taking his left hand into her soft right hand, and with deliberate purpose, gradually pulled his hand towards her.

Jack brought his right hand up to his chin to disguise his nervousness. He swallowed hard. He felt part of him becoming tumescent.

She brought his hand over to her and placed his hand high on her chest, just above her ample breasts, then quietly said, "No, Jack, it's the power of the heart."

Jack normally would have thought of several acerbic retorts, but he would never upset the energy that was coursing through his veins. Not now. He was at a loss of words, and that was the best answer he could have given her.

She leaned forward still holding his hand against her, now with both of hers, and in a whisper she said, "You may think you're hard as steel. You like to hide behind your wicked tongue, but deep down inside I know you're as soft as cotton. It's that vulnerability I find inviting."

Jack was spellbound. There was nothing she could possibly say he wouldn't believe. She had touched him where he had been hiding, where he always had hoped to leave but never had been truly tempted. He was protected, until now.

He looked into her eyes for what felt like the first time. They were bluer than all the worldly oceans. He looked below the surface into the fathoms of her spirit, and saw a compassionate being that was untouched by hatred or fear. She was confident, but not brash.

Walter was outside waiting when they exited the restaurant. They walked over not saying a word and got in. Walter pulled the sliding side door closed. On the way back, he asked if they were satisfied with the dinner, and they both told him they were more than satisfied, although not actually referring to the meal. Marnie reached over and took Jack's hand. They were quiet the rest of the short way home.

When Walter pulled up, Ila was in the front doorway. He dropped them off, and said he would see them tomorrow. They went in the door and told Ila they were going to bed. She reminded them about Attila.

They went up the steps. Marnie was in front. Jack followed. They went to the entrance of her room where she again took his hand and led him into her room. Jack always had the upper hand with women. This time, he was unexpectedly defenseless. Once she closed the door, Jack began to take charge of his senses. It was completely dark in the room. The outside lights were not visible through opaque curtains, which had been pulled across the windows.

Marnie simply dropped her dress to the floor and went to the bed. She had not been wearing anything underneath. She pulled back the covers. Jack took his time getting undressed. He was in no hurry. He was going to savor this moment.

He went over to the bed. Marnie was waiting. They felt each other in the dark.

Jack was a tender lover. No woman who had ever shared a bed with him was disappointed. He always gave his full attention and love to his lover, trying to give more than he received. He wanted his woman to be fulfilled. Loved. Secure. He wanted to please. It made him feel in charge.

She was on her back. He was on his left side, with his right leg draped over her right thigh. He could feel her soft pubic hair against his leg. His cock was hard, but he would wait. Her head was cradled in the bend of his left arm. His hand rested on her shoulder.

With eyes adjusted to the darkness, he looked at her, deeply. They were illuminated by the incandescent fire of love they were starting to feel. He took his other hand and gently stroked her cheek, never leaving the tender gaze into her eyes. Then he took his fingertips and ran them slowly across each eyebrow, then gently down the bridge of her nose, until he softly touched her lips.

She brought him closer to her until he kissed her. Tender, gentle. He then leaned back to where he was. This time he slowly ran his hand down her body, until he felt her breast. Her nipples were hard and erect. She continued to let Jack take charge.

Jack leaned in again to kiss her, but this time they opened their mouths to feel each other's tongue. It was unhurried. Each of them now knew their purpose. It would last beyond tonight.

After a few moments, he left her gaze. He moved with his tongue traveling down her neck, until he took her nipple into his mouth and gently sucked on it, causing her to make gentle sounds of pleasure. He continued to suck her nipples while moving his hand down, until he took his middle finger and played with her clitoris. He continued, and as she became more vocal, he responded by increasing the intensity of his actions. He started to gently bite her nipple and she became more aroused.

As Jack touched her lovingly, she became louder with excitement. Jack's penis was getting harder. He couldn't wait any longer. He leaned back and spread her legs. She was willing and wet.

He got between her legs and slipped his penis inside her. He started to pump, slow at first. Marnie was moaning with delight.

"Fuck me, Jack! Fuck me!"

Jack pumped harder and harder. She was holding her legs above Jack. She begged him to fuck her. She would continue to beg him until they were both spent.

Jack rolled off her. They were both soaked with perspiration, and their chests were heaving up and down, as they tried to catch their breath. Neither one could say anything at first.

"I know one thing. You were right about us being different," Jack said through labored breathing.

Marnie rolled her head towards Jack. He then rolled his head towards her, and saw the confused look on her face.

"What do you mean?" she asked while she was trying to catch her breath.

"I'm glad I'm a man and you're a woman!"

They both started to laugh, and then began to embrace each other. Neither of them wanted to let go.

41

It was morning. The sky was blue and absent of any clouds. The water was aqua-colored and clear. They were in water about fifty feet deep and they could see bottom. Immediately to the north about a mile was the island of Montserrat.

Bob Lewis and Duke Callison were getting ready for pay day. Today was the day they would meet with the camel jockeys, and get their money. They would get rid of some weapons that were already outdated. Knowing these weapons would eventually be destroyed allowed them to believe in their own virtue. One man's junk is another man's treasure. In the end, it's always about the money.

Bob and Duke were on their boat with the missiles about a mile from the meeting point. Half of the promised shipment of missiles was tucked below. The other half was within a day of delivery.

Tied next to their boat was another boat, with four men whom Duke recruited for this mission. They wanted to be prepared in case the young group of terrorists buying the weapons tried to get them for free.

The meeting was originally scheduled for ten o'clock in the morning, but Bob picked noontime. There was something nostalgic about high noon. They wouldn't agree, since they wanted to get the weapons early. Bob figured they were on some type of schedule, and didn't want to argue about something unimportant. Besides, this way Bob and his crew would get their money earlier so they could get on their way.

Bob and Duke had thought about getting something to eat for breakfast on a nearby island, but chose to buy the ingredients and cook onboard instead, due to the time constraints.

"What do you want for breakfast?" Bob asked Duke.

"What are you having?"

"I think I'm going to fry up some ham in honor of our new business partners, and then scramble some eggs with onion, peppers and cheese."

"Sounds good to me. What kind of cheese?"

"American."

"The only kind to have," Duke stated proudly.

Bob went down to the galley to start breakfast, and asked Duke to stay topside to keep a lookout for the terrorists. They weren't due yet, but you never knew if they might show up early as a surprise. He asked if the other guys were going to eat with them, but Duke said they had their own provisions. Bob and Duke were in a cove area, but they still had a good view of any boats passing in either direction.

After about twenty minutes, Bob brought the breakfast up on deck. The stern was large enough to accommodate a table with six seats. There was a blue canopy to shield them from the sun. They each sat down and started to wolf down their breakfast. Coffee and orange juice were on the table too.

"This is a pretty nice boat. How'd you get it?" Duke asked.

"I rented it. I didn't want to use my boat in case something happens," Bob said matter of factly. "What's the latest with Jack Dublin?"

"I haven't heard from my guy yet, but I did hear on the news someone was killed at the Hotel DuPont, and that is where my guy was headed."

"That's good, but we need confirmation. We need your guy to check in."

"I figure he's probably laying low for a couple of days, and then he'll call me. I'm not worried. I'm sure Jack Dublin is lying in some morgue by now," Duke announced. "In fact, I think we should drink a toast to the late Jack Dublin," Duke proclaimed, holding up a glass of orange juice.

"I'm glad you're confident, but until I know for certain," Bob answered evenly. "I am not going to toast to the death of Jack Dublin."

"So, what do you think?" asked Duke as he changed the subject.

"About what?"

"About today?"

"I think we give them their weapons, get our money, and get the hell out of here," Bob said as he sipped some coffee.

"You don't think they're going to try anything, do you?" Duke asked unconcerned.

"Those little shitbirds can't even shoot straight. We saw that with the way they shot the missiles. I can't imagine four of them could take us. Besides we have an ace in the hole. We're not giving them all the weapons until we have all the money," Bob said proudly.

"That definitely gives us a safety valve," Duke agreed.

"Yeah, ole Barney has the other shipment. By the way, does he know he has it onboard his boat?" Bob asked.

"When I told my guys to meet with him, I told them to tell him we needed supplies. Then they put the crates on board. I told them not to say what was in the crates unless he asked. Ole Barney probably thinks they're motor parts and booze."

"In those crates?" Bob asked. "He can see what it says."

Duke smiled. "No he can't. We transferred them to a regular crate without markings."

"Are they secured?"

"Yep. You'd need a crowbar to open it."

"Barney's leaving today to get here from St. Lucia," Bob informed.

"When do you expect him to get here?"

"He should be here by tomorrow."

"Why are we doing two shipments?" asked Duke. "Why don't we just get our money and run?"

"Like I said, I don't trust the towelheads. If this goes smoothly, then we can negotiate for the rest of the stuff." Bob didn't tell Duke his plan about selling information about the drones.

They finished breakfast, cleaned up, and then sat facing the opening of the cove, waiting for some action while finishing their coffee.

At 9:30, a boat slowly passed the entrance of the cove. Bob untied the connected boats and turned the motors on. Telling the other guys to stand by, he said he'd call them if they were needed. Steering the boat toward the entrance, he exited the cove, and followed the vessel that went west. It wasn't long before he pulled close, but kept a safe distance. It was Khalil and another of his cohorts.

Bob didn't waste any time. He got right down to business.

"Did you bring the money?" shouted Bob across the divide.

"Did you bring the missiles?" Khalil shouted back.

"Yes, but you didn't answer my question," Bob said.

"Yes, we have your money, but we need to have the weapons delivered onshore."

Bob didn't like the sound of the last comment. He told Duke to call in the other men. Duke got on the radio and advised them to respond.

"I see your friend talking on the radio. Why?" asked Khalil.

"If you want them on shore, we need help carrying them. Where onshore are you talking about?" Bob asked, trying to deflect the suspicion.

"Right over there," Khalil said, pointing to Montserrat. "You are familiar with the island, aren't you?"

"Yes, I am," Bob said, wondering how he knew.

"You're familiar with the exclusion zone?" Khalil asked.

"I see you've done some homework," Bob answered.

"What the hell is the exclusion zone?" Duke asked quietly.

"It's an uninhabited part of the island damaged by the volcano. It's forbidden to go there, but it is safe. The volcano is dormant for now. It's just rough terrain," Bob answered softly.

"Yes, we will need some help."

"That wasn't part of the bargain," Bob answered, just as the other boat with Duke's men pulled alongside.

"Well, I see you now have some more men to help."

"I've decided they don't do heavy work."

"Then why are they here?"

"To watch the operation."

"How better to learn, than to have some hands-on training?"

"We're not carrying anything," Bob said defiantly.

"I think you will."

As soon as he said it, three boats came out of nowhere, with nine armed men, all of Middle Eastern descent.

"Don't do anything stupid, men," Duke said before a gunshot rang out, and one of his men fell into the water with a splash, holding a pistol in his hand. No doubt his man was aiming at Khalil.

"Y'know, we need to play nice. That way everyone gets to go home at the end of the day," Khalil said pompously. "Now follow me to the unloading point, and everyone will be fine. Don't forget that my men will be on each side of you, so don't try anything stupid. I would hate to see another one of your men buried at sea."

"Let's keep cool until we see when we can turn the tables," Bob said quietly. "They haven't taken our guns yet."

Khalil turned his boat, and headed toward the exclusion zone. The rest followed.

. . .

It was the newest and largest cruise ship in the world. There were sixteen decks, with more than twenty restaurants. Over three football fields long, with more than 2500 rooms, and a capacity of over five thousand people, not including the crew, it was larger than a lot of cities. Truly, it was an impressive metropolis on water.

"Captain, this is an unbelievable ship," Senator Rothschild said, as he looked around the ship with disbelief. The small entourage went fairly unnoticed, since every passenger on the ship was mesmerized by the detail given to such a massive undertaking. Nobody was paying attention to a U.S. senator other than the captain who knew his identity.

"Thank you, Senator," Captain Nilsson responded. "I'm honored and quite fortunate to be the first one assigned to this ship. I'm sure I am the envy of all the captains in the fleet."

"I don't think there is anything anyone could want that they couldn't find on this ship."

"You're quite right. We have such a variety of stores and restaurants, it's like living in a city where if you need something, you just get in your car and go. The difference here is you don't have to drive. You can walk and see some nice sights. We have it all: movie theaters, bakeries, bars, dry cleaners, shoe shine, clothing stores, jewelry, casinos, and we even have a jail."

"How many years have you been with the cruise lines?"

"I'd say about thirty-two years."

"How long have you been a captain?"

"Seventeen years."

"What kind of medical services do you provide?" someone in the entourage asked.

The captain clearly enjoyed fielding questions. He could have given them a canned presentation, which he had done in the past, but it was more enjoyable, and probably more informative, to take questions.

"I know, most people don't think about getting sick at sea. Instead, people think of the places and sites they are going to see, but everyone should make sure they have their medications up-to-date and report any pre-existing conditions.

"Our medical staff is highly trained, and our equipment is state-of-the-art. We can x-ray broken bones, but we do not have a radiologist on staff to interpret the studies. So we send them digitally to doctors in Israel, who are members of what they call Night Hawks. They read x-rays for hospitals around the world."

"Why would a hospital hire doctors when they have their own staff?" someone asked.

"With today's economy, it's cheaper for hospitals to send an x-ray off site, and not have the expense of a radiologist sitting around all night with nothing to do. The response is quick. It's almost like having a radiologist on the ship."

"What if it's a grave situation?"

"If our doctors determine someone cannot be treated on our ship, then we have to make arrangements for them at our next port of call. If it is so serious that it can't wait, then we make arrangements to airlift them, which is quite expensive. It costs between ten and twenty-five thousand dollars on average, to airlift a patient from this ship to land."

There was a painful groan from everyone in the group. It didn't help when the captain told them most health insurance policies people have in their own countries do not cover the costs.

"What kind of security do you have onboard? I know you don't have anyone walking around with police uniforms, but I'm sure you do have law enforcement personnel."

"Yes, we do have a security contingent onboard and they're always watching. They are for the most part trained law enforcement personnel who enjoy traveling. There are always several people active, twenty-four/ seven," the captain said.

"What about terrorists? In today's world you never know. Do you remember the poor gentleman in the wheelchair on the Achille Lauro?" an older woman said.

"Didn't the terrorists toss him overboard in his wheelchair?" someone else added.

Senator Rothschild was getting tired of the Q & A and wanted to finalize it, so he could back to his cabin and enjoy the company of his mistress.

"Those days are gone. Yes, we still have threats from around the world, but I'm sure the captain would agree with me that security is at its optimal best, right Captain?" the senator asked.

"That's right, Senator," the captain said and before he could add to his answer, the senator interrupted.

"So, where is our next stop?"

"Tomorrow, we will be going to Antigua, but I want to mention we will be going past some other islands, perhaps most notable is Montserrat, where there was an active volcano back in 1995. Last year it rumbled again, but did not create anywhere near the havoc it created back in '95."

"Well, Captain, I want to thank you for your informative tour. I found it quite interesting," Senator Rothschild said, as he reached out his hand to shake the captain's. He wanted to send the message to the rest of the entourage that the tour had concluded. Some of them began to whisper, not realizing a U.S. senator was onboard.

Once the captain shook his hand, the senator left to return to his cabin where his naked mistress was anxiously waiting.

42

The boats moved up the rocky coast of Montserrat, traveling at a moderate pace. The view was distressing for Bob Lewis. Plentiful green vegetation and lively villages had been replaced with brown and gray volcanic residue. He had visited this island at least once a year since college until the volcano erupted. He had wanted to eventually retire here.

The former capital of Montserrat was Plymouth. It was destroyed from the lava flows that came down from the Soufriere Hills Volcano that began in July of 1995. The island had seen an economic growth derived mainly from tourism. A new port had just been completed to accept cruise ships and the financial bounty it would bring with it. The hopes and dreams of many were now nothing more than gray ash.

Now as they traveled past the coastline of the exclusion zone, the island looked like nuclear winter. Buildings could be seen as half- submerged tombs buried in what looked to be hardened charcoal mud. There was no sign of life at this end of the island with the exception of a few birds that soared overhead searching in vain for some type of meal below.

"Where do you think we're going?" Duke asked.

"My guess is we'll go ashore somewhere just south of civilization but still in the exclusion zone," Bob answered while paying attention to navigating. "Just north of Plymouth which is about where we are right now is a peninsula that juts out into the water. There was a bird sanctuary there. I'm guessing we'll go ashore just south of that."

"Why do you say that?"

"They probably have people onshore waiting for us."

"You think so?"

"We've underestimated them. We thought this was going to be a simple transfer of missiles for money, because they were just a bunch of young zealots with no conception of a business deal. We thought because they have deep pockets and some idiotic ideal we wouldn't have any problems. In hindsight, you don't get accepted in Georgetown for being stupid."

"Still, why do you think there are more people on shore?"

"Did you expect the other boats?"

"No," Duke said despairingly.

"Exactly! I'm thinking they want us to do something else, something additional."

"Like what?"

"I don't know but we'll soon find out. Right now I feel like Custer at Little Big Horn."

"One good thing, they didn't take our weapons yet. Maybe they're going to recruit us," Duke said with reservations.

"I wouldn't count on it. They will take our weapons. Believe me, they are not going to allow us to maintain our guns."

At that moment, Khalil looked back and motioned with his hand to start for the shoreline, just as Bob had suspected. They had no choice but to turn inland. Bob looked back and waved for his team to follow. Khalil's other boat was still following, monitoring their movements.

Once they approached the shoreline, four Chevy Suburbans were lined up in a row. There were four men waiting with them. They looked like they were islanders and not from the Middle East. They helped anchor the boats close to a dock that extended out to the deep water where Bob's boat had to remain due to its size. Everyone disembarked and walked to the shoreline.

Khalil went over to one of the men who had been piloting the boat behind Bob and his cohorts. He whispered in his ear and the man nodded his head in the affirmative before Khalil walked over to Bob.

"We need the missiles now," he said very assured. "We are not going to pay one dime until we make sure they are capable of being effective. We need your personal weapons also. Don't try anything stupid. We will not think twice about killing you," he said as he motioned to his men.

Slowly, Bob, Duke and the remaining three men removed their weapons as Khalil's men collected them. They were still standing on the shoreline.

"Do we have all your weapons?" Khalil asked.

They all nodded their heads with certainty.

"Put your hands behind your head," Khalil ordered. "Check them."

Khalil's men began patting down the men. One by one they were searched. As they got to the third man of Duke's crew they found a small Glock 9mm.

"Khalil," one the men said calling him over.

Khalil slowly walked over with an arrogance that spelled disaster. He took the gun from the inspector and looked at it in his hand. He placed it in one hand and then the other, weighing the situation, as if he was contemplating what action he would take while keeping everyone in suspense.

"Does it work?" he asked.

"Probably not," answered the guilty man defiantly.

"Let's see," Khalil said as he pointed it at the man point blank in the forehead and fired a single shot. The man collapsed immediately. What remained of his head was submerged in the water while the rest of his body was still on the shoreline.

"Is there anyone else who might be thinking of holding back?" Khalil asked with pleasure.

Nobody moved.

"Good," Khalil said. "Now let's get down to business. Mr. Lewis, I want you and your remaining men to get the missiles and load them into these vehicles," he said pointing to the Suburbans.

With those instructions, Bob, Duke and the remaining two men went onboard Bob's boat and retrieved the crates containing the missiles. With the help of the islanders, they carried them carefully and loaded them into the back of the Suburbans. Khalil gave seating assignments and they piled into their respective vehicles. They followed a road leading to Cork Hill. It would give them an excellent view of the ocean and any passing ships.

When the road ended at the foot of the mountain, they stopped. They decided not to take the vehicles any further due to the terrain. They exited their vehicles and stood next to them. Several of Khalil's men were in conference with him discussing their next move.

"Alright, I want you to take the crates out of the back of the vehicles and follow me," Khalil said.

Bob, Duke and the other two men looked puzzled and stood there.

"Did you not understand me?"

"Yes, we understand, but where are we taking them?" Bob asked.

"You're taking them up that hill," Khalil told them pointing up to what is known as Cork Hill. This area of the exclusion zone was close to the boundary of civilization on the island. It was like a tropical rainforest.

"You're kidding us right?" Bob said sarcastically.

"I'm dead serious."

"The vegetation is so thick we won't get those up there for hours."

"You're in luck, Mr. Lewis. I've planned ahead. My people have been down here cutting a path. It's just a matter of carrying the crates up there."

Bob looked at Duke and the other two. It was possible to get up there in a couple of hours with a path.

"Can I ask why we're taking them up there?" Bob asked.

"Because it is so isolated, you and your band of brothers are going to make sure they are not impotent like the other shit you sold us."

"You're going to just shoot them out into the ocean at nothing?"

Khalil smiled. "No, Mr. Lewis. There will be something to shoot at in a few hours. The largest cruise ship in the world will be going past here. We can't delay any longer. Get moving!"

They picked up the crates and began walking in the direction of the path leading to their destination. The sun was hot. They were tired and hungry, but mostly thirsty. Several times on the way up, they were provided with bottled water. It was late in the day when they reached their destination. The view of the ocean was spectacular.

They were ordered to set up the weapons and equipment, and then provide a remedial. Bob and Duke complied. They had no choice. Some of Khalil's men separated the other two men and walked them back down the path until they were out of sight. Shortly thereafter two gunshots rang through the silence. Khalil's men came walking up the path shortly thereafter. They were alone.

The group sat there waiting as the burning red sun started its descent. Khalil's men leaned against some rocks with their rifles trained on Bob and Duke who were sitting next to the missiles. They had about two more hours of light. Soon the largest cruise ship filled to capacity with an unsuspecting crew and tourists, including one U.S. senator, would be traveling right into the crosshairs of some maniacal militants with only death and destruction on their minds.

. . .

"I hope you enjoyed your tour earlier today, Senator," the Captain said as he sat on a chair in his private quarters.

"Very much so," Senator Rothschild responded as he sat on the couch facing the captain, with his mistress close by his side. "You have an amazing home here at sea. Do you ever miss living a normal life?"

"This is normal for me. I'm at sea six months of the year and home for the other six months. I get paid very well. I eat very well, as you can tell," he said while patting his barely noticeable stomach. "What is there not to like?"

"Do you have any family?"

"Yes, I have a son who lives in Norway with his mother. I get to see him quite often when I am not at sea," he said. "He's getting old enough now that I have had him stay with me on the ship."

"That's great," the Senator said, not really caring one way or the other. "I know there is an itinerary, but I seem to have lost it. When will we be getting into Antiqua?"

"At approximately 1 A.M.. I suspect you, like most of my passengers will be asleep. When you wake up, you'll be there. We won't leave again until 5 P.M. tomorrow."

"So we will have approximately eight hours onshore."

"Yes, you are correct. Would you like more hors d'oeuvres or wine?"

"I would love some more wine," the senator said, holding his glass out. "Would you like some more, honey?"

"Yes, please," the senator's beautiful blonde paramour said, smiling as she cozied up to him.

The captain motioned for the cabin assistant to bring more wine. Once their glasses were filled, the senator started to ask some more questions.

"What is one of the strangest things that's happened on your ship?"

"You mean this ship?"

"Any ship you have had under your command."

The captain looked intense as he was searching for a good story. There were many over the years.

"One time I can remember a college student decided to jump from an upper deck into the ocean on a dare."

"Did he live?"

"Yes, but wait 'til I tell you the whole story. He jumped at night. He was intoxicated and he didn't die on impact. His friends alerted a crew member and we had to launch a couple of search vehicles. You may have seen them elevated on the decks. We had to basically stop the ship and wait until our rescue boats searched the area. To make matters worse, we didn't have calm seas. Nevertheless, we miraculously found him in about a half hour. The problem for us was we had to alert the port we were coming in late. That never goes over well. It ended up costing our company a couple hundred thousand dollars."

"It must be a tremendous responsibility to keep everyone safe, including the ship itself," Senator Rothschild said contemplatively.

"It certainly is, but that is why I get paid the big bucks," the captain said smiling. "I hate to break this up but it is time I got up on the bridge. I want to thank you and tell you what a pleasure it is to have you both on board," he said as he rose from his chair. "If there is anything you need, please don't hesitate to get in touch with me."

"Thank you, Captain."

Shortly thereafter they left his cabin to go up on deck to enjoy the view. The setting sun tended to make the ocean glisten. Montserrat was slightly visible in the distance. It was quiet outside on the deck except for the sound of the massive ship cutting through the calm waters.

43

Jack woke up and instinctively felt someone staring at him. He slowly turned his head to the left and saw Marnie wide awake staring at him. He smiled.

"You look wide awake," he said facing her.

She gave him an agonizing look. Taking her left hand, and cupping it around his jaw, she turned his head so he was facing the ceiling.

"Are you trying to kill me?" she asked painfully.

"What? Are you saying I have morning breath?"

"Let's just say, it's bad enough to start peeling the paint in this room."

Jack laughed and hopped out of bed. He went down the hall after pulling on some shorts. She could hear him brushing his teeth. She waited for him in bed.

When he returned, Jack got back in bed and lay on top of the covers. He was still wearing his shorts. She looked disappointed.

"Does my breath smell better now?" Jack asked.

"A little," she said.

"You seem upset about something," Jack said.

"It's nothing really."

"C'mon, you can talk to me," said Jack happily, as he took his forefinger and crooked it under her chin to get her to look at him.

"It's just that I really care for you Jack, and..." she stopped.

"And what?"

"I'm just concerned about you."

"In what way?"

"As you know, my family was dead when I was young and I never got to feel the warmth of family."

"What does that have to do with me?" he asked, wondering why they were having this conversation at this moment.

"I want you to promise me before we leave this island, that you will attempt to resolve your differences with your father."

Jack sat up. He wasn't prepared for this.

"Why are you so concerned about it?" he said perturbed. He was getting tired of this topic, to the point that it was ruining the potential for a relationship with Marnie.

"Jack, I don't think you'll ever be a whole person until you mend the fence."

"I don't even know what I would say to him," Jack said flustered.

"You'd figure it out."

Jack was willing to make a promise to Marnie. Any promise. Just not this one.

"I don't know, Marnie. Can I think about it?"

She looked at him with a feigned pout. "I guess so, just as long as you have an answer before we leave this island."

"C'mon, we have work to do," Jack said as he pulled her out of bed. She was still naked, and the sight of her made it difficult not to hop back in bed, but right now, his life as a free man was hanging by a delicate thread. He knew they would have more time to "lock loins" as Billy put it.

Jack and Marnie walked down to the bay. It took them about ten minutes. They saw a charter fishing business called "Captain Barney's." They walked over towards the front door and saw a short, slender man who looked two days older than dirt, walk out. He had torn and tattered clothes and a baseball hat that looked like it had been shredded. His beard was long and unkempt. There was a remnant of a cigar in his mouth. It was probably a good thing. Cigar smoke smelled better than body odor. He was putting some rods on a boat.

"Excuse me," Jack said. "Are you Barney?"

The man hardly even looked at Jack and then said, "Whaddya want?"

"I want to know how much you would charge to take us to Montserrat and back," Jack said, pointing at himself and Marnie. The man stopped what he was doing and squinted at Jack. Then he looked at Marnie and back at Jack. He then took the cigar out of his mouth, and just continued to look at Jack before starting to laugh. Barney put the cigar back in his mouth and turned to finish putting the rods and tackle on his boat. When he was finished, he walked back to Jack.

"You're kiddin' right?"

"I'm dead serious."

"It's a long trip. Roundtrip cost you a couple thousand. Are you planning on doing any fishin'?"

"No. We just need to get up there and back. We might be there a few hours, and we would be bringing another person back with us."

"Twenty-five hundred oughta do it."

"Hold on a minute," Jack said as he took Marnie aside. "What do you think?"

"We're gonna trust that guy? He looks like he could have a heart attack any moment."

"If he does, I'll drive the boat. Not only that, but we'll get our money back."

"You don't even know where we're going, and besides, if he has the big one I don't want to be on the boat with some old guy rotting under the sun and smelling up the place."

"We'll put him in the water and tie him to the boat like in the "*Old Man and the Sea.*"

Marnie frowned at the joke.

"Alright."

Jack walked back to Barney and told him they would think about it and get back to him. Barney told him he was leaving for Anse Le Raye to pick up some supplies and they could leave from there for Montserrat. He gave Jack his cell phone number in case they decided to use him. Jack and Marnie walked back up to the villa. On the way back, Jack thought he saw someone familiar. It was someone he had seen at the Hotel DuPont but he'd dismissed it. Jack and Marnie talked about Walter and whether or not they should trust him. They were in unfamiliar territory and they didn't feel safe. After they talked about it, they decided they had no choice. Walter would have to be trusted.

"Walter, did you get an answer about Montserrat?" Jack asked when they got back to the villa.

"Mr. Hollingsworth said his boat is being serviced, but there is a guy down at the Bay named Barney who is the best man to ask."

"We just talked to him. He said he would take us. He said he was going to pick up some supplies at Anse Le Raye, but he did give me his cell phone number."

"Anse Le Raye is a small fishing village a short ride down the road. See if you can catch him. If not, we can meet him down there. It's pretty easy to get to, just a lot of winding roads. I'll drive you there myself."

Jack called him, but he was already on his way. He said to meet him there in about an hour. It would give him time to get his supplies, after which they could leave. Walter told them to take a quick shower if they wanted since they were going to be on the boat for a while. When they were ready, he would take them.

Jack and Marnie went to their rooms and took separate showers. There was no time for sexual Olympics. They met at the front door. Walter was nowhere to be found, yet the van was running. All of a sudden he appeared from around the house.

"You ready?"

"Yep."

They got inside the van and closed the door. Thankfully the interior was cooled by the full blast of the air conditioner. They started to pull out of the driveway when Jack made him stop. He went back to the front door, and grabbed the satchel that had his guns and ammo in it. He had forgotten it again. He took his Sig out which was fully loaded, and placed it in the small of his back before getting back in. He checked the Smith and Wesson and it was loaded as well.

"Sorry about that."

"You must be careful with a gun on this island. You will spend the rest of your life here, but it won't be on holiday," Walter said ominously.

"I'm leaving soon, so it won't matter."

They got to the end of the driveway when a shot rang out and broke the window next to Walter. He was hit. Jack looked to see where it came from and got out of the van, holding the Sig 9 mm. He used the van as cover. Slowly, he moved around the back of the van. Marnie was down on the floor. He saw another vehicle on the street. Nobody was in it. He realized whoever had been in it was walking on the property.

"Marnie, are you okay?" Jack shouted.

"Yes. I'm not hit."

"Get Walter out of the driver's seat and move him over."

Walter was moaning in pain but he understood Jack's command and slowly maneuvered out of the driver's seat over to the passenger side. Jack continued to scan for a shooter. He saw the same man from the Hotel DuPont poke his head out from the side of the house. Jack fired a couple of rounds as he got into the van. He put it in gear and pulled out of the driveway. Shots were returned but they missed the moving van.

"Walter, can you give me directions?"

Walter was moaning but Jack needed him.

"Walter!" Jack screamed.

"Take a right here," Walter said as Jack made a turn to a straight patch of road. He was thankful there weren't any turns for a long stretch. He checked his rearview mirror and saw a car speeding behind him. It looked like a Camaro. A further scan revealed two vehicles chasing him. The second car was a lot further back but it was apparent it was in the chase too. It looked like the Hummer he had seen the previous night.

The road took them through the middle of a banana plantation. There were cars coming from the other direction, but the only car on his side of the road was up ahead and it was turning left at an intersection. Jack checked his mirror. The Camaro was gaining ground.

Jack floored the van. It had some pick up but it was clearly outclassed by the Camaro. It was far enough away that Jack couldn't tell how many people were in the car. They approached an intersection.

"Hang on," Jack said as he blew through the intersection, just missing another car. The other car stalled in the intersection and the

Camaro had to slow down. It swerved around the stalled car and continued towards Jack and the van.

"You're gonna start coming into the town," Walter said through clenched teeth.

"Any ideas how we can lose the car behind us?"

Walter paused for strength. "There is another hairpin turn coming up. He won't know that. You'll have to be careful."

Jack began to slow down. The Camaro was close enough now that Jack could see only one person in the car. They approached the curve and the driver of the Camaro started to lean out of the window with a gun in his hand to take a shot. He shot one round off before he lost control and crashed into the wall on the turn. Jack looked back and saw the shooter get out of the car. Steam was coming from the crumpled front end. Jack knew he wouldn't be following any further. He started to relax and then looked at Walter, who was getting weaker by the moment from his loss of blood.

"Don't worry about me, mon, get on that boat. I have a sister who lives here. She'll get me to the hospital."

They were in the town already. The streets of Anse Le Raye were narrow and lined with buildings, which were fine examples of French and English colonial architecture. A local was walking down the street with a large snake dangling around his neck. He was approaching a group of tourists. A row of open air booths covered by a tin roof were nestled along the shoreline. Women were selling their wares which ranged from local straw baskets to clothing items. Behind them, Jack saw a long stone pier where Captain Barney's boat was tied. There were some smaller wood fishing boats anchored in the cove.

Jack parked at the end of the street leading to the pier. He got out and opened the door for Marnie. He went back to look at Walter.

"You sure you're going to be okay? You've lost a lot of blood. Maybe I should take you to the hospital myself. We can go to Montserrat tomorrow."

"NO! NO! You go now. There's my sister's house across the street. She has a car and she'll take me."

Jack paused, but he knew now was his only chance to find Bob Lewis. He looked at Walter with a kind sadness. “Thank you.” Walter nodded his head slightly, closing and opening his eyes as an acknowledgement.

“C’mon Jack, we need to get going. That guy could have walked here by now.”

Jack hurried. He went back and reached in for his guns and ammo bag. They ran down the dock to the boat calling for Captain Barney, but he didn’t answer. Then, they heard him calling from the base of the pier. He was behind them. They ran back to help him carry his supplies to the boat. All three of them were loaded down, barely able to carry everything.

Finally, they got on the boat and put the packages down. Captain Barney was storing some of the items away before he would start the engine. Jack looked back to the shore and panicked. He saw his gym bag by a tree at the end of the pier where he had left it when he helped carry the supplies .

“Shit! I need that bag,” Jack yelled as he jumped from the boat to the pier. Once on the pier, Jack sprinted down the pier about thirty yards to get his bag.

“Jack, hurry up!” Marnie screamed as Captain Barney turned the key to start his engine.

The explosion was deafening and the strength of the blast slammed Jack to the ground

44

Jack was stunned. He forgot who he was, where he was and what he was doing. All sounds were muffled. He didn't understand. Confusion took control. Looking around, he saw strange people running everywhere. It looked as though they were screaming because their mouths were agape but Jack didn't hear any sound he could comprehend. Their faces looked distorted like fright face masks. Jack just sat there, by the tree, trying to find his way back to reality, sanity. Nothing made any sense.

He turned his head towards the end of the stone and concrete pier. Splinters of wood started to rain down on him. There was a fire where the boat had been. Still, Jack did not understand. He couldn't. "Why am I here?" he asked himself. "What is happening?" He turned and looked back towards the street where he had left Walter. There were people surrounding his car. Slowly Jack emerged from the insanity of the moment. He remembered the car and then Walter.

Fear began to take over. It was a good thing. Jack now knew he had to get out of there.

He stood up slowly with difficulty, and brushed himself off. He felt for the gun he was carrying. It was still there. It gave him a sense of security and safety. He started to walk towards Walter's car. Then he remembered Marnie. He stopped, and then looked back at what used to be Captain Barney's boat. He had no time to mourn. It would have to wait. It was about survival now.

Jack turned and continued to Walter's car. People were surrounding the car. A woman who must have been his sister came running down the street with another woman. She was screaming. Jack was beginning to get his hearing back.

As Jack approached the car he noticed two men, a white man and a black man with braids tied behind his head. They were walking in his direction, looking straight at Jack, and not at the commotion around Walter's car. Jack started to back away. They kept their eyes on him. He couldn't wait any longer so he started to walk fast, away from the car, while he kept his eyes on them. They started to run in his direction.

Jack took off and ran down the street. When he got to the corner he turned left, looking for a place to hide. Up ahead and across the street he saw a cemetery next to a church. It had numerous vaults. Burials here had to be above ground. He looked over his shoulder and didn't see the men. Knowing his window of opportunity was small before they saw him again, he ran into the cemetery to hide.

He pulled his gun out and sat down with his back against a crypt. Jack started to question what would be worse, spending the rest of his life in jail for a murder he didn't commit, or being buried in St. Lucia? The clouds in the sky had dissipated. Birds circled overhead. All Jack could smell was smoky wood and burnt flesh.

He remembered what the colonel had told him on the plane. St. Lucia would not be a safe haven for him if he used deadly force. He didn't care. Survival was paramount. If the men chasing him approached, he would kill them. No doubt in his mind.

He waited a few minutes. As one of the men ran past, he heard the white man yell to the black man that he was going into the church. He thought about moving to another location while the white man was in the church, but he knew the black man was still lurking somewhere close-by. As he sat there, he tried to put together a plan of escape. He leaned slowly and cautiously to the left to look around the edge of the crypt to get a better view. Slowly and carefully he looked around and didn't see anyone. He felt a sigh of relief.

He started to return to his original upright position when he felt the unmistakable metal of a gun touching his right temple.

"Don't move or you'll be making a grave right here. Drop your gun slowly." It was the black man with the dreadlock braids from the Hotel DuPont.

Jack did as he was told. He was exhausted and worn out. There was not much fight left in him. Whatever his fate would be, he was resigned to it. The man took his gun and then called out for the other man, whose name was Dave, and was huge. He was at least six foot five, lean and strong at what looked to be two hundred and fifty pounds. He would have made a good linebacker or maybe a tight end in the NFL. He came over to Jack and got on his phone. Within a couple of minutes a black limo pulled up outside the church.

Dave got into the front seat while the black man, whose name was Charlie, sat across from Jack in the back seat. Jack was not cuffed. The window partition was down to allow Dave to watch the back. They all appeared to be in their thirties, including the driver. They were dressed in black T-shirts, tan utility pants and boots.

"Who are you guys working for?" Jack asked. There was no response.

"Where are we going?" Jack asked. Again there was no response.

Jack began to consider his next move, realizing he didn't have any. He was trapped and was going to die. He looked at Charlie and tried to read his thoughts. Would they just shoot him or would they torture him first? Jack knew if he had a chance, any chance for survival, he would have to do something different. At the worst, they would just shoot him immediately and get it over with. There would be no torture.

It was at this moment that Jack considered doing something that shredded every moral fiber he had. Never, never did he think he could say what he was about to say in a million years. He didn't live that way. He wasn't a racist, but he was angry and resigned to the fact that his assassin sat across from him. Jack didn't know him and it no longer mattered.

"Don't you talk.......nigger?" Jack asked hoping to rile Charlie but he sat almost as impassive as he did with the first two questions. Jack thought his eyes got wider and his nostrils flared but he didn't flinch.

Jack just sat back. At least they didn't load him in the trunk. It didn't matter who they were or who they were working for at this point. Jack was already dead. He may have been breathing, but he was dead.

The car drove up the mountain taking several sharp winding turns. It took about fifteen minutes before they stopped at the top of the mountain. Charlie still had his gun pointed in Jack's direction. Dave got out and opened the door for Jack. He too had a semi-automatic pointed at Jack.

When Jack got out of the limo he looked around and saw a long ranch-style home with all kinds of radio towers surrounding it. It almost looked like a mini-military installation. Beyond the tree-lined crest you could see the ocean. It was a beautiful view. There was a red Hummer sitting in the driveway with some other vehicles parked to the side of the home.

"You guys trying to get in touch with aliens or something?" Jack asked sarcastically as he looked up at the radio towers.

"This way smart-ass," Dave said, as he motioned Jack toward the house with his gun.

Jack walked slowly to the house. He guessed torture was on the menu. Maybe he could continue to aggravate them to just do it quickly and kill him.

Jack walked to the house and the door was opened for him. Once inside he couldn't believe his eyes. There had to be about ten people sitting at sophisticated tracking monitors the likes of which he had never seen before. This was no cheap organization. Money, lots of money, had been spent on this place.

A slender man who appeared to be in his early fifties walked over to Jack and held out his hand. His thick gray hair was short. His face had long dark features. He looked to be in top physical condition, wearing the apparent dress of the day: black T-shirt, tan utility pants and combat boots.

"Hello Jack, I'm Brian Oliver. I work for the U.S. Government. I'm in charge of this operation. You're quite a guy. We've been following you ever since the shooting in D.C."

Jack hesitantly shook his hand.

"I can see by the look on your face, you don't totally understand what is going on. Let me bring you up to speed. Bob Lewis was a rogue FBI agent. We almost had him once but he was slick. We know he is involved with an unusual terrorist group. Unusual because they are a bunch of American-educated college kids from the Middle East.

Currently, in thanks partly to you, we know he is down here somewhere. He's getting ready to move some rocket launchers. Can you imagine how bad we'll look if he is able to sell weapons that came from U. S. military installations to be used against Americans? The president would have a difficult time explaining to the American people how our own weapons killed our own people. Exactly what their plans are we don't know, but we want to minimize death and any collateral damage to the integrity of our government."

"Why do you need me? From the looks of this place you could follow anyone, anywhere," Jack said unabashedly.

"You would think so, Jack. You would think we could stay on top of things," he said while looking at the assembled bunch before returning his attention to Jack. "But Bob's boat is still in a harbor in Barbados. He used it as a decoy. We lost him and now we don't know where he is headed, but we do know that once he makes the transfer, the terrorists are going to strike somewhere. Obviously we need to interrupt the sale and transfer before people are killed. There are thousands of islands down here. It could be anywhere."

"My information is he is going to Montserrat," Jack said, and before he could say anything more, instructions were being barked to the men at the consoles.

"I don't know why we didn't think of that," Colonel Oliver said shamefully. "It makes perfect sense. Since the volcano erupted in 1995, the island is largely uninhabited in the southern part, particularly near the volcano which is still lying dormant. Nobody would expect it to take place there."

A man called out from the console. "They're on their way, Colonel."

Col. Oliver turned to Jack. "Listen, we have a helicopter landing here soon. You are to stay here until we get back. We're headed to Montserrat and we'll bring Bob Lewis back here to you so you can talk to him. He will be in the government's custody."

"With all due respect, I'd like to go along."

"Jack, this is going to be a high-level operation. We are going to have to rappel down from the helicopter and there may be a gun battle."

"Colonel, you say you've been watching me. You know how good I am. I can at least ride along."

"Can you rappel?" asked the colonel, expecting Jack to say no, killing any chance for him to go along.

"Yes I can. I was on the SWAT team and we practiced annually."

"When is the last time you rappelled?"

"About six months ago," Jack said with confidence.

"Can you handle an M-4?"

"I'm an expert with it," Jack said proudly.

The colonel looked around. "Rivers, you're about Jack's size. Get him some gear."

Rivers looked to be in his late thirties. He was a handsome man with a dangerous scowl, which let Jack he wasn't happy about him going along with the team. He took Jack into the locker room. "Here are some clothes to wear. What size shoe do you wear?"

"Size ten."

Rivers handed him some boots. Regardless of how the team felt about Jack going with them, he felt he deserved the chance to go. Either way Jack was going to respect their ground. He was the outsider and he knew he was lucky to be going.

Just as Jack was tying his boots, he heard the helicopter. Rivers came in and told Jack to get a move-on. Jack ran out of the room and outside to where the group was marshaling. The colonel handed him an M-4.

"Listen, it might be best if you stay on-board and hold cover for us."

"Once you're safely on the ground, I can come down, right?"

The colonel never heard him. The sound of the helicopter's blades washed out anything he said. Meantime, as the helicopter landed, everyone boarded. Seated next to Jack were Dave and Charlie. As he looked at everyone's face he knew it was serious. You don't play games with terrorists no matter how young they are.

Once the colonel gave his orders to buckle down and harness in, he gave the all-clear hand signal. The Black Hawk helicopter lifted off and they were on their way to Montserrat.

45

Time was critical.

The helicopter was traveling at about one hundred and seventy five m.p.h. Top speed was around two hundred and twenty. The doors were closed which didn't make it any easier to hear verbal commands. Jack was enjoying the ride, not thinking about the possible firefight that lay ahead. For now he was taking in the seriousness of his new comrades. Everyone was secured with their backs to the walls, staring across at each other. They were wearing blank faces. Obviously, this wasn't their first experience. They had been to Iraq, Afghanistan and the Gulf. The colonel had probably been to Vietnam as well.

Jack could see through the windows. They were flying low, so low he felt he could reach out and touch the treetops. He could see the waves below slapping against the sand, then turning into white foam. The sun, which had had a strong yellow burn to it all day, was now turning orange as it dipped towards the horizon, still an hour from touching it.

Periodically the colonel would converse with the pilot, Johnny, and his co-pilot. It was a private conversation.

"Alright listen up," the colonel shouted, turning his attention to his men. He was now capable of being heard via the headsets. Normally everyone was briefed before departure, minimizing conversation, but this was going to be a seat-of-the-pants objective.

"We just received some intelligence. Someone at a bird sanctuary reported seeing four Chevy Suburbans heading for the exclusion zone. Spotters said they believed these people were headed towards a low level mountain called Cork Hill. We have the coordinates. We will head there first to determine if our information is good since we have no other intelligence. Let's hope it's good. The sun will be setting soon and it may be difficult to find them in the dark. I have asked for a satellite confirmation and also a determination of weapons and type. I'll get back to you in a few minutes."

Jack looked at each soldier, eventually turning his attention to Charlie. Even though they were adversaries at the start of the day, they were now on the same team. Jack would remain onboard with the pilot and co-pilot while the rest of the team would engage on the ground. Nevertheless, he was part of something positive. He hadn't felt this way in a long time, forgetting about his troubles. He was focused.

After a few minutes, the colonel spoke again.

"Listen up, satellites have confirmed a group of approximately twenty people, as suspected, on the west side of the mountain. It appears they have automatic weapons, but worse, they have what appear to be two SAMS. Once we fly by, if the information is correct, we will rappel on the east side of the mountain. We don't want to take a chance they'll aim at our helicopter. We believe these people to be hostile. Check your weapons. Lock and load! Make'em hot! Careful on the descent. Cover and sweep. Remember to wait for my commands. Hand signals will be tough since we will be spread out. Stay on this channel."

There was a palpable change in the mood of each soldier. They checked their weapons again and prepared for the drop zone. They were minutes from engagement. Jack wished he was going with them but he also understood. They practiced together and knew each other's moves and tendencies. Jack would be a hindrance and he didn't want that.

"Jack, I want you to sit in the bay and utilize the M-4 as a cover tool. Watch our backs. We need you here. Make sure you're strapped in and maintain this channel. Give me thumbs up if you heard me," the colonel said.

Jack looked at him and gave him a thumbs up.

As they flew to the west of the still smoldering volcano, a cruise ship could be seen up ahead to the west approaching a parallel position to Cork Hill. The Colonel saw it at the same moment Jack did.

"Jesus Christ, they're going to aim for the cruise ship," the colonel screamed. "Johnny, put the pedal to the metal. We need to get there! See if we can communicate with the cruise ship and tell them to stop any forward progress. Let the captain know his ship's in harm's way. How long before we reach our target?"

"Four minutes out, sir."

. . .

"Here comes our target," Khalil said excitedly. "We need to wait until it's parallel. I don't want us to miss. Are you ready Mr. Lewis? You and your friend can have a little competition. Who will be the first one to hit the ship? Who will do the most damage?"

"You are the one who is going to shoot the missile," Bob said. "That's why we trained you."

Bob and Duke didn't want any part of this. They had agreed to coach them. They never wanted to be the ones who fired the missiles. They looked at each other, resigned to refusal.

"I'm not shooting at a cruise ship," Bob said boldly.

Khalil walked towards Bob with a semi-automatic in his hand, and pointed it at Bob's head.

"You will do as I say, or I will paint this mountain with your brains and blood."

Abdullah came up to Khalil in a panic.

"Listen, do you hear that?"

"Hear what?"

"A helicopter."

Soon everyone remained silent as they listened for the helicopter. Duke had heard it in the distance before anyone else. He knew from experience it was a Black Hawk. He knew it had to be U.S. military. Perhaps now they would be saved. He'd worry about the legal end of it later.

"Let's not make any quick decisions. Maybe it's just going to pass us by."

"I see it in the distance. It's coming right at us."

. . .

"Johnny, head right for them and see if we can verify the information. They'll probably think we're just passing through. If you see any of the SAM's pointed in our direction, take evasive action. Keep a good altitude. I don't want them to think we are on to them, if possible."

"Target at eleven o'clock," Johnny alerted the colonel.

Johnny could see the mountain in front of them. As he got closer, he saw several men with automatic weapons. They had their guns raised up as a warming sign, but they were not directly pointed at the helicopter as it zoomed overhead. "What now, Colonel?" asked the pilot.

"Circle back around, and get a visual on the cruise ship. Have we had any luck getting in touch with them?"

"Negative."

"When we go back, they're going to know we are here for them. Dip below the ridge, and find a location parallel to them on the east side. See if you can find us some clearing. Take a position as near to the top of the mountain as possible without risking exposure. Once you are in position, give me the signal, and we will deploy." The colonel turned to his team. "Alright men, this is it. Look for my signal and then descend as quickly as possible. Once the last man reaches the ground, we will reassemble to a new point and take cover. I will give further instructions at that time. Alright, open the doors."

As soon as the doors opened, it was too loud to hear anything. The Black Hawk was slowing down. The cruise ship apparently hadn't received any alerts yet, since it seemed to be maintaining its course. The helicopter began to hover at a point consistent with rappelling to the ground. The pilot had found a small clearing that allowed them to safely avoid any trees, and yet use them as cover. Jack was hearing all the information on his headset. He heard the colonel discuss the futility of using the two machine guns onboard. This was too dangerous. Friendly fire was the issue, and they didn't want to kill Bob and Duke if they could avoid it.

"Let's go!" yelled the colonel.

Upon hearing his command, they got into position, and without delay, they began to rappel. As the last man left the cabin, Jack moved into position with his M-4, and secured himself with a cargo strap. He kept his eyes on the ridge for any of Khalil's men. Once everyone was on the ground, Jack released the ropes to the ground as he was instructed. The helicopter would orbit safely, close to the ground objective. If necessary, Jack would engage in the firefight from his elevated position.

. . .

"Khalil, they have stopped on the other side. They are coming after us. We have to take action!" Abdullah said excitedly.

"Take some men to the top of the ridge and see if you can locate them," Khalil said, clearly concerned about his mission. "Kill them, if you see them!"

Abdullah gathered some men, and took off for the ridge, armed with automatic weapons. Khalil turned to look at the cruise ship coming into range. He then turned to Bob and Duke. "Get those missiles ready. We are going to change history. When I tell you to fire, make sure you do, or you will be dead men."

Just as he spoke, gunfire erupted on the ridge, getting his attention. He looked and saw two of his men hit and fall.

. . .

"We are under fire!" the colonel announced to Jack and the pilot. It didn't need to be said. Jack could see movement. In the impending darkness, he could see the flash coming from the barrels of the guns as they were discharged. He saw his team forging up the side of the mountain, engaging the terrorists. The helicopter circled, slowly moving closer to the action. Jack could see Charlie on the southern edge of the team near the corner of the ridge. He could see the enemy exchanging gunfire and then retreating. Experience was imperative here. Jack's team moved in concert, while the enemy seemed to be disjointed. The insurgents were clearly at a disadvantage since they did not have radio communication between them.

Jack heard the colonel barking commands to his team. They responded like a well-oiled machine, moving in rhythm with his directions. Jack focused on Charlie since he was closest to the helicopter's position. Jack's adrenalin was overwhelming. He momentarily couldn't believe he was at Montserrat watching a gunfight connected to his life from a Black Hawk helicopter. It was bizarre. Gunshots were loud over the radio and plentiful.

Jack wanted to help but he didn't think he would be able to add to what they were doing. They had everything under control. It looked like they had eliminated most of the enemy, even though they had the disadvantage of surging from a terrible starting position.

Just when Jack thought everything was under control, he spotted an insurgent making a low pass around the south corner of the mountain. Charlie was exposed and unaware he was about to encounter gunfire. Jack saw it, racked another round into his M-4 to make sure it was ready, and took aim. Quickly, he triggered an initial three-round burst toward the enemy who had just brought his gun into position to take Charlie out. Jack held his target and got off a couple more quick bursts until the ground kicked up by the shooter before striking him and rendering him harmless.

Charlie looked behind him and realized his life had just been saved. He looked up at Jack and gave him a thumbs-up. There were no more enemy shooters left at the ridge, and the team moved over the top in the direction of Khalil.

"Aim at the cruise ship and fire, now!" Khalil screamed.

The U.S. team was moving down the hill. Shots were fired by the two remaining men of Khalil's army, Amir and Mohammed. Bob pretended his launcher was jammed. Khalil continued to scream at him and Duke. Duke was not moving. Khalil was now standing between Bob and Duke, barking at them. He was infuriated. He turned, and shot Duke in the head. Duke's body collapsed limply. Khalil then turned to Bob. Shots were continuing to be exchanged behind them, before Amir and Mohammed were killed. Khalil and Bob both knew not much time was left. A bullet kicked up some dirt by Khalil's foot.

"Aim that fuckin' missile now!"

Bob started to take a position of aiming at the cruise ship but he didn't fire. Finally, Khalil was incensed to the point of taking it into his own hands. He turned to Bob, and shot him, but was simultaneously shot himself in the foot by an errant bullet. Bob fell to the side while Khalil picked up the launcher, defying the pain in his maimed foot. He took aim at the cruise ship. Just as Khalil pulled the trigger mechanism, he was struck in the back, but not in time to prevent him from pulling the trigger. The rocket missile was discharged toward the ship. Khalil would never know the outcome.

The glare of the missile in the twilight resembled a Fourth of July celebration. The team, which had arrived on site, could only watch in horror as the missile headed for the cruise ship. Nothing was said. They just stood agape in futility.

Onboard the bridge of the ship, the captain saw a stream of light headed his way. The crew on the bridge stared in astonishment as it was headed toward them. They could only watch. No ship, regardless of how technologically advanced, had enough evasive capabilities to duck an incoming missile. As it got larger and closer, their doom was apparent. Like a submarine heading blindly towards a depth charge, the crew could only pray for absolution. Finally, they stood and watched, as the fire in the air shot over the bow and traveled into the distant ocean before discharging into a plume of water.

They looked at each other for a moment before erupting into nervous but jubilant laughter and applause. Equally euphoric was the U.S. team on the mountain. In the air, Jack and the pilots, removed from the close proximity of the ground crew, were no less ecstatic.

Later, the Black Hawk was able to hover at the shoreline and take on the ground crew. They had to hurry since the helicopter needed to economize fuel for the return flight. A couple of the men stayed behind to secure the site until morning when a team could come in and assess the scene. The bodies would have to be disposed of properly. Bob Lewis was transported by an additional helicopter. He had suffered a gunshot to the head, but was still semi-conscious.

They would head back to the base camp from where they originated in St. Lucia. There, they would regroup and be debriefed.

46

It was a weary ride back to the base camp for most of the team, but not Jack. He was energized. The team had just prevented a media earthquake that would have placed the president in a very delicate political situation. Yet, for most of them, it was just another successfully completed mission.

Each one of them had played a specific, significant part in a play to which Jack had a ringside seat. He saw the entire event unfold dramatically in front of him from the side of a Black Hawk helicopter hovering above. It was something he would never forget, no matter how jaded he had become.

When they finally made it back to the base camp, darkness had taken over. Jack was a little apprehensive about landing on a mountaintop surrounded by trees, however, the lighting from the Black Hawk and the camp building enabled Jack to see the landing site without any difficulty, minimizing his anxiety.

They disembarked quietly but not quickly. They grabbed their gear, and were starting to walk toward the command center when Jack heard his name. He turned around and saw Charlie walking towards him. Charlie's size and manner were very imposing.

"Hey man, I want to thank you for saving my life. The pilot told me I would've been a dead man if you hadn't shot that bastard back there on the ridge."

"Don't worry about it," Jack said humbly. He put his hands out to his side in a gesture of conciliation. Before Jack could say another word, he felt a crushing pain in his chest. The next thing he knew, he was sitting upright on the ground. Jack looked bewildered. He looked up at Charlie who was standing over him wearing one of the meanest scowls he had ever seen. It was the kind heavyweight fighters give each other before a title fight.

"Don't ever call anybody a nigger again!" Charlie said glaring down at Jack.

Jack just sat there, continuing to look dumbfounded before realizing Charlie had punched him in the chest. Before he could answer, Charlie broke out into a wide grin and held out his hand. Jack took it and he was lifted to a standing position.

"You know, that was one of the cruelest things I've ever said, and I'm sorry."

Charlie just laughed and walked away. Jack started to brush himself off when he began to smile. He knew he had it coming to him. He felt his chest and knew it would hurt for days. *Son-of-a-bitch*!

He walked inside the headquarters. The rest of the crew headed for the locker area to drop and store their equipment. They were told there was food available in the dining area. Everyone was hungry and thirsty. Jack was last to get to the dining room where most of them had already started eating.

Once everyone was seated, the colonel got everyone's attention. He congratulated everyone on a job well done. He specifically pointed out Jack and let everyone know how important Jack was to the mission, and particularly to Charlie.

They all applauded Jack, the only civilian in the group. Jack was still riding the wave of excitement. Certainly he had been involved in dangerous situations before, from hostage situations to arresting murderers, but nothing felt quite as good as this.

Soon everyone was eating and enjoying the local Piton beer. Jack began replaying the entire experience, from the time they left in the Black Hawk helicopter, to shooting a terrorist and saving Charlie's life, and then back to the current moment. He cringed when he thought of his encounter with Charlie when they got back. Then, his thoughts took him back to the cemetery where he saw Charlie when he was running for his life. Ultimately, it brought his thoughts back to Marnie.

In the urgency of the moment, he was able to mentally escape from the horror of Marnie's death. Struggling for self-preservation allows you to focus away from the tragedy, but once the moment of safety arrives, you still go back for a mental review. He was experiencing a hodgepodge of emotions. He was elated to be alive, enraged at Bob Lewis for the position he put him in, and deeply troubled about the loss of Marnie.

Once the meal was over, and everyone started to leave the dining room, the colonel and Jack sat together at the table. Jack needed to talk with him about Bob Lewis and Marnie.

"Colonel, I need to ask you a few questions."

"Sure, Jack. I don't know if I have all the answers but I'll do the best I can," he replied.

"How long was I being followed by the government?"

"Jack, we received intelligence about an arms deal. It resulted in us trailing Bob Lewis. Ultimately, you came into the picture when the general's son was murdered in front of his house. We knew you didn't have anything to do with it."

"Yet, you let me get arrested, and put in a cell with a high bail."

"Long story short, yes."

Jack just shook his head trying to keep his anger in check.

"Why?"

"Jack, what you may, or may not know, is we believe Senator Rothschild is tied up in all this. We believe your arrest provided him with a false sense of security, which would lead to his ultimate downfall."

"In other words, it was all political."

"Yes and no. Yes, he is a politician but, he was also involved in a crime against our country. Imagine, a U.S. senator committing treason against the people he was elected to serve. Clearly, he was the big fish in the pond. You were useful to us to help get him. Jack, you are a hero. You made a sacrifice, willing or unwilling, it doesn't matter. You were helping us bring a corrupt senator to justice. I think you will agree, after legitimately shooting his doped-out son, and being the target of his vengeance, you have the last laugh. He is dirty, and needs to pay the price."

"How come I'm not laughing?" Jack retorted.

"I don't know if I would feel any differently in your shoes."

"Do you have enough to convict Senator Rothschild?"

The colonel sighed and looked away. It told Jack all he needed to know.

"You don't have enough, do you?" Jack asked.

"We're hoping Bob Lewis comes out of his coma so he can provide us with enough evidence to charge the senator."

"So, let me get this straight. I save a woman's life, I get arrested, thrown in a cell, almost get killed a couple of times, have to run for my life, literally and figuratively, save another man's life at the risk of my own, and perhaps most important, a woman loses her life, all because you want to get a senator arrested?"

"I know you're pissed, but you're missing the big picture."

"You're gonna sit there and give me *your* interpretation of the truth, and expect me to agree?"

"Jack, you're forgetting something else. We had terrorists who were preying on innocent victims that include Americans. You helped prevent innocent Americans from being killed. Don't you feel good about that?"

"Fuckin' great!" Jack answered scathingly. "Except I didn't save the one woman I loved."

They sat there for a moment in silence.

"Where is Bob Lewis now and what is his condition?" Jack asked, still fuming.

"Right now, he is in a hospital in Castries. As I said, he's still in a coma."

"Can I see him?"

"Why?"

"Because I want to look at the man who has been able to fuck up my life with the help of the U.S. government, and know he is about to go to hell."

"I don't know if that is a good idea, Jack."

"You owe it to me and, if that isn't enough, according to you, the people of the United States owe it to me."

"Let me think about that."

The colonel got up from the table and left the room. Jack continued to sit there trying to take it all in. He assumed he was now vindicated of all charges, but after what he just heard, he knew it wasn't safe to assume anything.

About five minutes after he left the room, the colonel returned with Charlie. It was just the three of them in the room.

"Jack, I'm going to let you see Bob Lewis. You'll only have five minutes. Charlie is gonna go with you, and make sure you don't do anything stupid. Remember, Bob Lewis may be in a St. Lucia Hospital, but he is still in the custody of the U.S. government. You are out of trouble now and I don't think you want to step into it again, by tampering with him. Do I make myself clear?"

"Crystal," Jack said sarcastically.

The colonel gave him a dirty look and said, "You will go by helicopter to expedite your visit. It's ready, so if I were you, I'd get your ass in gear."

Jack followed Charlie out to the waiting chopper, and they flew to the hospital in Castries. It wasn't far from the airport where Jack first arrived in St. Lucia.

Once they landed, Jack and Charlie went in and found a waiting team member who had accompanied Bob Lewis from the site on Cork Hill. They stood at the door leading to his room. The team member, named Joe, knew they were coming and allowed Jack to go in. Charlie followed right behind him.

"Jack," Charlie said, placing his hand on Jack's shoulder. "Please, don't do anything stupid."

Jack turned to Charlie, and gave him a look of compliance.

Bob Lewis was lying on a bed with tubes coming out of him and monitors next to the bed. His head was wrapped but his ears were exposed. Jack stood there for a few moments looking at a man he hardly knew, but knew well enough to despise. Jack realized the tubes were sending pain-killing medicine through his veins and he wanted to rip them out. Charlie stood in the back of the small room by the door. He was close enough to prevent Jack from disturbing anything.

Jack slowly walked over to the side of the bed and knelt down by Bob's side. He kept his hands behind his back, letting Charlie know he wasn't going to bother anything.

Jack stared at him. He wondered what made a man throw his family, friends and all his self-respect away for money. Greed, disrespect for others, and self-gratification were foreign to Jack. Generally, he had compassion for everyone, but he looked at Bob as a disgusting piece of humanity.

Jack slowly leaned forward to whisper in his ear. He gave a side glance at Charlie, who didn't move in his direction.

"Well Bob, I hope you can hear me. It's Jack Dublin. It was a nice try, setting me up for the fall, but I'm still here, enjoying life as a healthy, free man. You're lying there with a bullet in the brain and tubes coming out of your body hanging on to life," Jack said, without looking directly at him.

"I don't care if you ever say another intelligible word in this lifetime. Senator Rothschild will get his. I'll make sure of it. Marnie will not die in vain. Before I go, I'd just like to say, I hope you suffer and die, you miserable piece of shit. When you get to hell, make sure you save a place for your buddy, the senator. He won't be far behind you."

Jack stood up and walked out the door past Charlie. He was surprised to see the colonel standing there in the hallway.

"Jack, I need to talk to you."

Jack followed him over to a foyer where they could have some privacy.

"Jack, the plane taking you back to the states is waiting for you at the airport."

"What plane?"

"The same one you arrived on."

Jack didn't know what to say. It happened so quickly.

"What about," Jack paused. "Marnie?"

"Is that the name of the woman who was with you?"

"Yes."

The colonel placed a sympathetic hand on Jack's shoulder. "As you know, Jack, it was an incredibly powerful explosion, and a fiery one, too. Essentially everything was consumed in the blast, nearly vaporized. We understand local investigators and clean-up crews never found either of the bodies." Trying to find the right words, he continued the briefing. "All they discovered were....scattered remains...only shreds of human tissue. From our surveillance, it was quite apparent she meant a lot to you. I'm very sorry, Jack."

47

Jack sat quietly in the front passenger seat of the red Hummer. Charlie was driving, and had also been mostly silent the entire way. Occasionally, he looked over at Jack and saw him sitting there stiffly, staring straight ahead with a blank, impassive look on his face. Charlie simply allowed Jack to be alone with the many thoughts going through his head. He knew there was nothing he could do or say to help the man sitting next to him.

For several minutes, both men bounced about in their seats, as the narrow, tree-lined road became more poorly paved. After turning left and onto the access road to the private airport, Charlie slowed as they approached the security gate. A man in uniform stepped quickly from a small perimeter building, and simply waved the Hummer past.

As they passed through the security gate, an open-top jeep occupied by two more men in uniform was waiting just off to the right. At the wheel was the captain who had admonished Jack when he first arrived in St. Lucia. Now, after having been reprimanded by his colonel, the captain was providing escort to Hollingsworth's jet, already in position for takeoff at the far end of the runway.

With the Hummer in tow, the captain and his side-kick sped out onto the tarmac. Then, with tires squealing, the jeep whipped a sharp right turn onto the southwest taxiway and led the way to the waiting Gulfstream. The pilots had already commenced their start-up procedure, and the starboard side Rolls-Royce turbofan was screaming to life.

Charlie and Jack exited the SUV and Jack came around the front of the Hummer. As they approached each other, Jack held out his hand.

"Listen Charlie, I'm sorry for what I said back in Anse le Raye," Jack offered apologetically, having to yell the words over the din of the high-pitched turbofans. "I'm not that type of person. Really, that's not me, not even close," Jack loudly added.

"Jack, you saved my life," Charlie offered back in full voice, trying to speak over the irritating noise. "Nothing more need be said. You don't need to apologize to me."

"Yes I do, and I just did. It needed to be said."

Charlie smiled. "Take care of yourself, Jack. I hope to run into you some time."

"Just don't do it with your fist," Jack returned with a half smile, still yelling, as he rubbed his chest. "I'm gonna hurt for a week!"

"Perhaps it is me who owes you the apology," the big man told him.

"Let's call it even and forget it," suggested Jack.

Charlie only nodded his head in agreement, tired of yelling over the aircraft's howling engines. They hugged, and Jack trotted up the stairs and into the plane without looking back. He walked down the aisle and somewhat mindlessly took the same seat he had occupied on the flight down. However, unlike the flight down, Jack wasn't noticing the thick plush carpet, or the richly-upholstered over-sized seats, or the luxurious accoutrements everywhere throughout the posh cabin. His thoughts returned, ever so deeply, to Marnie.

"Can I get you something to drink?" asked the attractive flight attendant.

"Not at the moment, thank you. Maybe later," he answered vacantly, hardly noticing the young woman's beauty, and uncharacteristically paying more attention to fastening his lap belt.

With its engines pitching a higher shrill, the Gulfstream began to move, and taxied into position. Soon, Jack felt the potent thrust compress him in the seat as the powerful jet was racing down the runway. Seconds later, they were airborne and climbing out over the Caribbean. It was still early in the morning, and as the Gulfstream banked into the moonless sky to assume a northerly course, Jack watched as the lights of St. Lucia slowly faded and disappeared. He stared into the pitch black void outside, thinking only of what he had lost.

Fatigue had overtaken him. Jack was more tired than he could recall feeling in a long while. All his adrenaline had been spent, and his body felt like a bag of concrete that wouldn't move. His eyelids felt like lead, but somehow, Jack wasn't in the mood to sleep. He looked across at the seat Marnie had occupied only 48 hours ago. He could see her sitting there, and recalled her incredible smile, her easy laughter, and the unique sense of humor she possessed. Everything about her had made him feel so amazing, and had brought a special ease and focus into his life at such a difficult time. He thought about all the time they had spent together during the preceding days, what a wonderful companion she had been, and how fabulous she had made him feel. He had never in his life felt so attuned with a woman, so natural, so perfect. And, recalling the night they had enjoyed in each other's arms, when Jack knew he had truly fallen in love with Marnie, it was just too much to bear. His eyes filled with tears. It was the first time he had wept since losing his mother. Jack was certain he would have married Marnie, if she would have had him. But Marnie was gone. Forever.

48

"Mister Dublin?.....Mister Dublin?.....Sir?" the attractive attendant said softly in a soothing voice, lightly shaking Jack's right shoulder.

For a moment, Jack thought he was dreaming, but slowly awakening, he met the young flight attendant's eyes.

"Sir, we'll be landing in about 35 minutes or so, and the captain has asked me to bring you up to the cockpit."

Still somewhat groggy, Jack awoke a bit more, and thought to himself, "That was quick. I really must have conked out and slept heavily."

"What's this about?" Jack questioned, now more focused. "What does the captain want with me?"

"Sir, I'm really not sure. He just asked me to come get you. I'm certain the captain will explain," she answered politely.

Jack slowly stood, then followed the young woman through the opening in the forward cabin bulkhead, and into the forward crew compartment. Once through the doorway, Jack could see the cockpit, and noticed the co-pilot was flying the aircraft. The captain had already turned aft in his seat, to see the inquisitive look on Jack's face.

"Sir, go ahead and be seated in the jump-seat there. We might be descending through a bit of rough air in a few minutes, so please buckle yourself in."

Jack settled himself and secured the lap belt as the captain requested.

"Sir, I doubt if you noticed. Julianne told us you were asleep back there not long after we departed St. Lucia," the captain began. "We received a communication about an hour ago to alter our flight plan," he advised. "We'll be landing in St. Lucia...," he paused momentarily to look at the instrument panel, then back to Jack, "in about twenty-eight minutes," he continued. "We'll be landing at the same airport we departed three hours ago. I just didn't want you to become confused when we begin our final descent, and you see nothing but the Caribbean out your window, and then all the palm trees when we land. We didn't want you to freak out and wonder what was going on."

"What *IS* going on, if you don't mind telling me? What's this all about?" Jack inquired, bewildered about the situation.

"I really don't know myself, sir. We weren't provided many particulars, only that we were told to return to St. Lucia, and the change in our flight plan had been okayed by Mr. Hollingsworth. That's all we needed to know. When you fly for a man like Mr. Hollingsworth, you don't ask questions, unless it has to do with flight safety. You fly where you're told to fly, and do what you're told to do. There aren't many of us pilots in the world lucky enough to be flying a G650, and we love it, so we do what we're told," the captain explained, smiling. He turned to look at the flight instruments for a few seconds, and then returned his attention to Jack. "There is one thing, sir. When we land, you'll be met by a colonel...uh...," he paused for a moment, turning forward again to his co-pilot. The co-pilot had read the captain's mind, and was already handing him a small piece of paper. "Colonel Brian Olive; he's the man who will be meeting you. That's all we know. Like I said, this is typical when you fly for Mr. Hollingsworth. Go ahead back to your seat and strap in. We can delay our approach for a minute. As I said, we might pass through a bit of rough air during our descent. Nothing to worry about," the captain finished matter-of-factly.

Jack left the cockpit and returned to his seat. His mind had already started to work on the situation back in the cockpit. "What the hell is going on?" he thought. What could possibly have happened? Quickly, Jack's mind began to spin out of control with all the possibilities in rapid-fire succession. Why do they need me back in St. Lucia? The captain said Oliver would be at the airport. It must have something to do with him, or the group, but why would that have something to do with me? How could I help them? They don't need me; they're professionals. Then Jack thought, maybe Bob Lewis died. That can't be it, because they wouldn't have me return for that. Maybe Lewis came out of his coma and they need me to interpret something he said. That's it! But wait, I didn't have anything to do with the terrorists or weapons, and they know it. Hell, Oliver said they had been following me. He even said I was a fucking hero! Maybe it's the senator. Maybe Lewis said something about the senator. Jack pondered that for a moment, and then had a revelation. Maybe Lewis said something to implicate Jack. That fucking son-of-a-bitch! If he's not dead, I'll kill him myself! That's why the captain was so evasive. That's why he told me he didn't know anything. They didn't want to make me suspicious. They just want me to sit here like an idiot until we hit the ground. Come to think of it, he hadn't seen the flight attendant since he came back to his seat. Maybe they warned her to stay away from him. Jack was so exhausted he couldn't think straight. Nothing made sense to him. His mind was spinning out of control. But then, he thought of Rothschild again. Rothschild surely had powerful friends; hell, he was powerful himself. He knew all sorts of people, important people who could get anything done. Maybe it was Rothschild setting me up. He promised he would get me sooner or later. Maybe this was it. Maybe the senator had finally found a way to take me down for good!

Jack could feel the aircraft descending more rapidly now. He knew it wouldn't be long before they were on the ground. The urgency of the situation was really getting to him. *If I could only figure out what this is all about,* he wondered anxiously.

49

All the way down the final approach, Jack looked from the oval cabin window, pushing his head tightly against the glass, and peering as far ahead as possible. He strained to see if he could discover any unusual activity at the airport. Watching the island come up quickly to meet the airplane, Jack couldn't wait to be on the ground. He wanted to know what was going on. It didn't matter at this point; he just wanted to know what it was all about. This was a fucking three-ring-circus, and he wanted the show to be over.

It was another one of those grease-it-on landings, and the tires barely let out a peep. The pilot set down the thirty-ton aircraft so gently, had the runway been made of glass, he wouldn't have even cracked it. And, like the previous landing, Jack immediately heard the potent turbofans go into full reverse thrust, sending him forward in his seat as the big Gulfstream decelerated rapidly on the short runway. As Jack continued to look out the window, the red Hummer came into view and he saw Colonel Oliver and Charlie standing next to it. When the jet finally turned from the runway, and taxied to a parking area, Jack heard the engines shut down.

When the door was opened, Colonel Oliver, with Charlie close behind, came practically skipping down the aisle.

"Hi Jack!" the colonel greeted, in a voice so friendly and natural it was if nothing unusual was going on.

"Hey Jack!" Charlie followed immediately. "Long time no see!"

Jack was immediately disarmed, at least somewhat, thinking maybe everything was okay. He was dumbfounded, though, and his mind continued to spin wildly around all the possibilities he'd imagined ever since his conversation with the pilot.

"Okay, gentlemen, what's the deal? How long do you intend to keep me in suspense? I know you didn't fly me all the way back here just to say hello," Jack said sarcastically with a tone of irritation.

The colonel had taken a seat facing Jack. On their way into the plane, Charlie had stopped momentarily to speak with the flight attendant. He'd asked if she had a good single-malt scotch, and would she, please, bring a tall one back to Jack.

The young attendant arrived with the scotch, and offered it to Jack. Jack remained completely bewildered, and looked up at the woman with quizzical eyes. She shrugged her shoulders slightly, and returned a puzzled look telling Jack she didn't have a clue.

"Drink it, Jack," Oliver urged. "And please, Miss, bring another," he asked. "Please, Jack, drink it. You're going to need it, believe me," Oliver advised, staring Jack in the eyes.

Jack figured he'd never hear anything until he had the drink, so he banged it down in one long pull, and then disgustedly slammed the glass down on the small courtesy table.

"Okay, I've had the drink, whatever the hell that was about. Now what the fuck is going on?" he asked in an aggravated voice.

"Jack.....Marnie is alive," Oliver told him, but using a tone which told Jack there was more. "She suffered some pretty bad burns, and nearly drowned, but she's alive, Jack. She's alive!"

The attendant came, and Jack pulled hard on the second scotch, finishing about half of the burning liquid in one gulp. He was in shock. It was the last thing he'd expected to hear. He leaned forward in his seat, holding the glass now with both hands, simply staring at it catatonically. The moment was a complete aberration for Jack.

Colonel Oliver leaned forward, placing his hands on Jack's knees. "C'mon Jack, we're gonna take you to see Marnie. The doctors wanted to keep her, but when I told them we had a private jet waiting to take her back to the states, and a Navy medical team to accompany her, so... let's just go get her, okay? I pulled some strings and called in an old debt, so the medical team will be here before too long. Jack, did you hear me?"

Jack just sat there, not moving, looking at his glass, but then looked up at the colonel, and nodded his head slowly, affirming he had heard what was said.

"C'mon Jack, let's get going," Charlie said as he held out his hand to help Jack out of his seat. They began to walk down the aisle and as they approached, the captain held out his hand and Jack shook it.

"Congratulations, Jack," the captain said hopefully. "I hope everything turns out okay for you."

"Thanks," Jack said meekly.

Once they were in the Hummer, they bounced along the access road before hitting smoother pavement. For the first few minutes of the uncomfortable ride, Jack remained quiet, and kept to himself. Holding tightly to the egress handle just above his side window, he appeared to stare mindlessly at the trees whizzing by. Now, inexplicably, nothing seemed to make any sense, and none of the pieces seemed to fit together. Jack realized he should be feeling nothing but relief and happiness, but he was struggling to believe the events of the past hour, and fighting to overcome an unexplainable knot deep in the pit of his gut that was making him nauseous. He felt like puking out the window.

"Listen, Jack, I want to explain a few things before we get to the hospital," the colonel finally opened. "I'm sure you'll be interested to know exactly what happened down at the pier yesterday," Oliver added, also attempting to get Jack centered and refocused.

Jack looked at the colonel. He still appeared inattentive, and was wrestling with a wandering mind. He didn't look good at all.

"It was total chaos down at the pier and along the waterfront when the explosion went off. Complete pandemonium broke out," Oliver began, hoping to at least acquire Jack's partial attention. "A number of local townspeople were badly hurt; emergency responders arrived quickly and began tending to the injured. The blast was really powerful, Jack."

"Yeah, I was there, remember?" Jack said, his usual sarcasm beginning to show.

"From what I was told, nobody down there imagined anyone on Captain Barney's boat, or even near it, could have survived, so all their attention was on those they knew could be helped," Oliver continued. "We've already received back a lot of data and results from forensics. There wasn't much to evaluate and test, but everything recoverable and viable went up right away to the FBI lab. The explosive used was special stuff, something very new. It's all pretty much *Black-Ops* kind of research. And it's supposed to be way beyond even my security level, so you didn't hear it from me."

Jack sarcastically broke in again. "You know, all that sort of crap about something being above my pay grade is a skill I perfected a long time ago, Colonel."

Oliver wasn't sure that was the answer he wanted to hear from Jack, but he was heartened to see a bit of evidence of the Jack he'd come to know the past two days, so the colonel just kept talking.

"Somehow, Lewis had the right contacts to get his hands on that type of explosive material. I can't even talk about it, Jack. That's all I'm at liberty to say, all I am permitted to tell you," the colonel reiterated with emphasis.

Jack quickly interjected once more, "Colonel, you'd be surprised what cops hear sometimes about stuff like that, especially if they have friends on the bomb squad."

Oliver continued. "I doubt if you heard of this. It's highly classified, as I said. What I can say is that the stuff is designed to do exactly what it did, explode and create so much heat it vaporizes essentially everything. Do you catch my drift, Jack?"

"Yeah, I get it. It doesn't leave much evidence to analyze," Jack answered with increased attentiveness, and becoming more committed to the colonel's explanation.

"Exactly, and as I say, that's what happened, or at least nearly happened. The compound is tricky stuff, and is still being tested. I don't believe they've even determined how much to use, or what is necessary in various conditions, to produce specific types and sizes of blasts for varying purposes, if you know what I mean. So whoever Lewis had working for him probably didn't know much about the stuff, or how to apply it properly for their intended purpose. Even our R & D people aren't sure about it yet. I've already told you too much, Jack. Remember, this is highly classified," Oliver warned again.

Jack responded. "Yeah, I realize that, Colonel. Who am I gonna tell? Don't worry about me. Mum's the word," Jack said, mildly amused.

"Anyway, like I said, whoever was responsible for rigging Captain Barney's boat obviously had no idea what they were doing, and didn't have a clue what they were dealing with. Unfortunately, for Barney, he was apparently quite close to the blast origin, and was pretty much totally consumed, vaporized. And that's essentially what happened to most of the boat, at least what was above the waterline. The heat was so intense, everything burnable, which with this stuff is *everything*, was quickly incinerated. The rest, the remainder of the hull at and below the waterline, simply sank right away without burning. It went right to the bottom."

The colonel paused before getting into the incredible part of the story.

"Now we get to the amazing part, Jack. It's just a theory, at least that's what I've been told. Somehow, and by sheer accident, the manner in which the material was set to go off, sent mostly just a shock wave in Marnie's direction. There was quite a wall of heat sent her way, because she does have some pretty bad burns. But as I say, mostly all that was directed at her was a lesser-energy shock wave, carrying compressed, super-heated air, forced out and away from the blast center. But here's another piece of the miracle from a theory developed by the people at FBI HQ. Like I've told you, I can't provide every detail, but again, it all goes back to whoever set the charge on Barney's boat. I told you this is extremely problematic stuff, quite unpredictable. In order to produce a homogeneous explosion in which the blast event has a 360 degree similarity, the origin of detonation must occur at the precise center of mass, the center of the explosive core. Put simply, whoever set up the device would have to place the detonator at the exact center of the explosive material. And after analyzing everything we sent them, the folks at Quantico knew this didn't happen. They could tell from a simple site analysis, from what they were told about the local damage down here. Apparently, most of the blast wave released in the opposite direction was away from Marnie. If you look at the damaged area down around the pier and waterfront, it's very obvious. Had the device been properly prepared, Marnie never would have made it. Even so, the lower energy shock wave that struck Marnie was potent enough to cause poly-traumatic injury, and render her instantly unconscious. It carried her nearly a hundred yards straight up the waterfront, and luckily, over the water and not onto land. Are you following me, Jack?"

"Yep, I'm right with you," Jack answered quickly.

"Even more miraculous, right at the time of detonation, three guys in a skiff were pulling away from their dock. And get this, Jack: Two of the men just happened to be emergency room physicians from South Carolina, down here on vacation. Marnie landed in the water right next to them, only twenty feet from their boat. Both doctors went immediately into the water to save her. They were able to revive her by the time they got to shore and summoned more help. Now, what I mean by revived, they cleared the water from her lungs, established an airway, and got her breathing again, but she remained deeply in shock and had some serious injuries and burns. Is that totally amazing or what, Jack?"

Jack simply stared at Oliver with a rapt expression, slowly shaking his head back and forth in total disbelief of the extraordinary circumstances.

"Wait, I'm not finished, Jack. When she arrived at the emergency room, nobody knew who she was. She had no I.D., nothing at all to tell them anything about her. Obviously, at first, their only concern was getting her stabilized and beginning to diagnose and treat her injuries. Meanwhile, hospital officials had contacted local law enforcement, and quite an effort to identify Marnie ensued. Unfortunately, they had little to go by because there wasn't any evidence she was even on the island. The two of you came in on a private aircraft, and without passports, remember?"

"Yeah, how could I forget?"

Jack seemed to finally fully return to reality. Oliver could hear the familiar rough manner and sharp sarcasm in Jack's speech. He could see it in Jack's body language, too, and the colonel was glad to have the old Jack back.

"Finally, Marnie began to come around enough to be gently questioned, but all she talked about was Jack Dublin. She just kept calling your name and asking for Jack Dublin. And nobody had a clue who Jack Dublin was. It was only by chance that one of my men was at the hospital later last night. He'd gone to check on a couple of our guys who'd been hurt in the fire fight out at Cork Hill on Montserrat. He overheard some of the hospital people discussing that a badly injured woman had been brought in from the waterfront explosion early in the afternoon, and they had not been able to identify her. My guy began to put two and two together, and here we are, Jack. That all happened not long after you and Charlie and I were at the hospital for you to see Bob Lewis. Shit, Jack! Marnie was right there when we were, just on another floor of the hospital. I'm really sorry, Jack. If we'd only known then."

A look of apprehension suddenly returned to Jack's face, as Charlie pulled the Hummer to a stop at the hospital entrance. It was obvious he had deep feelings for Marnie, and feared what he would find inside.

50

They immediately took Jack to the ICU where Marnie lay unconscious. As he stood behind the glass window, Jack couldn't even tell it was her; she was almost entirely covered with burn wraps. There were several monitors attached to her which were constantly being supervised by various nurses.

"Jack, I just heard from the command center. They've been communicating with the Navy and coordinating the medical team's transport and arrival," Oliver offered, seeing the unremitting concern on Jack's face.

Oliver couldn't tell for sure if Jack was listening. Jack said nothing and his expression didn't change. His gaze was fixed on Marnie.

"I've been advised their aircraft just touched down at Hewanorra. The Navy wouldn't allow a landing at the airport here in Castries. The nixed landing had to do with flight safety, something about the airport fire category. My contact in the U.S. arranged for Marnie to be flown back on the naval aircraft. It's already equipped and set up with everything necessary to care for her during the flight. It makes a lot of sense."

"Yeah, I suppose," Jack replied in a preoccupied voice, never looking at the colonel.

"They're allowing you to accompany her, too," Oliver continued, trying to cheer Jack up a bit. "You guys are already big news, at least at the higher levels back in Washington. A lot of people are very grateful for the part you and Marnie played in the whole deal with Lewis and his people, the terrorists, and stolen weapons, and so forth. Apparently, the two of you have carte blanche; they can't do enough to assist you and Marnie. And get this, Jack. I understand there's quite a buzz started back on Capitol Hill regarding a certain United States senator," Oliver whispered in a lower voice, hopeful he'd get a rise out of Jack with that.

Never even blinking, Jack continued staring at Marnie, without a word or a sign he had heard anything the colonel had just said.

"Your private jet has been released, and already departed for Delaware, I'm told. I sent the Blackhawk to pick up the medical team. You'll be going back to our facilities in Bethesda. I'll check back with you later, Jack. Hang in there," the colonel said as he put his hand on Jack's shoulder.

"Thank you," Jack said gently.

He continued to stand guard over Marnie. Looking through the glass window, it was upsetting to see Marnie lying trapped and helpless in the complex and uncomfortable-looking contraption that was her hospital bed. Her bandaged head and face badly bruised and swollen so completely to disfigure her incredible beauty, was too much for Jack. She looked so vulnerable, with all the cables and weights suspending her limbs to position and immobilize them. And knowing of the burns beneath the air-blown sheets draped partially over, but not touching her, the entire scene completely overwhelmed Jack. It was impossible to contain what he was feeling anyway. During the last twenty-four hours linking yesterday with this moment, he had been more emotional than when his mother died.

When Jack first arrived at the hospital, the ER doctor, along with an orthopedic surgeon, had given him a synopsis of Marnie's injuries and current status at the time. They theorized she had hit the water three times, like a flat stone thrown and skipped across the surface. Along with the initial shock wave, which the doctors believed could be responsible for the rib fractures on her left side, it had been the first two impacts with the water that caused the extensive bruising and all the fractured bones. The combination of the high-decibel sound wave and shock wave of the powerful blast had also damaged her left tympanic membrane, the ear drum, and she remained deaf in that ear. They theorized one impact had involved her hip, lower back, and buttock on the right side which correlated to the fractures of both bones of her lower leg just above the ankle, and lower rib fractures on that side. The other two impacts involved her left upper back and shoulder. Surprisingly, none of the fractures was particularly serious, although the fracture of Marnie's lower leg was significant. The doctors had told Jack this was a minor miracle, considering the serious impact of Marnie's head hitting the water. A portion of her scalp had actually been torn away from her skull. All in all, considering what had occurred, the doctors told Jack that Marnie was an incredibly fortunate woman to have survived such a blast, let alone incur only the injuries she had sustained.

Jack began to think about the long recovery Marnie would have to endure. He would be ready to help her in every way. He was never going to leave her side. Jack was suddenly aware of a commotion up the hallway behind him. It was people talking, but one of them possessed a very deep and resounding voice. It was a voice so distinctive, clear and authoritative, he couldn't help but turn around and take a look. Already walking toward him was a very tall and quite handsome African-American man in a naval officer's uniform. He approached and held out his hand immediately for Jack to shake.

"Hello, Mr. Dublin. I'm Jim Willis, but most everybody just calls me Dr. J.," the Lieutenant Commander Navy doctor greeted in a friendly tone. "Being six-eight, I played a lot of round ball, so that's where the nickname came from. I had hair kinda like his, too, way back when. Unfortunately, I wasn't as good as Julius Erving, so I just decided to become a doctor instead," the pleasant commander continued, already joking with Jack. "I'm here to take care of your girl, and we're gonna see to it she gets the best," the tall commander finished with a big, reassuring smile.

As soon as the commander spoke, Jack somehow instantly knew the right man was on the job. Jack liked him immediately. It was impossible not to.

"Just to give you a little background: I'm from the western suburbs of Philadelphia. I attended med school at the University of Pennsylvania, and did a residency in emergency medicine there. Then

I did another residency in critical care at Johns Hopkins. Uncle Sam paid for a lot of my education, and I committed to the Navy. I fell in love with it, along with a Navy nurse. We both wanted to stay in, so here I am. I'm the assistant chief of critical care at Walter Reed in Washington D.C. That's okay with you, I hope?"

"Sure," was the only answer Jack could muster while being overwhelmed by Dr. Willis.

"I've already had a very good consult with the doctors here, and as soon as I do my initial exam and assessment, and go through Ms. Bloom's chart, I'll give you a thorough run-down, okay? We'll have plenty of time to get to know one another on the flight back. You are "the" Jack Dublin, right?" Dr. J. finished with a joke.

As the commander finished speaking, two Navy nurses arrived. One of them was pushing a wheeled cart, carrying papers and some medical equipment as they entered Marnie's room.

"Now if you'll excuse me, I'll talk to you in a little while," the commander politely said.

The tall doctor turned to enter Marnie's room, but almost immediately, he turned back to Jack.

"Sir, I'm sure Ms. Bloom looks quite frightening to you. As I said, I've already had a consultation with the attending and ER physicians, as well as the surgeons who repaired Ms. Bloom's scalp injury and treated her fractures. Ms. Bloom is going to be just fine, so please try to relax, sir. Everything is going to be okay. Ms. Bloom will receive the best possible care when we arrive at Walter Reed. I'll introduce you to Lieutenant Akers and D'Antonio later. They're both very fine critical care nurses," the doctor concluded, offering another reassuring smile before he turned to enter Marnie's room.

Jack was beginning to finally relax. Dr. J. had given the reassurance that was as good as a strong sedative. Jack even began to smile!

Just then, he heard familiar voices. He turned to see Colonel Oliver and Charlie coming up the hallway.

51

Jack sensed the helicopter slowing as its nose pitched up slightly to begin the descent. Then seeing the airport come into view, he could feel the chopper losing altitude more rapidly now on final approach to runway two-eight. All but the last few seconds of the approach was over water, as the runway threshold was only four hundred feet from the water's edge. Jack watched the gorgeous aquamarine Caribbean come up to meet the aircraft, and then suddenly there was land below. Within seconds, the pilot was swiftly hovering the copter across the grass between the runway and west parking area, to set it down at a location directed by the tower controller.

"That's the Navy plane," Oliver told Jack, pointing to the long and gleaming white jet with blue Navy markings.

"Holy shit!" was Jack's only response as he looked at it through the Blackhawk side window.

Jack had envisioned something smaller. The C-9 was the stretched military version of the civilian airliner used to transport airline passengers since the late 1960's. It was now known as the C-9B Skytrain II, used for aero-medical airlift.

During the short copter flight from Castries, and with headsets on, Oliver and Jack had discussed the happenings of the previous days, and had also offered each other parting words. There was nothing left to say, as the Blackhawk set down and Jack jumped from the cargo door after shaking the colonel's hand. Once beyond the whirling rotor blades, Jack turned to salute him one last time, before heading across the tarmac to the waiting C-9. Charlie remained behind for a minute or so, receiving final instructions from the colonel. He would be accompanying Jack and Marnie across the Atlantic.

Marnie and Commander Willis, along with his medical team, had made the flight to Hewanorra on the Blackhawk earlier in the day. This had given them time to get Marnie situated in the C-9's intensive care unit, while the Blackhawk made the round-trip flight to Castries to pick up Jack and the other two men. With everything now completed, the C-9 was ready to depart as soon as Jack and Charlie boarded.

Once aboard and walking down the slightly off-centered aisle, Jack saw there were four sleeping stations on the left, like a pair of bunk beds situated end-to-end. Other than the beds and the quite complex-appearing forward crew station, nothing seemed too extraordinarily different in the C-9 compared to a civilian passenger plane. But as Jack moved further aft and opened the bulkhead door, it was like entering another world.

The intensive/critical care transport unit, one of four in the forward part of the cabin section, appeared to be better equipped than one would expect to find at the best trauma center. In fact, this was the case. When transporting critical patients long distances by air, it was necessary to have many items on board that would not necessarily be immediately accessible in a hospital ICU. And although this caused the cabin to seem cluttered, every last item was custom-designed and specifically placed for its intended purpose and particular need onboard the C-9.

As Jack stood at the doorway and took in all the sophisticated equipment, he was approached by an inviting nurse whose full-tooth smile gleamed at him. "Hello Mr. Dublin. I'm Lieutenant Nurse Leah Akers. I'll be covering the care unit for Ms. Bloom, along with Lieutenant Andrea D'Antonio. Don't you worry, we'll take good care of her," she said as she turned to look at Marnie. "Why don't you come on back,? Andie and I will show you around, once we're airborne and can unbuckle," she advised, gesturing Jack through the bulkhead doorway and into the astounding critical care cabin.

Jack saw Marnie tethered and well-secured in a specialized kind of bed, the likes of which he'd never before seen or imagined. She had electrodes and sensors attached all over, and tubes, drains, and multi-colored cords and electrical wires coming from everywhere on her body. The device which held and restrained her, looked to be an amalgamation constructed from a hospital bed, an articulated examination-surgical table, and a reclining lounge chair. Incredibly, Marnie appeared to be amazingly comfortable, although Jack wasn't sure if it was the drugs or the device causing such to be so.

Dr. Willis turned from Marnie where he had been tending her along with Lieutenant Nurse Andrea "Andie" D'Antonio, who also quickly turned her head and smiled at Jack. The commander took the several steps toward Jack necessary to offer a handshake with a big, friendly grin in his usual gregarious manner.

"Chopper ride okay, Mister Dublin?" the tall doctor began, still smiling as he always seemed to be. "Ms. Bloom is doing just fine. No problems on the way down, and we've got her all hooked up, strapped in, and ready to go," Dr. Willis continued. "Everything's A-Okay as they say at NASA. I'd like to get going as soon as possible. We'll talk once we get in the air and up to our planned flight level. Out here over the ocean without all the congestion and other air traffic, the captain will probably shoot right up to cruise altitude, so it won't be long at all."

Just then, two quick beeps came from an overhead speaker in the ceiling only a few feet away. Then two seconds later, over the same speaker, came the pilot's voice.

"You folks ready back there, Commander?" the C-9 captain asked in a friendly and casual voice.

Immediately, and without touching anything, Willis responded in a similarly casual and informal tone, "Yep. We're good to go. Just need a couple minutes for everybody to strap in," the commander advised, with his chin slightly elevated, and appearing as if he were talking to someone who wasn't there.

"ErrrRoger that," the captain quickly returned, more in an airline pilot kind of voice. "We'll wind'em up momentarily then. And Commander, our planned flight time to Andrews is three hours and fifty minutes. We'll probably trim a little time off of that due to some favorable winds aloft. Maybe cut it down to around three hours and thirty," he added.

"Thank you, Captain. We'll be good to go back here in zero two," Willis briefly returned.

The C-9's engines pitched louder and D'Antonio strapped in without much fuss, as the aircraft began its taxi to the active runway. And immediately becoming serious and busy, the Lieutenant gave full attention to the screen displaying Marnie's vital information arriving continuously from all the sensors attached to her.

For nearly an hour, Jack simply sat and stared at Marnie, and watched Lieutenant D'Antonio constantly checking her. Jack appreciated D'Antonio's dedicated attentiveness. Akers then asked him if he could go up to the forward cabin for a while. They'd be changing some of the bandages on Marnie's burns. Jack was thinking a little time in one of those comfy seats up front might not be a bad idea.

"Just give us about ten minutes, Mr.Dublin," D'Antonio told Jack, offering him a big grin that accentuated her cute dimples.

Jack headed to the bulkhead door. Entering the forward cabin, he immediately recognized the dreadlocks visible above the back of one of the wide club seats. Jack settled into the chair next to him.

"How ya doin' Jack?" Charlie asked, seeing the accumulated fatigue and strain on Jack's face.

"Hangin' in there, buddy. Just tired, I guess. They're doing some stuff with Marnie and wanted me to be scarce for a while. I'm really worried about her. I know Willis and the medical team are excellent, but I can't help thinking something just isn't right," he offered.

Charlie looked at Jack and wondered what to say. "Jack, ya just gotta let it go. I mean, there are only so many things you can control. Right now, Marnie's condition is one of those things you can't control. For this situation, she has the best doctors looking after her. After that, it's in God's hands."

"Yeah, you're right. But there are other things too."

"Like what?"

"There was a lot of stuff going on in D.C. when I left. Although the colonel said the government had taken care of a lot of it, I'm still not sure what that means and what is going to happen when we land," Jack said contemplatively.

"Jack, yesterday he filled me in on a lot of details regarding what has been going on in the states. Apparently he spoke with someone in the CIA who it appears knows your father and..."

"My father?" Jack interrupted.

"Easy, Jack," Charlie said trying to calm Jack down. "The colonel was trying to get some particulars and wanted me to convey to you that all the legal matters for you and Marnie have been resolved. There is no need for you to worry about that anymore. You just need to focus on Marnie."

"That's fine, and I appreciate it, but I still can't understand how my father is involved, and fits into any of it, in any way. I mean he was just a banker, for crying out loud," Jack offered in a more subdued voice, yawning and stretching.

Jack had been sleeping soundly for nearly an hour and a half when Commander Willis came forward to give an update on Marnie. Seeing Jack asleep, Willis decided to delay the talk, and spoke quietly with Charlie. Jack was aroused, hearing the low tone of Willis' voice. He immediately straightened in his seat and looked to the commander.

"How ya doin', Mr. Dublin?" the commander inquired. "Just came up for a minute to give you a little run-down on Ms. Bloom's status. She seems to be doing fine. My only concern is her level of consciousness. It seems that, even though I ordered a mild sedation from the doctors in Castries for her ride to Hewanorra, they may have administered more than was necessary. As a result, she is a little bit out of it, but she should be coming to before long. And once she does, we'll have you come back and sit with her for..."

Just then, Lieutenant Akers opened the bulkhead door to see Willis speaking with Jack and Charlie.

"Sir, will you come back here, please?" she interrupted.

"One minute, Lieutenant," Willis told L.A., not turning to see her face.

"Sir, I think you should come now," Akers iterated with urgency.

The commander moved past Akers, who held the door for him. As he passed, Akers was staring into his eyes with a telling expression of doom. Jack picked up what was going on and got up to follow. When he tried the door handle, he realized Akers had locked it.

Shortly after assessing Marnie's condition, Willis and his Lieutenants worked feverishly to stabilize her. Once she appeared to calm down, Willis hit a button at the monitoring station, then waited.

"What's the problem, Commander?" the pilot asked right away.

"Our patient has gone critical. What's our ETA to Andrews?" Willis asked.

"About thirty-three minutes if we go to max cruise airspeed," the captain came right back.

"Our patient needs emergency surgery, and she needs it right away," Willis advised.

"Roger that. We've just gone max cruise, and we'll keep pushing it as hard as we can. Presently, we're showing a ground speed of six-twenty. And I'll get an emergency clearance direct to Andrews," the captain promised.

Willis exited to the front cabin to talk with Jack. It was a difficult situation he had faced many times as a physician. Relaying bad news was never easy. He was met with a concerned but hopeful look on Jack's face.

"Mr. Dublin, Ms. Bloom's condition has deteriorated rather substantially over the past fifteen minutes. We have her stabilized, but her status is quite critical," Willis began, trying to drop the bomb as gently as possible. "Ms. Bloom's injury, in particular the head trauma she sustained, is considerably more severe than we originally thought and had been able to ascertain. The CAT-scan studies showed she was doing fine. However, if she had been in the states, better equipment would have been available and other tests and procedures would have been performed that simply were not available. But like I say, we just felt her status to transport was appropriate."

Jack interrupted. "You're really not telling me anything, Doctor. What specifically is her condition?"

"Ms. Bloom has an intracranial hemorrhage. She is bleeding inside her skull. The blood is occupying space, putting pressure on her brain. Unfortunately, this kind of pressure affects vital functions. Right now, even though she can breathe on her own, we have placed her on a ventilator. This allows her to maintain the proper level of oxygen throughout her body...."

Jack interrupted. "Doctor, what are her chances?"

"She needs to get to surgery as soon as possible. Our captain is pushing the aircraft just as fast as it will go, and has already been given emergency priority clearance directly to Andrews. We're doing the best we can."

Jack slipped into a kind of stupor. Hearing of Marnie's sudden and unexpected downward spiral, Jack was angered, and his mind became confused and disoriented. Seeing Jack's pallid face, Willis realized he was going into a temporary shock where the brain simply shuts down due to being overwhelmed with sensory overload. Willis knew his brain would eventually reorganize itself and reboot. They just needed to stand by in case Jack needed them.

Soon the captain came over the speakers. "Commander, we're about eighteen miles out, on final descent to begin our approach into Andrews. Better get ready for landing back there, okay?"

52

Once they landed, Jack returned to a state of normalcy. He sat with Charlie and tried to stay out of the way. He didn't want to interfere with the effort to get Marnie the urgent care she required. Several emergency personnel were present at Andrews AFB when they arrived. A medical helicopter was standing by, revved up and ready to go. Jack learned later it was about a forty-minute drive from Andrews to Walter Reed without traffic. Marnie didn't have time to wait.

The efficient lieutenants, Akers and D'Antonio, moved in concert with the ground medical staff. In a matter of a few minutes, Marnie was removed from the aircraft and placed onboard the helicopter. The unmistakable sound of the rotors increased as it lifted off the ground and gained altitude. Soon it was just a dot on the horizon.

Since Dr. Willis went with Marnie in the helicopter, another doctor, Dr. Gambrill, came forward to Jack and advised him further. "Mr. Dublin, Marnie is being transported to Walter Reed where they have a wealth of knowledge and provide outstanding care for persons with head trauma. It's where our service personnel who have suffered devastating injuries on the battlefield come to recover and rehabilitate. If you and Charlie want, you can catch a ride with me to the hospital. I have a car waiting."

Charlie looked at Jack. "Sounds like a good idea, doesn't it?"

Jack just nodded his head affirmatively.

Once they arrived at Walter Reed National Military Medical Center, a young military officer from the Navy was waiting for them. He escorted them to a solarium area closest to the room where Marnie would be sent once her surgery was complete. While they were being escorted, Jack couldn't help but notice the many officers who were missing limbs. They struggled to walk, yet seemed determined to minimize their infirmities. Deformed as they may be physically, their tough spirit was quite alive. It gave Jack pause for his self-centered attitude. In his heart he knew Marnie was a fighter, and he needed to be strong too.

As soon as they entered the waiting area, Jack saw Mr. Prescott standing by the window looking out at the grounds in contemplation. Excusing himself from Charlie, Jack walked over to Mr. Prescott, not sure what to say. He looked almost withered and beaten.

"Hello, Jack," he said without any sign of emotion while still looking out the window, obviously seeing Jack approach in the reflection of the glass.

"Hello, Mr. Prescott," Jack responded. "I'm sorry."

Mr. Prescott turned to look at Jack and then looked at the floor for a moment.

"She had a very troubled life but had turned it around. She was quite fond of you Jack," he said as he returned his attention to Jack.

Mr. Prescott could see the confusion on Jack's face. "No, Jack. She is still alive as far as I know, but her life is irrevocably changed. Whatever progress she made has been wiped out. She will never be the same."

Jack looked at him with a variety of feelings. Did Mr. Prescott blame him?

"Jack, you will be pleased to know I have been in touch with the prosecutor's office and all the charges against you have been nolle prossed, dropped."

"Thank you."

"I will be in touch," he said before turning to walk out of the waiting area.

"You're leaving?" Jack asked in disbelief.

Mr. Prescott stopped, and then slowly turned to Jack before walking back towards him.

"Aren't you going to wait to see how she makes out in surgery?" Jack asked modestly.

"Jack, you still don't know, do you?"

"Know what?"

"Marnie is my daughter," Mr. Prescott said plainly, looking at the astonished look on Jack's face. "Maybe not by blood, but I've raised her since she was a little girl. Her parents were very important to me for reasons I don't want to get into. But when they died, I made it my life's mission to make sure Marnie had the best life has to offer. I now feel that I've failed. No offense, but being in your presence is a painful reminder."

Mr. Prescott paused for a moment, and then turned and left, leaving Jack in his wake.

Jack stood there speechless. In his emotional turmoil, it now became apparent how Marnie was assigned to watch over him. She worked for her stepfather.

Within five minutes, Dr. Willis came to talk with Jack. As he entered the waiting area, Charlie joined them.

"Jack, they are still operating on Marnie," Willis informed him. "It will be quite some time before she is able to communicate with you. I suggest you go home and get some sleep. You are not doing anyone any good by waiting here. Go home, get some rest and come back tomorrow."

"How is she holding up in surgery?" Jack asked.

"Right now, as well as can be expected."

Jack wanted more information, but he was too tired to ask.

He knew the doctor was right. He would be better off going home and recharging his batteries.

"Jack, do you need anything?" Charlie asked.

"No. I think Dr. J is right. I need to go home. Are you going to be okay?"

"Don't worry about me. The government has taken care of my accommodations," Charlie said. "I'll be here. If anything changes, I'll get in touch with you."

"Thanks."

"Jack, there's a car to take you home. You'll be given a number to call when you want to return and a car will bring you back here," Dr. Willis said.

. . .

Once he was on his floor, Jack got off the elevator, happy to be back at his condo. Exhausted, he just wanted to crawl in bed and sleep, not wanting to be bothered talking to anyone, especially Ms. McGarrity. If she came out into the hallway to start a conversation, Jack didn't know if he could maintain civility. Walking softly past her door, there was no sound coming from her place. Perhaps she was out.

Finally getting to his door, he opened it and started down the steps that led to his living room. Remembering Guinness was with Carla, Jack was disappointed that his dog was not there to greet him. He would have to call later to make arrangements to pick up Guinness.

While descending the steps, it was comforting to see in the distance the Washington Monument with the Capitol behind it. Everything still looked the same in the living room. He walked over to the sliding glass doors and sighed. It was good to be home.

"Hello Jack," came the baritone voice behind him in the dining room.

He slowly turned around and saw a dignified looking man sitting at the dining room table with the chair turned to face him. The years had been kind to him. Jack had really hoped he was dead, but there he was, in the flesh.

He had not seen or talked to him in twenty years. The man was in an expensive Armani suit. Now in his late sixties, he had an impressive head of silver hair to go with his refined looks.

Standing next to him was an imposing black man, who stood about six feet five, and must have weighed about three hundred and fifty pounds. He was dressed in an ill-fitting black suit, white shirt and black tie. His head was bald but he had a full black beard. He was not smiling.

"How did you get in here, and what the fuck do you want?" Jack asked testily.

"Please don't talk to me like that. I'm still your father."

"You're not my father. Fathers don't desert their families."

"Listen Jack, I know you hate me and some of it is with good reason, but we need to talk."

"Why?"

"It's time you heard my side of the story."

"I'm sure it's a story, alright."

"Jack, all I ask is an hour of your time. After you've heard me out, if you don't want to talk to me again, I will disappear from your life and you will never see or hear from me again."

"You've done that for the last twenty years. What makes this different?"

"Because I've decided I don't want to go to my grave without you hearing the truth. You need to hear me out."

Jack said nothing.

"Listen, I know you've been through hell the last week or so. Why don't you let me take you out for brunch?"

"How do you know what I've been through?"

"Jack, you'd be surprised at what I know." There was a pause and then Jack's father stood up, turned the chair under the table and spoke again. "C'mon, I'll have Roosevelt here take us into Georgetown and we'll get some brunch, and afterward I'll have him bring you back home."

Jack pondered the invitation. He was tired but hungry, and curious to find out how much his father actually knew. He reluctantly decided to go. They went downstairs to the lobby while Roosevelt brought the black limo around. They didn't talk while they waited. Jack's father got in first. Then Jack got in, and sat opposite his father who was facing toward the rear. The Sea Catch restaurant was less than five minutes away.

On the way, Jack's father tried to make small talk, but he could see Jack was ignoring him so he tried a different approach.

"It's a shame what happened to Marnie. Almost the same thing happened to your mother," he said as they pulled up to the Sea Catch restaurant.

"Listen, you son-of-a-bitch, I don't want to talk to you about my mother or Marnie."

"Jack, there *are* some things we need to discuss about her."

"No. Not with you. You no longer have that right," Jack said angrily. "I can't believe I agreed to this. I'm not having a meal with you. Just have your driver take me home."

Just then the door opened and a young adult voice said, "Hello, Grandpop."

Jack's father held up his forefinger as if to say, "Give me a second", and then looked at Jack and smiled. Jack was confused. He knew Connor was his father's only grandson, unless, of course, he had one out of wedlock. His father started to brush imaginary lint off his pants and then began to exit. He took one final look at Jack, "Are you sure you don't want to have brunch with me?" he said with a devilish grin.

Jack just stared ahead, almost catatonically, at the empty seat next to his father. He didn't answer. He was trying to process the information.

"It's a shame, Jack. I think you would have found it informative and interesting. Take care, Jack. I truly hope you have a good life. Roosevelt, take him home," he said as he grabbed the stirrup handle and pulled himself out of the car.

He got out and shut the door, without turning back.

. . .

After some tedious moments throughout the numerous hours of meticulous neurosurgery, Marnie was taken to a private ICU room. She was heavily sedated, or so it seemed. Her prognosis was tenuous. The doctors had done everything they could and remained cautiously optimistic.

Several nurses were painstakingly setting up her monitors and IV's. They had performed these procedures hundreds of times, and understood her situation. "I think this is the woman who was in the papers," the older nurse said as she was hooking up her monitors.

"What woman?" the young, plain-looking nurse asked.

"The one who was involved in the investigation of the senator and the terrorists," said another nurse, who was adjusting Marnie's bed.

"Oh," the young nurse responded while hooking up the IV.

As they were talking, Marnie's lips started moving and the nurses heard some slightly audible sounds. The older nurse put her ear next to Marnie's mouth to try to determine what she was saying.

"Can you understand what she's saying?" asked the youngest nurse.

"It sounds like she's saying "Jack" but I'm not sure. Wait! She's mumbling something else. I'm not sure but I think she said "heart"."

. . .

Roosevelt started to slowly pull away from the curb. Jack looked out the back window and saw a young man about his son's age, walking with his father in the direction of the restaurant. Jack was still stunned. He didn't know what to think or say.

Then he felt Marnie's gentle whisper in his ear. "Go Jack, you'll figure it out... It's the power of the heart."

"Stop the car!" Jack said to Roosevelt. Once the car came to a stop, Jack opened the door and practically vaulted from the car, jogging towards the restaurant.

CPSIA information can be obtained at www.ICGtesting.com
Printed in the USA
BVOW11s2045270614

357611BV00014B/382/P

9 780615 597669